SCIMITAR RISING

By Trey Percynter

Copyright

Scimitar Rising

Copyright © 2016. All rights reserved.

Fourth Edition: February 2019

This is a work of fiction. Names, characters, places, and incidences are either the product of the author's imagination or are used fictitiously, and any resemblance to locales, events, business establishments, or actual persons—living or dead—is entirely coincidental.

Dedication

I dedicate this book to all who inspired me to write it. First and foremost, my lovely wife 'Bebe,' who functioned not only as my biggest cheerleader, but also as my critic; for the truth is always better than a well-meaning lie. And, to those that took the same oath I did and still hold true to the same; "… to defend the Constitution of the United States against all enemies both foreign and domestic…so help me God."

Appreciation

To my friends and family, who were subjected to raw drafts of this work and pushed to provide feedback; especially Dougie and the Insane Canine. A special thanks to Christa S., the amazing graphic artist that designed the cover of this book and to Richard C. for editing. Finally, to Angery American; author of the Going Home series—thanks for the advice and guidance.

Foreword

As you read this book, you will find similarities to the current political culture and even individual players of the culture. For the story to be continually relevant and not locked into a particular date in history, I did not assigned dates; only seasons. The story is meant to be at future state and time—just a few years from now, though not far, so as to intertwine current events.

This book does not intend to identify or imply any particular individuals currently living or dead. However, some of the characters identified by name (e.g. al-Baghdadi) are known historical figures and are added for realism. Certain events and documents listed in the book are also real and are supported with dates and/or sources. For the storyline in this novel, these were interpreted by the characters to advance the plot. I encourage the reader to research these and determine their own opinions or interpretations. While it was my personal intent to provoke thought; this book is a work of fiction and intended for entertainment value only. I hope you enjoy it—I certainly enjoyed writing it for you.

God Bless America!

-Trey Percynter

Table of Contents

CHAPTER 1

"Greater love has no man than this; that he lay down his life for a friend." John 15:13, Holy Bible

The Marine F-35B fighter quickly closed the distance to the wayward civilian aircraft. As the pilot gained visual contact, he slowed so as not to overrun the plane. His wingman followed suit. Major "Sheets" Duncan had been scrambled from Beaufort, South Carolina to intercept the aircraft as it reportedly lost contact with ATC over an hour ago. The flight plan filed by its pilot had it departing from Destin, Florida and landing in Savannah, Georgia. However, now the plane was over the Atlantic Ocean having never descended to the intended destination. As Sheets approached the aircraft from the starboard side, he tried to contact the pilot on guard frequency. There was no response. He came abeam of the turbo-prop driven aircraft and his fears were realized—the windows were frosted up. *'Damn, this seems to be happening more frequently,'* he thought to himself. He selected the inter-aircraft squadron frequency.

"Digger, you seeing what I'm seeing." Sheets transmitted.

"Roger that." Digger replied.

They both knew the fate of the occupants was sealed with the failure of the aircraft pressurization system. Captain John "Digger" Jones had first-hand experience with the issue two summers ago during pilot training. While engaged in a 'dog fight' with six other aircraft, his pressurization system had failed. He ignored the warning for only a few moments as he was actively engaged in mock combat. He should have called 'knock it off' right away, but he was in a good position to make a kill and didn't want to lose the opportunity. The OBOGS system would have provided him the necessary oxygen to negate the effects of hypoxia, but it too had a problem. The combination of the two malfunctions at 40,000 feet gave Digger about 15 seconds of useful consciousness. He recognized the effects immediately and went to the backup system, but not before nearly passing out. Slowly, his color vision returned, and the radio chatter became clear in his ears. He descended to 10,000 feet and declared an IFE or 'Inflight Emergency.' The incident was called a 'brown out' but could have easily been a 'blackout.' If not for his training and experience in the altitude chamber, Digger would not have recognized the symptoms in time; suffering the same fate as the occupants in the aircraft now just off his right wing. *Tragic,* he thought; *civilians should really get this training before strapping on an aircraft like this one.* He wondered how many people were in the plane with the pilot. His thoughts were interrupted by Sheets transmission.

"Atlanta Center, SWEDE 26." Sheets transmitted.

"SWEDE 26, Atlanta; go."

"Roger, aircraft is confirmed at flight level two-eight-zero and contact unresponsive. Uhh...the windows are frosted up pretty good, Center...it doesn't look good. We'll try and wake them up, but...ahh..." He paused, "...ahh, standby."

Digger was already positioning. Sheets watched as Digger's afterburner fired and the Lightning II accelerated up and away. The roar would have been deafening in the cockpit of the civilian aircraft. If anything would wake them up, that would be it. Sheets tried the guard frequency again. Nothing.

"Atlanta Center; SWEDE 26." Sheets transmitted.

"26, Center; go."

"It's a negative...no response." Sheets reported. "We're going to call home...what would you like us to do?"

"26; Center...request you stay on station if possible...assist emergency services in locating the aircraft."

"Center, 26; affirmative...will call with intentions after calling home."

Sheets contacted the Command Post at Beaufort and was told to stay with the aircraft as long as possible or until it crashed into the ocean. He had no idea how long that might be or who would run out of fuel first, but he was pretty sure without a tanker to tag up with, the civilian aircraft would outlast him. The fighter was not designed for endurance and maintaining the relatively slow speed of the stricken plane was not the most efficient fuel management scenario for the Lightning II. Sheets had about half an hour before 'Bingo Fuel,' meaning; that he had enough fuel to safely return to base, plus 30 minutes. Then, he would have to leave the civilian plane to continue by itself. Digger transmitted on the inter-plane frequency.

"Sheets…he's going in."

Sheets saw the propeller slow and automatically feather. The airplane began to descend with its wings level at first; the auto-pilot trying to maintain altitude. It slowed down until it approached stall speed. At some point the auto-pilot kicked off and the plane appeared to be in a stall buffet. The F-35's could not stay with the aircraft as it was flying too slowly. They could transition to STOVL flight, but that would require more fuel. Sheets tried to keep the plane in sight as he departed. The last thing he saw was the plane nose over, roll, and spiral earthward.

"Digger, I'm going down to have a look." Sheets said as he began to descend.

"Think that's a good idea?" Digger responded, gently prompting the senior officer.

"I know what you're thinking, Digger…" Sheets answered, "…but I feel like I have to."

Sheets descended to a safe altitude and initiated STOVL conversion as he approached the crash site. The stealthy jet began to open doors and gear wells, redirecting thrust downward in anticipation of vertical flight. He slowed as he got closer to the area where he thought the civilian aircraft may have come to rest. He kept his altitude high enough to observe a wide area but low enough to be able to pick out someone floating in the water; thankful the sea state was relatively calm. It was taking a lot of power and he dare not go slower. The aircraft was capable of hovering, but not at this weight. Suddenly, he saw something off his port side—a wing! He vectored the jet toward the debris to get a better look. Yes, it was; a wing, the tail broken off and bobbing, and some other smaller pieces he really couldn't identify. The wings had separated from the fuselage but, only one was floating. The cockpit and engine had slipped under the surface. Aircraft that run out of fuel over water will many times have their wings float because they are empty and trap air inside. Sheets began scanning the water for survivors, but it appeared they likely sank with the cockpit and engine. He set up for another pass over the wreckage. This time there were fewer pieces as he went by and he noticed the wing was floating lower than before. He figured it must have had a small rupture. Sheets marked the spot in the aircraft navigation system as a waypoint for future reference.

"You okay down there, boss?" Digger inquired. It was more of a reminder than a question.

"Affirmative, coming up. I'm bingo…let's go home."

Fuel was critical now, they had to leave. Sheets made the call to give coordinates of the downed aircraft. *Damn*, he thought, *they never had a chance.* Initially, they heard the Emergency Locator Transmitter on the guard frequency, but soon lost the signal as they returned homeward.

Over the next few days, the search was on. Unfortunately, there were no ships in the immediate area as it was nowhere near an active shipping lane. The Coast Guard was on scene within six hours, but found no trace. Seas were fairly rough by then with an approaching storm, so even an oil slick would have been difficult to find. After a reasonable period of time, the search was called off and the occupants of the aircraft, Robert and Katrina Wallace and their pilot Rick Kitchenmaster—were considered lost. One year later, they were officially declared dead.

The lawyer's office was dark and intimidating. Books lined an entire wall encased in fine oak shelving. This guy was definitely old school. Probably knew dad forever and a day. They were childhood friends—lifelong—though dad didn't spend much time with him as the lawyer lived in Montana; not Florida where dad and mom lived. It was beautiful up here in the mountain west. The family spent quite a few vacations here as dad was originally from this area. He and mom actually owned property up here somewhere. David had never seen it, but knew the area. Dad invited him several times, but the military and all manner of trivial things just never seemed to align with his schedule. He regretted it now.

The lawyer looked intently at his computer. The dim light from the screen cast a large shadow on the wall behind him making an intimidating man seem even more so. He hadn't moved in several minutes except for the occasional shift of his head up and down to peer through the reading glasses perched precariously on the tip of his nose, ready to slide off at any moment. David hated the silence and the waiting. His sister Leigh was always late, why should today be any different? He looked at his brother and sister sitting across from him; both were texting on their phones and seemed quite comfortable with the delay, showing no sign of impatience. The lawyer had informed them that until all were present the reading of the will would not be accomplished. David wondered what the others would want to do with the property here in Montana. He would like to keep it for sentimental reasons. Mom and dad loved it so much. In fact, they spent a lot of time up here over the last 3 years. Again, he regretted not accepting their invitations. Now, he really wanted to see the place they spent so much time up here so he could try and connect with them somehow. He really missed them.

The huge door opened at the back of the room and Leigh walked in ushered by the legal assistant. She looked stressed, probably because she knew David would give her static about tardiness. Oh, he would definitely do that—but later. Ross and Carrie looked up and smiled at their oldest sister strutting toward the empty seat that separated David from the other two.

"Sorry I'm late," she said sheepishly glancing at David, "Tanner was being a pest."

"It's okay sis, the lawyer only gets $250.00 per minute waiting for brats," David slid in sarcastically.

The lawyer peered over his glasses at David, the corner of his mouth curled up slightly to hint that he approved of the humor. Leigh glared at David displaying more disgust than she really felt, then rolled her eyes and fluttered her eyelids.

"Whatever." She sneered, promptly sitting down in the large leather chair.

The lawyer turned away from his computer, opened the desk drawer immediately to his right and produced five rather plump legal sized manila envelopes. He placed them in the center of his desk and fanned them out, then took the very top one and opened it. David could tell the top envelope had been accessed many times before as if reading its contents was a common occurrence.

"I've read this document several times," the lawyer spoke deliberately, "…and I will admit that it intrigues me each time I read it." He paused and looked at each of the four siblings. "We live in perilous times, I'm afraid. Your parents' were visionaries…prophets, if you will. They bequeath to you something of more value than anything I've ever heard of…in fact, I have followed suit on a personal level. I was a skeptic at first, but now…" He trailed off, slipping into deep thought.

He had the attention of the four now. David felt himself leaning forward as if to hear just a bit clearer. He turned to look at the others, who were now looking back at him. Ross shrugged slightly and raised his eyebrows. Carrie cocked her head to the side inquisitively and stared directly at David as if he knew something. David responded by also shrugging slightly and moved his head from side to side to convey he had no knowledge of what was about to be disclosed. All wanted to interrupt the lawyer's apparent daydream, but the commanding persona of the man intimidated them. This only worked on David for a few moments before he took control.

"But now…what?" David asserted.

It broke the concentration of the stoic man. He stood and distributed each of the remaining envelopes to the recipient whose name was on the outside. It was obvious they had been sealed and unopened. Carrie proceeded to open hers and was promptly stopped by the lawyer.

"Wait,'" he said, sternly. "These are to be opened at a later time by each of you individually when you're by yourselves. It contains a copy of what I'm about to read plus a personal message for each of you. Your father sealed them himself, I do not know the contents beyond the document I'm about to read." He addressed the document in front of him, "The Last Will and Testament of Robert and Katrina Wallace…"

David was still staring at Carrie who was tearing up. He felt a lump begin to grow in his throat. They were gone—they were really gone. One would have thought the memorial service could give closure, but no; it was this reading of the will. They all felt it. The lawyer droned on. It was mostly legalese at first, delineating the division of equal shares in the estate. Mom and dad were not rich, but they had accumulated a respectable upper middle-class inheritance for their children. Honestly, none of them cared about the money. They would all rather have their parents' back. The lawyer mentioned a few personal things to be given to particular individuals. Items that none of them would contend should be for anyone but the intended recipient; items that meant more to the recipient than anyone else and had little monetary value. As they listened, the same question formed in the back of their minds—*what in this document impressed the lawyer so much?* Certainly, they had not heard anything to this point lending to such implied profoundness. They would steal a look at each other occasionally when an item was identified, as it prompted memories. Carrie and Leigh were into their second round of tissues when the lawyer paused. He looked up at each of them intently. It was almost uncomfortable. The effect was tempered with anticipation and impatience by the siblings.

"The final portion of the estate has 'special legal conditions' that cannot be undone," he stated flatly. "This is because your parents' set up a trust that includes me as overseer. It cannot be sold or liquidated even with the consent of all of you. It involves the property and all contents therein. You may reside there indefinitely as a permanent resident; one or all of you and your families. But, you cannot sell or lease the property to anyone else."

David and Ross exchanged stares. The boys had been able to literally finish each other's sentences from an early age. It was likely true that both were now thinking the exact same thing; *we gotta get up there and see what's going on.*

The lawyer went on, "The taxes have been paid on the property from the trust—in advance—for the next 20 years. There is no implied liability for any of you concerning costs with regard to the property. Your parents' wanted one or more of you and your families to live on the property at the earliest convenience, but it is not a requirement to satisfy the will or the trust conditions. However, if one or more of you do reside on the property, there is a modest account set aside for set-up, moving, etc. I will, however, require approximately 30 days' notice before you intend on exercising this option as the account consists of actual gold bullion and must be liquidated to allow for tangible spending. Also, like the trust itself, this account can be used for nothing else except for the purpose described to you."

Ross looked at David with a puzzled look that said *'what the hell?'* David was thinking about what his parents' had preached to him for the last several years and what this was might be—a redoubt; a prepper's escape location in the middle of nowhere. *That's what this must be about...but why didn't they move there?* As far as he knew, they just spent summer vacations hanging out in the mountains. Now, his interest was really piqued. He glanced at the manila envelope in his hands and wondered at what it might contain.

"Yesterday, a shipment of boxes was sent to each of your homes. They contain items that will make sense to you after you've read the contents of your envelopes," the lawyer continued, "...and please consider this as sacred as the property, though I cannot keep you from doing what you will with it."

The lawyer finished up with the legalese in the document and had each of the four siblings sign a document saying they had been presented with the will and the envelopes. The legal assistant notarized the document and returned with copies. Then, lawyer gave them each a card with his contact information on it and wished them well. They didn't say much beyond thanking him for everything and let the assistant herd them toward the lobby. David turned back to look at the lawyer just before leaving the room. The man had an expression on his face that David could not read well. They had just met the man, yet there was a feeling of closeness like he was family. Concern—yes, that was the expression—he seemed concerned. But, that was not it entirely. It was more like a look you would get from someone who dropped you off at the airport and knew it would be a long time before you met again. It was like that.

The lawyer held his gaze and gently nodded to David, who nodded back. "God speed, David…God speed," the man boomed so that David could hear, "…to all of you." Then, he turned and clasped his hands behind his back as the door closed shut. For an instant, David considered going back in and engaging the lawyer one on one. He had the feeling that there was more to be said—privately. But, what would he say to the man? He didn't know.

"Was there something else?" The assistant inquired. It broke David's concentration and he looked back to see his siblings staring at him.

"No…no, I'm good," he said, looking down at the lawyer's card in his hand. "I just need to digest everything."

They all shuffled out into the parking lot and formed a loose circle. Carrie spoke first. "That was weird."

"Yeah, like a Stephen King novel kinda weird," Ross piped up. He looked at David to catch his eye, but he was looking down at the card in his hand, slowly moving his thumb back and forth across the raised print. Ross wondered what he was thinking.

"Well, I'm hungry…let's go get some coffee and food somewhere," Leigh said with her strong Arkansas accent. "I want to talk about this…see what y'all are thinking."

There was agreement amongst the group and conversation started to flow, all except from David. He was still in deep thought. Their voices were bouncing off his head like so much background noise at a bowling alley. He needed to know more—now—not later, and this manila envelope was at the center of it. What was it the lawyer said "…a personal message to each of you to be opened…when you're by yourselves?" David wanted to get off by himself and rip the envelope open more than he wanted air. He looked at the seal on the envelope and the tape his father placed himself.

"I can't," David interrupted the group and their droning. "I have to make a few calls back to the base…er…work. Let's meet for lunch."

"How about dinner, instead," Ross asserted. "I think we all need to get off by ourselves and read our packages…we need more info and I don't know about you guys, but this thing is burning a hole in my hand." He shook the envelope.

"Well, me and Carrie are getting breakfast and…" Leigh started.

"Fine…it's settled then," David cut her off. "We'll see you at the hotel restaurant at say…seven?"

"Fine, whatever." Carrie retorted, "We just thought…"

"Quit thinking so much, sis, you might break something." David chided. She didn't like it, but accepted the quip as only siblings do.

"We good then…7 pm at the restaurant?" Ross pressed. "Good," he popped, before anyone had a chance to respond. "I'm riding with David." No one said anything. It fell into the 'silence is concurrence' category.

The girls hugged the boys and they headed for their cars. David was glad Ross laid out the plan. He knew his older brother had calculated the time to allow for them to get a look at the property. He was curious about it, but even more so about the contents of the envelope.

16

Neither of them spoke as they made their way to David's Jeep. Both were thinking about the property. By contrast they could hear the girls chatting a mile a minute, speculating as to what they might find.

"Why do they do that?" Ross spoke. "They want to figure everything out before they get all the info. Then, they'll try to say they were right about this or that as they uncover the facts. What does it matter?"

"Exactly," David said dryly. "I can't imagine being a woman."

"So whadda ya think…we go back to the hotel, you make your calls, we read our stuff here…," Ross said shaking the envelope, "…and we make a run up to the folks' place?"

"Yeah, sounds good," David replied. "Dad gave me the GPS coordinates a while back. I looked at satellite imagery of the property on Google, but since it's not a residential area the resolution is not very good. I got a topo map of the area too. It's basically surrounded by National Forest."

The boys split up at the hotel and agreed to meet up in half an hour and they didn't want their sisters to see them leaving. They would all go to the property together, maybe tomorrow, but right now the boys didn't want to be hindered.

David settled on the corner of his bed and began to open the envelope. Again, he considered the tape that sealed it and his father's hands in the act. He treated it gently, with reverence, as if tearing it open was sacred in some way. He poured the contents on the bed and assessed them. There was a copy of the document the lawyer read from, a CD or DVD of some kind, a red key, a topographical map, and another document; the personal message the lawyer talked about. He stared at the message; wanting to pick it up and read it immediately, but hesitated. This would be the last communication David would ever get from his parents'. After this last one thing, there would be no more. Nothing. He almost wanted to save it. Waiting a few moments more, he picked it up and read the heading.

Dear David, if you're reading this it means that I've likely gone on to my reward. Weird, huh? You should feel what I'm feeling right now just writing this. Mom wrote one too, it's a few pages into this document. I want you to pay particular attention to the third part, directly after her message. There are instructions in it that are very important...'

CHAPTER 2

"On my honor, I will do my best
To do my duty To God and my country"
— Boy Scouts of America

Leigh looked blankly at Carrie across the booth. She was trying to digest what her sister had just said. What was she suggesting? *Is that what the lawyer meant by her parents' being 'prophetic?' Or worse; did they purposely fulfill prophesy?* Leigh poked at her pecan waffle for a few moments, contemplating the conversation.

"So, you're saying mom and dad knew they were going to die? How could that be possible unless they did it on purpose?" Leigh said a little too loudly. The Waffle House cook looked up at them curiously.

"No, no…I'm saying that mom was preparing for something…something big. Because they were getting everything in order, paying stuff off, etcetera…" Carrie paused, "All I know is that mom can't keep a secret, you know? And, she kept hinting at something coming up. It wasn't just about paying stuff off…it was like, well…they were getting rid of stuff too. Not like a garage sale or anything…it was trying to find a home for pictures and keepsakes. Stuff she would never give up, unless…"

"There you go again. When you say 'unless', you allude to them dying, right? Because why would mom want to make sure the pictures and stuff got taken care of?" Leigh quipped.

"I don't know…I don't know." Carrie was now confused herself. "But, that's what she was doing…and, she told me not to tell anyone about our conversations…I mean, how weird is that?"

Leigh was still trying to unravel Carrie's assertions. She wanted just the facts, not theories. Although, the facts were puzzling; why would she be trying to resolve all these things and not want Carrie to say anything to anyone? What were mom and dad involved in? Was it illegal? Were

19

they planning on escaping something or someone? Were they then—murdered—before they had a chance to escape?

"Okay, okay…let's look at only what we know. Don't get into *'unless,'* okay? That just muddies up the water." Leigh said, trying to be the voice of reason. "So, why were they going to Savannah?"

"I guess cuz dad went there a few times and liked it…he wanted to take mom," Carrie responded.

"Did mom seem nervous about the trip?" Leigh asked.

"Yeah, she did. Like, a lot more than normal. Remember how she backed out on that cruise with dad at the last minute? Like, that kinda nervous." Carrie trailed off a bit in deeper thought.

Leigh contemplated the conversation and then remembered the manila envelopes. She wondered if there might be more answers there. She was dreading the read and had already been a blithering idiot; crying over the loss several times. She knew the message in the envelope would probably put her over the cliff again and she was tired—exhausted.

"You know, we should go," Carrie broke the silence, "…and read these things." She tapped the envelope.

"Yeah, I know. I was so anxious to read it in the lawyers office, but now…" Leigh hesitated.

"Like, you want to save it, cuz it's the last thing you'll ever get from them?" Carrie was making a statement more than a question.

"Right." Leigh mumbled, still staring at her sister's envelope.

"I don't want it hanging over my head…gonna get it over with." Carrie stood, making the gesture to leave. "It's eating me up inside."

Leigh didn't speak. She slid out of the booth and paid her bill. Then, they left in Carrie's rental car and made their way back to the hotel. Other than a quick hug and a promise to meet for dinner, there wasn't much conversation. A lot was on their minds.

Damn this road was rough, David thought. The Jeep he rented had a stiff suspension that added to the hard ride, but the vehicle still groaned as it cleared the rocky trail. Mud had been splashing up over the sides; he would have to clean it before he took it back. Ross just grinned at his brother each time they were launched against their seat belts. A particularly hard bump popped his Coke out of the cup holder next to him.

"What the hell?" he grumbled loudly. "No wonder they didn't actually live up here. Can you imagine getting back here in the winter???"

"Pretty cool though," Ross responded, "...beautiful. Like when we were kids and we camped almost every weekend."

They came to a creek and David stopped. It didn't appear too deep, they could see to the bottom through the crystal clear water. Rocks lined the area and it seemed safe enough. Clearly, it had been shored up for passage, but it still might be deep. Ross got out and surveyed the crossing. David switched off the Jeep and followed him. The stream was making the only audible sound.

"Think this is okay to cross?" Ross queried.

"Yeah, unless you want to walk it first?" David said dryly.

"Yeah...no," Ross puffed, "...you first. That water is colder...how did dad say it...than a well diggers...?"

"I know that's right...bet we could drink it, too...right out of the creek." They headed back to the Jeep.

David started the Jeep and moved forward slowly. As they entered the water it was clear the sub-surface rocks were just as rough as the trail leading to it. About half way across the right front tire slipped into a hole and water splashed up into Ross's side of the vehicle; soaking his right side and face. He quickly leaned inward to avoid more of the same, bumping David's arm off the steering wheel. The Jeep careened into the deeper part of the creek and water began to fill the floor boards. David grabbed the steering wheel with both hands and gunned the 4-wheel drive; knowing that momentum was the only thing that would save them from getting stuck…or worse. He was driving straight down the creek looking for a bank to climb out of, but trees lined the whole area and blocked him. The only saving grace was the fact that the creek did not seem to be getting deeper. The Jeep bounced and jerked with each boulder they hit.

"What the hell are you doing???" Ross cried.

"Trying to save us, you idiot! You knocked my hand off the steering wheel!" David retorted, still fighting the creek and its rocky bottom.

"Well, don't flip us!" Ross said, contemplating baling from the struggling vehicle. "If the water gets to the air intake of the engine we're screwed."

"You wanna drive???" David grunted as they hit a larger rock.

"Nope, you're gonna get us to the scene of the crash just fine…" Ross paused, "…There! On the right; a break in the trees!"

"Got it!" David acknowledged, as he made his way toward the opening. It was steep, but they would make it. The engine revved as the tires clawed their way up the bank, bucking and slipping. At one point it wasn't looking good; the Jeep lost traction on the right side and began to roll. David turned into the roll to keep it on all fours, but now they were headed toward the trees. He turned the wheel sharply to the right again and they found themselves back into the creek; this time returning toward the original crossing point. They continued to bounce everyway but backwards and both were now soaked. Eventually, they got to the crossing and David turned hard right again. The Jeep didn't like it much and groaned as it popped up onto the rocky shore. The right rear tire was still in the creek when it began to spin. David again tried to accelerate, but now all the tires were spinning. Suddenly, the left side tires bit hard into the rock and launched them forward; but not before the vehicle rolled up onto the right-side tires. The engine strained and the Jeep teetered on only two tires as it careened up on the trail. Just as it looked as if they might roll over, the terrain met them and all four tires were on the ground again.

The Jeep bounced hard and both men were thrown into their seatbelts. Ross's head bumped the dashboard.

"Just like I planned." David grinned at his brother, who was now rubbing his forehead.

"Whatever! I'm walking across there on the way back. That way I can tell the insurance company how you died," Ross said sarcastically.

"I was thinking of buying this Jeep, but after that, I think I'll get a different one…I think this one is bent," David joked. They both laughed and Ross fumbled at the laces of his shoes, wanting to get them off his feet. They were cold now and the shade from the trees blocking the warm sun seemed to make it colder. After another 20 minutes they came into an opening—a meadow—that stretched for an eighth mile in all directions. David entered the meadow and drove to what the geographical center would be. He slowed to a stop and pulled out his GPS. After a minute, Ross asked, "Are we there yet? Are we there yet?" He tried to imitate an impatient child on a long road trip.

David studied the GPS for a few more seconds and then looked up, then back down to the device. "Yeah, we're actually close," he paused to look up. "See those trees over there on the North end? That's the center of the property…we're actually on forest service land right now."

"It's beautiful," Ross said, looking around. "I don't see a house or anything…where did they stay when they came up here?"

"Get in," David ordered. I'll show you…I think."

"You think?" Ross said quizzically.

"Yeah…" David trailed off, still thinking about what the GPS was telling him. "Did you read your package? I had a different GPS coordinate in the package than dad originally gave me a few years ago. I'm thinking it must be where they stayed."

"I saw one in my package, but I don't own a GPS…well, except for my phone, but that only helps with cities and roads. It's not like that one; a topo tactical type thing for outdoor woodsy stuff," Ross said. He looked at his phone—no signal. Not like it needed one to function as a GPS, but phone-based GPS devices also triangulate off cell towers to get initial location info. In addition, they get the ephemeris data through the cell towers as the data takes about 14 minutes to completely download from the satellite—too long a time for a cell phone to wait.

David continued toward the trees and the area his GPS directed him. *The ground was fertile and the soil rich here*, he thought. *Nice place for a garden—a big garden.* As they approached the location identified on the GPS, a cow elk sprinted from the timber. David stopped to admire the animal. She was prancing proudly and swiftly with her head up and slightly back to keep a wary eye on the Jeep. Within seconds she disappeared into another stand of timber.

"That was cool!" Ross piped up.

"Yeah, and be tasty too," David added.

David thought about his package and the personal message: *"…the area is perfect for long term sustainment. Plenty of game for meat, pure water, and rich soil for growing vegetables and fruits; though the growing season is short…"*

They continued to drive towards the GPS coordinate. Only 150 feet to go, but he could see already there was no structure in front of them. They passed into the stand of trees and just slightly out the other side of them into a smaller meadow—about the size of a half a football field. David slowed the Jeep to a crawl until he came to a stop. The GPS showed he was at the point in the package.

"We're here." David said, as he shut off the vehicle and slid out.

"Bout time." Ross said, trying to get his shoes back on.

David surveyed the area. It was a perfect place for a homesteader, though he bet the winters were pretty harsh if you weren't prepared. He pulled out his binoculars and searched further up the mountain. It was a beautiful place, he knew why dad liked it so much…mom too. But, man was it out of the way…*way out of the way.* As he glassed the tree line to the West, he saw something in the timber. The shadows cast there prevented him from it seeing with clarity, but what he saw was undoubtedly a structure of some kind. He bumped Ross in the arm, handed him the binos and pointed in the direction of the structure.

"Hey, over there…there's something over there," David said as he started walking. Ross glassed the area and responded, "Don't you want to drive over there?"

"Nah, I'm tired of driving…I need to walk a bit." David mumbled.

They headed in the direction of the structure, taking in the lay of the land—David from a more tactical perspective than Ross, but he didn't verbalize it. There were some high points about the property where a highly skilled sniper might take for a hide, but the shot from that location would be upwards of 2000 meters and would likely require a Barrett or a Lapua.

"It's a cabin." Ross said with enthusiasm, "Very cool." He started picking up the pace. David let him go on, still interested in the tactical position the cabin was in and how he would defend it. It wasn't perfect from what he could see. He thought about his dad and why he would have picked this place for a cabin. Dad wasn't stupid. He would have thought this through and he had the tactical knowledge to do it. David stopped and turned around looking back at the Jeep and then again at the cabin. He continued into the trees and near the front of the cabin, then again looked back at the Jeep. This cabin was not meant to be more than a temporary home. It was too small to house a family for anything other than short term. He walked around to the back. There was a small stream running from the meadow to the back of the cabin and down into the timber; dad would have called it a 'crick.' *Ahh*, David thought, *irrigation*. The smaller of the meadows was for the garden, not the larger as he thought earlier. Also, once he got a better look at the tactical side of things, this was a pretty good place. Especially if others were built in a perimeter to support this one. '*Pretty smart, old man.*' David smiled. Suddenly, he missed his dad again, thinking he would have wanted to compliment him for choosing such a good location. David continued around the small cabin until he arrived at the front door.

"It's locked." Ross said disappointingly. "Maybe we can get in through one of those windows." He was pointing to the windows high on the wall, but too narrow for them to squeeze through.

"Yeah," David said, "…or we could use this key." He pulled out the shiny red key from his package. David tried the key in the lock. It was not a match.

"Doesn't fit…not even close." David said quizzically, "I wonder what this is for, then?"

Ross was already looking around for a hidden key, finding one of all places—under the mat. The key fit perfectly. David looked sheepishly back at his brother.

"What a dork." Ross said as he pushed open the door.

CHAPTER 3

"Soon shall We cast terror into the hearts of the Unbelievers, for that they joined companions with Allah, for which He had sent no authority." -Quran (3:151)

Achmed walked quickly toward the back of the mosque. This would be a day of days; the day he would lead an effort to destroy the infidel. It was only right as it was mostly his idea. He only needed help from the financiers to implement the plan—and now they would provide the funding. Frustrated at first, because he knew the idea was sound, the leaders finally agreed after a lengthy period to decide for action. It was a bit strange that they now seem to be in a big hurry. Apparently, his mission was to be coordinated with others of a different type. He wondered about them and what they might be. He would know soon enough, the meeting would start in just a few minutes. He did not want to be late for his own mission brief. That would be unacceptable.

As he entered the room, he scanned for who he might know. Sitting front and center was Abu Bakr al-Baghdadi. He froze. It was unthinkable; walking into a room to brief a mission and seeing the supreme leader of the Islamic State. He knew the man from his picture only. This was surreal and he had no idea what the protocols were; does he acknowledge him, shake hands, bow, and kneel…even approach him? Still frozen he now continued his scan in hopes he would be prompted what to do. No one moved.

"Achmed." The voice came from back in the doorway to his left. He turned and saw Ari motioning to come back outside. Achmed glanced back at the Emir, who seemed uninterested in his presence, likely because he didn't know who Achmed was at this point. That raised a question; *would he still be the one to brief the mission?* He doubted it now. He was too insignificant. His heart sank a bit but he was strangely relieved at the same time.

Someone grabbed his arm firmly and continued to marshal him toward the door. The man was huge and had a large scar on his face that went from his forehead and across his left eye, stopping on his cheek just above the jawbone. From the look of it, stitches were not part of the healing process. Achmed didn't struggle or resist in anyway. In fact, he increased the pace toward the doorway to convey to his usher that he was very willing to accept his terms. Ari stepped back through the door as Achmed approached. The large man loosened his grip only after Achmed cleared the room. Certainly, this man was a bodyguard. He looked at the man with as much respect as he could project and nodded. The bodyguard's expression did not change, he only displayed a look of disdain; the eyes were cold and dead. Achmed had seen that look several times before—it was the look of someone who could kill without any conscious thought—a condition achieved only through conducting that act many times. He could terminate Achmed's existence on the earth with no more cognition than flushing a toilet. Achmed felt like a demon crossed over his soul.

"Achmed…what are you doing???" Ari was stressed by what just happened. "You cannot just walk into this place like you own it!"

"I have been here many times over the last few weeks, and never have I encountered this…" Achmed turned back to look into the room just as the door shut. "What is happening? Is that not the Emir?"

"Shhhh, aieee! This is a secret meeting. They are to discuss many things…to include your ideas. I have heard them say your name several times." Ari pulled him further away from the door.

"What is going on…what am I to do?" Achmed inquired, his voice trembling now.

"I am unsure…but for now, just stay right here. We will wait for instructions." Ari said, trying to calm his friend.

Achmed needed to smoke a cigarette in the worst way. It always calmed him. He thought of asking his friend if he could, but already knew the answer. He would have smoked a whole pack before he came had he known of the situation. That reminded him; *what was the situation?* The door opened and the scarred man looked to the opposite side of the room from where Achmed stood. He motioned to

Mohammed; a local business man Achmed had known since he was a child. Mohammed snapped to and quickly moved toward the door. What would he be doing here? And, why would the Emir want to see him? There were so many questions and so few answers, his head was spinning. He needed to sit down…was that permitted? Could he at least squat?

About thirty minutes passed and the door opened again. Mohammed emerged and walked slowly into the center of the room then paused and looked toward Achmed. His face was emotionless for several seconds before he simply nodded, then he seemed to come to his senses and left quickly without a word. This made Achmed's heart race again and he felt himself sweating like when his father was about to take a cane to him for disobedience. He was feeling nauseous now.

"Ari, I need to sit down." Achmed said softly. Ari looked at his friend and could visibly see color draining from his face. He held Achmed's arm and helped him down to a squatting position.

"Achmed, what is wrong with you? Ari sounded more puzzled than concerned.

"I think…I think I am just afraid." Achmed sputtered. It felt good to at least squat. He felt that if he had not, he would have fainted.

"Afraid of what…do you not know that if you were in trouble they would not let you be here?" Ari was still confused at Achmed's behavior.

Achmed contemplated what Ari just said. He was right. If he had done something wrong, the last place he would be was here, in the presence of the Emir. He started to relax and his breathing began to return to normal. The sweat now was cool and almost refreshing. He was glad Ari was here.

"Ari…I'm better now…" he paused, "You are right, I didn't expect this…you know?" Achmed slowly stood to his feet. "I was already excited before I came here and I did not sleep well in anticipation of the briefing. Thanks be to Allah that I did not know of this…with…" He stopped short.

"This is a great day for you, my friend. Your name will be uttered on the lips of many jihadi in the days to come." Ari boasted for his friend.

It was just an idea, Achmed thought. He almost wished someone else had thought of it and was uncomfortable with the accolades. Pride was not a good thing, he had been taught that from a very young age. He was experiencing pride before he walked in here, now he only experienced…what was it…fear? Yes, it was fear. Yet another thing he was not supposed to feel.

The door opened again and the man with the scar appeared. He scanned the room, finally stopping on Ari but saying nothing. Ari turned to Achmed and nodded. The bodyguard's steely gaze now bored holes in Achmed. Once again, he began to feel sweat flee from his pores, but managed to maintain his composure. The bodyguard opened the door wide and stepped to the side—a gesture for Achmed to enter. As he stepped forward, Achmed drew in a deep breath and slowly exhaled, then he moved toward the open door and the specter holding it open for him. The bodyguard raised his hand to stop Achmed before he entered. It was not a threatening gesture; clearly he wanted to say something.

"You do not approach the Emir unless he motions for you to do so. Once you are in position to brief the room, you will acknowledge him first—non-verbally—before you start, and last before you leave. Do not dwell on him during the briefing—brief the room. Do you understand?" The huge man seemed less threatening now. Achmed nodded affirmatively and he started into the room. The bodyguard stopped him again.

"What you are doing is a great thing and admirable. Allah is with you; both in this room and on your mission. Know that and be comforted." The man seemed almost human now. Still, the eyes were dark and empty. Again, Achmed nodded to the man, unable to think of an appropriate response. He turned and walked into the room with as much reverence as he could project—if that were possible.

The cabin was plain, but functional inside. There was a Majestic wood cook stove at the end opposite of the door and a table with four chairs in the center of the room. The west wall had two bunks; one queen sized on the bottom, and a twin on the top. The east wall had a countertop running along it. Other than that, it was relatively empty, save a selection of various tools hung on the walls. They were not for decoration. Everything seemed to be functional of purpose. Ross wondered about the four chairs. It was just mom and dad up here, who would have needed the other two? Now, that he thought more about it; why two beds?

"I expected more," Ross said, referring to the basic amenities. "Didn't you?"

"This may not be the only one…if I'm guessing, this was the first building and was designed simply to work from." David replied. "A functional shelter…judging by the age of the logs, this would have been built shortly after they bought the property."

"You think there's something else?" Ross seemed surprised.

"I don't know what it is—a cabin, or otherwise—but they spent a lot of time up here over the last three years and I doubt it was to hang out in this." David referred to the meager means.

David took note of the loft above one-half of the ceiling area. He looked for a ladder and spied it hanging under the counter, on the wall. He unhooked it and set it up to climb to the loft. Reaching into his thigh cargo pocket on his pants, he produced a small tactical flashlight and began to climb the rungs. As he placed his weight on the second rung, it broke and he fell into the ladder and slid to the floor. Ross laughed at his brother's position; face resting on the third rung.

"Damn, I almost bit my tongue off!" David exclaimed, spitting a small amount of blood. The age of the ladder and the failed rung confirmed the age of the cabin. It was likely the ladder sustained more aging as clearly it had been used outside, and the elements had accelerated the rotting of the rungs. Not to be outdone, David scaled the ladder again, but this time he placed his feet on the rungs as close to the risers as he could to alleviate stress. He also transferred more weight to the risers by using his arms; just in case another rung gave away.

"Whoa, I didn't expect that!" David said, looking into the loft. "This is crazy!"

"What is it???" Ross was excited.

"Look for yourself" David jumped down to the floor.

Ross quickly moved up the ladder as he had just seen his brother do. As he looked into the loft he knew he had been duped. There was only another bed…a queen sized one—exactly what one would expect to be in a loft. He loitered a few moments longer, letting his eyes adjust to the low light just in case there really was something else. There wasn't.

"Nice, dork." Ross said sarcastically. "Were you hoping another rung would kill me or something?"

"Something like that." David jibed, spitting more blood, this time out the open door.

Ross pushed out from the ladder and jumped to the floor, but not before a moderate sliver from the riser embedded itself in his hand. He cussed. David laughed as Ross dug at the menacing shard.

"Karma." David asserted.

They went outside and searched the area. There was a small shed—empty—and an outhouse. Nothing else was in sight. They followed the stream from below the cabin and into the pines. There was a trail, but it had not been maintained in some time. For the most part it paralleled the stream.

"We need to get back soon," David said. "We'll be late for dinner."

"Yeah, I just want to see where this goes," Ross plugged. "It's the tracker in me."

"You couldn't track a freight train." David joked. Ross whipped a pinecone back at his brother and tripped, nearly falling on his face. He cussed again.

"Karma." David said, as if it were a fact.

Suddenly, Ross caught a glint through the timber in front of him. A few more steps and its source was evident—a lake. Well, a pond really, but it was a good sized one. Just as they fully cleared the pines a pan-sized trout broke the surface and splashed back into the crystal water. Rings of ripples emanated from the center of the re-entry point where the fish had been.

"Rainbow?" Ross asked.

"Cutthroat." David responded.

They both stared at the water, trying to see where the fish had gone. While the water was absolutely clear and the sun glinting off the ripples made it difficult to see. David pulled out his polarized sunglasses. After putting them on, he just grinned.

"There must be fifteen of them…right there!" He pointed in the direction of the splash. "Check it out."

"Yeah?" Ross said excitedly, "Well, check that out!"

David looked at his brother to see where he was staring. Across the pond to the northern shore was a cabin—a nice cabin. It was recessed back into the timber making it difficult to see, but it faced the water and had a nice covered porch. Still, it was rustic looking; not like a kit or a modern log home. David wondered about the satellite image he used when he surveyed the area and when this cabin had been constructed. Surely, it was after his image was taken; he would have noticed it.

"Come on dork!" Ross spouted, already continuing down the trail that now took a sharp right turn and followed along the bank of the pond.

"Whoa, cowboy," David cautioned. That cabin is not on our land. Our land ends on this eastern bank; the northern bank belongs to someone else."

Ross stopped, clearly disappointed. "Well, let's go meet them anyway…being new neighbors and all."

"It's late, we don't have time. Besides, I want to do a little research first…find out who owns that and other properties up here." David again spoke with a reserved caution in his voice. "We're going to come back up here again tomorrow with the girls anyway. That will give me time to check things out and if we do go over there, it might appear less threatening if they are with us. Besides, if we meet them now and then later, it will be evident you and I came up here today…Leigh and Carrie don't know, remember?"

"Oh yeah, that might be bad, huh?" Ross chuckled.

They took a last look and turned up the trail the way they came. As they approached the Jeep, David was thinking about the GPS coordinates and why his father gave him the one where the Jeep now rested. It didn't seem to have any significance. He decided to take a closer look and told Ross to as well. At first, they thought it might be a focal point for something else on the property, but nothing seemed obvious to them. David fired up the Jeep and they headed back down the mountain. Ross didn't walk across the creek crossing as he had threatened earlier. David seemed to get across it without much problem this time. As he crossed, he thought about how easy it would be to remove the rocks from the crossing; it would deny most vehicles from passage, thereby forcing any unwanted trouble to finish the trek to the redoubt on foot—which was about eight miles or so. He made a mental note of it.

They pulled into the parking lot of the hotel restaurant at ten minutes after 7 pm. They were late and had no time for a shower. Their plan was simple; go in through the bar entrance, get a shot at the bar, and act as though they went to the gun show and had a good time. They hoped the girls would buy it.

They didn't.

The sun was setting on the western edge of the pond. It was always beautiful and consoling. This time of year, sunsets coincided with the smell of dinner being prepared. The pond was calm; not a ripple in it, save the occasional fish jump. He stepped out onto the porch to get a better look. The air was crisp and he filled his nostrils by drawing a slow, deep breath; a wisp of smoke in the air from the fireplace mixed with the scent of dinner. It was the perfect place on earth to be, yet in the back of his mind he was troubled. Things were not yet settled and he was reminded of it by events earlier in the day when he saw two men standing on the eastern edge of the pond. Though it was a couple hundred yards away, he had a good idea who they might be. He resisted the urge to use the binoculars to confirm his suspicions. He looked back through the screen door at his wife, now filling the plates with what would yet be another great meal. He didn't tell her of the sighting; it would ultimately only upset her. Still, the day would come when the men would find a way to their cabin. He was glad it was not today. Much more must come to pass before that time. He looked back onto the water and the sun, now below the crest of the mountain. The colors were a cobalt blue with a transition to orange as they touched the retreating sun. The pond reflected both colors. A loon's haunting song broke the silence. His mind now drifted away from today's event and into the environment now bonding with him.

"A penny for your thoughts, honey." The voice came from the other side of the screen door. He turned to see her face as she pushed open the door and joined him; wrapping her arms around his waist. He heard her take in a long breath as he had done earlier and felt her warm breath on his neck as she exhaled. "I love this time of the evening." She said, still smiling.

He hugged her back and drew her closer. "Yes, it is a paradise…God cannot be outdone. Nothing man-made could ever compete with this, could it?" She nuzzled her head deeper onto his chest. He thought about telling her of the sighting. "Dinner is getting cold…we should go in." She said, loosening her arms. "Yes, I'm hungry." He smiled back at her. He almost said something; it would have been a mistake. Still, he would have to tell her sometime, wouldn't he? If he did, the longer he waited the more angry she would be, knowing that he knew earlier. Yes, he would keep it to himself. If they did return and come to their cabin he would not disclose that he had seen them. He was torn, but he knew it was best they did not come back until…well, more had to happen, didn't it? She called again, wanting him to join her. He took one last look through the screen door as he let it gently close, not wanting to disturb the moment extending beyond the porch. "Ahh, pheasant dinner...my favorite!" he pretended to be surprised. He had killed the roosters earlier that morning. She rolled her eyes and slid the plate in front of him. "Yup, my very favorite."

CHAPTER 4

"Be not weary and faint-hearted, crying for peace, when ye should be uppermost, for Allah is with you..." -Quran (47:35)

Mohammad reached into his backpack and produced his Quran. He would read to quell his fears and to demonstrate to his captors that he was indeed—one of them. Were they his captors? He didn't know. It was true they were restricting him from leaving this facility but yet they were treating them well. *Them*; the other jihadi from America. There were about fifty or so. Mohammad was from Sanford, Florida. He was part of a trend of American citizens volunteering to join ISIS; a militant Islamic group recently exposed on the international scene as the next big threat to the West. Mohammad came to fight with those now invading Syria and Iraq. He was not alone in his desire to travel a great distance to aid his 'brothers in arms.' Muslims from all over the world were joining the jihad. He was uncommon because he was white and born in the United States.

John Wesley Jones—his given name—came from generations of American born family. They were strong Southern Baptists and they voted Republican. Anyone in the family that disclosed anything else was looked at askance. To convert to Islam—well, that was way off the reservation! He kept it a secret for nearly a year, but as he grew stronger in the religion he became bolder until finally he felt he would burst when listening to other family members talk trash about the 'rag heads' in the Middle East. "Kill them all; and let God sort 'em out!" was the typical statement. He hated them for it. At one point he plotted to kill them just before he left for the jihad—a true bridge burning for sure. But, he didn't and because of that decision he was joined with these fifty odd others. 'Johnny' Jones was in this room because everyone here could return to the United States with very little scrutiny; they were all American born citizens, with American passports, and all were of non-Arabic descent. Johnny—or Mohammad, as he called himself—hadn't legally changed his name yet, as demonstrated by his passport. He intended to change his name as part of his 'bridge burning' strategy, but thought better of it when considering his 'escape' from the United States. There were those being detained by U.S. Customs for openly declaring their intent to join ISIS; or ISIL, as the President called it. Mohammad decided to keep a low profile in order to successfully complete his plan. He even adjusted his travel itinerary to avoid scrutiny by first flying to Italy, then to Cyprus, and to his final destination.

Mohammad's conversion had been peaceful at first, but he met another 'Mohammad' while attending services at the mosque. This man subtly introduced a more ominous side of the Quran. Pointing out obligation to destroy the infidel and join jihad. "It is the written word of Allah," he had said, "You cannot pick and choose to your own liking, what you will believe and what you will not... what you will *do* and what you will not." It made sense to Johnny. He felt convicted and incomplete as a true Muslim. At one point he wanted to meet with the leadership of the mosque, to confirm this tenet of his new found faith, but 'Mohammad' told him not to do so, "...they must maintain plausible deniability...to approach them would compromise that." Were they really silent supporters of this tenet? He didn't know, but at some point it didn't matter. He decided that if it wasn't true, then Allah would not have included it in his holy scriptures.

This, of course, is the fatal flaw in the Muslim religion with regard to extremism; the Quran *does* contain these passages and as long as they are there, they can—and will—be exploited by those who would embrace them. Some mosques covertly support these tenets, while others do not appear to, but in Johnny's experience there was always somebody in the congregations that did, whether the leadership was directly involved or not. He had travelled to other mosques with 'Mohammad' and was introduced to those that believed as he did. He really didn't like the secrecy of it, but understood in American society why it had to be this was way—for now. One day they would be openly recognized as pioneers of the American Islamic Movement— forefathers' of a new world order, in which all nations of the world would be Muslim. That would be a glorious day for sure.

"Are you well, my brother?" One of the guards addressed him and shook him from his daydream. Mohammad looked up to see him smiling. He returned the smile and the sentiment.

"Yes, I will always be well as long as I am in the holy lands…my brother."

The guard moved on, continuing to engage the others as he passed them. Mohammad felt a bit more comforted. He had thoughts of having his head removed on television as had several people recently. *Yes, but they were infidels*, he told himself, *captured—not willing jihadi like himself.* Still, he felt like he needed to prove who he was somehow in order to avoid a similar fate. He was reminded of one of the decapitated victims being a cameraman who was in fact, a practicing Muslim. However, the man was not a professing jihadi like Mohammad. He was a western journalist, living a life of comfort and likely did not subscribe to jihad. If he were in fact 'innocent' then he would be a true martyr of the faith, but only Allah can judge.

'On a chilly night, the 16th April of 2014, a small group of highly trained and educated personnel crawled into manholes near a San Jose, California sub-station and severed the fiber optic communications lines that served to provide security alerts for the sub-station as well as 911 services to local residents that would soon hear gunfire. In the 19 minutes that followed, over 100 rounds of ammunition were expended at select targets inside the fence of the sub-station; 17 giant transformers and several junction boxes supplying power to Silicon Valley were taken out in what was clearly a surgical attack. Small piles of rocks were used to mark the firing locations for each of the transformers; a clear indication the operation had been well planned and practiced before it was executed. The transformers were methodically targeted in a way that would disable the sub-station and they would not explode, but instead overheat and shutdown. It took 27 days to bring the sub-station back on line.'

Dirk Madison lifted his fingers off the keyboard of the computer terminal and leaned back in his chair, still staring at the report he was writing. *This is bad*, he thought to himself, *and no one is paying attention.* He looked at the clock on his desk; 11:36 pm. He really needed to finish this, but he was tired and previous attempts to 'educate' his superiors had resulted in nothing...nada. In fact, he was chastised and told to stick to his own area of expertise. In short, they didn't want 'that kind of signature on it.' *Signature? That's a term used by political mongers!* He shook his head. *They don't realize the gravity of this incident. It was highly coordinated and executed—a Special Forces type of operation.* He should know, he spent six years in 'the business' before he blew his knees out and was medically retired. He sat up and addressed the keyboard again.

'Concerning future attacks, of the 55,000 substations located in the United States, as few as 9 being hit in a similar manner could take out the entire US power grid for weeks or even months. This reported by the Federal Energy Regulatory Commission Chairman.'

Dirk again paused. *I'm wasting my time here,* he thought, *I've said this all this before. Even NPR and several periodicals reported it. No one cares...now, but they will...because it's coming; and soon. What could he do?* He closed the cover on the laptop and rubbed his eyes. Quite honestly there was only one thing to do—not be a victim of this train wreck. No, he didn't want give up trying to get them to listen, but he needed to prepare himself for the inevitable. He'd read several books on the subject and disliked the whole 'prepper' thing, but he had to admit that having a plan was something he could no longer ignore. Living in the D.C. area was also an issue; if the power went out here, 50% of the population would likely die in the first couple of weeks—either by natural or 'unnatural' means. He thought about his retirement checks and his pension. They would be worthless in the economy crash following the power grid loss. So would his 401K. He should liquidate it now...get something out of it. Time was short.

He stood and looked out the window. The streets were empty; just a dim glow of foggy lights trying to illuminate the dingy streets below. *"I really have to get going on this plan"*, he said, mumbling to himself, *"Now."* He turned from the window. Grabbed his coat and headed for the door. He would sleep on it for now, but his mind was fairly made up; he would draft the resignation letter tomorrow. No more procrastinating. This was just too serious. If he was wrong, then his retirement would be a bit more meager than he planned—growing his own food and living in the wilds of Montana. But, if he was right, that existence would be more than 95% of the United States citizenship would enjoy. He was never a gambler, but those odds were worth wagering on. At least he was guaranteed to be alive. Yes, he would do it.

Turning to look into the office that would soon belong to someone else, he clicked off the light and locked the door. He felt an immediate release from his decision to leave; for him this was all the confirmation he needed.

Mason sat on the edge of the bed and listened to Leigh read from the package she'd received from the lawyer. He was stunned for the most part, yet he wasn't really surprised. He had had many conversations with Robert Wallace about preparing for catastrophic events. Prior to those conversations Mason had been a skeptic; making fun of 'preppers' on television. The show sensationalized everything and clearly targeted 'idiots' for the purpose of entertainment. Seldom did they have what he thought to be legitimate preppers, on the show. Part of that would have been because no legitimate prepper would expose himself and his efforts on a national television program. To do so would compromise everything. When things got bad and everybody was out of food, they would know who had some and eventually come to take it out of desperation. Robert told him to covertly acquire guns, ammunition, food, medical and dental supplies, etcetera, and to have a plan to escape the city to a safe "bug-out" location. He quoted a study done under President Reagan citing that 90% of city dwellers would be dead within a few weeks and that only a 'bad element' would survive there—looting, killing, and worse. He stared intently at the floor, wondering what he would have to do if he stayed in that environment. Certainly, it would involve lethal means to protect his family.

"Hey, are you listening to me?" Leigh squawked.

"Uhh, yeah…I was." He retorted.

"U-huh, so what did I say???" she challenged.

"Uhh, yeah, well you were talking about your dad's letter and the Montana thing." He was in trouble now, struggling to recall that last few words she read.

"Riiight, and what was the last thing I said?" The challenged had been upped. He would go down in flames now.

Going for broke, he resorted to humor. "Uhh, your underwear was too tight???"

"Mason! You think you're funny, but you're not. I'm being all serious and our life could change soon. You need to pay attention and tell me what you think about this stuff!" Leigh was stressed and his joke didn't help. He felt bad about it.

"Okay, I'm sorry. I was thinking about stuff your dad said earlier. I am serious about this…more than you know. I think about it all the time—how I would protect you and Tanner and get to a safe place." He was serious now, she could see it in his eyes.

"Well, that's what this is about…a safe place." She continued. "The land in Montana is a where he's saying we should go."

"Yeah, I know," he said defensively, "If something happens, then we have a place to go…I get it."

"No Mason," she paused to consider what she was about to say, "…now!"

"Now…What do you mean, now?" He wished he had been listening. His head was trying to reconcile everything, but he was more confused than ever.

"Dad is saying it's time to move to the redoubt now." She stated.

"Now?" He said incredulously. "But, I thought it was when something catastrophic happened. I don't understand. Did something happen? Wait…read it to me again." Leigh raised her eyebrow and cocked her head. He knew what that meant; '*here it comes, boy…get ready.*' She took a deep breath and flipped the documents at him. "Here, you read it!

I'm going to check on Tanner…tell me when you're done." She boomed.

Landon watched his wife fumble around the hotel room. She did that kind of stuff when she was unsettled—trying to act busy, as if that would somehow manifest itself into the reality that it would make her busy enough to forget whatever was bothering her. *Kind of ironic if you really think about it,* he thought. He knew where this was going; she wanted him to engage her in conversation about the whole ordeal, but he'd had enough already. Carrie always centers on the minor details; he just wants the Reader's Digest version. She would keep this up until he either caved-in—starting the inquiry—or she would blow up and find an excuse to get mad at him. He was in peril either way. Still, it would be less painful to engage in conversation, knowing that after the 'blow up' he'd end up there anyway.

"So, I'm confused about something…how would your dad know a year after his death, when his will was read, that it was the time to move to the…what did you call it?" Landon groaned inside.

"Redoubt." Carrie popped back, clearly pleased he asked. She made her way to the bed and sat beside him. He knew what it was, but it was a segue into the scenario. She pulled the document from the manila folder and started reading.

"I cannot go into detail here, particularly the facts. For you to know these things would put you in danger. The same kind of danger I am in. I've put your mother and myself in a position of peril and there are those who would not want this information to become public…" Carrie continued to read the document as Landon listened. He had read it before, but as he listened to her speak, a thought occurred to him; *this part of the message wasn't specifically for us— it was for those who might believe we were made aware of the facts…Wallace added this text to protect us…he knew it might be read by someone else. And, by making this statement, he was implying that he hadn't disclosed anything to us.* Landon stiffened and felt an uneasy feeling start to build. *Were the Wallace's murdered?*

43

"What was it your sister said?" Landon interrupted her. "She said your mom knew about something…was preparing for…"

"Yeah, she was like, getting things in order for something big." Carrie responded, looking quizzically at him for cutting her off. "Why…what do you know? Wait; what?"

Landon stood and looked around the room, though he didn't know for what. He felt slightly ill, driven by the essence of fear. It was the fear of being watched. His mind reeled as he tried to reconcile everything that had happened. Every conversation he had with Wallace—every inference concerning politics and conspiracy. It was so subtle, yet to put it all together; it made sense. Wallace didn't overtly assert conspiracy, but it was implied in little hints here and there in his assessments of current political events. He was a patriot and had passionate respect for the Constitution as well as a disdain for those who tried to erode its tenets for their own lusts. Landon just kind of went along with the conversations to appease the man, but now he wished he'd listened more critically.

"What is wrong with you???" Carrie broke his concentration. He looked back her, she was still scanning his face for understanding. His eyes narrowed and as he brought his index finger to his lips and mouthed, "shhhhhhhh…" He turned the television on and brought the volume up to a good level. Then, he grabbed her hand and guided her into the bathroom. He looked around and until he saw his reflection in the mirror. He felt foolish; what did he know about any kind of devices or spying or whatever? Yet, he felt threatened—that was real.

"Get dressed. We're going out to dinner." Landon said emphatically. Carrie scrunched her eyebrows and mouthed, "What's going on?"

Landon whispered back so she could hear, "I don't know, but I don't think we should talk here. Just get dressed. We'll take a walk and I'll tell you then."

She thought about pressing him on the issue, but he was clearly stressed about something and she had not ever seen him act like this. "Okay," she said rather loudly, "I'm starving."

Landon smirked and rolled his eyes—she wasn't good at this spy stuff, either.

CHAPTER 5

"If ever the time should come, when vain & aspiring men shall possess the highest seats in government, our country will stand in need of its patriots to prevent its ruin." –Samuel Adams, Letter to James Warren, October 24, 1780

"So what the heck's going on?" Carrie spit out, not wanting to wait another second. Landon looked back at the hotel room door, they were barely 20 feet from it.

"Geez, I said a walk, not 'let's go out in the parking lot!'" Landon quipped back, as he marshalled her by the arm toward the trail that led into a small wooded area. She complied, but her lack of patience was clearly visible.

The trail meandered along the edge of a small pond. It was quiet except for the birds singing in a nearby tree. Landon was starting to feel foolish again about his 'spy' behavior and was re-thinking his initial knee jerk reaction to get out of the hotel room. Was it just his imagination, or was there something really to this? Carrie broke his train of thought.

"Well Matahari, don't you think this is far enough?" she chided. He felt even more foolish now.

"Yeah, …look, I don't know if there's anything to this, but just think about it for a second; the conversation you had with your sister, the way your mom was getting things in order, the business your dad used to be in…and probably still was, they never really retire…and then this paragraph in the letter." He produced the document and had her read the statement. She slowed her gait and came to a stop. He scanned her face as she read. He could tell by her eye movements that she read it twice. She paused for a moment, and thought about what she just read. Her eyebrows raised and her face brightened as she slowly looked up.

"Wow…" she said, pausing again, her eyes darting back and forth across his face. He knew she was putting all together, so he didn't interrupt her thoughts. He watched as her face gradually changed; the realization of what was a logical conclusion now rolling through her mind. A tear now forming in the corner of her eye, confirmed to him that she had reached the same conclusion as he did and he didn't feel foolish anymore.

"You think they were murdered for what they knew?" Her voice cracked. It was more of a statement than a question. "He was protecting us, wasn't he…I mean; this statement here wasn't just for us, was it?"

"No, I don't think it was for us at all." He confirmed.

"Who then? The lawyer?" She sounded as though she was trading sadness for anger.

"No, I don't think so. The envelopes were sealed and besides; they were childhood friends—your dad trusted him." Landon sounded sure. "It was likely that your dad knew a soft version was easy enough to extract…be hacked…whatever." Landon worked in IT for several years before making a bold career change in becoming a pilot, so she was fairly confident he would know that to be true.

"But how? They were in a plane and the fighter pilot we met with told us how things happened…unless…they were shot down and he lied to us?" Carrie said thinking out loud.

"No, not likely. Remember, they were supposed to land in Savannah. They would have descended well before they got there. The plane flew a long distance—at altitude—over the ocean. The air traffic controllers tracked them out there before the fighters were dispatched." He paused to reflect a moment, thinking of how it might have been done. "It wouldn't be hard for a mechanic to sabotage the aircraft pressurization system…maybe some kind of timer or altitude trigger to…wait until…" He didn't finish the sentence. She nodded, another tear rolling down her cheek made him regret the suggestion.

"It doesn't matter." She said. "They're gone and they're not coming back." She thought about Landon's earlier statement in the hotel room. How would her dad know that his will being read—a year after his death—would be the critical time for them to move to the redoubt? Dad had insisted—strongly.

"The redoubt." He was raising the issue just as she was thinking it through. "He would have had to have known within a short period of time that he and your mom would be…" he trailed off, knowing he had yet again made the suggestion of murder. He felt bad, but how else to reconcile the redoubt issue without discussing the likelihood of murder, or at least foul play? It would have to have been timed near perfectly. Unless Wallace knew if he were murdered, that it would somehow coincide with events resulting in the social-economic collapse of the United States…or even the world. That was what he was always talking about; the inevitability of an event that would result in TEOTWAWKI; a substitute used by preppers and stood for 'The End Of The World As We Know It.' This was not necessarily Armageddon as mentioned in the Bible, but Robert Wallace believed the United States would not be a factor in Armageddon as they were not mentioned in the Bible to be a contributor in that event. He felt that our own technology and our reliance on it would be at the center of our demise. Landon heard Wallace preach this many times—the idea that regardless of the initial trigger—the ultimate result would be an eventual loss of the power grid. This is why he believed that if you prepped for loss of the grid, you would be prepared for any event, regardless of what caused it.

If the event were an enemy nuclear strike in the upper atmosphere, the EMP—or Electro Magnetic Pulse—would destroy the power grid and any controlling computers that manage it. All electronic devices would be permanently disabled. Cars, buses, trucks, trains, planes, and all communications would cease—all at once. If the event were to be an outbreak of a virus or disease, those that weren't infected would be fearful of contracting it and refrain from going to public places to include work. Power plants require workers—no workers; no power. If the event were economic collapse, eventually people would not go to work as they wouldn't get paid. Instead, they would do like everyone else and forage for their families or stay home to protect them as civil unrest would be rampant.

Landon started to formulate a possible scenario, "What if your dad knew of a specific event that was due to be carried out or initiated on a certain date…like if he had intelligence information."

"Maybe…," she replied, "…but then how does that explain how he knew the date over a year in advance?"

"I don't know," he responded, "All I know is that I don't feel as safe as I did before we came up here."

"Me either…" she agreed, handing the document back to him, "…Me either."

Dinner was good. David loved barbeque, especially smoked brisket. Yes, it was good, but not as good as his father's. Dad made the best. Still, the relational interaction around the table was what made the night complete. The four siblings laughed and talked and laughed some more. It was typical Wallace shenanigans all around. Teasing, telling embarrassing stories about each other and pretending to be incensed. It would have been perfect, if mom and dad had been there.

They would all head home tomorrow. Earlier, they had spent the day on the property. It was fairly uneventful. David returned to the GPS coordinate again. This time he discovered a rebar marking pin driven into the ground; its painted red tip protruding only slightly. The jeep was parked over it the first time he and Ross were there and was the reason he didn't see it before. David watched the video message from his father and it just about broke him, but the information on the DVD was specific. He knew what was under the rebar and the purpose of the shiny red key. The others obviously didn't watch their DVDs or they certainly would have mentioned it. David wasn't sure why he didn't say anything, only that he didn't want to get into conversations about digging it up. Dad was clear about when that should happen— and it wasn't today. Besides, they didn't have shovels; well, except for the one he saw in the cabin under the long shelf. He thought about the

DVD. It was hard to see his father again and know he was gone, but the disturbing part was what his dad had said about the Department of Homeland Security (DHS) and FEMA. David knew about his father's plans and preparations, and about concerns of 'tyrannical posturing.' That's what dad called it.

Several of the Executive Orders coming out of the White House as well as scores of 'Presidential memos' had illegally legislated actions; setting up ominous powers to a sitting President. These essentially orchestrate a take over the country and run it from a single point of control—in other words; a dictatorship. With the stroke of a pen, the President could enact martial law, temporarily suspending the powers of Congress, and place complete power in—the Presidency, and the secretaries of the six primary departments of government: Agriculture, Energy, Health and Human Services, Transportation, Defense, and Commerce, as well as the members of Defense Production Act Committee: Secretaries of State, Treasury, Defense, Interior, Agriculture, Commerce, Labor, Health and Human Services, Transportation, Energy, Homeland Security, Director of National Intelligence, Director of the CIA, the Chair of the Council of Economic Advisors, the Administrator of NASA, the Administrator of General Services, and the Attorney General. None of these individuals are elected and all are appointed by—and report to—the President. The President only needs to leverage an excuse to enact the process. This is even more disturbing when considering "Executive Order – National Defense Resources Preparedness" dated 16 March 2012, Section 103(c), which states; "…in the event of a *potential* threat to the security of the United States, to take actions necessary to ensure the availability of adequate resources and production capability, including services and critical technology, for national defense requirements." In short; that could mean everything and anything interpreted as 'critical.' David was skeptical of his father's interpretation until he looked it up himself on whitehouse.gov and verified it. The executive orders state, among other things, that all resources to include the US military could be employed to force any civilian entity to surrender services, resources, materials (even privately owned), and personnel (labor)…*without compensation*, regardless of ownership. This includes any and all food resources, water sources, and anything required in the production of them; to be distributed or redistributed as deemed necessary.

David thought about the additional patch he had noticed on several police uniforms lately—they were augmentees for DHS. He remembered hearing they were looking for volunteers from police departments, fire departments and emergency services. A friend of David's—Sammy Jessop—recently left the Air Force and became a police officer. He told David about the special qualification. After selection, he was trained to un-package "FEMA Camps" and put them into operation in short order. David was a fan of history and it didn't take much for him to realize these were nothing more than internment camps, much like those of the Second World War used for Japanese Americans. In fact, David actually found a copy of Army FM 3-39.40 "Internment and Resettlement Operations" dated February 2010. It was then David realized his father's conspiracy theories were more than just theories. Still, he didn't really act on anything himself until the President lost the support of the Congress in the last election and stepped up his efforts to incite civil unrest, reduce public fears of Islamic extremism, and essentially allow ISIS, al Qaeda, and others to go unchecked. In short, he was setting up the country for a catastrophic attack, or economic collapse whereby he could enact executive orders and memos. All elections would be suspended and the Constitutional government as currently defined would be replaced 'until order could be restored'—a perfect time to then create a new government and a new constitution with a more socialist agenda. Who better to destroy the Constitution than a self-proclaimed constitutional lawyer who became President?

David remembered a favorite quote that his father had posted on his office wall; *"If ever the time should come, when vain & aspiring men shall possess the highest seats in government, our country will stand in need of its experienced patriots to prevent its ruin."* –Samuel Adams, Letter to James Warren, October 24, 1780. The quote was made into a poster with David holding an American flag on the pinnacle of a Hawaiian peak. Just now, it seemed a little prophetic.

Leigh's laughter broke David out of deep thought; he mentally returned to the table and his siblings. He laughed too, though he didn't know what for—that alone made him laugh. Everyone was having a great time. He didn't want it to end; no one did. He looked around the table and felt a sense of responsibility to protect them. They didn't know what he knew; at least not yet. And they would be skeptical, especially Ross. As close as they were, Ross subscribed to a more liberal mindset. It was the only thing that really separated them at times. David would have to convince his brother and that would likely prove difficult. As a professional musician, Ross would be reluctant to leave his profession of playing to large cities full of his fans to reside in the Montana wilderness and play his sax for the coyotes.

David drifted back into thoughts of the DVD and his father's insistence that he contact Dirk Madison; a counter-terrorism expert and intel analyst working somewhere in DC. He would do that tomorrow. Apparently, dad had worked closely with Dirk on a project to provide Surveillance Detection to all the US embassies world-wide. They remained in close contact even after they went separate ways; Dirk to Washington and dad to some kind of classified program for an intelligence agency. David was young when his father was employed in that world and dad never talked about what he did. The DVD didn't give any indication why David should contact Madison, only that it was very important and it should be post haste. He had never met Madison, that he knew of, and felt awkward about cold-calling the man, but Robert Wallace was a thorough planner when it came to details concerning work related efforts. And because of that, the counter-terrorism expert would likely be expecting the call. David smiled thinking about his father's planning skills at home; because there were none. Mom did all that and dad just left her to it. Mom used to say she didn't know how dad could run a company, but couldn't organize the kids schedule or stay on task at home. David smiled at the thought.

"Hey…where are you?" the inquiry came from Carrie as she waved her hand in front of his face. You're supposed to be a badass killer; a freight train could have snuck up on you just now!

David slipped from his thoughts again to a table full of silence; everyone staring at him. He smiled sheepishly and said, "Yeah, I was thinking about mom and dad."

"Dude, what a buzz kill," Ross quipped, "...you gonna be like that all night?"

David raised his glass and proposed a toast to break the tension and reset the mood. "To me! May I never again be negligent in my duties to lead the Wallace Clan to perfect harmony."

The toast earned him groans from multiple sources and a dinner roll bounced off his head, fired from Leigh. They all laughed and the party continued well into the night. David didn't stray from the festivities again except for once; when he contemplated the toast he made. It was meant to be a joke, though now he realized it was likely a reality.

The next morning, David got up early as he was anxious to contact Madison. He wanted to know why this man was so important to his father as well as why it was urgent he contact him soonest. David watched the section of the DVD that had the phone numbers. The first number he called was Dirk's office which produced a recording stating the number was no longer in service. The second number was a personal cell phone. It was answered after only one ring.

"Yes." The voice was curt and business like.

"Mr. Madison?" David inquired. There was a long pause before David broke the silence. "Hello?"

"I'm not interested." The voice stated.

"Wait, I'm not selling anything...I'm just looking for Dirk Madison. My father gave me this number." David paused and he heard the voice draw a deep breath, but he did not answer right away. This made David uncomfortable as he realized just because he called this number did not mean he could expect to converse with the intended party. The man was being careful—evasive—and that tripped David's caution sense.

"And, your father is…?" the voice was demanding. David did not feel comfortable spitting out his father's name. He wished he had called from a pay phone rather than the hotel room as anyone with simple resources could easily find out who was calling. He decided too much of the 'cat out of the bag' had already been disclosed. He decided to trust the voice.

"Robert Wallace" David said in a monotone voice. Another deep breath from the voice, this time with no hesitation to respond.

"I'm sorry about your father. He was a good friend," Dirk offered. "Which one are you?"

"David Wallace."

"Yes, that makes sense." Dirk said,

This sparked David's interest; *he had been expecting me to contact him.* Things were becoming more mysterious—even ominous. It didn't feel right and he didn't want to be in the dark.

"Make sense how?" David said quizzically.

"Yeah, well…I…" Madison paused, "…tell you what—you're in Montana now, correct?" David thought for a moment and wondered how the man knew his location and then remembered the area code from the hotel phone would have tipped Madison off on his caller ID.

"Yeah, but I was leaving this afternoon to…" David began, but Dirk cut him off.

"Change your plans." The question was directive and not a request. David could extend a day or two, but nothing more; he was expected back at the squadron.

"Where?" David was now curt. He was only slightly annoyed, but it would be an imposition. He didn't like fact he would have to wait to find out anything.

"There's a place your dad used to call his 'favorite escape'…know it?"

David thought about it. The only place he knew his father referred to by that name was a backpacking location—and it was a big location— miles of primitive area in the East Rosebud...or was it the West? He needed more information.

"That's a big place. Can you be more specific?"

"There's a large structure at the end of the road. Follow me?" Dirk sounded friendlier now, but the mystery of why they had to meet at such a remote location still concerned him. David knew Madison must be talking about Mystic Lake dam.

"Yes, my sister hates that *damn* place because dad would insist on vacationing there every year!" David was being cheeky, but he needed confirmation and sliding in the inference was all he could come up with at the moment. None of them had ever been there. It was where dad backpacked when he was young. David had always wanted to go there after hearing the stories, but he never made it.

Madison laughed, "Yeah, well I can see that. Teenage girls have different ideas on vacation. They spell it S-H-O-P-P-I-N-G." He had caught the coy reference to the *dam* and smiled. The kid was quick, like his dad.

"Yes," David chuckled, "You know them well!"

"Meet me there tomorrow at noon...at the top of the structure. Do not bring a cell phone with you...even in the car." Madison was speaking more mysteriously again.

"Roger that." David confirmed.

"Until then." Dirk said curtly again and the line went dead before David could sign off.

"Yeah, see ya...don't be a stranger...love you too!" David joked with himself as he hung up the phone.

"Marital bliss in chaos?" Ross was standing in the now open doorway. David had left it slightly ajar. He thought about what he had just said and thought about how it must have sounded. He decided to go with it.

Yeah; no…just a spat. She wants me home…you know how that goes?"

"Not really," Ross joked. He wasn't in a relationship at the moment, let alone married. Neither was David, but Ross didn't know that. David's girlfriend of five years had recently decided things were too stressful and so she broke it off. "We're ready to go if you are. Girls are already in the Jeep and it is packed full!"

David drove them to the airport. The girls went right through security as their flights were in 45 minutes. Ross's flight was an hour later, so they found a bar and had a last beer together. David thought about the call with Madison and considered saying something, but thought better of it. It wouldn't serve any purpose except to raise a bunch of questions and likely engage them in a conversation that would end on a poor note. He didn't want that, it had been a good visit—no reason to spoil it. He also decided not to disclose the information he learned from the county recorder's office, earlier that morning. The land with the cabin on it next to theirs belonged to Race Kitchenmaster—which was very interesting considering Kitchenmaster was the last name of the pilot flying the plane his parents' perished in. The boys said their good-byes and David watched his brother go through security and out of sight. He didn't look back. David understood.

The drive to Red Lodge was long. He had too much time to be by himself after being surrounded by family and it made him sad. He cranked the radio, rolled down the windows, and even sang along, but it didn't help much. After arriving in Red Lodge he found a motel and got a room using cash he'd drawn out at the airport ATM. The trip to Mystic Lake was still a trek and he would need to get up early. He set his alarm for 5 AM, took a shower and went to bed. It would be a long night; there were a lot of thoughts to keep him awake.

CHAPTER 6

"The Prophet... was asked whether it was permissible to attack the pagan warriors at night with the probability of exposing their women and children to danger. The Prophet replied, "They (i.e. women and children) are from them (i.e. pagans)." -
Bukhari (52:256)

Achmed and Ari entered the room where the American jihadi were held. They had been kept under supervision for quite some time now and it gave the feeling of captivity, though they were treated well. Still, there was visible tension on their faces and Achmed could see it. Ari was seemed stressed as well. Their plan to 'escape' was still thin and needed to be fleshed out more to ensure success, but it did give them hope. The large bodyguard with the scar that protected the Emir was there—and he was armed.

These jihadi were unwitting fools at best. They would be all be martyrs shortly, but didn't know it. Achmed wondered if Allah would reward them the same as those who chose to be martyred, like suicide bombers. *Only Allah can judge them*, he thought to himself. He glanced at Ari who was talking to the Americans; smiling and shaking hands. It seemed to provide comfort. Achmed almost felt sorry for them, their deaths would be horrible—his too, if their escape plan didn't work out. He shuddered inwardly and swallowed hard. If he could reverse time and retract the whole thing, he would. He felt guilty about it and for having planned an escape. Yet, he was considered a hero by his peers. Such mixed feelings confused him.

"Greetings, my brothers. I am Achmed and this is Ari. I hope you are well?" He waited for indications from the jihadi. They nodded. "Good. We have considered your willingness to join the jihad and how your contribution could best be served. While we need everyone we can get on the front lines, we've decided because of your unique background there is a special mission in which you would be better utilized." Achmed paused for effect. He expected them to be excited, but that is not what he saw on their faces. It was fear. This caught him off guard and he was puzzled. 'Scar face' picked up on it too and shifted his weapon from a cradled position to one more ready to use. It came to Achmed that after this long period of captive supervision and his statement of a special mission, they must be thinking they might be used as hostages or even executed. He needed to defuse this immediately.

"You will be boarding trucks outside and travel to a training camp just over an hour from here, where you will train for your mission." Again, Achmed paused, "And, you will be returning to your homeland."

There was some relief, Achmed could see it, but they were still unsettled. Certainly, they had to be confused. He turned to Ari, who was smiling back at him because he was enjoying the suspense. Ari was kind of sick that way. Achmed returned a very subtle smile, only allowing the corner of his mouth to curl up. He glanced at the scar faced man, who was not amused. That completely drained any feelings of humor out of Achmed. He quickly readdressed the jihadi.

"Upon returning to your country, you will be assigned to contacts in various locations and you will receive orders to conduct operations against the infidels. Because of your unique status as natural born American citizens of non-Arabic descent, you will be able to move among them unnoticed, making you the most effective weapon we have ever waged against them. They cry over the few thousands lost in the 9/11 attacks, but this is minor compared to the numbers of casualties you will inflict simultaneously across your nation. They call us terrorists…well, they have not experienced terror yet. We will bring them to their knees and they will fear us everywhere. No one will feel safe. It will shut down their way of life. They will not know safety in any place, nor will they be able to rest. They will know the wrath of Allah and the penalty of unbelief!"

The mood in the room had changed greatly. Achmed observed Ari standing tall with his arms crossed staunchly over his chest. He turned to the scarred man who smiled and nodded. Achmed continued.

"We regret only that we cannot disclose these operations now, as operational security must be maintained. The training will give indication of the types of missions, but location and dates must be withheld. You of course, understand why we do this. If one of you were captured or compromised, the whole of you must be able to continue. This is a great day, my brothers, arise and stand with me!"

The room was now filled with excitement—and relief. It was questionable how many of these 'jihadi' would have been good soldiers anyway. The reality was that after being here for the last few weeks, many likely wished they had never come. The fact that they would be returning home—well, that was just the best news they could get. Achmed had done his job very well and the Emir would be pleased. Now, he and Ari must strengthen their plan. That would be his focus for the next few days while the Americans were in mock training. Yes, they would shoot weapons, learn tactics, and play with explosives. But, they would never be employed to use any of it.

David looked down at the map. It showed the road end just ahead. He looked up and there was the dam. It was bigger and older than he thought. On the far side of the canyon was some kind of tram tracks, though they didn't look like they had been used in some time. As he approached the base of the dam and the end of the road, he saw only one vehicle—it was a doozy. It looked like a military grade camper. He backed into the spot next to it—force of habit in case he needed a hasty retreat.

David got out and stretched as he looked around. The drive was long and the Jeep wasn't known for touring comfort. It was beautiful here, really breathtaking. He walked around the RV and was impressed. It was a custom job of some sort. *Very capable set up*, he thought, and wouldn't mind looking into it himself. It appeared to be on a four-wheel drive Mitsubishi truck chassis, probably 1-ton, very heavy duty with a huge fuel tank; probably diesel. AATREC was written on the back. He'd make a mental note of it and research it when he got back to use his computer. It also had Wyoming plates on it. There was a metal plaque near the door to the camper that said "Insane Canine." Other than the two vehicles, there was nothing else around except a couple of small buildings and what looked like a power station for hydro-electric generators; they were locked. David looked toward the dam and where the trail to the top might be. He glanced back at the tram and decided that even if it worked, he'd rather walk. It literally went straight up the cliff. If the cable broke it would be all over.

Finding the trail head, he started climbing. He wasn't worried about Madison being a threat, his father trusted the man with his life, but he was concerned about the way Madison had been careful and evasive. David picked up on the man's cautious nature quickly. He decided that he would keep his SA—or Situational Awareness—on 'high.' Whatever made Madison cautious just might be out here, though he really didn't think anyone listening on their phone conversation earlier could have ascertained where they would meet. Still; who owned the AATREC? Did Madison make it here at all?

The climb was challenging, but not really difficult. He remembered his dad telling stories about the grueling climb up the trail and on to Slipper Lake, thinking it was an exaggeration until he recalled the trips were weeks long. That would have required their pack weight somewhere in the neighborhood of 70 pounds or even more. David's day pack weighed only 25. He looked at his watch; 10:22 am. He had plenty of time to get to his destination and still scope things out. *Yeah, this would have sucked with a heavy pack on my back,* David thought. He paused to look back at the base of the dam and his Jeep. The AATREC had a solar array on its roof; he'd really like to check that thing out and wondered what it cost. As he was about to start back on the trail, he saw two vehicles coming up the road a half-mile away. They looked like Suburbans—black of course. He didn't like it. Madison wouldn't have brought anyone with him. David picked up his pace; he didn't want to be visible to the vehicles occupants when they arrived at the base of the trail. He was near the top of the dam and the trees would be good cover to observe the newcomers. The trail was steep and the rocks were shifting under his feet, which slowed his progress. He turned to look back to see them round the corner into the parking lot. Clearly, they were in a hurry.

David finally made it to the trees and moved into a position of cover where he could observe. Reaching into his pack, he produced a tactical monocular. The men in the vehicles exited quickly and set up a perimeter in true military fashion, however no weapons were visible at this point. David raised the monocular to view the scene more clearly. His heart was pumping harder now; not so much from the climb as from the threat. It was a threat, wasn't it? He didn't know for sure, but one thing he did know, his mind and body were in 'tactical mode.' He hadn't felt this since Iraq and Syria.

The vehicles both had multiple antennae. Each vehicle produced two men; none of them were dressed for hiking which made David feel somewhat better, though his rental Jeep was still down in the parking lot. David tried to read the license plates but it was too far for the monocular. Two of the men pulled out large binoculars and began looking up in his direction, while the other two checked out the AATREC. They didn't seem to be interested in the Jeep at all. That might be good for him and may mean they were after the AATREC owner. Was that Madison? He thought about how elusive the man was on the phone—secretive even. Yes, it was likely now that Madison did own the vehicle and these guys were looking for him. David eased behind a tree when he saw the men with the binos scan in his direction. They could probably see into deep space with those things; certainly better than his monocular.

The men assembled at the back of the AATREC and were having a conversation and pointing toward the trail head at the base of the dam. He noticed one of them point to the tram, but the others shook their heads. David cracked a smile. That's what he thought too. He looked at their shoes and thought how miserable it would be to climb up here in street shoes. Maybe they wouldn't try it. He continued to concentrate on their gestures to determine what they were planning. Suddenly, they broke apart and two of them started toward the trail head. The others stayed to watch the parking lot. David slowly rose to his feet and was about to turn toward the trail when he realized someone or something was behind him. He heard the slide on the auto-pistol go forward.

"Don't turn around." The voice was low but firm. "Who are you?"

David thought he recognized the voice, but the seriousness of the weapon being ready to fire still kept his attention. He started to slowly move his hands away from his body and toward the sky.

"Don't move at all." The voice was more forceful. "Answer the question."

"David...David Wallace," he said slowly. "Madison...that you?"

The voice ignored the question and the pause was unnerving. David couldn't believe this guy got the drop on him. He should have been more careful, but his focus on the men below had distracted him.

"Your dad had a nickname for you...what is it?" The voice demanded.

"Ahh, Sniff...or Sniffy." David replied.

"Oh, I thought it was 'dork.'" The voice chuckled.

"Oh... well, to dad, everybody was 'dork.'" David said sarcastically as he turned around to see the man holstering his weapon. Madison was older than dad by probably 10 years, but he was clearly in very good shape. David bet he could handle the 9mm Sig on his hip pretty well. The man extended his hand to David. David stepped forward and nearly tripped over a rock to shake hands. Madison had a grip like a python—a real man's handshake, his dad would have said—and he looked David square in the eye.

"Listen kid, we gotta get going," Madison said hurriedly, "...looks like we got company for dinner."

"Yeah, I figured they were friends of yours," David quipped back, "...but I wouldn't worry too much, they weren't dressed very well for dinner and were wearing street shoes."

"You mean the two coming up the trail from the parking lot? Nah, I'm not worried about those two...you probably didn't notice one of the vehicles stopped on the curve down there briefly and at least two more got out," Madison said, as he turned to go. "...and they were dressed for dinner, as well as bringing their own silverware."

62

"Long guns?" David asked.

"ARs of some kind, probably AR-10's judging from the mag size. I could kick myself…I left my heavy stuff in the camper. All I have is this nine-mil," he said patting his holster, "…and a couple of spare mags."

"I'm packing the same." David said. "But it's in this." He pointed to his pack.

"Well, it'll serve you much better out here. You got a holster for it?" Madison asked. David nodded affirmatively. "Good. We gotta make haste here. I'm thinking they'll judge us for average travel and not expect us to close the distance to them. They'll still be moving fast and less stealthy. That's where we'll hit them."

David's radar went into full tactical mode. His instinct would have been to circumvent the men and make his way down to the parking lot. Madison was planning on terminating them.

"Hit who?" David asked, trying to hide the reservation in his voice.

"Kid, I don't know how much your father told you about what he knew, but I can tell you without doubt; the same organization that murdered your parents' sent these guys to get us!" Madison barked.

"Us?" David retorted, "I don't think they know about me. They seemed disinterested in my rental Jeep—only your camper." Madison's pace was strong, but hearing that he paused and looked at David.

"Good point. I'll bet they don't know about you. Although, they know there's somebody up here because the Jeep is in the parking lot. Did you notice if they checked any of the buildings when they got here?" Madison's mind was in high gear now.

"They didn't. They only studied your camper…and by the way, what the hell is that?" David shifted the conversation.

"I'll show it to you later, but we gotta plan this right." Madison shifted back to the task at hand. "Okay, I think you're right; they aren't planning on two of us…we can use that. It'll give us the edge we need.

So do you want to be the prey or the flanker?" He waited for a response. David thought about it for a moment, catching the inference—did he want to be the target these men were hunting, or the surprise waiting to flank them when they engaged?

"Prey, I guess." David responded.

"Okay, then let's keep moving. We gotta find the right spot. These guys are pros and will recognize potential ambush sites subconsciously." Madison was moving fast now, his head wheeling back and forth as if he were scanning and processing every bit of terrain and flora. "We'll only get one shot at it, I'm sure of that. A worn-out old green beret and a kid against some pro shooters..." he paused, "...but I think we're going to be okay."

David was impressed at the way the 'sixty-something' man was moving—fast and quiet. He was about to get in a gunfight with a man he'd just met—against who? Madison hadn't really said. And, he confirmed a suspicion that David had of his parents' being murdered. He wanted to know more about what Madison thought—or knew—about his parents' demise, but this wasn't the time or place. They made their way through the forest for over an hour before they came to a natural rim with about a thirty-five foot drop. Madison surveyed it for several minutes; walking along the edge. He looked off in the direction he anticipated the men would come. Then, he went back up the mountain in the direction he and David had just come from. Nodding his head, he spoke.

"This is it. Come on." Madison said as he made his way back up the mountain. They hiked about 20 yards before Madison stopped. "Okay, so you see that log on its side up there by that cluster of boulders? You're going to hide behind those rocks...I'm going over here." He pointed to some rather dense underbrush.

Madison explained the whole plan to David and told him when to initiate contact. David nodded and took his place. Madison was impressed with the young man's candor and apparent lack of nervousness. They were about to get into a firefight with the intent of killing these men and the kid was rather calm—as if he did it every day.

David made his way to the spot Madison selected and got settled. He was holding his fears well and wondered if the old warrior knew or sensed that he was nervous—fearful even. The truth was that David felt like he was in some kind of shock. Everything was surreal. He thought about what the Green Beret had said; that they had to take these guys out, because if they didn't, they would never get off the mountain alive. David knew it made sense and that he was probably right. Even if they circumvented the men and made it to the parking lot, they would have to deal with the two men guarding the vehicles. If they managed to get through them, the others would be in short pursuit. Trying to escape in a Jeep or a camper wasn't a viable option. David wondered if Madison's plan was to take all six of them out. He hadn't mentioned the two climbing up the trail with street shoes on. They would be moving slower and were probably not anywhere near the top of the dam yet. Also, they would have to make their way back down and by that time the fight would be over; David and Madison would be long gone. Was that the plan? He wished he'd asked.

Suddenly, David saw Madison's sign—they were coming. David felt a little sick and wished he was somewhere else, but he put that aside and took control of his fear—there would be time to deal with those feelings later, after the fight—he hoped. Madison started moving diagonally down the mountain toward the rim and away from the direction the men were traveling. He had found a natural breach in the rim that he hoped the men would climb through. But he also knew the men would see this as a potential ambush point and be on high alert, making the ambush less likely to succeed. He and David had pistols; these guys had high-powered assault rifles.

Madison made his way down through a chimney in the rim about 20 yards away from the spot the men would be climbing up through the rim. If the men were ambushed at this point, they would expect to be flanked from the left or right and from an elevated position. Madison would wait until they cleared the rim and felt safer. With their guard somewhat down, they would proceed further up into David's position at which time David would surprise them and hopefully take one out. Madison would by then have positioned himself diagonally below the second man, but within pistol range. When the second man retreated to the cover of the rim, Madison would take him down. If he charged David, then he would flank him with the same result. It had merit.

David heard voices. The men were actually talking. He couldn't make out what they were saying, but it was clear these two believed they were a long way from Madison. David had doubts now. Maybe they weren't there for Madison. Maybe they didn't even have guns. Could these guys just be up there for fun? He thought about the street shoes, the sneaky way that two were dropped off on a hidden corner...their interest in the camper...no, these guys had bad intentions. David began building up his resolve to do what had to be done. He took a deep breath and let it out slow. His palms were sweating. He wiped them on his pants and checked the status of the weapon in his hand for the last time. David peeked through the rocks and saw the two men coming, their rifles mounted to their chests with a single-point sling. He thought about what Madison said about them being pros. Another 20 yards and David would fire on them. His heart was pounding like a bass drum and he could feel the pulsing in his head and neck. They were walking and talking low, but too relaxed to suspect they were near where they anticipated Madison to be. Pausing, they were looking up the mountain far past David's hiding place.

Madison was now near the top of the rim, having climbed back up behind and diagonally from them. He needed only to take one more step up to be in position to see and fire on the men. Even if David missed them and they charged forward, Madison could get them both. If they retreated, then they would run directly into his fire. He slowly lifted his leg to take the last step up when the rock under his other foot gave away. Madison caught himself without losing any ground, but he was still not in a position to fire. Worse; the rock was falling and would certainly make noise at any second. He decided to scramble up quickly and hope he could at least get one of them.

The falling rock popped loudly as it hit the base of the rim below. The two men turned quickly, swinging their weapons up at the ready. The one on the right saw Madison's head and began to fire. Had the man actually gotten the weapon to his shoulder it would have hit Madison, but he fired too quickly; rookie mistake and a wasted bullet. Still,

Madison could not return fire in this position. Knowing the next shot would be different and the second man would be firing soon, Madison had no choice but to let himself slide back down the rim.

David heard the rock pop and watched the men turn towards Madison and fire. They quickly advanced toward the rim. He knew once they got to the edge it was bad for Madison—there would be few places to hide. David thought for a second about firing from his position and likely getting one of them, but without Madison flanking the second one, success was slim. The men made it to the rim and began firing heavily. David considered the noise from the ARs and took the opportunity to jump out of his position and close the gap to the two men before firing. As he sprinted toward them, he could see they were wearing body armor. His gun arm was up as he ran, though he had not chosen a specific target—he was waiting to see which would turn toward him first. He worried about the crunch of pine sticks and needles under his feet. To him it sounded like a rhino running through bubble wrap, but the men did not hear him or know of his approach. As he reached them, instinct took over and he fired at the head of the man on the right and kicked the back of the man on the left. The bullet struck at the base of the skull of the first man and he fell instantly. The second flailed wildly trying to gain his balance, but it was of no use. He fell off the rim and twisted backwards, looking directly into David's eyes as he fell. It was a look of total surprise. David crouched, expecting the man to fire at him like some kind of movie villain, but it never came. The man hit the base rocks of the rim, bounced over his own feet and rolled for about two yards before Madison's pistol ensured he would never move again.

"You took your time, dork!" Madison yelled up the rim, stepping out from an under crop. David looked down and saw the man was smiling for the first time since they met.

"Well, where the hell were you?!?!" David said, gasping for air. "I thought we had a plan?"

"Plans change…adapt or perish." Madison said flatly. "Go through your man's gear; take what you need and let's get moving. It probably sounded like World War III up here."

David turned to look at the man he had just killed, laying crumpled on the edge of the rim. His eyes were partially open and a fly was already crawling in the blood soaked lichen on the rocks. He rolled the man over to view the weapon underneath him. The mag was much larger than the M-4 David carried when he was deployed—it was an AR-10 as Madison had predicted. He picked up the weapon, clicked the safety on, and released the magazine. The .30 caliber rounds inside were much larger than the .223 round David was used to, then he noticed the green tipped bullets—armor-piercing rounds! Damn, who did they think they were after? David looked down at Madison methodically stripping his prey, checking every pocket, nook and cranny. He marveled at the efficiency of the survey, pausing briefly to scan things and then he would either pocket an item or pitch it. Madison stood and looked up at David as he slipped something into his pocket.

"Get the armor too," he barked at David "I only heard one pistol shot; where'd you hit him?"

"Base of the neck." David responded.

"Did it go all the way through?" Madison continued. David looked down at the dead man again. The round was fully jacketed and had passed all the way through the neck and exited out in the timber somewhere. The exit wound was larger than David expected. It probably hit the C-1 or C-2 vertebrae and turned it into shrapnel.

"Yeah. Clean through." David responded.

"Good. Hurry up. Get any documentation you can find…and try to find the cartridge for the round you fired—bring it with you." Madison barked, as he tore at the Velcro straps on the dead man's armor.

David glanced to his right where the cartridge would have ejected. He didn't have to look long as the sun was glinting off the brass. He picked it up and put it in his pocket and then continued to strip his victim. As he was removing the armor he heard a voice again. David held his breath and strained to listen—what direction was it coming from? Above or below, he didn't know. Then, he heard it again; it was coming from the body—a radio.

"Don't answer that!" Madison commanded. "Just take the radio."

David found that a bit humorous. What would he have said? *"Hi, yeah, we just smoked your buddies and now were comin' for you!"* He took the radio and the additional mags for the AR-10. The tactical vest was a nice one, David thought about taking it too; it sure would be easier to carry the mags. He took the man's wallet and opened it. Couple of credit cards, driver's license, and some cash. 'George Robinson' was the name on all the documents. David looked down at the man. "Yeah, you look like a *George*." He muttered to himself sarcastically. He thought about what would have happened if things had been different; this man standing over David and looking into his wallet.

David decided to take the tactical vest as well. The armor was a pretty good fit as he was about the same general size. The dead man was taller, but that didn't matter. The plates in the armor were lighter than what David was used to, *probably composite*, he thought. He would check that out later, provided he didn't get killed today.

"You ready to didi?" Madison called up to David, using a term from his Vietnam days, meaning 'get outta here.' David made one last survey of the scene and started thinking about what had just happened. He noticed he was shaking a bit and felt faint; then realized why. He needed to get his blood sugar up. All the adrenaline and excitement exhausted it. He reached into his pack and pulled out a couple of Clif bars and began chewing on one. His dad used to call this 'buck fever.' David got it twice before; both times after a short lived, but very intense firefight when he was first deployed to the desert. After that he just seemed to get used to it. He guessed it because it was different, being here in the US and these men being Americans and not 'hajis." He was being hunted by Americans—that really struck hard. *What the hell was going on?*

"Dork!" Madison was being a little more forceful now. David popped out of deep thought. He turned his head away from the dead man and narrowed his vision toward Madison. He missed being called 'dork' but it seemed strange coming from this man.

"Yeah, coming." David said, moving toward the chimney formation in the rim. "You alright...I mean from the fall earlier?"

"I didn't fall, I slid on my face." Madison quipped. He raised his cheek to show the scrape.

"That's good, no loss there." David joked.

Madison put his hands on his hips and cocked his head to the side. "I see why your dad called you dork, now."

"Yeah, well now I know why he called you Mad Dog." David fired back. The both chuckled as David walked up. "I get it now...about what's written on your camper. 'Insane Canine'...Mad Dog. I didn't put it together until just now."

Mad Dog looked at David for what seemed like a long time. The smile on his face slowly faded, as the man's mind was drifting elsewhere. He lowered his eyes to the forest floor; his gaze darting from left to right as he contemplated something deep inside himself. David thought he must have said something wrong. Then, Mad Dog looked up at David took a short breath through his nostrils and cocked his head to the side. It was hard to read the expression on his face, but there was definitely emotion.

"Your dad gave me that name...Insane Canine." He said, slowly. "We worked on a security project together using Surveillance Detection principles. We needed a LLC company name so your dad took my nickname from 'Nam'—Mad Dog, and spun it—and had the graphic artist create a whole marketing brand around it. He called it 'Insane Canine Productions.' The first time I saw it, I asked who that was because I didn't get it at first either. He just grinned at me." Mad Dog shook his head and smiled. "Only your dad, kid...only your dad."

"Yeah." David said, taking a deep breath.

70

"Come on," Mad Dog said, as he quickly shifted out of reminiscing mode, "...we gotta get moving. Those two clowns with the street shoes are either headed back to the parking lot or headed toward us. I want to take them on two at a time, not all four at once." He shifted his newly acquired armor around, trying to get it comfortable. "Set that radio up so you can hear anything they say, but DO NOT transmit. This set up has a GPS capability. If you key the mic it sends an embedded signal with your GPS location..." He examined the radio closer, and then reached over and turned David's off. "On second thought, this one looks different—newer. It may report position without keying the transmitter. Let's go, we'll have to plan the parking lot assault on the way. We can't go directly to it, they would expect that...we'll go back to the point these stiffs were dropped off." He said, pointing back at the dead men. "They may think there are comm problems in these mountains and if they see me tracking that way maybe they'll believe I'm one of them." He looked at David with one eyebrow raised.

"Sounds weak." David said, being a little more candid with the older veteran.

"Yeah...you're right, but I don't think we have many other options...or time." Mad Dog said flatly. With that, he turned and started down the mountain.

David was apprehensive about the lack of planning, but logically Mad Dog was right. This one had to plan on the fly. He thought about what had already happened and what was about to happen. It was not the time to resolve the events—they were still ongoing. He needed to focus on the next imminent event. That's what his dad taught him. He could still hear him saying, "When it is safe to reflect and resolve; then take the time, but don't let those events affect your focus if danger still exists." David looked at the veteran stealthily moving in front of him and wondered if the ol' guy still 'had it.' He was no spring chicken anymore, but he was moving pretty good. Hopefully, he would hold out. Still, this wasn't going to be a battle won by strength and endurance—it would be about experience and David decided that regardless of Mad Dog's physical condition, he was the most experienced of all the players. The 'old dog' just might have some 'old tricks' the young dogs had never seen.

CHAPTER 7

"But if any provide not for his own, and especially for those of his own house, he hath denied the faith, and is worse than an infidel." -1 Tim 5:8, the Holy Bible

"What's all this stuff...what did you order now?" Landon said sarcastically. There were several large boxes haphazardly spread across the living room floor. Some were already opened and what appeared to be camping equipment was stacked in a pile by the dining room table.

"I didn't order anything. This is the stuff my dad had sent...you know, the stuff in the will. I told you, remember?" She said defensively.

"Oh yeah. Well, what is it? Looks like camping gear." He changed his tune a bit now. She was annoyed at his initial assertion and he knew it.

"It is...kinda. You know my dad was into the survivalist thing pretty heavy—probably because of his military special ops stuff." She continued, "So I guess he expects us to move to Montana as soon as possible."

"You sound like you just talked to him or something...he's...they've...been gone a year now." He said, slowly.

"I know, it's just the video he left me." She mumbled, pawing through the pile of gear. "It was pretty convincing." She looked up at him. "Really...you should watch it."

Now, it was he was getting a bit annoyed. He'd heard a lot of what Robert had to say about preparing for disaster and even some of the conspiracy theories that the man had concocted—well, that's what some of them sounded like—concoctions. Okay, so they weren't that wild and he did have good information that the public didn't seem to have, but Landon wasn't about to just drop everything and move to Montana. He would need proof or something that got his attention more than just a few stories.

"So, what then, I just quit my job and we backpack to the sticks with all this...this crap???" Landon had slipped to the next level and would likely pay for it, but he wasn't about to cave on this one. "That video was made at least a year ago, if not longer...and nothing has happened! What?—your dad looked into his crystal ball and made the damn video because he predicted his death and knew they wouldn't read the will for a year afterwards...all the while knowing the perfect time to run away to Montana and escape catastrophe would be when *you* watched the video??? Really???" He sounded exasperated at this point, but he also knew he'd gone too far. He braced for impact. Carrie slowly lifted her head from the box she inventorying. He expected to see fangs bared and claws drawn. But, she was relatively calm and unaffected except for a tear running down her cheek.

"He said you'd say something like that...almost verbatim." She managed to push out the response. "Then, he said for you to watch the video. He also said the reason he sent all this 'crap' was because you will wait until it's almost too late...and we'll need this to survive on the way to the redoubt." She paused. He felt terrible for hurting her, but he was a long way from being convinced. He was developing an apology when she presented an ultimatum. "I won't speak to you again until you've watched the video," she said, "...so don't even talk to me until you've done it...I mean it." And she returned back to the box.

Landon was mad. He wanted to throw the DVD into the street and smash it. He stood there looking blankly at her for almost a minute, but she never looked up again. It kind of unnerved him because he had never seen that kind of resolve from her in previous arguments. Then again, he'd never acted like this before either. He thought about asking where the video was, but he wasn't going to cave just yet. After all, he was still mad! He turned and stormed away and into the garage, though he didn't know what he would do when he got there, but it would be something manly—something she couldn't do. *Yes, man stuff.* He hadn't reached the door yet when he knew he would return eventually and watch the video. He hated that he knew that...and he hated even more that she knew it too. *Damn!*

Ross put the key in the lock just as he saw the delivery notice hanging precariously from the wooden panel on the door to his flat. It said the neighbor on the other side of the building had it. 'The neighbor,' he smirked to himself—it was his ex-girlfriend. Well...on-again, off-again girlfriend. Currently; it was off. He really didn't want to go over there. As he pushed the door open a horrible smell hit him like a lead sap.

"Jeez...what the...?" He gagged to himself.

It smelled like a mixture of something dead and something with bowel problems. He dropped his keys on the table as he made his way to the kitchen area. There was dog crap everywhere and the refrigerator door was wide open. A brush against his leg confirmed the guilty party.

"Mateo! What are you doing here?" Ross said in a scolding tone. The dog seemed glad to see him and from the looks of it, he would have been happy to see anybody at this point because clearly he'd been by himself in the flat for at least a week.

Mateo belonged to a fellow musician and friend, Chino. He toured a lot as well and would frequently ask Ross to watch Mateo. Ross was supposed to be back by last Tuesday to watch the dog, but he forgot about the commitment when he met his siblings in Montana and stayed a bit longer than he'd planned.

"Yup," he said under his breath, "...about a week...aww, man you gotta be kidding me!"

Mateo just wagged his tail and followed Ross through the flat. Stuff was everywhere. Pillows were torn up, cushions were on the floor and the food Mateo could reach in the open fridge was either half eaten or scattered and rotting. In the corner was a huge bag of dog food which was also torn open. Urine and fecal matter was represented in every room. The kitchen island had a note lying next to the sink. It was from Chino:

Ross: I guess your flight coming in was late, so I left Mateo and a bag of food. See you in two weeks. C-man

"The neighbors have been complaining to the super…" a voice came from behind Ross, "…about the smell and the noise."

Ross turned to see Hallie standing in the doorway. She was dressed to go out and looked hot; as hot as any ex-girlfriend should look if she wants to get back together…or make her ex-boyfriend wish he was back together. Ross wasn't sure which it was this time. Either way, he could feel the ploy working on him. He smiled sheepishly.

"Oh, and your stuff," she paused, smiling back at him, "…the boxes, from the…wherever…are in my apartment."

"Yeah, well thanks. At least those are safe from this monster." He said, scratching Mateo behind the ears. "This is bad. This is sooooo, bad." Ross assessed the chaos in front of him again.

"Well, I was about to go out. You can't stay here." She pointed at the mess. "You can stay at my place…umm—on the couch…until you get this cleaned up."

The couch? Did she have a new boyfriend now? Ross never stayed on the couch before. The offer was always to share the bed even when they were in 'off-again' status. Of course, one thing turned into another and things quickly went back to 'on-again' status. That was always her plan. And, it was always her plan because he was always the one to advocate 'off-again' status. She never did it. But, the couch? That was new.

"Yeah, umm…if you don't mind…should be just one night. I'll get started on this right away," he slowly replied, still trying to figure out her current 'status.' What was that he was feeling just now? Was it jealousy? Nobody 'got' him like Hallie. He could be real with her, but she had some issues that would just irk him and build up over time and he would change their status to 'off-again.' It was really the only thing they argued about—well, except when he would break up with her. She contended there was another woman or women involved. Ross took strong exception to that. He'd always been loyal—to any girlfriend, not just Hallie. He just couldn't prove it. Such was the life of a popular musician and the mysterious 'life on the road.' Certainly, he'd gone through a phase where his hotel bed had a revolving door in the early days, but never when he was promised to someone else. Besides, he had a real problem with shallow women in love with the 'stage persona.' That wasn't the 'real him' up there.

"Okay, well...you have a key. So, just let yourself in. I'll see you in the morning." She said it like he was a patron in a dentist's office and she was the receptionist. She patted his shoulder, turned and walked down the hallway. Yes, she did look good—really good. He watched her until she made the turn to the elevator. She never looked back.

"Damn," he muttered, again scratching the dog's ears. He felt jilted. But, how could he feel jilted if he wasn't 'on-again?' She'd always been there when he came back. He didn't like it. Was it a new ploy? If it was, he knew one thing; it was working.

He thought about starting to clean up tonight, but he was tired from the trip to Montana. He'd only landed back in Boston a few hours ago. Maybe a good night's sleep would be best. Besides, he wondered about the deliveries in Hallie's apartment and what they might be. Reaching into his pocket, he produced the key ring and fumbled though them until he found the one he needed. It had a big pink heart on it. He felt the feelings of loss again. Was it too late? He didn't know.

"Okay, buddy. You have one more night alone in the dump. I'll see you in the morning." He tried to sound upbeat like it was something Mateo wanted too. However, the dog's true feelings were revealed after Ross locked up and started down the hall to Hallie's apartment. It was pretty loud and would certainly result in yet another complaint to the 'super.' Ross didn't care and he kept walking. Mateo would stop when his throat got sore. That made Ross smile.

Hallie's apartment was well kept and neat. That was a surprise. Usually, it had at least some clutter. This place didn't even look lived in, like it was a staged model home. Ross surveyed the place for his deliveries and finally found them in a corner covered with a neatly tucked blanket. It was the same one they had used for picnics. He recognized the wine stain on the corner of the blanket and remembered the day it happened. *Best date ever*, he thought. They had so much fun back then. He wondered if she purposely chose the blanket to entice him. There was that feeling of loss again. He wondered where she went—who she was with right now.

The first box he opened was the smallest one. There was a note on top. It read; *"Read this book first and don't take your time…there's not much time left."* He looked under the note and found "How to Survive the End of the World as We Know it"—by James Wesley Rawles

"Come on dad, you've probably sent three copies of this to me over the last couple of years." Ross muttered. "I did read it—twice." Ross lifted the book out of the box. There were several other books underneath. They were all centered on survival themes. He recognized some newer ones in the Going Home series by Angery American. He'd read the first one and really wanted to read the rest—they were more fun to read than the fictional manual types. On the bottom was a series of topo maps. It appeared they covered a route from Boston to Montana. On closer examination, he found there were hand written notes and markings on the maps. The last map, the one that would have contained a location of the property that he and David had visited—was completely unmarked. OPSEC, Ross thought. The old man was always about secrecy and security. There would be some coded message in all this stuff of how to get there, he was sure of that.

"All this end of the world stuff…" He shook his head. Ross didn't totally dismiss his father's ideas on the subject and it was true that being prepared for short term disaster was something he and dad agreed on, but he always felt his dad was overboard on things. He blamed it on the business his father had been in and the exposure he received from it. Dad probably worked for, or with, one of the intelligence agencies; especially when they lived in Phoenix, but he never said anything.

Ross eyed the two larger boxes. He opened the first one and it had a large backpack inside. It was fully packed like it was ready to go out the door. He knew exactly what this was; a Bug-out-Bag, or BoB. Some folks called them GOOD, or Get Out Of Dodge bags. Ross unzipped a few of the pockets and peered inside. It had everything, even freeze-dried food. There was a note in the bottom of the box that told him to inventory the contents and get familiar with it. Now, he eyed the other large box and wondered what that could be. In a bugout situation, he knew he could only carry so much.

He opened the box and found a teddy bear on top. Underneath was a note resting on a similar, but slightly smaller backpack. It read; "For Hallie…or whomever. She is welcome too." Ross took a slow breath and released it. Mom and dad liked Hallie. They liked the effect she had on him. That wasn't the case with several others. The only thing they didn't like was if she spent the night. It was a Christian thing, and for the most part, he honored it. Still, there were times…there was that feeling again. He held the teddy bear and rubbed its abdomen with his thumb. Suddenly, he heard something to his right and spun around quickly.

"We're back!" Hallie stood in the doorway watching him fondle the bear. "You left the front door open, silly." She looked so good to him at the moment and he smiled at her. Then, the smile quickly left his face as it registered to him that she had said, '*We.*'

"We?" he said, "*We* are back?"

"Hey dork." A voice came from behind Hallie. It was Kate; Hallie's best friend. Kate was actually responsible for originally setting up Ross and Hallie. They all got along at first, until he and Hallie got closer and Kate lost out on 'Hallie-time.' Then, the barbs started to manifest themselves, even to the point that Ross was convinced Kate was trying to break them up. He liked Kate in general, but the relationship was always strained when he and Hallie were 'on-again.' Once during an 'off-again' period, he and Kate almost hooked up. She had just been dumped by her boyfriend and came by waiting for Hallie to get off work. Ross felt sorry for her and invited her in to his place. He listened intently to her as she mourned the relationship and at one point held her close to comfort her. That's when one thing led to another and they almost…

"Hey Kate." Ross popped back, rolling his eyes. He handed the bear to Hallie. "From my parents'." He pointed to the boxes.

Kate looked at Ross with a quizzical expression, but Ross didn't answer right away. She looked good too. Really good. "It ahhh…well it was a condition of their will being read and all…and since they couldn't be declared…" He paused, a knot filling his throat. "…for one year after…"

"Aww baby." Hallie gave him a big hug. "I'm sorry."

"Hmmm, nice." Kate said, surveying the boxes. "But are we still going out, or what?"

Ross looked puzzled. "Yeah, why did you come back here?" he asked, addressing Hallie.

"Her idea," Hallie quipped, thumbing at Kate. "She wanted you to come along…wanna go? Come on, it will be good for you." Hallie hung her purse on the corner of a chair. He didn't have time to respond before she spoke again. "Good, it's settled…I really have to pee…I'll be back." She quickly headed for the bathroom.

"Your idea?" Ross looked confused. Kate turned slightly away and avoided eye contact. He didn't know what to make of it. Kate wasn't much of a drama queen, so he didn't suspect anything dirty. He watched her poke around in the box with the books, pretending to be interested in them. Ross was staring at her and she knew it. After a few moments she looked up and broke the silence.

"Well, I knew you just got back and about the stinky mess and, well…it would be good for you." She looked up at him. He blinked a couple of times and then his expression turned to that of skepticism. She picked up on it and before he could interject, and continued. "Okay fine. Hallie is hoping to meet this guy she's kinda hot on…and he's a real douche." She paused and looked Ross in the eye.

"Hmmm…" he smiled at her, "…you mean a bigger douche than me?"

"Way bigger…way!" She responded. "And, I know that seems impossible that someone could be a bigger douche than you, but…"

"Okay, ready to go?" Hallie was walking back into the room. Ross was staring at Kate who was still displaying some measure of false attitude,

80

accented by an appropriate amount of toe-tapping. Hallie looked at them both and raised her eyebrows. "You two having a moment? Okay then, get over it and let's go." She pointed to his keys on the table. "Last one out the door has to lock up." With that, she quickly went out the door into the hallway.

Kate turned to go out the door, but Ross grabbed her hand. She turned back toward him and he kissed her on the cheek. Nothing big; it was just a peck. She didn't say anything. A small smile started from the corner of her mouth. He pushed her out the door and turned to lock it.

"Just when you think you have enough evidence on someone to justify disliking them, they go and do something like that...and then you have to start all over!" Ross squawked as he pretended to appear upset.

As they walked down the hallway, Kate reached to Ross' hand and squeezed gently, then released it. She really was a nice person. Hallie wouldn't have her for a friend if she wasn't. Ross made a mental note that if he and Hallie were on-again, he would include Kate more.

They entered the elevator and Ross looked at them both. There was a lot of 'feel-good' going on right now and he felt an overwhelming need to break the gooey sweetness of it all. So, just as the doors closed, he passed a rather large quantity of gas that could be heard three floors down.

"Ewwww, pig!" Kate piped, punching him in the arm. "Why do you let him get away with that??"

Hallie covered her nose with the sleeve on her arm and giggled, but said nothing. Ross loved it. Kate was clearly not amused.

"Cuz she does it to me all the time!" Ross chuckled. Hallie appeared surprised at the accusation, but said nothing. She just started laughing. It was a subtle admission of guilt.

"OMG!" Kate fired back. "You two disgust me! Who does that?" She pretended to get fresh air from the crack in the elevator door. "You guys really do deserve each other...Seriously!"

The elevator continued down to street level as the 'off-again/on-again couple' began to laugh at their incensed friend. It was good to be back, and it was good to be on-again—if that's what it was. Ross thought so. And, it was good to get the endorsement of Hallie's best friend. He hadn't expected that.

As they walked down the street toward the entertainment district, the girls were rattling on about something Hallie heard at work. Ross' mind drifted back to the boxes and their contents. What did dad really expect? Could he have known about something that was about to happen from over a year out? It just seemed like if something were going to happen, it already would have. Ross didn't know, but he would keep the boxes and their contents…just in case.

CHAPTER 8

"I will cast terror into the hearts of those who disbelieve. Therefore strike off their heads and strike off every fingertip of them" -Quran (8:12)

Achmed opened the door and was greeted by the afternoon sun shining in his eyes from its perch just above the horizon. Before he could raise his hand to block the bright light, it was eclipsed by a familiar shape—a rather large shape.

"Achmed; you are to come with us immediately." Achmed knew the voice well, though he had only scarcely heard it before. His eyes began to focus on the telltale scar for confirmation.

"Yes, yes…I will gather my things…" Achmed barked compliantly.

"No, now." The voice was strong and insistent.

Achmed was ushered out to the street and into a waiting SUV. As he got in he noticed two men in the furthest back seat on either side of another man. The man in the middle had a black bag over his head. Achmed felt his blood run cold. Before he could inquire where he would sit, a bag was pulled over his head and he was pushed to the center of the middle seat. A man got in on each side of him. He was going to say something, but thought better of it. No one spoke.

After about five minutes, the vehicle stopped and Achmed and the other hooded man were moved outside and told to stand with their arms outstretched. The men in the SUV began to search their pockets. Their cell phones were taken away from them and given to someone who drove off on a motorcycle. Achmed heard a beeping sound moving up and down and around his body. He was no expert at spy craft, but imagined it was some kind of sweeping device checking for bugs. It was hot under the bag, he could barely breathe and it didn't help he was afraid.

Moments later, Achmed and the other man were back in the SUV. After what seemed an eternity of twists and turns, they arrived at their destination. Still not allowed to remove the bags, they were again ushered down a hall and up several flights of stairs and then back down to ground level. Achmed knew this because he counted the steps, both up and down. He was starting to feel better now, as he realized being bagged and ushered gave a strong indication of a return trip—they weren't necessarily going to kill him. Eventually, they arrived in a room and were made to sit at a table. The bags were removed.

Achmed's eyes focused slowly and Ari's face came into view sitting directly across the table from him. Yes, he should have known the other bagged man was Ari. He looked to his left and the Emir sat at the head of the table. The only men in the room were the four that sat on either side of him and Ari in the SUV, the man with the scar, and the Emir; Abu Bakr al-Baghdadi. Only the Emir, Ari and Achmed sat at the table. The rest stood.

"Are you well, my brothers?" the Emir said genuinely. They both nodded affirmatively. "I apologize for the way you were brought here. We have learned over time about the infidels' tactics and means of targeting us. They continually tell us how we are hunted by bragging to their press corps and this only serves them poorly as we learn and compensate. Your belongings will be returned to you later."

The Emir was an impressive man, even if one did not know who he was. His demeanor and visible resolve were evident in the way he carried himself. Born Awwad Ibrahim Ali al-Badri al-Samarrai, this most dangerous man asserted he was a direct descendent of Mohammad the Prophet. The respect he carried was not only from the blood line, but from his academic prowess as well as his track record as the leader of the restored caliphate. 'Doctor' al-Baghdadi was a graduate of Islamic University in Baghdad in Islamic studies and history. He had led the most aggressive and successful group of Islamic militants to victories in Syria and Iraq and formed what is now recognized as the Islamic State of Iraq and Syria; or ISIS. All other leaders before him to include Ayman al-Zawahiri paled in comparison. Only Osama bin Laden himself is recognized as a greater leader—but that was about to change. There was a no more ruthless killer than al-Baghdadi. His plans to destroy the 'Great Satan' would make the twin towers look like a minor event when compared to what was about to ensue. If successful, the United States of America would be no more—rendered totally ineffective and vulnerable to their Chinese and Russian adversaries.

His strengths lie in the ability to strategize and recruit. In fact, al-Baghdadi had successfully recruited a massive force away from al-Qaeda, al-Shabab, and from all over the globe—to include sects in the United States. His hatred for America and the West is unparalleled; captured by the US and having survived a four-year captivity in an Iraqi prison, he met and recruited other al-Qaeda fighters. Unlike al-Zawahiri, the Emir is charismatic and known for getting his hands dirty, choosing to fight alongside his men, rather than hiding; although he remains somewhat anonymous. Many have met him and fought with him, unaware. He is smart, shrewd, and cunning. If America ever had a more deadly foe, al-Baghdadi was it. Even Hitler would not inflict more death and destruction on a global level when Scimitar was fully realized.

"You are a relative of our brother Ayman al-Zawahiri, is that correct?" the Emir queried Achmed.

"Yes, Emir. He is a distant uncle." Achmed answered only what he was asked.

The Emir nodded. Achmed fidgeted slightly in his chair. He knew the two leaders were not friends, or even comrades. Al-Zawahiri had tried to assert rank over al-Baghdadi, but the Emir would have none of it. He was a man of action and felt the leaders of al-Qaeda were too cautious. So, he started his own al-Qaeda splinter group.

"You are close?" the Emir continued.

"I met him twice; when I was very young. I doubt he would know me except by name." Achmed paused, looking at the scarred man for affirmation, but he didn't reflect disdain so Achmed continued, "...my father sent him a letter, announcing that I had joined the jihad."

The Emir said nothing and shifted his gaze to Ari. Ari sat up taller in his chair in anticipation of being addressed—but it never came. The silence was deafening. Achmed could hear his own heartbeat pound in his chest and throb in his temples. The four men that had previously ushered Ari and Achmed in the SUV, moved uncomfortably close behind each of them in anticipation. Still, the Emir just stared at both of them. Whatever was about to happen would be dependent upon how they answered the next questions; they wouldn't have put bags over their heads if there was no possibility of return. However, there was no guarantee and that was evident with the encroaching proximity of the men behind them.

The Emir nodded. Scarface left and returned with Mohammad, the local business man that was at the first meeting with al-Baghdadi. He was forced to sit on the opposite end of the table from the Emir. It was dark in the room, but Achmed could clearly see the man had sustained 'wall-to-wall counseling.' His blood stained shirt was torn and soiled as if he'd been a human mop in a gulag. Mohammad didn't look at Ari or Achmed; only down at the table in front of him.

"This son of a whore," the Emir began, "was valuable to us at one time. He managed funding for our efforts, even your operation, Achmed…but at some point, he decided to partake in activities that resulted in the lining of his own pockets." The Emir nodded and Scarface grabbed the man's right arm and placed it on the table. Aside from the rest of the shirt, it looked normal—except for the stump where once a hand resided. Ari turned his head away. The Emir cut his eyes toward Ari. "This bothers you?"

Ari had no time to answer before one of the two henchmen pushed his chin in the direction of the handless man. He began breathing heavily and was clearly distressed. Achmed chose not to look at his friend for fear he would see some horrible torture inflicted on him too. He stared only at the stump.

"We are in the greatest jihad of all. We don't have time to reflect on events or actions of the past years, months, weeks, days, or even minutes. We move forward…forward to jihad until the last infidel is wiped from the earth. Allah demands our action, not our cowardice. If we are careful to strike and fade—citing that it is better to fight another day—then we are cowards and no better than the infidel. If we are distracted by the riches of this world and steal from our own, then we are worse than the infidel. For this demonstrates a false faith that acts like a cancer and tempts and infects a man's family— producing more of the same behavior." The Emir stood to his feet and continued to pontificate as he made his way around the table. "But, it didn't stop there. Upon interrogation of his wife and children, it was learned he talked too much as well. He is a braggart."

Emir nodded and Scarface grabbed the man from the top of his head and dug his fingers into Mohammad's nostrils, prying open his mouth. Blood spilled onto the table; the open mouth revealed the man's tongue had met the same fate as his hand. Achmed would have vomited were it not for fear keeping it in check. Mohammad began to weep. The Emir was unfazed and continued.

"This son of a whore will not see another sunrise, nor will his family— they precede him in death." Emir nodded again and Scarface produced a large knife and began chopping at the nape of Mohammad's neck. The sound was grisly and grotesque. The man didn't even try to resist; clearly, he just wanted it to be over. Bits of bone and flesh flew from the wound as Scarface continued to swing the blade, finally finishing the job. He placed his hand on the severed head and jammed the knife into the base of the skull. Then, he held it up like some kind of jack-o-lantern. The eyes were partially open and appeared to stare at the table in front of Ari. As Mohammad's heart continued to pump, spurts of blood cascaded onto the table, the smell of fresh blood filled Achmed's nostrils. It was a horrific experience.

"Do you know why I do this? Why you are here and witness this?" The Emir addressed Ari rhetorically. But, Ari answered anyway. "Because you demand our loyalty?"

"No, my brother," he seemed agitated, "Because Allah demands your loyalty!"

87

The final few pumps of blood left Mohammad as the man's heart quit. The Emir waved his arm and the men behind Achmed removed the body back through the door that Mohammad had originally entered. Scarface wiped the bloody blade on Mohammad's beard and lobbed the head toward the door. It made an unforgettable thud as it careened off the wall. The Emir was seemingly unaffected by the events of the last few moments.

"My brothers…we believe we have eradicated all those who may have been told of our plans. However, we cannot take chances and so we must accelerate the timelines. Are you ready?" Again, the question was rhetorical. Ari didn't answer this time, but Achmed did by nodding just once. "Then tonight, you will enjoy an earthy pleasure as Allah intended for his jihadi." Al-Baghdadi returned to the head of the table and nodded. The two remaining sentries produced the bags for Ari and Achmed, but the Emir waved them off. "These men are to be trusted, for they leave tomorrow. Take them to the appointed location." Achmed and Ari were taken to the SUV and driven off to spend the night with infidel concubines recently acquired from the village where they served as aid workers from the United States.

The Emir sat at the table and motioned for Scarface to join him. "Achmed will serve us well on two fronts, Mushreq," he said confidently, addressing the scar-faced man. "First, as the leader of the Scimitar Group to spread death to America, and secondly to send a message to the Islamic nation that al-Zawahiri's own flesh and blood chooses to serve ISIS, rather than an ineffective leader. He hides like an old woman in Pakistan and waits for what? He deals out a hand full of pesky annoyances to our enemies in an attempt to remain relevant in al-Qaeda. He has become a joke and forgets it is Allah we serve." With that, he discussed the acceleration of the plans and how they would interact with each other to compound the impact. "Millions will die, Mushreq…millions! For over a decade they've lamented over a mere 3000 dead. What will they do when millions die at our hands?"

Across town, Achmed lie in a bed listening to jihadi men rape and beat the women in the brothel. His own concubine on the floor at the foot of the bed remained untouched. The events of the day were too much for him to perform. She would be spared his advances for now. Perhaps in the morning he would try. His mind would wander back to the room and Mohammad's horrific torture and death. He wanted to be a million miles from here right now and wished he'd never had the idea; now communicated as a mission called Scimitar. Tomorrow he and Ari would lead the new jihadi to the land of the Great Satan. In a turn of irony, he looked forward to it because he would feel safe there. *Well, at least compared to here.* Still, he worried over how he and Ari would avoid the same fate as the Scimitar jihadi. It would be difficult. And, what if they did survive, would they return here? How would they be received?

He wondered what Ari thought now. Achmed was almost too afraid to discuss a survival plan with him after what they both had witnessed. Ari might turn on Achmed…it was possible. And, then what? Would Achmed's fate be as was Mohammad's? He shuddered at the thought.

He thought of the young woman at the foot of his bed and felt somewhat sorry for her. This was a sharp contrast to how he'd fantasized in the past, about what he would be doing in this situation. His desire to be with a woman was on his mind almost constantly…but now…he just didn't know.

"What is your name?" He called out in the dark room. There was no response. He sat up in the bed and called out louder, "I said, what…"

"Callie," she called back, in a whimper. "It's Callie."

"Where are you from, Callie?" he said as he fell back onto his pillow.

"Umm, Destin…Destin, Florida." She responded.

"Is it nice there?" He asked, not really wanting to know, but just to strike up a conversation—anything to get Mohammad's death out of his mind.

"Yes…it's one of the most beautiful places in the world…to me anyway." Her voice cracked.

Achmed again felt sorry for her. She would never see her home again; of that he had no doubt. He wondered if she knew that. It wouldn't much matter. The Scimitar plan would very likely destroy her town and all that lived in it anyway. Achmed thought of her sandy blonde hair. Maybe he would try now.

"Callie, how long have you been here…here in this place?" he asked.

"Five or maybe six months, I think. It's hard to tell in here. But…long enough to…to…" She stopped.

Achmed sat up in the bed again. "Yes? To what?" he was interested now.

"To get pregnant." She replied softly. "I think I'm pregnant."

Achmed didn't expect that. It stopped him cold. When they find out they will likely kill her. He rolled back onto the pillow again and thought about how that might be done. It would be the same thing he witnessed this afternoon, except they would video the event and send it out to the internet. Her family would see it too, undoubtedly. He took a slow deep breath. Why should he care, she is the infidel. This is God's plan for the infidel.

"What is your name?" she asked. There was no response for an uncomfortable amount of time.

"I need rest. Be quiet and go to sleep." Achmed ordered. "In the morning, I will tell them you were compliant and enjoyable. They will not harm you." He knew that was probably a lie. The next jihadi would likely be a different experience for her than tonight.

"Thank you," came her reply from the dark, "God bless you."

CHAPTER 9

"A well regulated Militia, being necessary to the security of a free State, the right of the people to keep and bear Arms, shall not be infringed." -Second Amendment of the US Constitution

"I ask, Sir, what is the militia? It is the whole people. To disarm the people is the best and most effectual way to enslave them." –George Mason, co-author of the Second Amendment, June 14, 1778

"If the representatives of the people betray their constituents, there is then no recourse left but in the exertion of that original right of self-defense." Alexander Hamilton, Federalist 28

"That ain't good." Mad Dog whispered, looking down at the parking lot from his vantage point high above. The area now had five vehicles and another nine men. Two looked like park rangers, four were from the sheriff's department, and three more government types carrying AR-10s had joined the hunt. Madison wondered what the government guys told the local boys.

"Change of plans?" David whispered back candidly.

"Yeah, unless you want to be Butch Cassidy…I'll be the Sundance Kid."

Another vehicle approached from around the last bend—a wrecker. The two fugitives watched for several minutes as the wrecker was directed to remove Mad Dog's AATREC from the parking lot and take it to some unknown destination.

"Got any ideas," David asked.

"Well, we got this little pack of mine with 100 ounces of water and four Clif bars. We also have these nice little beauties and a limited amount of ammo." Mad Dog referred to the AR-10s. "And, I'm thinking that ain't enough to live out my life in these mountains for very long." He paused, continuing to glass the area with his binos.

"We can't take these guys...we can't run very far, so..." He stopped suddenly. David saw a wry grin start to form on the older man's lips.

"Why aren't they searching for us yet?" David asked.

"Because they're waiting for reinforcements...maybe even aircraft. The fact they haven't used the radio in over an hour is indicative they know it's been compromised." Mad Dog pulled the device off his neck and placed it on a large flat rock and smashed it. "Can't take the chance, especially if we're going to pull this off."

"Pull what off...wanna clue me in?"

"That your Jeep?" Mad Dog ignored the question, asking his own.

"Yeah...well...it's rented."

Anything in it you can't live without?"

"Just my clothes, toiletries, and..." David paused, his blood ran cold. His thoughts went to the package given to him by the lawyer. It had everything in it; video, GPS coordinates, etc. "I gotta...I mean I have to get something from it." David seemed desperate. He had hidden it inside the storage cubby hole under the jumper cables because he knew the removable fabric and plastic shell wouldn't be much of a deterrent to a thief.

"Sorry kid, I don't see that happening. Not if you want to live, anyway. Sentimental value stuff?"

"Nope. It's critical info." David explained what it was and how it could lead these men to the redoubt. He also thought about the threat to his siblings as well.

"Well, maybe we could destroy it...burn the Jeep." Mad Dog went back to glassing the area. "If we could just get a little break here, we might be able to spray the Jeep with these ARs and get a fire going and...wait a sec..." He lowered the binos and then raised them again. The wry grin started to return. David looked to the area Mad Dog was surveying and saw the second wrecker coming down the road. He wondered what Madison was thinking.

"Come on, we gotta haul bacon here," Mad Dog said as he gathered things together. "I'll explain on the way; we don't have much time if this is going to work."

They made their way down the mountain, but not in the direction originally planned. Instead of the parking lot, Mad Dog had them headed almost the opposite direction. They were in thick timber now and could not see the parking lot or the road anymore. Their pace was very aggressive and as a result it was difficult for the older man to hike and talk. So, David got the highly condensed version of the plan.

"We're gonna hijack the wreckers." Mad Dog puffed.

"What about the other vehicles? Won't they follow?" David panted back.

"I don't think so. I'm betting they won't spare a man to ride in the wreckers either. They're already waiting for reinforcements. The wreckers know where they're going, they don't need escort...they'll just take the vehicles to a impound yard and lock them up. Meanwhile, we intercept them on the road and drive right off!" Mad Dog's big toothy smile was infectious and David felt the corners of his mouth turn up. It was a pretty good plan and it was simple. The best ones always are. Besides, there was no other viable option. Even Jeremiah 'Liver Eatin' Johnson wouldn't have much of a chance out here with the amenities they had. *And, he was from here!*

"If we have to fire, the gig will be up, though." David cautioned.

"That's right, kid...you're thinking it through. I like to see that."

"What about the drivers?" David queried, a bit afraid of the answer.

"We'll hold them at gunpoint and make them take us to a place in the middle of nowhere...somewhere it will take them a long while to get back to a phone. We'll be long gone by the time they walk out."

Landon watched the rest of the video and felt like the wind was knocked out of his sails. Carrie's dad was right and his argument was strong. He didn't expect Landon to just move to Montana based on his say so. But he did want him to "have a plan" and even outlined it. It was a pretty good idea and it involved grand theft, but if it really was going to be the event that Wallace said it would be, then no one would really notice or care anyway. The world would be in chaos. So, Landon was fine with that. He would wait until the SHTF before he made a move. Simple. Now, Carrie would get off his back.

"Well?" Carrie inquired.

"Yeah…I'm on board. It makes sense." He started to head for the living room to watch the Diamondbacks/Rockies game.

"Then, where are you going? We gotta build this bugout kit…put everything together."

"Now?" He whined.

"You said you were on board, remember?"

He sighed and dropped to his knees and picked up a box that said "Solo Stove" on it and started reading the description. She watched him open the box and put it together. Then, he carefully put it in the pouch that came with it and discarded the box. He looked at all the other materials and again sighed; it would be a long afternoon.

Mad Dog halted and dropped to a crouched position while simultaneously raising his hand to eye-level with a closed fist. David instantly recognized the sign and froze. They had been moving so quickly that they nearly ran into the road. Was there something or someone in front of them? David didn't know, but just in case he moved the selector switch on his weapon to semi-auto. He tried to slow his breaths to be quieter, but they had been exerting themselves heavily and it was difficult—*probably sounds like a steam engine climbing a mountain*, he thought to himself. Mad Dog emphasized the closed fist again, and moved forward very slowly. It meant that David was to stay while he checked things out. He watched as the older man moved like a cat toward the road—it was impressive. Any quick movements would catch the human eye and Mad Dog was clearly a master at moving in such a way to minimize anything that could cause them to be discovered—and not just him—but anything that could brush up against him. A pine bough whipping free might as well be a waving flag in this circumstance.

David lost sight of Mad Dog and decided to check their six-o'clock position for anyone who may be tracking them. He watched for several minutes but saw nothing. Then, he moved slightly left of his position to try and view Mag Dog. He was about to reposition again when he saw movement, though he wasn't sure what it was. David moved his eyes offset from the area he initially saw the movement; this would aid him in detecting additional movement. It was a technique he learned in night psychological training. While it wasn't night just yet, the technique still worked.

There it was again—movement. He focused on the area intently now and raised his weapon slowly to use the optic—a pant leg dressed in khaki—it was Mad Dog moving up the bank to the edge of the road. He was prone and moving painfully slow. David wondered if it was necessary. Still, a discovery of any kind would essentially mean death for both of them at this point. Suddenly, David heard a vehicle coming. The gravel under the tires made a sound that indicated a fast approach. Would they see Madison?

The vehicle raced past the place Mad Dog laid—another black Suburban. Dust and dirt filled the air and clouded David's view of the area. It was evident they didn't see the older man along the road or they would have certainly stopped. After a few moments the dust began to settle and David strained to see his companion.

"Well, you gonna sit up here all day and watch, or are you gonna get with the program???" Mad Dog said from a position behind David. David jumped visibly and turned to see a toothy grin.

"Damn, that wasn't smart." David puffed, as he clicked on the safety of his weapon. Mad Dog looked down and saw the muzzle pointing directly at his abdomen. The grin faded slowly as he realized the younger man could have easily spooked and killed him.

"Hmmm...perhaps you're right about that, youngster," Mad Dog whispered, "perhaps you're right...I apologize. That was a rookie move."

David thought about what had just happened. The old warrior leveraged the dusty camouflage and noise to move tactically to a position of advantage. Had David been an adversary, he would certainly be dead now at the edge of Madison's knife. It sobered him. Yes, he was a well-trained special operator in the ways of calling in air strikes and supporting SOF teams, but what Madison just did made him realize he needed to learn a lot more. They can only train you to do so much; learning from 'old-timers' and gaining experience is what takes a guy to the next level. He would learn from this man; today and in the future.

"Okay, so now that we have these things packed, what do we do?" Landon's sarcasm escaped.

"We put them in a central location, along with the other items." Carrie responded.

"What other items? Isn't this all that was sent?" He pointed to the bug out bags and all the empty boxes.

"No, we need to make some more 'acquisitions and supporting armament.'" She quoted her father from the video Landon had just watched.

"You mean a gun." The statement was not a question. "We talked about this years ago and decided we didn't need a..."

"That was before...and this is now. You heard what he said and you know he's right. Dad died a year ago and made predictions that are happening right now. That's indicative that the next events are very soon." She opened her eyes wider to make a statement. "We need a freakin' gun! Now, get your shoes on and let's go."

"Go where? Are you a gun expert now? What kind of gun?" Landon was not happy. A few hours ago he was getting ready to watch the

Rockies play the Diamondbacks. Maybe drink a beer or two and relax. Now, he was completely rattled with all this survivalist crap and about to go against something he previously believed very strongly about—owning a gun! What the hell???

"Dad provided all that in the letter. He knows we're not gun experts. The store he suggested is only 15 minutes from here." Carrie slowed her roll. "Look, I don't like it either, but it's going to happen and we have a choice to stay here and die, or do what we know is right. Besides, if dad is wrong, we just sell the gun."

Landon thought about it. She was right…Wallace was right too. It was too big a risk to stick their heads in the sand and hope nothing happened. He just didn't like the 'gun thing.' He took a deep breath and exhaled through his nose slowly and purposely avoided her eyes, but eventually his eyes found her through a quick glance. She was grinning.

"I don't like guns either…but…" She started.

"Alright, alright…damn. The next thing you know I'll be joining the military. Let's go get the stupid gun." He strode off to find his shoes.

"Uhh, 'guns.' You mean 'guns'…as in plural. Dad said we both need one," she corrected. He didn't even look back.

It would be dark soon. David mulled over the plan they were to execute; when the wreckers come down the road they will step into view with their guns leveled at the driver, but separated one and a half times the width of the wrecker. This will send a message to the driver that he better stop as at least one of the men would get him, even if he ran one down. The separation ensured he couldn't get them both. Pretty smart, David thought. *Where does somebody learn this stuff?*

"Here they come." Mad Dog said as he clicked off the safety on his weapon. The wreckers were traveling together as Mad Dog thought they would. David used the 3X optic to verify the drivers were alone in the cab. That was a welcome sight.

Mad Dog stepped out first as the wreckers crossed a point where he thought they could recognize a man with a menacing gun, but still have the distance to stop. David followed; his weapon trained on the driver's chest. Through the optic he could see the surprise on the man's face—it was horror.

The wrecker nearly lost control. Mad Dog's AATREC started to jack-knife in the road, but the driver compensated and brought the big rig to a sliding stop right beside the old warrior; the barrel of his weapon pointing squarely at the driver's head.

"Whoa, whoa, whoa!" the driver cried loudly. "Hey, wait a minute. We're with you guys! Don't shoot!"

Mad Dog immediately picked up on the inference. The driver thought he and David were part of the government group back at the dam. The second wrecker came to a stop beside the first, David trained his weapon on the driver. Mad Dog was thinking on the fly and needed David to pick up on the direction he wanted to take. Mad Dog lowered his weapon.

"Hey, can you shut that thing down so I can hear myself?" Mad Dog yelled at the driver. The driver turned off the noisy diesel and motioned to the second driver to do the same. David was confused at Mad Dog's posture, specifically the lowering of his weapon, but he took the hint and also lowered his to point at the ground. Mad Dog was pleased, now he knew David could hear the conversation.

"Sorry, I've had a bad day and yelling over that thing wasn't making it any better." Mad Dog said apologetically.

"No problem, man. I just didn't wanna get shot. Your guys back there seemed pretty jumpy, especially when they heard the shots and couldn't get a hold of you on the radio." The driver was still a bit rattled.

"Yeah, well, we've been up there all day and the batteries gave out on the radios and..."

"...AND, he got us lost!" David yelled out followed by a chuckle.

Mad Dog flashed a disapproving look toward David for the benefit of the drivers. *Awesome; the kid picked up on it beautifully*, Mad Dog thought. David pulled the weapon from his shoulder to a less threatening position.

"Do you want us to take you back?" The first driver said.

"How far is it back to the dam?"

"About ten minutes."

"How far to town?"

"About thirty."

That's perfect, thought Mad Dog. He pretended to mull it over and glanced at David with a quizzical look. David returned the gesture with a shrug.

"Nah, screw them. If they really cared about us they would have come looking. They can wait an additional thirty minutes for us to call. Your radio won't reach the dam from here, will it?" Mad Dog was fairly sure it wouldn't. There were no repeaters out here and there was a mountain between them and the dam. It was risky, but he knew they would offer.

"Nope, I already tried," the second driver spoke up. "Must be a dead spot here."

Mad Dog hadn't specifically thought about the radio threat as they were running down the mountain to the road. That could have been disastrous. He would make a mental note of it. The situation could change as they got closer to the town and hit a repeater. Mad Dog motioned for David to get in with the second driver. David nodded and moved towards the passenger door of the second wrecker. The kid was smart. Mad Dog knew he wouldn't let the driver use the radio if something came up. He would have liked a private conversation with David before they left, but it would have aroused suspicion and he didn't want to take the chance. They could always control the situation with weapons if needed, but this was a better scenario and would buy them more time. Mad Dog needed to think about their next move and the bigger plan. Would there be men waiting at the impound yard? Would they pick up an escort? He hoped not. He also wondered about transportation and where they would go.

The diesels fired up and started for town. David was dying to know what Mad Dog was thinking now and wished he could talk to him. This was a better situation than what they'd planned, but there was a lot to think about. What would they do next? Where would they go? He thought about the redoubt. Also, he needed to get to the package in the Jeep—if it was still there. He hoped so.

"Yeah, I wanted to see one of them drone things…pretty cool, right?" The driver broke David's concentration.

"Huh?" David said. "What did you say? Sorry, I was falling asleep over here…rough day."

"I'll bet….no, I was sayin'…I wanted to be there when the drone showed up. I think they had it in the last Suburban that I passed on the way out from the dam."

Of course, David thought, *a drone was what they were waiting for to aid in the search*. He had worked with teams that had them before—awesome little things with IR cameras. They could hover over an area and pick up everything. Since they knew the general area where the shots were fired, that would be the first place they'd send it. They'll see the bodies, but won't know who they are until they direct a team there to make identification. That wouldn't take long; not much longer than it would for the wreckers to get to town. David felt his stress level rise again. Mad Dog needed to know.

"Mind if I borrow your radio?" David asked casually. The driver motioned affirmatively by pointing at the headset.

"Mad Dog one; this is Mad Dog two…you copy?" David cringed inside. He had just thrown COMSEC out the window.

"Two, this is one; go." The response came. David took a slow breath, this needed to sound less professional and more cavalier…funny even.

"You know why those lazy fools didn't come to help us? Because they were waiting for the drone! I never waited for that thing…and half the time the batteries aren't charged when it shows up! We could have starved before they found us! David glanced at the driver to see if there was an inkling of suspicion. He only laughed.

 Mad Dog was uneasy now. He needed time to think this through, but recent intel that his pursuers were using a drone reduced that time significantly. Once the drone located the bodies of the men they killed, it would be obvious what direction they headed. Also, the drivers would play into it; if they went missing or didn't get the vehicles to the impound lot in a reasonable time, the game would be up. He really wanted to use the AATREC for his escape, but it was much too uncommon a vehicle. The Jeep wasn't much better. In addition, he still didn't know how they originally tracked him or David to the dam. To take either vehicle would not work. To steal a car would be just as bad. They were up against pros with the latest technology and resources; resources to find a needle in the proverbial haystack—and fast.

CHAPTER 10

"The fifth angel poured out his bowl on the throne of the beast, and its kingdom was plunged into darkness. People gnawed their tongues in agony." -Revelation 16:10, the Holy Bible

Achmed watched as the American jihadi filed into the makeshift auditorium. Training was over and inoculations were complete. The graduates learned to shoot AK-47s, create IEDs from various items, learned tactical operations, etcetera. It was the same training all jihadi received except for one significant difference; the inoculations. Saline solutions were substituted for most of the vaccines; only one contained a vital component for the mission and that one—ironically—was not to prevent illness. Rather, it was to instill one. Achmed and Ari were not made to receive the inoculations, but they would be traveling with those that had for the next several days. Most would be traveling back in the way they came using commercial airlines. There were some that would require the use of Mexican coyote comrades as their names had shown up on U.S. Customs watch lists. Those would take longer to travel and Achmed was concerned about the close proximity with the infected, because he and Ari would be with them. *The infected, yes,* thought Achmed, *that's what they are; infected.* These jihadi were a different kind of solder for the cause; one that had never been employed in any war. It was true that biological warfare had been used, but the ordnance in this case was to be human, and the agent—Ebola virus.

The Emir himself would brief these jihadi; in Arabic. It was up to Achmed and Ari to translate later. The hope was to motivate these men by demonstrating their importance with a personal sendoff from the supreme leader. Achmed was somewhat comforted by the gesture as it confirmed the jihadi were not yet contagious, even though they carried the deadly virus in their veins. The Emir would not be in the same room with them if they were, he was sure of that. He and Ari had been told the jihadi would not be communicably infectious until they became symptomatic and that would be two to three weeks. He hoped so.

"You leave tonight…very good. The Emir is pleased and will communicate your plan and contribution in the coming months." Mushreq had surprised Achmed again with his stealthy approach. "To do so now, would of course endanger the mission."

"Of course," Achmed said nervously. This man was attempting to encourage Achmed that he would get credit for his 'contributions.' He looked up at the big man and wanted to say. *'Yes, I am to be trapped in a nation dying of unimaginable plague while you and others tell of my contributions.'* It was almost humorous. Almost.

"You are okay?" Mushreq queried.

"Yes, just tired…and excited. Not much sleep to be had in the last two weeks."

"Your test group was a success. You should be proud of the accomplishment."

"Test group?" Achmed was genuinely surprised.

"Yes, your idea had to be tested before we could commit to releasing more of the groups. Even now there are many others that will graduate training in 3 days. In all, there are hundreds of American Jihadi that have joined our cause since the nation of ISIS was born. The American Homeland Security officials put the number in the thousands and while we have not seen that many in our ranks, they are clearly in the hundreds."

Achmed was caught off guard with the comment. He hadn't considered there would be more groups. Based on projected statistical models, the original Scimitar group would easily do the job. The addition of more groups would accelerate the effort greatly. He thought of the makeshift plan to escape that he and Ari made. This new information would jeopardize it.

"Allah be praised," Mushreq uttered, as he turned and entered the auditorium. Achmed didn't follow right away. He wanted to talk to

Ari. They needed to re-plan their escape from the plagued nation—if there could be such a plan.

"Your dad said on the video that by September 11th of this year we would need to be at the redoubt." Mason argued. "I think we should go earlier than we talked about. It's going to take time to get there and we have to sell stuff...pack...there's a lot to do!"

"I know, but what if dad was wrong? What if we wait and see...like, you know, we just get ready to go and if it happens then we hit the road." Leigh countered. She really wanted to believe her father, but he was gone now. What if he was wrong or things changed? She was reluctant to give up their friends, jobs, comfortable lifestyle for a 'cabin in the woods.'

Mason looked at her and understood; he had similar feelings. If Wallace were still here to converse on the prediction it would be easier to have confidence, but as the video explained; the date was too important to the bad guys to be shifted—it has to be *that* date. This gave Mason a thought.

"Okay, so I'll meet you halfway on this. How about we go on vacation to Montana in a few weeks? If things go your dad's way, we motor on in to the redoubt. If not, then we come back home." Mason paused and studied Leigh's face. She was digesting the proposition. Mason continued. "So think about it. We don't quit our jobs...we don't tell anybody about our plans. Everybody thinks we're going on vacation to Montana for two weeks, right? If nothing happens we come home and plug back in...no big deal. Now, I know we're going to burn vacation time and some of our savings, but if we don't go and we're wrong..."

"I get it..." She said softly. "...then we're dead because we can't get there." She nodded. "It makes sense...okay, but I don't want to sell anything. If it happens, the money we get from the sales would be worthless anyway."

Mason had wanted to use the money for ammo and other things, but the redoubt was supposed to have everything they needed...*except beer*

104

and cigarettes! He sighed. That would be tough. He did need to quit smoking and there was the beer making kit he bought plus the case of Everclear 190 Proof he could put behind the seat. He would cut that and make it last until he could make his own. But, he really needed a still and hadn't managed to accumulate all the components yet. There was time; they had about a month before they had to be there. If worse came to worst, he could just put it on a credit card.

"Okay, then we will leave on the 7th of September." He said. "No one has to know about anything…we good?" She nodded affirmatively. He hugged her close. "It's okay, babe…we're going to be okay. I hope your dad is wrong; I really do! But, vacation time and money are a small price to pay to be sure."

Confidence was high and the jihadi were excited. The Emir's speech had the desired effect. Achmed thought that some of the enthusiasm might also stem from anxiousness to return home. A few of the jihadi clearly had adjustment issues with the standard of living. He even felt that a couple of them would not likely respond if activated. That wouldn't matter would it? They were unwitting biological ordnance; their fuses were lit and could not be put out. It would now be up to Achmed and Ari to see they made it to their targets.

"Brothers…" Achmed began, "…In less than an hour, we will part ways for a little time. 9/11 is exactly four weeks from now and as previously discussed, we want to you spend time in congested areas documenting times and locations of the highest flow. Transportation stations, social events, musical concerts and other events of high density attendance. Funding will be provided for tickets, fees or costs. For instance, if attending a rock concert, move through the crowds in various places. Think about where to get maximum casualties and still escape undetected. Then, on the 8th of September, you will make contact with your counterparts using the phone number provided. At that time, you will be given further instructions and materials to accomplish your mission. More will be understood when you receive your instructions. For security reasons, now would not be a good time to know the full mission. When you make contact, you must also be careful not to disclose what you know about the mission to your contact—he only knows his part of it. They are only to provide you materials and another contact. It will be up to you to select targets based on the timeframe we want you to act. We did not train you to be suicide bombers and that is because they can only be used one time. We want you to be used many times. Coordination and security are the most important. I can tell you that September 11th is the day some of you will strike. The rest of you will strike on successive days until America is brought to its knees!"

The jihadi erupted into a roar of approval. Achmed joined them, though for a different reason. The mission would be great and Allah would be pleased, but it would not unfold as these men had just been told. The disease will have consumed all of them before the 8th of September. By the 11th of September or "9/11", thousands of the second and third generation infected would become symptomatic and a rush on the American medical system would be overwhelming. If only a third of the jihadi were successful in exposing thousands of people; 80 American cities would be under siege from the most deadly virus known to man. No country could prepare for that—none. It is the perfect weapon as it will deliver millions of casualties but, the Americans will not have a smoking gun or an adversary to retaliate against because they won't know who attacked them. Certainly, not everyone would die. There will be isolated pockets of people who survive, but even they would eventually die as all commerce would stop; shipping, manufacturing, and food processing would halt. With nothing to eat and no clean water to drink, the rest would perish; save a few farmers. The Great Satan would be no more. Other nations of the world would have no choice but to quarantine the ailing country; separated geographically by oceans.

Achmed's optimism was strong and his hopes were high, but he only knew half the plan. Even now, as he and the additional jihadi groups were about to embark on a devastating mission, the Emir was finalizing the second phase of the campaign; a force multiplier for the infected jihadi that would ensure the plan had maximum effect. The first two phases of Scimitar were relatively simple and logistics were easy; thanks to the American traitors—now jihadi—and the poor immigration policies of the United States. The American politicians and their greed for money and power would be their downfall; failing to close vulnerabilities in favor of importing voters that were otherwise illegal. All for the greater good; but whose greater good? John Stuart Mill's philosophical views were about to be realized in the US political system; there are no moral absolutes, no rules that can't be broken for the greater good. Both political parties believe their way is the best and that it doesn't matter how it's achieved if the end result is for the greater good. But this is only a ruse, for they lie to themselves; substituting greater good for personal gain. Yes, it is about power and greed and self-service. The Emir grinned to himself and thought of how close he was to watching America implode on itself. Soon, they would not be a factor and Israel would not have an ally capable of protecting them. This was truly the era of Islam; Allah would deliver the infidel into the hands of the faithful.

"Nice big barn. Looks like it's about to fall over." Madison said, pointing at the structure about 200 yards off the road.

"Yeah, that's the old Swanson place. It's been abandoned for 30 years. I'd like to get in that barn before she falls down completely. It's empty except for a 1934 Model "A" John Deere tractor in there…and in pretty good shape too." The driver said enthusiastically.

"Really!!! Man I'd kill to see that thing!" Mad Dog piped. "Do you mind?"

The driver looked at Mad Dog for a moment and responded, "Well, hell I guess if you guys don't mind getting back a little later, then I don't." With that, he slowed the wrecker and made the turn. The second wrecker slowed and stopped on the main road, but did not turn. The radio crackled in Mad Dog's wrecker, "Hey, what are you doing?"

"Yeah Drew, this dude wants to see that old tractor."

David asked his driver what this was about and he told him about the tractor and their dreams of restoring it. David had a good idea what Mad Dog was up to and expressed a desire to see the tractor as well. The driver seemed a little annoyed, but complied and turned off the road where the first wrecker did. As they approached the barn, it was clear that Mad Dog was holding a gun on his driver, who was now making ready to unhitch the AATREC. David's driver turned to him with a surprised look and was greeted with the business end of a Sig 226.

"Just relax. We don't plan on hurting anybody unless they decide to play hero…are you a hero Drew?" David asked rhetorically. The driver shook his head negatively. "Good. Then, why don't we see if we can help your buddy."

David kept an eye on Drew as he rolled out of the cab of the wrecker. The man was very compliant but clearly upset. The AATREC was now separated from its captor and Mad Dog motioned for the driver to pull the wrecker into the barn. He made the driver keep his door open so Mad Dog could see any shenanigans. David told Drew to disengage the Jeep; he was unsure of Mad Dog's intentions for it at this point, but it would fit easier into the barn if it weren't attached to the wrecker. As Drew was lowering the Jeep to the ground, David peered inside and noticed his backpack was open and its contents spilled into the back seat area—it had been searched. Then, he glanced at the cubbyhole panel. It didn't appear to have been opened; the government spooks likely did a cursory search and saved the complete teardown for later. He wondered about the AATREC.

"Dork!" The voice came from the barn. "Bring your boy in here." David complied; Drew was clearly even more upset. David figured the man was thinking it would be his last moments on Earth. He needed to quell Drew's fears; not just for the purpose of easing his anxiety, but because a man that feels like he's about to be killed will get desperate and try something as he has nothing to lose.

"Drew…hold up a second." David said as he lowered the weapon, but keeping a safe distance. Drew slowly turned thinking the worst and seeing the gun was not in his back—relaxed visibly. David saw that his eyes were welled up.

"I've got kids man, ya know?" Drew's voice was quivering.

"Dude," David began, "I'm not going to hurt you if you do what we say…trust me. I already killed two today and I'd rather not add to the count, but it was necessary. You and your buddy there are just good folks trying to make a living like anybody else…like me." He paused. Would it really matter if David gave an explanation to what happened on the mountain; probably not, but he would do it anyway. "You don't have to believe me—and I don't care if you do—but those clowns back at the parking lot are not the good guys. They are rogue government thugs working for a corrupt administration. I believe they killed my parents' because of what they knew, and now they want to do the same to me. I'm not going to tell you anymore, because it will put you in danger. If they think you know *ANYTHING* at all, they will kill you and make it look like Mad Dog and I did it. Believe it!"

Drew nodded affirmatively, indicating he accepted David's explanation. They continued their walk toward the barn, David's weapon was still at the low, but he maintained a position behind the driver just in case. As they approached the barn, David heard Drew mumble something.

"What?" David said, "Did you say something."

Drew cleared his throat. "I said…we're Three Percenters…Nate and me." He pointed to the bumper of the wrecker in the barn and the sticker that displayed "III" in Roman numerals.

David knew the reference. It was becoming more and more popular these days in response to anti-government sentiment. The affiliation was in reference to the original three percent of the population in America during the Revolutionary War that actually fought the British for independence. An incredible fact; most Americans today are under the impression that all able-bodied men joined the fight—they did not. The term 'patriot' was assigned to the 3% that carried the war to victory. It essentially separated them from those who merely survived the conflict; which is much like the delineation today between the 'preppers' and patriots. The general perception is that preppers want to retreat to their redoubts and be left alone, but the patriots feel compelled to rise against the government to restore and protect the Constitution. David had been in contact with several of these modern day 'patriots.' He considered half of them to be whack jobs or wanna-be's that hoarded guns and ammunition; the other half had some merit. To date, he avoided affiliating with any of them because even some of the better groups still had whack jobs in them. Those would be a security risk at a minimum. Facebook was full of those that joined overt anti-government groups and local militias, bragged on their guns and ammo, and just generally spit a constant regurgitation of government hate statements. This ensures only one result; their inclusion on government watch lists. If there was a tyrannical takeover by the government, these guys would be the first to be rounded up and either be terminated or sent to internment camps. David was positive that legitimate groups existed, but very difficult to find as they would have strong adherence to OPSEC and COMSEC principles. Sizing up Drew and Nate, he would assign them to the 'wanna-be, but well-meaning' category. They were both mid 30's and a little plump, but that could be deceptive. Still, he would probe a bit.

"Any military experience?" David asked directly.

"75th Ranger…both of us. Nate was a Pathfinder." Drew said dryly.

David smiled. *Nice.* He stopped. "Well, thanks for your service…I'm Air Force…a JTAC…or was until this all happened." Joint Terminal Attack Controllers—or JTACs—direct combat aircraft in air to ground and close air support (CAS) operations.

Drew stopped and faced David with a big toothy grin. "No kiddin?' Man, you guys saved our bacon a bunch of times. One of my best friends was a JTAC in our unit; Jake Burrelson…know him?"

"I know of him…Medal of Honor winner in Afghanistan; died in the line of duty." David was very familiar with the legend, as were all JTACs.

"I wasn't with him that day…wish I had been, but probably wouldn't be here if I was; they had over 50% casualties before it was over. Nate was on the QRF that went in after the Warthogs and Spectre finished up on the hajis. He said it was the worst thing he ever saw…and smelled. He said the smell haunts him even more than what he saw!"

"How did you both end up here?" David asked, as he holstered his weapon. Again, it was a risk, but he was sure Drew was not a threat at this point. Drew noticed the gesture and appeared visibly relieved.

"Aww, well, I'm from here. Nate was from Arizona and really didn't have any family left, so I told him to come out here and we started a business together. Ranger Wrecker and Salvage, Inc." He pointed to the door on the wrecker where the magnetic sign clung to a rusty metal finish.

Now, all four men stood together in the barn. David looked at Mad Dog and smiled. "The old geezer here was a green beanie." Mad Dog had been watching and partially listening as they approached and observed David establish a rapport with Drew. He thought it risky that David holstered his weapon, but waited to pass judgment. Upon hearing David's declaration of Mad Dog's military experience, he pretended to be incensed.

"Geezer??? I'll show you what this geezer can do to a washed up wing nut." Mad Dog barked, as he holstered his weapon. He extended his hand to Drew. "Mad Dog; 1ˢᵗ & 10ᵗʰ Special Forces…this here, is 'Dork.' He's *Air Farce*."

Mad Dog shook Drew's hand and then Nate's. There were smiles all around and a little shuckin' & jivin' but, still some nervousness on the part of the wrecker crew. Nate was the first to break the ice. "You boys seem to be in a bit of trouble…what's the plan?"

"We would appreciate any help we can get, but you and Drew don't need to get involved. Trust me. These guys are pros and they are ruthless. The less you know the better." Mad Dog hesitated for a few moments and then continued. "I was going to hide the wreckers and

Jeep in here and then tie you guys up. I figured it would give us a few hours anyway."

Drew sized up the big white AATREC. "You ain't gonna get far in that thing, they'll find you too easy." He looked at Nate and rubbed his chin for a moment. "Tell you what let's do. We'll leave the wreckers and the Jeep here and go to my shop. I have a down-draft paint stall there and we could get a new set of clothes for this ol' girl in about an hour. We'll pull a Montana license plate off last week's roll-over wreck and it'll look totally different."

"What about you guys?" David said, "They'll know you helped us."

"Not if you take us hostage and drop us off in the middle of nowhere." Nate chided. "By the time we walk out, you'll be out of state."

Mad Dog looked at David and nodded. The idea had merit. "What about our government friends, won't they be waiting at the impound yard?"

"The shop isn't co-located with the salvage yard. It's at my place a couple of miles outside of Red Lodge." Drew responded.

"Okay then," Mad Dog chimed, "...you got cold beer at this shop?"

"Beer???" laughed Nate, "Oh yeah! We got lots of beer...hell, we even got a still!"

David went to the Jeep and repacked his gear in the backpack. His military gear seemed to be intact also. Everything was there except half a dozen Clif bars. *Jerks!* The package in the cubby was safe and appeared to have been undiscovered. He was relieved, but still concerned about how he would contact and warn his siblings. Virtually any contact at this point would compromise him and Mad Dog. Also, it remained unclear how the government thugs came to be at the dam; David was starting to think he might have been the one led them in, either by GPS tracker or tail. They would need to know the AATREC was clean before they arrived at the shop.

"Did they ransack your AATREC?" David said, watching Mad Dog come out the door of the camper.

"No, we would have known it. Got a claymore mounted just inside the door for unwanted visitors." He chuckled. "If you don't know the secret and pop the door open…"

David shook his head. "Yeah, they probably guessed you had something like that and left it alone."

Drew spoke up. "Oh yeah. They told us not to touch anything or let anybody near them." He reached into the wrecker and pulled out a coil of rope. "We're probably gonna need this to make things look legit." He started using one end of the rope to chaff his wrists.

Mad Dog smiled. "You guys think of everything."

"Well, not everything. I still needed you to turn your head for juuuuuust a second…" Nate reached under the seat of the wrecker and pulled out a Colt Python .357 magnum. Mad Dog instinctively jerked his hand toward his holster, but restrained from drawing the weapon, seeing the ranger turn the 'hand cannon' butt first to David. "I was waiting for Drew to start something, but he never did. Good thing, I guess…this whole thing might have turned out differently."

"Yeah," Drew said looking at David, "I was close…real close. But I was pretty sure the kid would have popped me. I just wasn't gonna go down without a fight."

David studied Drew's face. Yes, he had sensed Drew was to that point, and it was the reason why he decided to reduce the tension. It would have been bad; David would have killed Drew, but then the distraction would have likely allowed Nate to pull the Python. He held the shiny pistol in his hand now. It was well maintained. He thought about the potential events and how they would have ultimately played out; it shook him up a lot more than killing the two thugs earlier. He handed the pistol back to Nate, who then replaced it back in its hiding place under the seat. David could tell that each of them was contemplating the close call. The silence was awkward.

"Beer! Where's that beer??" Leave it to Mad Dog to break the stall. They all laughed. David was grateful for their new allies and the comradery. Though, he appreciated the help they offered now, he would soon learn their contribution would be much more than he could have imagined.

CHAPTER 11

"Make allowance for each other's faults, and forgive anyone who offends you. Remember, the Lord forgave you, so you must forgive others." –Colossians 3:13

Achmed hated flying. The flight was particularly frightening with the bad weather they encountered while crossing the Atlantic. His hands ached from gripping the armrests and he was exhausted. Ari slept most of the way. The dusty ride in the van to Juarez wasn't much better. There was no air-conditioning and food was not offered.

The coyote was very insistent they get through the tunnel into El Paso before dawn because the scheduling window for avoiding US Customs checkpoints was tight. Achmed and Ari did not have passports and the American jihadi with them were believed to be on watch lists. This meant they could not use commercial airlines to disperse into the country and would have to use ground transportation. Achmed wanted to have a day of rest, but was thankful it would be one less day of exposure to the infected jihadi. They would become contagious soon. He stared at one of the jihadi who seemed to have picked up a nagging cough. Ari noticed it too.

"Do you think…?" Ari whispered to Achmed, but purposely didn't finish the sentence.

"I hope not, maybe it's just a cold." Achmed tried not to breathe as deep, as if that would help. "In a few hours we will be at the place where we part with him and those others. We continue to Dallas on the I-20 road and they go to San Antonio and Houston on the I-10 road."

Ross stared at the private message on his Facebook page; "Can't wait to see you climb the ladder and bite your tongue." It was from 'Dorkboy Sniff.' *There was only one person that could be from—David. But, why didn't he use his regular account?* Ross didn't know. He drafted several

115

responses citing cute references, but none seemed right, mostly because he felt something was wrong. He typed a short response and looked at it for several moments before sending it. Ross knew where—it was the cabin where David broke the ladder. He sent a response, it read simply; "when?"

The response came back in less than a minute; "Now would be good."

Ross sat back in his chair and stared at the message. *What the heck? Was David in trouble? Why didn't he just call? Well, that's just crazy,* he thought. His curiosity was eating him up. He looked at his schedule and there were gigs through the rest of August and September. It just wasn't practical. He sent a message back; "Can't...got gigs"

The response again was immediate; "now, and bring BoB with you...tell Gator and Bug to come too"

BoB? Who was BoB? Ross knew Gator and Bug; those were nicknames for Carrie and Leigh. He racked his brain for a few minutes before he recognized the "o" was little, then he put it together; BoB stood for 'Bug out Bag.' David was making reference to the stuff his father sent that was in Hallie's apartment. Ross looked back at the schedule. Hallie was in Orlando until the end of next week. Then, they were to go to a major gig Ross was playing at Madison Square Garden. Things were going well and he didn't want to miss her—or the gig.

He typed a message; "can u wait 2 weeks?"

The response; "if necessary, but no longer"

Then, as suddenly as it appeared, 'Dorkboy Sniff' showed offline. Ross sat back and stared at the screen and re-read the entire conversation again. He thought about the reference to the BoB—*that's what this was about; getting to the redoubt.* He looked back at the calendar, this time September 11th jumped out at him. It was only 3 weeks away now. *Time flies, doesn't it?* He got up and went to the bedroom to find the DVD disk his dad included in the package. Ross had tried to watch it before, but in less than a minute he got choked up and turned it off. David had told him earlier that he needed to watch it because it was important. The DVD was still in the player where he left it. Picking up the remote, he took a deep breath and muttered, "Well, here we go..."

"Do you think he got it?" Mad Dog said, looking over David's shoulder.

"Yeah, he's pretty smart that way." David answered as he exhaled forcefully.

"Okay, let's get going, just in case somebody figures that mess out, I couldn't understand any of it and that might be a good thing." Mad Dog shook his head. "You guys are a little touched, I think."

They left the library and got in an old '72 Plymouth Fury that Drew loaned them and drove off. Mad Dog wanted to observe the library for a few hours to see if anybody came poking around, but that would serve no real purpose other than to satisfy his curiosity. It would have been risky too, but old habits die hard. He was deep into surveillance detection mode. In fact, he had made a living at it working for the State Department to protect US embassies worldwide.

As they drove outside the city limits, two black Suburbans drove around them and sped down the road. David looked at Mad Dog and laughed. "Dude, you look like you ought to be tending your liquor still in the outback." Mad Dog had an old oversized coat on with grease stains on the front, a dumpy looking hat sporting a three inch sweat band stain and big bug-eyed sunglasses.

"You looked in the mirror lately?" he said dryly as he hung his arm out the window. "You ain't no peach, yourself."

David shifted the rearview mirror so he could get a look at himself and busted out with a belly laugh. That got Mad Dog going and they both laughed until they had tears rolling down their faces. It was good, and they needed it. As they continued on, they drove past the salvage yard. The two Suburbans were parked there along with a sheriff's car and four men were standing next to it. Mad Dog cranked the stereo in the Fury to blast C&W music. The men turned to look at the car and saw

Mad Dog with his arm hanging out the window tapping along with the beat. The men immediately turned to ignore the redneck and began engaging in conversation. David was beside himself.

"Are you crazy?" He turned the radio down to a dull roar.

"Best place to hide, kid...is in *plain sight*." He warbled.

"Yeah, well you are a *sight*!" And they started laughing again.

Drew and Nate had been dropped off on an old logging road about 8 miles from town by David and Mad Dog. As they walked, they used pieces of rope to rub their wrists and make it appear as though they had been tied up. They told Mad Dog and David to go to Drew's mother's house and hide there. The property had been unoccupied since she died 11 years ago, but Drew kept up the minimum maintenance on the house so it didn't rot away. The AATREC had been stashed in a pole barn at the back of the property and covered with an old parachute. Dirt, old rancid hay and a few weatherworn planks were strewn over it to give it the appearance of having been undisturbed for at least a decade. The original plan was to paint the AATREC and send the fugitives on their merry way, however the activity in the town and surrounding area required a snap decision to stay put near Red Lodge until the heat was off.

"What if they're intercepted before they get to your mom's house?" Nate was having anxiety.

"Yeah, I thought about that too." Drew replied. "If they give us up, we won't go to jail for aiding and abetting...if what Mad Dog said is true, the government boys will assume we were told things and waste us too."

"Yeah, maybe we shoulda just let them tie us up in the barn with the wreckers."

"Too late now, we're in it up to our necks. Besides, I honestly believe we're doing the right thing." Drew said, rather patriotically.

"Yeah, me too. And, you gotta admit, we ain't bored no more." They both laughed and continued to trudge toward town.

Mohammad hated the Northeast. There was nothing but a bunch of rude yankees up here. While it felt good to be back in the United States, he would have preferred something a little further South. Even back in Sanford, Florida would be nice. Still, because he didn't like these people, he enjoyed the idea that he was going to terrorize them somehow. They already enjoyed the efforts of his Muslim brothers during the Boston Marathon. Achmed had told him this assignment was special, as he would be avenging the brothers that bombed the race.

Boston Logan International Airport was smaller than he expected for a city the size of Boston, but it was very busy. He looked around for an ATM and found one near the restrooms. There was a cop standing just a few feet away. Mohammad thought about going somewhere else, but then remembered he was invisible in his white skin to the enemies of Islam. They would never expect him to be a threat, unlike the couple that just now passed in front of the cop. Mohammad watched as the policeman sternly focused his attention on the man; his wife wore a full burka and trailed slightly behind. The irony of the scene made Mohammad crack a smile. This policeman was clearly engaged on what was probably a harmless Muslim couple, and yet the real threat stood just feet from him—hiding in plain sight.

Mohammad fondled the debit card between his thumb and forefinger. He wondered how much money was in the account. They gave him a few dollars before he got on the plane for food or whatever, but the real money was supposed to be on the card. He was to use it to find a place to stay, buy food, and mingle in high traffic areas to gather intelligence for potential missions. Concerts, fairs, expositions and movie theaters were all on his list of places to scope out.

The card slipped into the ATM slot and he was prompted to enter his pin. He punched in four digits and the welcome screen displayed his given name—John W. Jones. It annoyed him. He selected balance and a few seconds later the account balance appeared. He was somewhat stunned; it was just under six thousand dollars. It seemed a bit excessive. He was told the amount in the account would have to be enough until he met with his handler in just under three weeks. He could live like a king on this, go to a concert every night, and still not blow that amount. He smiled to himself again and selected the amount of $200.00 dollars and withdrew the cash. This had two functions; first he needed the money, and secondly it was a confirmation to those monitoring the account that he had safely arrived and cleared U.S. Customs without incident. Now, he would proceed to the Boston Common Hotel on Trinity Place; just a few blocks away from Berklee College of Music. There, he would try to connect with the music scene. As he was making his way to the doors labeled 'Public Transportation' he spied a rack of brochures and free entertainment rags that advertised all kinds of events he could attend. He grabbed several of them and was about to leave when he also noticed a rack across from the first one. Apartment Finder was right on top. This was a sign from Allah. All was being laid out for Mohammad to accomplish his mission down to the smallest detail. He felt wanted. He felt needed. He felt important.

He climbed into a cab and gave the name of the hotel. Settling back into the seat, he opened one of the entertainment rags and flipped through the pages. There were so many options and choices; he would be busy for sure. But, he wanted a big venue. As they crossed the I-90 Bridge from the harbor, he thought he'd ask an expert.

"So, what's to do in Boston if you want to see a concert?" Mohammad queried.

"What, tonight? Not much pal…tomorrow is the big draw. Fenway Park for the DURP Band…heard of 'em?"

"Yeah, I think everybody has…that's cool. It's not sold out, is it?" Mohammad hoped not.

"Might be…probably is…but you can always get with the scalpers if you wanna go bad enough!"

That wouldn't be a problem for Mohammad; he had six thousand dollars in the bank! He liked the DURP Band. They rocked. This would only be a fact finding outing anyway, the DURP fans would be safe. But what of a couple of weeks? He didn't know.

"So, will there be more concerts at Fenway soon? Mohammad inquired.

"Yeah, for the next few weekends until the weather gets bad. The Sox didn't make the playoffs this year so Fenway has been open for other stuff."

Mohammad smiled to himself as he dropped the entertainment rag and picked up the Apartment Finder. Once again, he was stunned. The rent rates were crazy high. A small one bedroom was $1600.00 per month. Considering he would have to pay first and last month's rent in advance plus a deposit; it didn't seem like the $6000.00 in the bank was so excessive now. He would have to shop around or maybe move away from downtown. Taking the train in and out of town wouldn't be a bad idea anyway. It would give him the opportunity to scope out public transportation as well. The cab driver looked in rearview mirror and noticed Mohammad reading the Apartment Finder.

"So, you looking for a place to live?" He seemed excited.

"Uhh, yeah. I just flew in from over...over Florida way...Orlando. Why? You know a place?"

"Yeah, well my cousin just lost his roommate last month and the rent is killing him. He's looking for somebody. You seem like an okay guy. It's $800 plus half electric...it's a great place; right across from Berklee...you should call him."

Mohammad looked out the window and smiled. It was starting to sprinkle and the drops on the glass distorted the lights from the businesses as they passed and it reminded him of Christmas lights. Yes, Christmas would be different in America this year. *If they only knew*, he thought.

"Yeah, that might work. Give me his number, I'll check it out."
Mohammad was again feeling as though Allah was lighting his path.
"Yeah, that just might work."

Things seemed like they were getting a little slow after the events of the
last few days. David and Mad Dog settled into "mom's place" fairly
well, except there was no cable TV; just what they could get across the
air waves. It was just too hot for trying to leave the area, as there were
still several government thugs roaming around. Drew and Nate had
been thoroughly grilled and re-grilled until the thugs were satisfied they
didn't know anything more. That said a lot about them and their
allegiances. David breathed a little easier now. Their new friends were
smart and only visited once since the big event at Mystic Dam; and
then it was to drop off an old truck next to the house as if business as
usual was the order of the day. They didn't enter the house and
pretended to clean up the front yard of trash that had blown in since
the last visit. Under the tarp in the truck was a supply of food and
beer. There was even a bottle of George Dickel whisky. It would have
been an excellent resupply mission had they included toilet paper. Mad
Dog complained about that little oversite frequently. David's biggest
complaint was that they could not turn on the lights at night as the
house was supposed to be unoccupied. It made for long nights and he
could only sleep so long. They moved the TV into a small back storage
room with no windows, but that got old too because they could only
get two channels out of Billings, and one of those was fuzzy—KULR;
ironic because phonetically it sounds out "color," but the TV was black
and white.

David was itching to know what Mad Dog knew about current intel
surrounding the events that drove his father to orchestrate
development of the redoubt, as well as anything he might know
concerning his parents' death. Mad Dog had hinted that when it was
safe, he would give David a Sit-Rep; or situation report. Now, seemed
like a good time as there was no imminent danger and they were quite
bored. He had decided that if the old spec operator hadn't volunteered
anything after dinner tonight he would start the conversation himself.

David cleaned his gun twice and was now sharpening his knife on a small Arkansas stone when he heard Mad Dog call him from the kitchen.

"Dork, or Sniff, or whatever…come in here a minute," Mad Dog began, "…I wanna talk to you about some things." David walked into the kitchen to see that Mad Dog was yet again cleaning his gun. It was something to do.

"Love the smell of Hoppe's Number 9, don't you?" David said, as he took a deep breath.

"Been using it as cologne for years!" Mad Dog joked. "Have a seat, youngster."

David pulled up a chair and contained his outward excitement as he had a good idea what was coming. He loved getting intel briefs; though there was a thread of apprehension with this one, which was understandable as it was of a personal nature.

"You know what I was doing…what my job was before I left?" It was more of a rhetorical question, but David still nodded, "I think so…but you might want to enlighten me." Mad Dog looked up from the lower receiver he was inspecting. He gently placed it on the table and began.

"So, I've had a few different jobs in my life. I started in the Army…infantry officer; spent a little time in 'Nam.' Got into Special Forces…Green Beret, but it was not long before I was recruited into a CIA offshoot that essentially equates to the Air Marshalls of today. Back then—the '70's—it was hush hush…nobody knew about it. There was a lot of hijacking going on. The Cubans were hijacking east coast airliners and taking them to Cuba. It was getting rather common before somebody got the idea we should stop it. It would take time to get metal detectors and such in all the airports, so as a stop gap measure they got the idea to use spec ops guys to fly on airplanes and neutralize the hijackers quietly. It worked…well most the time. I had to use the stewardess…er, flight attendant in confidence once. Took out a hijacker and she covered for me while I got him offloaded in the Sky Chef truck. Anyway, that was my intro into the spook world.

Over time I became a counter-terrorist expert and advisor, and finally an analyst when I just got too old to 'jump fences' anymore. I met your dad when we worked together on a surveillance detection program. I was working as a consultant then and trying to adapt surveillance detection principles into the civilian world. Your dad had the idea of marketing the program to the National Labs...particularly, Los Alamos. They loved the idea and promised to get back with us after the Christmas break. They called it operation; 'Volant Band.'" He shook his head. "But, after Christmas they didn't contact us as promised, because it was their intent to steal the idea and do it in-house. The problem was they didn't have the expertise and the program ended up just being a shell with no teeth. Your dad called it, 'Violent Band-Aid.'" Mad Dog chuckled. "Your Dad...he was always coming up with crap like that. In any case, the company your dad worked for decided to part ways with my consultancy, but your dad and I remained good friends..."

He rolled one of the 7.62 rounds between his fingers now, seemingly lost in thoughts of the past. David studied the man's face. It was like a taking a tour; every scar, crag, and line seemed to lend credibility to the man's life. He was the real deal; he had 'been there and done that.' There was no urgency, so David didn't interrupt. His thoughts now drifted toward his father and the relationship Mad Dog had with him. He could see his smile and almost hear his laughter. He imagined the two of them having a beer together and solving the world's problems. Those must have been good times.

"So, your dad ran a facility in Phoenix where he was exposed to several different guys like me; each of them from various worlds and groups." Mad Dog continued, "And, they were not necessarily related. Add that to his previous career in spec ops, and you have a pretty good network. You see now days, everything in the intel world is so compartmentalized to thwart foreign agents from getting intel on us, that it's very difficult to put things together...and that's by design. It's also created a very dysfunctional intel gathering force. For example, 'analyst A' at the CIA discovers a piece of intel on a new effort to destroy the U.S. by using a suitcase nuke bought on the black market. 'Analyst B' in the NSA finds a communication that talks about smuggling something in on an airplane painted and flagged as a U.S. carrier. 'Analyst C' who is a military intel officer looking at satellite photos discovers an aircraft that matches the type believed to have been lost in the Indian Ocean, in a remote location on the African continent; but he dismisses the possibility of it being the lost jet because he's looking for Air Malaysia and the one he's looking at is clearly marked Delta Airlines. These three analysts are stove-piped in their organizations and cannot get access to the others' intel…and by the way, while I just kinda brought this up as an example, I really believe this one is being worked right now, but it's just a theory." He paused and took a deep breath. "Anyway, your dad had a lot of friends from different worlds; spec ops, CIA, NSA, SOCOM, me of course, and several others that would under normal circumstances—not have crossed paths. He was one of the best networkers I've ever known and he kept close contact with all of us…just the kinda guy he was. So, imagine that he was friends with each of the analysts in my example, he would be able to put it all together, right? Well, I think that's what he did…he put a lot of things together from multiple sources and normally, that would be a good thing, but…" Mad Dog picked up the rifle round again and rolled it back and forth. Clearly, he was struggling with something. David wanted to push, but he knew it wasn't the time. This was something the man had to resolve within himself.

"Well, we can take a break," David started, "You want something to eat?"

"No…no. Sit down, I gotta get this out." Mad Dog said clearly under duress. "Your dad…well, he discovered a terrorist plot that crossed multiple 'stove-pipes' and sources. Unlike the attacks of 9/11, he described them as much simpler to execute, but infinitely more devastating. He believed it would be the fall of the United States and recovery would be impossible. And, he knew the timeline…to the day…"

"September 11th of this year." David stated flatly.

"Yeah." Mad Dog agreed.

"Why didn't he just communicate what he knew to the others in his network?—stop the threat. Then, there would be no need for the redoubt or the fall of the U. S. It doesn't make sense to me, he was one of the strongest patriots I know. Why would he allow this to happen?" David was visibly upset. *Was Mad Dog struggling to tell him that his father wasn't who he thought he was…that he was a traitor to his country?*

"Settle down. It's not what you think…it's not." Mad Dog was firm and stern in his answer. "It was…is…an impossible situation. Perhaps if he lived he might have figured a way, but all avenues to him were closed. And, there were those of us that…he tried to protect, but it was too late."

"Too late? Too late for what? What are you not telling me?" David was now frustrated also. He wanted to tell Mad Dog to just spit it out, but he was afraid it would close down the conversation and he would never know.

"Okay Dork, this is complicated and it's not easy for me! I'm getting to all that. Maybe I need to shift to the other side of this thing…from the top down." He frowned and looked David in the eye. "Remember when I said, who better to tear down the U. S. Constitution than a president who was also a constitutional lawyer?" David nodded. "Well, that's what we got, but it's worse than that—he doesn't want to stop at the Constitution—he wants to change the entire culture of the United States and the world. He knows his time is short and there are those that believe mental illness is to blame. One of the intercepts I analyzed came from high level German intelligence and had been briefed to the Chancellor. The German experts and psychologists believe POTUS is unstable and has displayed symptoms of mental illness. They base a lot of the premise on the fact that only a maniac would commit the slow suicide of his own country. The actions POTUS is taking deliberately destroys the fabric of the country, not only internally, but also weakens us for external threats. There is no upside to his actions."

"Is that what you think?" David asked.

"Mental illness? No, I disagree, but then because of your dad I have information they don't. Yeah, POTUS wants to knock the U.S. down a

126

few notches and change the culture too, in short, it's a power grab from a fool that doesn't realize what he's doing will create a chain reaction the country can't recover from. Oh, he'll change the culture alright…or rather 'they' will; his political party is buying into a lot of what he's trying to do, but they don't know his whole plan. Bringing in illegal aliens and giving them voting rights, appeasing radical Islamic groups through political correctness, inciting racial bias, and making as many government dependent citizens as possible because they always vote for those that give them 'free stuff'…these are all deliberate plans to create a bomb called 'dependency' and ignite it with civil unrest. He's been in the office for six and a half years and only has a year and a half left. His hope was to create a civil unrest situation on a national scale whereby he could activate actions from the executive orders he and other presidents have written!" Mad Dog was on a roll, but he recognized he was losing perspective of what he wanted to convey to David. He stood up, took a deep breath and began digging through the supplies left by Drew and Nate. Eventually, he found what he was looking for—George Dickel. "Martial law…he's got to get the country to a state of martial law. Then, he can dissolve the current government and put it in the hands of the minions he appointed; that essentially being his cabinet." Mad Dog took two glasses from the cupboard and poured about two fingers in each glass. David didn't hesitate, nor did Mad Dog. They gestured a toast and downed the pale brown liquid. Mad Dog filled the glasses again and sat down.

"Thing is…POTUS knows he ain't gonna make it in time. He needs a more aggressive plan, but with aggressive action comes unintended consequences…and those consequences will be the downfall of this country—we will not recover." Mad Dog took a smaller sip of the whiskey. "But, of course POTUS thinks differently."

David followed suit, but his sip was more of a gulp. He looked at Mad Dog a little askance. As convincingly as the old warrior delivered the rant, David still didn't have enough of the puzzle to completely buy in. He knew Mad Dog was going to get around to the final points, but David was getting impatient. *What did this have to do with his father being ex-pat, if he even was?*

127

"Okay, so let me back up a little…Your dad uncovered several phases of a terrorist attack by compiling intel from several of his friends; me included. Then, he disseminated the compiled analysis back to each of us. We were blown away! Phase One was to cripple the power grid in such a way that it would additionally cause damage to itself and essentially leave the country without electrical power for months…maybe years. And, it's not hard to do. If just nine strategic sub-stations are hit simultaneously with simple rifle fire, the cascade effect will do exactly that. This was briefed to the President and to the Congress. It was even televised on CSPAN. And, it came in the wake of an actual event—an attack on one of the known stations in what was called 'a strategic military operation by highly trained and educated personnel.' Some speculated Russian, while others thought Chinese. Doesn't matter really, it was a test and a very successful one. Yet, we've done nothing to learn from it—not really. The vulnerability is still there. Your dad put together the date—9/11—from another source. Even if there was not a 'Phase Two,' studies show the result of power outage for this length of time would cost millions of American lives and destroy our major and moderate sized cities. In short, two-thirds to 90% of the population in the United States would be dead in a year. Personally, I think it would be higher, but what do I know? Everyone weighed in on the study; the CDC, DoD, etcetera. It made enough of an impact that the concept of 'FEMA camps' was born. Basically, they're internment camps for the surviving citizens, run by Homeland Security and FEMA. This is a prime example of preparing to treat the symptoms, rather than the problem. These FEMA camp kits or stations are all over the United States. They contain everything from concertina wire, food, tools, tents, and even coffin vaults. They need only to be deployed in the event of a national emergency…or…civil unrest." Mad Dog toasted the sky again and finished the Dickel in his glass. David once again, followed suit. Mad Dog filled them once more.

"Your dad didn't know what Phase Two was exactly; only that it was the second part of something called Scimitar. The intel he had was not conclusive, but what he did say was that the bad guys believed it to be much more devastating than Phase One. I have a hard time believing

128

that anything could be worse, but your dad thought maybe chemical or biological attack of some kind. We know that Saddam's bio-arsenal was moved to Syria and other locations and can assume they have been compromised by ISIS, but the quantities and logistics involved to create the impact that was implied would be tough even for the United States. So, I don't personally put too much stock in the threat…not such as I just described it anyway. Even my theory of a suitcase nuke flown into New York or Los Angeles on a stolen airliner wouldn't qualify for a more catastrophic event than that of the power grid." He looked at the glass and the intoxicating liquid and decided not to pick it up at this point, he was already feeling the effects of the first shots. "Phase Three…well, that's the destruction of Israel. With no USA to fly cover for our friends in the holy land, the assault of Israel by all Islamic nations is inevitable."

David was now feeling the effects of the whisky too. He contemplated what Mad Dog had said, and put it together with what his father conveyed. He was buying in, but he was still confused about his father's inability to get the word out.

"Why couldn't you get the information back upstream? You had the information…you had the whole package." David almost sounded as though he was accusing Mad Dog of failure.

"Ahh, and there's the crux: So did POTUS!" Mad Dog hesitated to allow his statement to sink in.

David looked back at the old soldier in a puzzled manner. What did that mean? Of course he did, because dad's friends' gave it to him. He thought about the last thing Mad Dog said. Then, the light came on.

"You mean the president already knew about everything?" David said incredulously.

"Now you got it." Mad Dog responded. "Imagine that you *want* a certain event to take place in order to accelerate your plan because things aren't moving fast enough. You didn't initiate it, but you didn't stop it either. Not your fault—it was a terrorist attack—and the country is in turmoil. Time to bust out the executive orders conveniently put in place, and BINGO! You are now supreme dictator of the United States of Socialist America! What a legacy!"

"Wow! So then, they came after dad because he was going to blow their plans...so, how did they know he was the one behind the intel compilation?" David was still perplexed.

Mad Dog lowered his head in his hands and sat motionless for several minutes before looking up at David. "Because of me," he looked down at the table. "It was because of me."

"I don't understand." David shook his head.

"I was the one that took the compilation to my superiors, who in turn elevated it until it reached some level at the White House. I was summoned to the Director's office and asked where I got the information and I told him. That led to a White House visit...I thought we were going to be commended in some way, but it was just the opposite; demeaning and pure political slime. I was told to shut up and that our meddling could result in the loss of all the Department of State was trying to accomplish in the Middle East; that we weren't cleared for the level of secrecy of the efforts in motion, and that in time we would watch it unfold and understand." Mad Dog paused, looking David directly in the eye. "It was because of me that they knew about your dad...and the others too." He straightened up and prepared himself for the next statement, as if bracing for impact. "I think they killed your parents'...now, they want us." David didn't say anything. He was trying to digest everything he'd just heard. He didn't blame Mad Dog for his parents' death but, it was clear that Madison blamed himself. In some way, he looked to David for forgiveness.

"Us?" David queried. "So, you think they know about me?

"Oh yeah, by now they've put it all together." Mad Dog answered. "Remember, they towed the Jeep too, and they went through your things. Probably been reported AWOL as well...yeah, I'd say you're blown."

David thought about the AWOL part of it earlier. He felt compelled to contact his unit, but knew that would be bad at this point. He also thought about trying to contact some of his comrades privately, but they might be watched or bugged. The thing that was really on his mind was if they suspected him, they were now watching his siblings…or worse. Ross might have gotten the clue from the cryptic message David had sent, but he bet Leigh and Carrie were burning up the phone lines concerning the redoubt. And, that wasn't good.

"We've got company, kid!" Mad Dog said hurriedly as he assembled the AR-10. David turned to see a Schwan's food delivery truck slow on the road and turn to enter the drive. Mad Dog was already clearing the table of anything that made it appear as though someone was living in the old house.

"What the hell? You don't think our Ranger friends decided to have food delivered, do you?" David said incredulously.

"I don't think they're that stupid, but I do think our government thugs might be, so be on your game."

CHAPTER 12

"The goal of socialism is communism." -Vladimir Ilyich Lenin

"Socialists ignore the side of man that is the spirit. They can provide you shelter, fill your belly with bacon and beans, treat you when you're ill, all the things guaranteed to a prisoner or a slave. They don't understand that we also dream." – John Wayne

The Emir stood looking over the table in the dim room. The only light in the room cast illumination on the table like that of a pool hall. Reports were spread haphazardly in front of him. He was pleased with what he saw as it was indicative the plan was going well. Still, he was shaken up about the previous day's events when he was nearly killed in an attack by western forces. In fact, they had declared his death to the world. It was close, and he was wounded, but he was far from dead and only superficially injured except for his right ear, which was still ringing from the explosion.

"Mushreq…have the second and third waves confirmed yet?" The Emir was impatient and expecting the scarred man to have good news.

"Not yet, Emir. But, they have been trickling in slowly. Remember, this is a much larger group, 160 in all. It will take time." Mushreq responded.

The Emir merely rocked back and forth on his arms over the table, contemplating potential failure. Would it be a failure? No, he didn't think so; the first group alone would cause catastrophic damage by themselves. He had to send them a bit early because of the potential compromise caused by Mohammad—*that son of a whore!* Emir knew timing would be critical for maximum effect. The Center for Disease Control must not sound the alarm before the power grid fails. If even one of the jihadi is diagnosed with Ebola before that event, the impact could be significantly less. Americans must not know of the epidemic—the loss of power and resultant communication would severely restrict them from effectively warning the public. He considered pulling the trigger on the grid attack early to ensure success, but the date was too important to him. It had to be 9/11.

"Something to eat, Emir?" Mushreq asked.

"No, Mushreq. My appetite for anything other than news of success consumes me."

Mushreq nodded and withdrew. The Emir continued to scan the papers in front of him, desperately expecting them to change before his eyes and somehow console him with additional news. If the compromise highlighted ISIS as the instigator, the entire world would be against them. This had strong potential to focus negative attention on Muslims around the world and that concerned him deeply. It could reverse internal takeovers in all the countries. This was the perfect time and must be carefully executed.

The plan had been simple, but fragile at the same time. Through immigration to western countries, infiltration has been sufficient enough to be gravely significant. Muslims are breeding at much higher rates than their hosts. Studies show Muslim cultures are growing in these host countries at a rate of 8.1 children per family, as opposed to the hosts themselves at a rate of 1.6 to 1.8; which is indicative of a reduction. To sustain an existing culture, this rate must be a minimum of 2.11 or higher. Nearly all of Europe and Russia are infiltrated with Muslim immigrants and the result will achieve a majority in less than 8 to 15 years. Then, political control would be established and Sharia Law would be the law of those lands. Resistance would be futile; without Second Amendment rights; any of those considering a patriotic front would be nullified. The fragility rests on continued political correctness to protect the rights of the Muslim communities and the only thing threatening that is if Scimitar were to be linked to ISIS.

Scimitar should render the United States useless; even defenseless against her enemies. They had tested the plan on a single sub-station with a Special Forces team. It went flawlessly. Arming ISIS with this information gave the Russians plausible deniability in the event it were thwarted or compromised. There was no trail back to them. Even with the loss of the grid, the American nuclear arsenal was still quite capable of delivering a devastating retaliation. But, if the grid attack were to be successful, the Americans would not know who to retaliate against. Over a relatively short period of time, the social fabric of America would come apart under the conditions of her affliction—and she would be rendered helpless; a non-player on the international scene. To add the Ebola epidemic in the mix would assure a stake in her heart, as without electrical power there would be no internet, no media, and very poor communication to alert her citizens. Everything would eventually crumble; social programs, government assistance, police forces, and finally the military. With the rest of the world already under Muslim control, only the Chinese remained to be conquered. Eventually, they too would succumb to Allah and Islam over time. But, it all hinged on bringing down the Great Satan.

The weather was great for this time of year. Fenway was nearly full for the concert and Ross was stoked. The temperature was just a little cool, but under the hot lights it was perfect. The first five songs DURP Band played had the crowd in a frenzy. The song Ross was currently playing, Carolina's Serenade, slowed things down a bit. The solo was particularly soulful and Ross usually played it with his eyes mostly shut. However, Hallie was below in the crowd and he wanted to acknowledge her personally—play to her. She and Kate were standing together, when he went to the front of the stage and sat down on the edge. He looked right at the both of them and gave his best. The solo was longer than normal for this song, but the band took it in stride. Hallie smiled back at him and blew a kiss. The crowd noticed the interaction and hooped and hollered as expected. She felt special, just like he wanted her to and the crowd pulled back to have the two women standing by themselves with a bit of space around them. Kate gave him a thumbs up. *What a great night,* Ross thought. *I wish it could be like this every time I play.*

Mohammad moved around the crowd like a predator. At least that's how he felt. It was pretty cool. Nobody knew him or how powerful a jihadi he was…yes, that's how he felt; powerful. It was packed down in front. He had to push though in several places, but nobody cared because they were all engaged with the band. He thought about how easy it would be to drop an explosive device with a timer. No one would notice until it exploded; then they would know—the whole country would know!

As he came up toward the stage, the sax player stepped out and sat on the edge and began playing to someone in front of him. He pushed through to see two women holding each other and one blew a kiss to the player. He stood and watched until the solo was over. The crowd cheered loudly and it hurt his ears. It was a great solo, though. He really liked this band and wondered who the two women were. He thought about engaging them by starting a conversation, but it was too loud, so he moved back through the crowd and searched for more potential target areas. Perhaps if he could carry several charges and drop them near the exits. If they all went off at the same time the crowd would panic and surge away from the exits. This may get more casualties though trampling or suffocation by compression. It was a thought. He would make a note of it.

Landon eyed the flight schedule as he always did on Sunday nights; Carrie usually helped him. It was something they did together. It would have been ops normal, except for one thing; Landon was considering not just this week's schedule, but the following week as well, since it contained a very important date; 9/11. Carrie didn't say anything, but she had an idea why he was looking.

"So…" she started, "…you think you should schedule anything on that date?" Her finger hovered over the computer screen above the suspect date.

"Hmmmm…I don't know. I mean, if something does happen on that date, then nobody would fly anyway. And, if it is as catastrophic as your dad predicted, nobody will care they missed the flight…even the student." Landon was looking at the schedule a little differently than Carrie, but he didn't want her to know what he was thinking—just yet, anyway. They finished the week's schedule and Carrie said she was tired and ready for bed. Landon told her he had to work a flight plan for the next day's flight in case the student didn't do a good job and messed it up. Carrie went to bed and Landon went to work, though it wasn't on the plan he had mentioned to her.

The next morning after his first student was debriefed, he scheduled the Piper Seminole for 0600 on 9/11 and requested max fuel. This would ensure maintenance would prep the aircraft the night before to include the fuel load. If nothing happened, he would cancel, but if it did…well, they had options. Then, he made a call to a close friend in Fort Collins, Colorado. They talked for a long time about various things before Landon changed the subject and made a strange request. He knew no way to talk around it, so he just blurted it out. The line was silent for about half a minute.

"You're kidding, right?" Landon's friend Derek said slowly.

"No…I'm not. I can't go into any more depth, but I really need this favor, dude…and I need you to be quiet about it too. I'll pay for everything. I know you and Karen are into backpacking, so pack like you're going on a very long trip, but no Gucci gear. We must be weight conscious." Landon waited for a rebuttal, but it never came. That surprised him.

"Okay…okay. I'll do my best." Derek said, still clearly confused.

"Thanks, bro…that's all I can ask for. I'll call you in a few days to finalize things. If anything comes up before then, I'll call you sooner."

Landon hung up and thought about what he was planning and the ramifications of his actions. He could go to jail and certainly would get fired. However, if this thing goes off like Wallace said, there would be nothing to get fired from and in the end, no one would care about any of it. He was getting moderate anxiety over it, to the point where he was distracted while teaching his students to fly and that was dangerous.

Derek had been Landon's best friend since they were kids in Colorado. They played baseball together on club teams. However, as they got into high school, Derek developed into a man's man type; preferring to be a jock, while Landon turned to his interest to cars. Still, they remained very close and hung out together most all the time. People wondered how the two observably different 'buddies' got together in the first place.

Derek's girlfriend of the last several years, Karen; was a man's woman. Landon liked her, but she was too outdoorsy for him—almost masculine. Derek referred to her as a 'beast,' though she didn't look like one. Karen was a looker; at five foot nine inches tall she was statuesque and muscular, but not so much so that she looked masculine. She was also smart; having just completed her education as a physician's assistant. In short, she was beautiful, but tough. Carrie liked her because she wasn't a drama queen and felt she could trust her, but there was little in common to talk about between the two except that Carrie was a nurse and Karen a PA. This in turn usually meant they talked about work to keep the conversation going. Landon expected any day to hear that Derek was engaged, knowing they were waiting until she got her first job as a PA.

Landon was drinking the Kool-Aid now. He was more than 50 percent sure Wallace's prophesy would come to fruition, but not so much that he would act before the event was to happen. He had to have 'an out' if it didn't. That was the best he could do. He didn't tell Carrie about his plan because it included bringing two more people to the redoubt and he wasn't sure that would go over so well. Still, adding a carpentry skill and a medical capability seemed like it was within the scope of what a redoubt should have. He would eventually have to tell Carrie of his plan because she would see the financial transactions for items Landon needed to purchase. He would tell her then.

Ross and Hallie were cuddled on the couch and sharing a bottle of wine. The two were on again; mostly. Ross' personal solo to her had helped facilitate the rejoin; the wine didn't hurt either.

"So, I need to talk to you about something…" Ross began, "…it's a little awkward since we're just kinda getting back together."

She sat up and looked at him a little askance. "You 'kinda' think we're back together?"

He was in trouble. This had all the makings of a 'soup sandwich.' He thought about the coming event and what it entailed. It was too important and for that reason alone he decided not to tiptoe around it and commit all the way. If he was rejected, then so be it. If he was well received, then he saved a lot of precious time, but what he really didn't need right now, was a fight.

"I want us together...not just kinda, and I'm hoping you feel the same. I don't want to slowly feel things out or test the waters...or have ambiguity about our relationship. I'm committing to you, and I'm hoping you'll commit to me." He braced for impact.

She didn't explode, that was good, but she still had a strange look on her face. She sat up and slid slightly away from him. That wasn't good.

"So, you think our previous relationship didn't have commitment?" Her tone was indicative of a full out assault.

This had to be good; everything was about to get real. He had to think quickly and it had to be smooth. He decided to lay it all out there.

"Commitment from me...I never really afforded you that, and I'm sorry. I recognized your commitment, but I didn't..." he paused because he could not think of how to close the sentence with his thoughts, so he just decided to start a new one. "It's just that I wouldn't blame you if you said no, after how I've been in the past. And I was hoping that you still might be willing to take a chance on me." *Oh, that was good!* He thought. *Where did that come from?*

Hallie stood up and looked at him for a few seconds before averting her eyes to answer. "I don't know how to respond to that." She said in a low voice. Clearly, his statement had disarmed her. "I mean...who are you??? Where is all this coming from, and why now?"

It was a legitimate question, but one he didn't feel he could answer honestly. If he told her the truth, she might think he was only responding to pressure that it was the end of the world and he didn't want to be alone. And, that made him think, *what is the truth?*

"I don't know...not exactly." He replied. "You know, I got to thinking about us when I was on tour...and I thought about how you and I 'get' each other...it's not like any other relationship I've ever been in, you know? And, well I'm comfortable with you...I don't have to be somebody else. People seem plastic to me...fake...but not you...so, when I came back this time, all I wanted to do was see you. But then I had to go to Montana for the reading of my parents' will..." he paused to see if anything was registering with her, but her expression hadn't changed. "...and, I've recently learned about some things—serious life threatening things—that have...accelerated..."

"You have cancer or something...what?" she shook her head, "I don't understand."

Ross decided to go for broke. He had her sit down and told her the whole story, to include the recent cryptic message from David. She didn't interrupt; not even once. Which, made Ross a little nervous because he wasn't getting a read on her or what she thought. He finally finished the explanation with the fact that his father had included an additional BoB for her as well as the teddy bear.

"Look, I was already wanting to be 'us' again and this came up to compress things...and I don't expect you to believe me when I say..."

"I'll go." She said quietly.

"What?" He wasn't sure he heard her, but it made his heart beat faster.

"I said, I'll go...I'll go with you...but I want Kate to go too."

Mason was going over the list they put together. It was too much stuff and wouldn't fit—no way. It would take a much bigger vehicle. He dreaded going to Leigh about it as it would be a fight. They only had a few days before they would have to leave in time to get within a 'one-tank-of-gas range' to the redoubt as they had planned.

"Babe, we got a problem," he started. "You know…all this stuff on the list…it's…well, it's not gonna fit." She was cooking dinner and seemed to be unfazed by his comment, preferring instead to play with Tanner and his castle of Tupperware in the center of the kitchen floor. "Did you hear me…what I said?"

"Yeah so, use your work truck," she answered without looking up from Tanner.

He was stunned. He hadn't even considered that. Mason worked for a major heavy equipment company and had his work truck; a huge beast with a hydraulic crane, every kind of tool you could think of, and a lot of storage space. It had huge auxiliary fuel tanks—and a company credit card to fill them up. It was an idea. A pretty good one, but he would need to think it through. This would be a very handy thing to have at the redoubt and if everything crashed on 9/11, no one would know or care if the truck was missing. On the other hand, if 9/11 was a false alarm, he would have to explain the fuel costs on the company credit card. It was a risk, but the tanks were big enough to essentially make the trip; well, almost. They could actually leave the day before 9/11 and travel for a few hours, fill up and then wait to see what happened. If nothing, then just come back—*hey, probably wouldn't even notice that little increase.* But if something did happen, they would have enough fuel to get there easily and have fuel left over to use the truck for constructing cabins.

Mason went into the kitchen and kissed his wife. "Good idea, babe…oh, and by the way; we don't have to leave until the day before, now. So, Tanner can go to that birthday party for Kinsie."

She smiled and told Tanner; he was pleased. Mason went back to the packing list. *Let's see, a case of ammo and another case of Everclear…that should do it…*

Saul Alinsky had been dead for over 40 years, but his dream of socializing the United States was in the final stages of reality. His books, designed to arm radicals, were quoted many times by left-thinking political figures in America, to include the sitting president. A hoax was attributed to Alinsky citing a fictitious list; "Eight Rules of Control." However, a popular fact-checking website debunked it and suggested that it was really a document found during the Second World War titled, "Communist Rules for Revolution." While Alinsky didn't write them, the president found them to be interesting because they did seem to align with his own agenda—though he would never admit it. To date, all had been implemented except for one:

1. Control healthcare and you control the people.

2. Increase poverty levels and provide the poor with everything they need.

3. Increase the national debt to unsustainable levels.

4. Take guns from the citizens so they can't protect themselves from the government and impose a police state.

5. Create a welfare state.

6. Get control of the media to filter or slant news to the masses.

7. Remove religion from educational institutions and government.

8. Divide the rich from the poor to create dissent.

The President looked out the window and contemplated these 'Rules of Control' and smiled to himself. Only the 4th rule was unrealized, but that would change soon. Guns would be outlawed and those that resisted would succumb to the military.

There was some reservation in allowing the grid to be taken down; yes, lives would be lost, but he believed it necessary for the greater good. Soon, he would enact the executive orders and declare martial law. The existing government would be suspended and he would replace it with his cabinet—essentially a politburo—from where he could orchestrate the birth of a new government—*and a new Constitution*. This was his legacy—this was his destiny.

Most the staff had little knowledge of his true intentions, though some had suspected. There was a very small group of trusted collaborators that knew the entire plan and they would remain silent as their reward for doing so was significant—the penalty for non-obedience; severe. In a few days he would raise ThreatCon levels, claiming new intelligence of imminent attack. This would be expected as 9/11 was a known favorite date to the terrorist communities and involved putting the military on high alert. Recalls would be initiated to ensure maximum response in the quickest way possible; not to protect as implied, but rather to be redirected in an effort to quell civil unrest.

History will remember him as a president responding in a great time of need; a hero of the people. No one must know of his negligence to protect against the assault on the grid. The smile slid from his face as he was reminded of two men that were armed with this knowledge. Perhaps he would soon know of their demise. The door to the office opened and the Chief of Staff entered.

"Mr. President; the Director of the CIA is here." The president motioned for him to enter.

"Mr. President." The greeting was curt and the Director continued, seeing impatience. "We still have not apprehended Madison and Wallace, but we believe them to be incapable of communicating at this time as we believe they are in a very remote location in Montana."

"You believe," the president said flatly.

"Yes sir, we intercepted a communication we believe came from Wallace to his brother in Boston, telling him to join Wallace in what we believe to be a very remote location."

"You *believe*," the president said slightly more emphatically.

"Yes sir, but we've not seen any activity in terms of preparation to travel from any of the Wallace family and why we believe…" The director was cut off.

"People *believe* in Santa Claus. People *believe* in the tooth fairy, and people *believe* in God! I don't want what you *believe*; I want facts! I want action! I want these two nullified now! The ramifications of them getting public interest is serious, do you understand that?!!"

The Director only nodded. The President turned back toward the window and took another drag on his cigarette. He rarely smoked in the Oval Office, but these trying times—more than usual. His wife would not approve, but she was in a Jordanian sandstorm and wouldn't be back until tomorrow.

"So, what's the plan?" the President asked, a bit more calmly.

"Well, we've moved most of the team from Red Lodge to the area of interest. Based on the mileage from Wallace's Jeep, we've subtracted the known driving distance he made to the dam and that left us with a radius of several hundred square miles of wilderness to search. We're employing drones to accelerate the effort, and we beli…" the Director hesitated, not wanting to use the word. "…Uhh, we have reduced the area of interest significantly." The President did not turn around and the Director took that as he was wanting more information. "Ahh, we left one man back to surveille the library where Wallace sent a message from, in case he returns. We have not located the camper Madison traveled in, but we…we have a reasonable assertion it has either been destroyed or abandoned; this based on constant monitoring of all roadways."

The President turned back to face the Director. The look on his face implied he was still less than impressed with the information. He took a final drag on the cigarette and put it out in the ashtray on his desk.

"I need results. If you can't find them, then make sure you keep their heads down for another week. I don't care how you do it. After that…it won't…" He didn't finish his sentence. "Use any resource to find these two. Contact my Chief of Staff if you need anything." With that he motioned the Director toward the door and turned again to the window. He left without hesitation. Upon seeing him leave, the Chief of Staff entered the office and stood behind the President, waiting for orders.

"Get my wife home." The President said without turning around. "Use military aircraft if you have to, but I want her here before things get bad. A sandstorm shouldn't be able to stop the Air Force." The Chief of Staff promptly turned around to attend to the order and left the office. The President reached into his jacket pocket and retrieved another cigarette from the pack. *This effort has been in the works for over a year now. It was hard to believe these two 'loose cannons' could be in a position to thwart the whole thing. Better start work on a plan of action just in case things go south.*

Major "Skip" Helm trotted across the ramp toward the big gray airplane. Its significant nose radome made it nearly impossible to mistake for a standard C-130. She was one of the last of the Combat Talons still in the inventory. Skip bounded up the crew door and up the stairs to the flight deck.

"Boys, we're being re-tasked," Skip puffed, nearly out of breath. "…going to Jordan."

The flight engineer and the navigator looked at each other for a moment and their nonverbal postures said it all; Skip was pulling another fast one. The pilot was well known across the spec ops community as a prankster.

"Riiiiiight, I got yer Jordan…" laughed the flight engineer, "…right here!"

"Here's the flight plan…" Skip threw it on the Nav table. "The mission is legit…National Command Authority direction." He jumped into the left pilot seat and began to run his preflight checks. The Nav started reading the flight plan and after a few seconds looked up at the engineer and shrugged. Skip looked back and saw they were still unconvinced, so he reached into the flight suit pocket on his right leg and produced a document. He thrust it into the Engineer's hand, who in turn opened it up and after a few seconds, handed it to the Nav.

"Let's turn and burn, boys!" Skip called across the intercom, "We don't want to keep the lady waiting."

The APU fired up and the loadmaster stumbled out the crew door fumbling with his headset. The electronic warfare officer, or EWO, heard the APU and popped up the stairs from the cargo compartment.

"What's the hurry? We don't need to take off for another two hours!" The Nav pushed the two documents in front of the EWO station for him to read and continued to align the internal navigation system. After reading the first few lines, he too scrambled to run his checks and then went to wake up the co-pilot, who was sleeping on a web seat in the back.

The big plane taxied toward the runway and promptly took off. The mission was simple; fly to Amman, Jordan and pick up the First Lady. Then, fly her to Incirlik Air Station, Turkey. From there, she would transfer to State Department aircraft that would again take her to Washington, DC. There was just one issue; a sandstorm had hit Amman and reduced the visibility to "0/0." A designation meaning zero visibility for zero distance. Only one aircraft large enough to carry the First Lady and her entourage was capable of accomplishing that task; the Combat Talon II. This spec ops bird was designed to penetrate virtually any environment, under any conditions. Its terrain following radar and IR sensors allowed it to see safely through weather, darkness of night, or even a sandstorm. The radar would have attenuation issues with the sand, but the navigation system would get them close enough to burn through with the radar and 'paint' the runway when they got there. Though the aircraft was designed to make a 0/0 landing, it was not something practiced or welcomed. It would still be a challenge—but it was capable. Skip had actually only done a real 0/0 once before; in Morocco. The fog was so thick that after they landed, they could not see the ground from the cockpit and had to de-plane the loadmaster to walk in front of the aircraft and direct it using the intercom. The difference was that fog didn't cause issues with the radar. There were other aircraft capable of flying and landing in these conditions, mostly because they were capable of vertical flight—like the CV-22 Osprey—but they couldn't carry 67 people and gear. A Combat Talon could.

"Howdy!" The intercom declared the warning from the Flight Engineer. It wasn't enough of one as the smell had already invaded the nostrils of the crew. The 'howdy rule' was simple; if you pass gas, warn the crew with a brief transmission using the greeting, "howdy." If you didn't and the crew figured out you did it—you had to buy beers for the entire crew upon landing.

"Oh dude! That was a bad one. I'm going on oxygen." The Nav squawked. Skip turned and looked back at the engineer, now proudly grinning at the accomplishment. He shook his head.

"You better get that out of your system before we pick up 'Herself.' That won't be appreciated, I'm sure." Skip said, candidly. "I would appreciate it if you would go to the back next time."

"No way! I don't want him back here!" piped the loadmaster. "Make him hold it in!"

"Actually, that's a good idea. You need to hold it in." Skip said, "That's an order...I mean it." He eyeballed the engineer who was still grinning. "Well, don't you have something to say?" The pilot was expecting a proper 'yes sir' in response, though the two were good friends and anything could be expected. After a moment, the engineer's response came.

"Howdy!"

CHAPTER 13

"All that is required for evil to triumph is for good men to do nothing." – Sir Edmund Burke

Mushreq had good news for the Emir; all but 6 of the 112 jihadi in the second wave had pulled money from their accounts. Now, over one hundred cities in America were being exposed to the deadly virus. It would only be a week until the country went black without power and the spread of the disease would grow exponentially without a reliable way to warn citizens—cell phones and internet were their lives. All contact with the any surviving jihadi would be severed just before they expected to be activated; accounts closed, no way to contact their handlers, and by now they were symptomatic and very contagious.

What Mushreq didn't know, was that two different hospitals had reported potential Ebola cases to the CDC with verifications pending. However, the voluntary hush order leveraged by the White House—observed by a willing press corps—was still in effect. The idea being that panic would only add to the problem—which would also be another nail in Americas coffin. The Emir was aware of the hush order and believed it would work in his favor. He was right.

"Don't answer the door…and be prepared for anything. I'm going to check our 'six.'" Mad Dog referred to the back door and yard area. He slowly approached the back door at an angle; careful not to silhouette himself in the window. The sheer curtains that hung there would be susceptible to any light wind movements and would alert adversaries that the house was occupied. He expected a flash-bang to pop through the window at any moment. Slowly, he peeled the sheer curtain just enough to view the porch and backyard area—nothing. He wondered about David up front.

Suddenly, the front door opened and rather than gun fire, Mad Dog heard laughter. Then, voices. He moved cautiously toward the kitchen threshold and did a quick peek maneuver, then dropped his gun to his side.

"Just when I thought you two couldn't get any dumber…" Mad Dog began, directing his jibe at Nate and Drew. He glanced at David, who was still laughing his head off; clearly amused at something and gave him a somewhat serious, but quizzical look. David sensed the agitation and decided to put the old warrior at ease.

"Look; they come bearing a gift!" David said as he pointed out the window.

"You guys steal a Schwan's truck or something???" Mad Dog said sarcastically.

Drew chuckled and responded, "It's not stealing if somebody gave you the keys."

"Well, who would be dumb enough to give you clowns the keys to anything?" Mad Dog asked as he made his way to the window.

"You did." David responded, and then laughed again.

Mad Dog pulled back the curtains to get a better look and stared at the large vehicle sitting in the driveway. "Holy Mother of God! What did you idiots do to my truck???!!!"

The AATREC had been painted to look just like a Schwan's delivery truck. The windows, too. They also added some kind of sheet metal skirt around the bottom and made flared areas around the rear wheels so it didn't look like a high-clearance 4-wheel-drive vehicle. Mad Dog was dumbstruck.

"Don't worry…it comes off easy…just pop-riveted on. The windows have a plastic film on them that will peel right off too." Drew said, still chuckling. "And, there's two cases of military grade spray paint cans inside…flat green, olive drab, dark tan, and black. You can repaint it later when you get where you're going. Just leave the film on the windows and solar panels until you're done painting…then just peel it

148

off…there's a tub of Bondo and sandpaper too, so you can fill the holes made by the pop-rivets."

Mad Dog just blinked and stared. The laughter trickled down to grins as they waited for him to respond. Mad Dog dropped his chin to his chest and smirked. He looked back up and commented, now starting to chuckle himself. "Well, I gotta say, that's thinking…but what about the thugs? Think it'll fool them? They might have seen you drive up to a supposedly abandoned house."

"They're gone…well, all except the one guy hanging out at the library. He's waiting to see if you come back there." Nate said.

"How do you know he's one of them?" David asked.

"Well, Roxy…the librarian, has been fending off his advances since he showed up. He tries to act like he's from Bozeman, but when he gets to talking faster, his east coast accent slips out. Roxy asked him if he liked the Pickle Barrel sandwich shop and he didn't know anything about it…*EVERYBODY* knows the Pickle Barrel in Bozeman."

Mad Dog shook his head in amazement and smiled. "Well, you two do good work. I guess we need to plan our next move." He gave David the high sign. "Boys, we gotta have a talk. You need to know about some things that are about to happen. Life is going to be a little different soon…for everybody."

Mad Dog took them through the entire story, to include David's father and his involvement. Several times, the men glanced at David and nodded; acknowledging approval. The only part left out was the existence of the redoubt. David thought about what would become of Nate and Drew. They might be alright and seemed capable, but a Montana winter was coming. There would be no power, no natural gas—eventually, since the pumps required power as well—and no food, medicine, etcetera. Hunting would help and they were clearly capable, but David knew that wasn't enough. The hoards would migrate from Billings and follow the interstate in search of safety and food, eventually finding Red Lodge and of course Nate and Drew.

When Mad Dog finished, the two just sat there. A long silence ensued before Drew spoke up. "So, there's no way to stop it? We couldn't just go to one of the sub-stations and take out the hajis?"

"It wouldn't help. We know of some of the prime targets, but they will likely hit those and more. Stopping one or even two would have little effect." Mad Dog responded gravely. "Millions would still die and the grid would be down for months…maybe years."

Drew stood, clearly in deep thought. He spied the half empty bottle of Dickel on the counter and got two more glasses out of the cupboard, placed them on the table and poured. They kicked around a few ideas and drank. David sided with Drew; he thought doing something was better than doing nothing. Mad Dog thought their time would be better spent preparing for the event and its aftermath, as little time was left. There would be runs on the stores almost immediately and he felt they should stock up. Nate didn't say much and just listened. After a while, he noticed the television was in the storage room and all manner of aluminum foil was hanging off the 'rabbit ears.' He chuckled and pointed to the contraption.

"What's that old TV doing in the storage room?"

Mad Dog looked back over his shoulder at the TV and responded. "We didn't want light to leak out into the house, as it was our only link to the outside world."

"Yeah, but it's black and white, right?" Nate responded, looking now at Drew.

"Yeah, mom didn't see so good, she just liked listening to it as she tootled around the house. I got her a digital conversion box so it would work. She really didn't need anything other than black and white."

David thought of his previous joke about the irony of the station being phonetically pronounced "color" and the fact that nothing but black and white was on the screen. Suddenly, he stood up.

"Color!" David said enthusiastically.

"Naw, it's black and white…trust me." Drew countered.

"No, KULR…K-U-L-R." David exclaimed.

"Channel 8?" Nate said, now confused.

"Yeah…" David said, sitting back down and looking at Mad Dog, "Channel 8."

Mad Dog looked back at David. The kid's gears were still turning in his head. He knew what David was thinking, and while it had merit, it was risky. Mad Dog shook his head.

"Risky…not sure of an upside…at least not one that warrants throwing away your father's plans for you and your siblings." Mad Dog seemed as serious as David had ever seen him. Nate and Drew sat back and looked at each other; no idea what was being communicated.

"How so?" David didn't quite get it.

"Kid, in a few days the world is gonna change drastically. The thugs left town and are off our trail. Once the 'event' happens, they have no reason to continue their search for us." He paused, "We do this…and it's not likely you will ever make it to the redoubt. Your siblings may not survive either."

That made David angry, but he contained the emotion. He was very disappointed in Mad Dog; this wasn't about saving a handful of people so they could live out their lives in a redoubt. This was about saving the country from a greedy tyrant. That would take patriots; lots of patriots. He considered Mad Dog in that category without reservation—until just now. David stood up and spoke with conviction, "If we could get the word out that the President was sitting on an attack so that he could throw the country into martial law and dissolve the existing government to make himself king—it would change everything. No longer would he be viewed as a savior that reluctantly had to institute these measures—he would be viewed as an instigator for a coup. A revolution would certainly ensue and POTUS would be stopped before he could start. The only option for POTUS would be to deny the coup and stop the attack. He could then claim he was in control the whole time and that the coup rhetoric was just rightwing spin. Regrettably, he would look like a hero for stopping the attack, but in a year and a half his term would be over and he would be out!"

David didn't want to look at Mad Dog, he was too upset. He could feel his face flush and knew it must be apparent to the others. He was formulating a barbed response for Mad Dog, but couldn't help glancing at the man. When he did, he was greeted with a big toothy smile. Then it hit him.

"You…you said 'we.'" David exclaimed, as he felt the anger leave him and drain into the floor. "You said, if *WE* do this."

"Yeah…when do *WE* want to leave?" Mad Dog started laughing.

"Wait, what?" Nate said quizzically. "Where are we going?" David started laughing too.

Drew had picked up on it by now. He looked at Nate, who was the only one not laughing and patted him on the shoulder.

"Nate Dog, my friend…we're gonna be TV stars!"

Johnny "Mohammad" Jones was as sick as he'd ever been. He could hardly get out of bed to go to the hospital without the help of his roommate. As they walked to the bus stop, they passed Wally's—the venue he was to scope out tonight. He would have liked to have gone, as the DURP Band was playing again. Also, it was less than a week until 9/11 and he had decided Wally's was probably the target he would hit, but without his counterpart available yet, he didn't know how he would get the explosives. For now, he was too sick to do anything except swing by the ATM on their way to the hospital. He was thankful for Remy, his roommate, who was starting to feel bad too. Mohammad hated that he passed on the flu to him.

They rounded the corner and entered the convenience store where the ATM was in the back corner. Remy had to help Mohammad put the card in the slot and it took a few moments for him to enter the pin code. The screen popped up and Mohammad shook his head and cancelled the transaction. Then, he tried the card again and re-entered the pin. The same screen popped up.

"Something wrong?" Remy asked.

"It says 'Account Closed' and that can't be right. I still have over a thousand dollars in there!" Mohammad was distraught. What was happening? Did the operation get compromised or something? Did they think he was a traitor and maybe cut him off? He thought about who he could contact—there was nobody; not a single person aside from the phone number they gave him, but that was not to be used for a few days. The excitement used up what little strength he had and he dropped to his knees. Remy tried to catch him but was unable and Mohammad rolled onto his back into a state of semi-consciousness. There were people all around who took notice, but only the shop owner responded, "I'm calling 911."

Landon had about half an hour before his next student so he decided to wander into the hangar and check on the aircraft he scheduled for his escape. One of the A&P mechanics was working on the bird and had the left engine cowl open. Landon's heart sank.

"Hey…it's Dave, right?" He remembered the mechanic from an incident that involved a bent prop during a hard student landing.

"Yeah." Dave turned around to see Landon walking up.

"Problem?" Landon pointed at the engine.

"No…no, I was just getting her ready."

"Oh, I wondered because I'm on the schedule for it." Landon was relieved.

"She'll be ready for ya. I know it isn't for a few days yet, but I had some time and thought I'd get a little ahead on this one. I'm going to tow her out in a few minutes and fuel her up…hey, just to confirm; you wanted a max fuel load, right?"

"Yeah, yeah…I'm going on a long cross country profile."

"Oh ok, no problem. Normally, we don't pump 'em up that far for you guys. I'll make sure she's topped off."

"Cool, thanks man." Landon smiled and started back toward the office. He was really hoping Wallace was wrong. He'd catch some flak for cancelling the flight if nothing happened, but it was better than shelling out all the money for the use of the aircraft and fuel. Every day they got closer to 'doomsday' the anxiety level increased. He just wanted to ignore the whole thing—stick his head in the sand, but he knew in his heart that he couldn't do that. Landon was 80% sure it would happen. He just wished for a little more confirmation—it would come, but not how he expected.

"That's it, babe…we're loaded for bear and ready to leave for the great redoubt!" Mason exclaimed, as he walked into the house.

"Good. I'm ready for a vacation." Leigh whispered back. "Hey, be quiet. Tanner's taking a nap."

"Sorry," he whispered back, "I didn't know…hey, you need to go look at the truck—looks like the Clampetts' are headed to Beverly Hills."

"Well, I know it's a lot, but we're not coming back, so I wanted to save a few precious things."

A few precious things, Mason thought. *More like everything!* He didn't argue the point. Everything was already loaded anyway—including his 'stash.' That made him smile.

The drive to Billings was not long. They would be there soon. Mad Dog and David were up front in the AATREC while Nate and Drew rode in the back. David was thinking about the conversation in the kitchen and about second guessing Mad Dog's loyalty.

"You know, you had me thinking you weren't on board back there…not a patriot. I feel bad for doubting you. Even if it was just for a few seconds." David chuckled to soften the comment.

Mad Dog didn't say anything at first, as if he were contemplating something. It was a little uncomfortable. Mad Dog turned to look back at the two ranger boys in the back, now in a conversation about what they were going to do after the event. He turned back to look down the road.

"David, I'm going to assume you share your father's faith in God here." He looked at David sternly. David nodded and gave a thumbs up. "Because, your dad and I share that faith…and I don't know if he ever had this talk with you or not…but in his absence…" He paused to check the auxiliary fuel tank indicator. David knew something was coming and hoped it wasn't about his father being less than a patriot.

"I love this country; so did your dad. We both fought for it…to preserve it…for what it stood for…but, at some point you need to recognize that your ultimate allegiance is to God, and in the event you had to choose sides between your country and your God; you better choose God."

David contemplated what the old warrior said and while he wasn't necessarily confused by the statement, he didn't want to be misunderstood in his own position on the matter. He wanted clarification, but rather than ask questions, he decided to make a statement of his own.

"This is the way I see it," David started, "I align myself with those that started this country, fought for this country, and support the Constitution as it was intended by the founding fathers. I believe they were inspired by God and that God blessed this country. I believe our flag represents all those things. But, I do recognize there has been a significant erosion; a concerted effort to bring this country down and away from what God blessed. I gave an oath to support and defend the Constitution of the United States, such as it was, not necessarily what it might become by the perversions of a tyrant and his minions. I recognize there are those that would disagree and may even consider my statement as treasonous. I understand the President is the Commander in Chief and that implies that I follow his orders. However, as I said before my oath is to the Constitution; not POTUS. So, if he stands against the Constitution, then I am at war with him."

"He already has." Mad Dog said simply. "It's been a slow methodical process, but that's what he and others have done and continue to do—to use your words—'significant erosion.' When is it you'll decide not to follow him to defend the Constitution?"

"I already have…I'm standing with you, aren't I?" David responded. "We're risking our lives at this very moment to thwart POTUSs' plans. He also gave an oath to support and defend the Constitution. He's the traitor—not us."

"Touché, kid." Mad Dog smiled. "I agree with everything you just said, but you didn't really respond to my original statement, and so I'll ask it in a question; if it came down to God or country, how would you choose?"

"My country—the one I'm fighting for—would always choose God, so there is no choice to make." David asserted.

Mad Dog broke into laughter. He wasn't going to pin the kid down so easily and was amused at his tenacity to avoid being put in a box. But, there was a critical point he wanted to make with David because he believed the kid would be faced with this decision at some point in his lifetime—and likely soon.

"You're implying that '*your country*' is made up of those in the United States that think and believe as you do…it's those you fight for and defend. I get that; I have felt the same way. If I were the last true patriot on the continent, I would display our flag and die for what it meant and stood for. But again, that's not what I asked you, and so I'll present you with a scenario—a very real one that I believe will happen in the near future. If you as a military member were ordered to apprehend or kill Christians as a result of 'political correctness' and the laws supporting it; would you?" Mad Dog's aim was now very direct. There was no room to wiggle free.

"No, because again; my country is made up of those very Christians and those that believe they have a right to exercise their faith freely. They are not a house divided, therefore, there is no decision to make." David still avoided answering, but it opened another window that Mad Dog wanted to address.

"Ah, so you fight for and represent only those who think like you do—not the whole country. The rest of the country should not have the right to think freely. We should force people to be Christians…to go to church. Is that what you're thinking? Because, that's what you're saying. Our forefathers' lived under that kind of oppression, David. King George demanded that there was no religion but his—that was Christianity to him—and you know how that went over."

David was silent and thinking about what Mad Dog had just said. It seemed right, but it didn't quite sit well with David. He should have the freedom to fight for who he wants to fight for—not the socialist thugs trying to rip down the country for their own personal gain. Mad Dog could see he had given the kid something to think about. He smiled to himself, because at some place in his life he had struggled with the same issues. He decided to splash just a little more fuel on the fire.

"At some point with that line of thinking, you will find yourself against God." Mad Dog turned his head to look out the window so David wouldn't see him smile. The statement had the desired effect.

"Now, you're starting to piss me off!" David began, "You know that God said, 'He would that no man should perish.'"

"Yup, you're right." Mad Dog fired back. "So, if that's true, and He's God and can do anything, why are men going to perish if God doesn't want them to?"

"That's circular logic." David shot back.

"Is it?" Mad Dog said with skepticism. "There's an old story theme we see in books and movies. It has become a cliché these days and it's about a king who can't find genuine love because he's a millionaire and everybody knows him. He can't trust if they really love him—or his money. So, he disguises himself as a poor average schmuck and he meets several people, most of which treat him like dirt. But, there's a kind soul that feels sorry for him and she treats him right—and she's probably a babe too, right?!" Mad Dog chuckled. "Anyway, they fall in love and he knows it's not for his fortune and fame. He puts on a glass slipper or kisses a poison road-apple or whatever…you get the drift—they live in a castle happily ever after. The moral of the story, my young warrior, is that the woman was given a choice without undue circumstance or influence and she made the choice to love the frog before he was a prince. And, that equates to real love. Get it?"

David busted out in laughter. "You really should have read more children's stories when you were a kid, cuz you really jacked that one up!" They both had a good laugh and after it faded, Mad Dog continued.

"You're right kid, God doesn't want anyone to perish, but the one thing He won't do is override your freedom of choice; to choose Him or reject Him. The founding fathers'—most of which were devout Christians—understood that all too well. And, for that reason, they wanted to ensure that no one would infringe on that right, and so the First Amendment was born. The problem is the socialists believe that religion needs to be eradicated for true socialism to exist, so they twist and erode the verbiage and meaning of the amendment. It says, *'Congress shall make no law respecting an establishment of religion, or prohibiting the free exercise thereof'* and goes into freedom of speech and the press, etcetera. But, our liberal friends have got the country believing it says simply, *'separation of church and state.'* The meanings are quite different. The founding fathers' didn't want the state to establish or respect one religion over another, though it's fairly obvious from their personal memoires they expected that would be in the scope of Christian denominations. Still, the most important part of the amendment was *'…or prohibiting the free exercise thereof.'* Meaning, if a coach wants to assemble with willing Christian athletes and pray at the end of a game or a little girl wants to pray silently in class before a big test; they should be able to do that. But the phase *'separation of church and state'* has a different connotation and lends to the argument that allowing a little girl to pray in school is 'respecting establishment of religion.' Which, it does not, but we've allowed them to get away with it."

"That makes me really mad." David said emphatically.

"Me too, kid…me too." Mad Dog said as he patted David on the shoulder. "I didn't mean to get preachy on you, but I wanted you to understand where I'm coming from and that your ultimate allegiance is to God; if the choice ever came to that." Mad Dog's smile slipped from his face and he got quiet for several minutes. David could see the change in the old warrior's demeanor before he spoke.

"If POTUS and ISIS are even partially successful with their plans, this nation is probably done for, as we know it." Mad Dog said with dark despondency. "Many believe the United States is not mentioned in the Bible because it will not be a factor in the end of days…and I think they're right…I believe they're right that America will not be a factor"

"Not a factor? It's the most powerful nation in the world, even with POTUS efforts." David replied.

"I believe the Bible's lack of a direct reference to America was intentional. She will be ineffective and without influence…maybe even destroyed. I don't want to preach anymore…look it up for yourself…but the event we're trying to prevent—in conjunction with whatever Scimitar is—is exactly the kind of event that could be responsible."

Ross meandered around the REI store with a checklist of items in his hand. Hallie and Kate followed close behind. The list Ross carried was identical to the items sent by his father for him and Hallie. When he couldn't get the exact item, he substituted with what seemed right. Kate had done some backpacking and pointed out a few issues.

"Uh, you know you need a fuel canister for that stove," Kate tried to sound humble and not confrontational.

Ross picked up the MSR butane stove and turned it upside down to view the port on the bottom. He was not an expert on this stuff. All he knew is that there were no fuel canisters in the kit his dad had sent.

"Ok, well, then we need to get some of those for my stove too." He responded. "Which ones fit the Solo Stove?"

"The Solo Stove is a bio-stove; it burns wood, twigs, pinecones and stuff like that. You're dad probably understood that fuel would eventually be unavailable for conventional backpacking stoves, so he included something you could use indefinitely." Kate responded.

Ross looked at her and smiled. "Cool."

They continued around for better part of an hour until they had most of what they needed. Ross thought it was kind of fun, but Hallie thought it was exhausting. Kate was just plain thankful as Ross was paying for all of it. They still needed to fit Kate with hiking boots and cold weather gear, but time was getting short for Hallie as she was due at work in a half an hour, so she hugged them both and left. Ross thought it funny she felt the obligation to go as they were leaving in a few days—forever. But, Hallie didn't want to 'leave anyone hanging.'

After Hallie left, Kate was acting strangely. Ross picked up on it, though he wasn't sure what the deal was, so he decided to ask.

"You okay Kate? If you're tired we can do this tomorrow…we have time." Ross said, trying to be sensitive. That was hard for him as their relationship in the past was edgy, but now it seemed Kate had wanted him around her best friend, rather than compete with Ross for her.

"No, sorry…it's okay. I'm just…" She turned her head away so he couldn't see her face.

Women! What the heck??? He thought, suppressing his urge to challenge what he perceived as drama. *It must be that time of the month!* He took a slow breath and used his Wagamama restaurant persona—the one he used on difficult customers.

"Can I help you with anything?" He managed to squeeze out without sarcasm. She turned to face him and he could see tears had welled up in her eyes.

"I'm sorry, I guess after watching your dad's video...it's all just...crazy. We've really come to this? This is it?"

Ross sat down next to her and began loosening the laces on a boot she was about to try on. "I know it's a lot...Hallie and I have had time to digest it. This just kind of hit you between the eyes, so I can understand why you're emotional about it."

She wiped her tears on the sleeve of her jacket. "No...that's not all of it...I just..."

"Then what?" he asked.

"Why?" she queried. Her eyes darted across his face as if she were looking for her answer there.

"Why, what?" he asked back.

"Why are you taking me with you?" She continued to scan his face for an answer.

"It's not as noble as you might think, Kate. Hallie insisted you go with us."

"She said you thought it was a good idea and agreed willingly...so, why?"

"Oh I don't know, I guess because you're family...here, anyway. All we have is each other and when considering what's about to happen...well, how could we leave you behind? Let's not make this weird, okay? I just want to get this stuff and..."

She threw her arms around him and hugged firmly. He couldn't hug her back because in her haste she had pinned his arms to his sides. He looked around and some people were noticing the 'moment.' He felt foolish and probably looked like he'd just been tackled by a linebacker. The only hand he had free was the one on her hip, so he just kind of patted her with it in response. It was awkward. She sensed that he was uncomfortable, smiled to herself and pushed back; stripping his hand off her hip.

"Yeah, well don't get any ideas, Slick…and keep your hands to yourself," she said as she plopped herself down to put the boot on.

Mad Dog parked the AATREC two blocks from the television station and they walked around the area to check things out. David reached in his day pack and pulled out a foil pouch. Mad Dog watched intently as David opened the pouch and pulled out his cell phone. He inserted the battery and turned it on. After it booted up, he typed out a quick message and sent it. Once he was sure it had been sent, he removed the battery and placed the phone back in the pouch. Mad Dog gave David a disapproving look followed by a skeptical smile.

"I should take that away from you and ground you for a month," Mad Dog cracked, "but, I understand. It won't matter now anyway, the gig is up."

Their plan was simple—just walk right in and ask to talk to the manager. They would explain who they were, what they wanted to broadcast and why. Then, just leave. It almost went like that…

…almost.

CHAPTER 14

"Make the lie big, make it simple, keep saying it, and eventually they will believe it." –Adolf Hitler

Achmed watched the television with intense focus. Fox News was repeating a story out of Billings, Montana. A man claiming to be an intelligence expert working in Washington had critical information about an imminent attack by ISIS. He claimed the President had been made aware of a terrorist plot to bring down the power grid on 9/11, but was choosing to ignore it. The man claimed the president was allowing the attack in order to establish martial law. Ari walked into the room.

"Ari, what do you think of this?" Achmed said curiously. "This man claims the power grid will be attacked soon, by ISIS…on 9/11." Ari froze. He had overheard a conversation in Syria between Mushreq and another man concerning the taking of electricity from the infidels. Could that be it? Ari turned his attention toward the television.

The police cars streaked past the four as they pretended to walk into Outback Steak House on the corner of Overland and King Avenue. They were literally 200 yards from the AATREC, parked at Perkins Restaurant just across street. Mad Dog used the window as a mirror to see if the cops had taken notice of them. They didn't seem to and continued racing toward the television station. After the police were out of sight, they continued on to cross King. Mad Dog wanted to run, but that would draw attention; as would the four of them together. He told Drew and Nate to walk over to the bridal shop and he would pick them up. They looked puzzled, but complied. More sirens were coming, they may not be so lucky this time. David looked down at the corner and saw a piece of cardboard that had "Homeless – God Bless" written on it. He picked it up and faced the street.

"Go," David told Mad Dog, "Pick me up here…get the truck."

Mad Dog kept walking and seconds later, another squad car raced by; this time the cop looked directly at him. Had the cop actually seen the broadcast, the gig would have been up, but he had not and continued to the television station. They were looking for four men, not one old man walking down the street. He didn't even glance at David. Drew and Nate were standing in front of the bridal shop on the other side of 20th Street and watched the whole thing pass in front of them.

"You gotta admit; those guys are pretty smart." Drew said, clearly relieved. They stared at David, still standing on the corner holding the sign.

"Yeah, I wonder if anybody will give him money." Nate joked. They both laughed nervously.

"We have approximately 85 confirmed cases in 16 cities, Mr. President," said the Secretary of the Department of Health and Human Services, "…as reported by the CDC. This is worse than an epidemic, sir…it's deliberate."

"How do you know that?" the President asked.

"Statistically, it is impossible for these cases to emerge simultaneously in that many cities across the United States. In fact, anything above 10 cases in two cities is at the threshold of credibility. But 16 cities…"

"An attack. then. You're saying it's an attack." He pushed.

"I see no other explanation, but of course I can't say how it was accomplished. There would have to have been some willingness to participate by a lot of people…I see no other way possible." She answered.

Mad Dog picked up Drew and Nate first. Then, pulled into the gas station on the corner where David was still standing and began to fill up the tank. David eyed the faux Schwan's AATREC and wanted desperately to drop the sign and bolt for the camper, but the cops were everywhere. One even stopped to ask David if he had seen anything. They needed to get clear of here as it was only a matter of time before surveillance cameras from various businesses would be analyzed and every Schwan's truck would be a target. David waited until the AATREC was full and Nate pulled the hose; he turned and walked slowly toward the gas station. It was the longest walk of his life.

"Mr. President." The Chief of Staff said hurriedly as he rushed into the Oval Office. "We have a problem!"

The President looked up from his desk—he was annoyed. The Secretary of the Department of Health and Human Services and her staff were still outlining a plan to contain the outbreaks. He told her to take a break. She stood and looked at him in disbelief. *What could be more important than this?* She thought. After she left, the President leaned into the desk and waited for the next bit of 'good news.'

"Mr. President; Madison forced his way into a television station in Billings, Montana. The broadcast has been re-played by FOX and CNN. For now, they're taking the position that he was a quack, but in a few days they will know better."

"Dammit!" the President pounded his desk and stood up. He stared down the Chief. How did this happen??? I told the Director..." he stopped and went into deep thought, "What did Madison say?"

"Essentially, everything; date, event, who, etcetera....and he claimed you were aware and allowing it to happen!" The Chief braced for impact, but it didn't come. There was a long pause before the POTUS spoke.

"Thoughts?" the President queried.

165

"Go public. Stop the attacks to the grid—make Madison a liar. You say we were always planning to stop the attack, but now Madison compromised the operation and national security—make him the bad guy. We have no choice."

The President mulled it over for a few minutes, pulling out a cigarette and lighting it. As he exhaled a cloud of smoke, he spoke very deliberately. "Call the staff in ASAP and set up a press conference for 7pm tonight. Get the Pentagon on the phone, tell them I want the Joint Chiefs in my office in an hour." He paused to think. "We can still pull this off, but we'll just use a different reason." The Chief looked at him curiously. "Ebola…that's our play now…our reason for locking the country down…get the Secretary back in here."

Mushreq moved quickly down the hallway and toward the Emir's quarters. The news he carried was not good. The Emir would not be pleased. As Mushreq entered he could hear sounds that indicated the Emir was not alone.

"Emir; I have urgent news," Mushreq said assertively, "It demands your immediate attention."

"What is it???" the Emir boomed from the darkness.

"It is sensitive…for you only." Mushreq responded.

"Go to the meeting room…I'll be there in one minute."

Mushreq walked down the hall and waited in the meeting room. He thought about what should be done with the new information. What could be done? He wasn't sure at this point. The Emir would not be pleased. He heard a scream from the hallway, but knew better than to respond—it was a woman. Shortly thereafter, the Emir entered the room.

"Our sources in America are reporting that our effort is compromised concerning the power grid. National news media is reporting an accurate date of 9/11 as well." Mushreq paused. The Emir would ask questions now and didn't like to be told mass quantities of information.

166

"Mohammad…that son of a whore! His big mouth has caused this." Emir said emphatically.

There was silence for several minutes. The Emir paced the room contemplating the news. Mushreq was surprised that he didn't ask questions. Finally, the Emir spoke, "Activate the teams—they will go in now; three days early…you say the date was communicated?"

"Yes, Emir…9/11…they also claimed the President has known of it for some time but has chosen to allow it to occur." Mushreq was offering additional information as he didn't want the Emir to make a rash decision without knowing all the facts. The Emir looked up at him with a puzzled look.

"I must see this myself…and get an interpreter. We must move quickly."

David walked past the AATREC and into the convenience store associated with the gas station. He picked up a bag of pistachios and turned to look out the window. Drew was sitting in the driver's seat staring at him. Mad Dog and Nate must have been in the back. That was good. Mad Dog's face would be all over the news now. David went to the counter to pay for the nuts. The clerk was looking at the piece of cardboard tucked under David's arm. "You could have gotten a hamburger for what you pay for those pistachios, ya know?" David restrained himself from speaking. He didn't want the clerk to remember anything about him in the event he was interviewed. After he bought the nuts, he turned to see the AATREC slowly moving out of the parking lot toward the north end of the building. David went out the door and clear of the cameras in the store. He looked back toward the television station and then caught up to the AATREC and got in. They drove off down King Avenue to get on I-90. As they approached the on-ramp, a police check point was set up. Several cars were in front of them as they crept toward it. Mad Dog spoke from the back.

"This might be it, boys. I don't want to fight it out and hurt innocent policemen. We surrender if it comes to that."

No one said anything. David thought about the nine-mil tucked in his pants. He wished the road block was manned by the men in the Suburbans; that would have made things different. Only one car was between them and the road block now, David's heart was pounding in his chest. Drew rolled down the window as they moved forward. The cop motioned them up. He looked intently at Drew and then David.

"What's the big ruckus?" Drew started first. "I got stuff thawing out back here."

"Aww, somebody tried to take over the TV station…you got anything besides food back there?" the cop asked.

"Nope…and I'm guessing I shouldn't pick up any hitch hikers today, huh?" Drew said rhetorically.

"That would be a good guess." The cop said, now looking critically at the AATREC. "This a four-wheel drive?"

"Yeah," Drew replied. "We service the East Rosebud area and the snow makes it pretty dicey up there."

"Yeah, I'll bet." The cop said as he motioned them through.

They all breathed a sigh of relief. After they got on the interstate, Drew looked at David and cracked a smile. "We gotta get to Red Lodge and paint this truck, ASAP!"

The Emir watched the broadcast twice before commenting. It was already on YouTube. Mushreq said nothing. "Whether the President was going to let it happen or not is of no consequence at this point; he has no choice except to prevent the event. I'm sure even now that he moves his military to stop us…" the Emir paused, his fingers tapping the table while he mulled over what he'd just seen. "There are tens of thousands of sub-stations in America. Protecting them all would be

168

impossible, yet they know which are most critical and would surely move to protect those first. When did this broadcast first air?"

"About two hours ago, Emir." Mushreq said.

The Emir nodded, "The logistics for them would be a nightmare; even for America. There are any number of combinations they are considering and they expect a 9/11 date…but of course, they know we would not be foolish enough to strike then." He looked at one of his advisors. "Has the President addressed this yet?"

"No, Emir. We are being told through Al-Jazeera sources that his press secretary plans for a 7pm address to the nation…7pm Washington time."

"Then, we must move fast. Tell the teams to strike at that time; 7pm. If we wait, every gun-toting American will flock to protect a sub-station near where they live. Tell the jihadi not to worry about taking out the communications networks as planned—it would only highlight the intended targets sooner." The Emir stood and stared down at the map in front of him. "Yes, tell them now. They will only have a few hours to mobilize."

"Emir," Mushreq cautioned, "You know that means the west coast states would still be in daylight operation. Those sub-stations might even have workers in them."

"Yes, it is unfortunate," Emir began, "their escape is jeopardized; I know this. But, they are jihadi solders of Allah…and their fate is with him."

"Every one of them???" the President said incredulously.

"Yes sir. We've traced most of the Ebola victims as recent travelers to Syrian or near-Syrian locations; several were already on watch lists," The Director stated. "It is likely they were unwitting pawns, though they appeared to be radicalized as they willingly made the trips."

"How many of these 'pawns' are there?" The Chief of Staff asked.

"There's no way of knowing for sure, but based on the timeline and comparing traveling profiles; over 300 at this point. If we consider a wider, more recent profile; then considerably more. We're tracking them down now." The Director pulled a document from his briefcase in anticipation of the next question. He anticipated correctly.

"How many cities are we talking about here?" the President said, holding his head in his hands.

"Uh, well, they seemed to disperse to anything with a population at or above 100K…about 240 cities coast to coast…give or take…only Alaska and Hawaii seem to be spared. We just don't know exactly which ones they picked or how many were in each city." The President didn't move or look up, so the Director kept going. "Also, second and third generation infected are difficult to predict and track. They too, travel."

"Have FEMA and Homeland Security been staged as I asked?" The President still didn't look up.

"Yes, sir. Upper management levels have been briefed and lower levels believe they are preparing for an exercise. They know not to initiate for real-world actions until just prior to 7pm. The National Guard has been recalled and similarly postured. Police and emergency services personnel will be alerted—without specific details—about 30 minutes before your national address. The Joint Chiefs…well, you know about them." POTUS looked at the men in the room; their uniforms adorned with all manner of ribbons and badges. The President addressed the Chairman of the Joint Chiefs.

"Recommendations?"

"Mr. President, I recommend we move the fleets out of Pearl and other harbors to disperse our assets. In addition, I recommend we bump up to DEFCON 2. Our enemies need to be sent a strong message that we are not weak or vulnerable. We would be viewed then as a coiled snake, rather than one caught out sunning on a rock waiting for the proverbial boot to the head. Also, we need to recall all military leaves and seal all bases and posts against potential infection. You, your family, and critical cabinet staff should leave immediately for Camp David after the national address. Depending on the public response as well as foreign adversarial posturing, I would then recommend you and your staff transfer to multiple E-4B "Nightwatch" aircraft indefinitely, or until such time as stability is established. There are two on alert at Andrews AFB as we speak."

"Let's go with that, all except DEFCON 2; I think mobilizing our entire fleet sends a loud enough message. We'll bump up to DEFCON 3 for now. I'll make the appropriate calls to the Russians and the Chinese just prior to the address. General; make similar arrangements to apprise NATO."

The President looked around the conference table. This was not how he envisioned things just a few hours ago. The CDC had painted a very dismal picture of life in the United States with an Ebola epidemic of the magnitude they were facing. To lose the power grid at the same time was to lose the nation. That just could not happen.

"General, what's the status on protection of the power grid?" The President said, trying to hide his insecurity.

"Sir, we are mobilizing now and will be covering most if not all of the critically identified targets before noon tomorrow—certainly well before the 9/11 deadline. There are over 55,000 substations in the United States, and so many of the smaller remote stations will be vulnerable. However, their potential impact is small and relegated to smaller areas as well. It might not be a bad idea to ask the public to aid us in this endeavor."

"Absolutely not!" The President barked. I won't have them or the NRA taking the opportunity to trump up the gun rights issues. I won't hear of anymore suggestions about this—are we clear?" He scanned the room; no one indicated otherwise. "Fine. Now, what about the establishment of martial law?"

"Mr. President," Chief of Staff began, "After consulting with the legal team, we feel it's better to include a curfew in your speech tonight, rather than officially declare martial law. In a sense, they are enforced the same way, but the term is not used or implied. It can be elevated quietly at some point and have less political impact. We just go with 'curfew for public safety' and declare a 'national emergency.' Those are the terms I would repeat frequently tonight."

"Anything else for now? I've got a speech to practice for…oh, and I do want the teleprompter for tonight. I want to look directly into the camera as much as possible." No one spoke. "Okay then, how much time do we have?" It was rhetorical as he glanced at his watch while saying it. "An hour and a half. Let's get this done, people."

Leigh's phone buzzed in her purse. After a few minutes, she finished with the last patient and checked the phone. The message took only a second to read. David had sent the 'get out of dodge' announcement. "Okay, little brother…I hope you're right." She said to herself as she forwarded the text to Mason.

Ross glanced at his phone for a third time, but he still didn't move. Hallie saw him do it and said nothing. They were watching a movie and she didn't want to start a conversation that would require yet another pause; it was just getting good. It was a horror flick and kind of stupid, but the characters were entertaining—the zombies could have looked more realistic, though. The part that made her swallow hard was when the hero and his group ran into another group of survivors that were even scarier than the zombies. They weren't slow like the zombies and they had the same diet—live people! Cannibals; it made her shudder. She paused the movie.

"So, you gonna watch the movie, or your phone?" She said sarcastically. Normally, he would have fired back with something equally snide, but he didn't. He just sat there with a serious look on his face. She turned and sat up facing him. "Something wrong?"

"David just sent the 'get-out-of-dodge' message." He said, still not moving.

172

"Wait…what? Let me see." She reached for the phone. He handed it to her and she gazed at the glowing screen. 'Miss you guys.'

Ross got up and retrieved the COMSEC sheet from the Bug-out-Bag and sat next to her. He pointed to the phrase 'Miss you guys' and slid his finger across the page to the correlated message. 'Critical -- Leave immediately for redoubt.'

"What are we supposed to do now?" she said.

"I think I'm supposed to authenticate with this." He said sliding his finger further to the right on the line. It said, 'Pansy.' The response was different for each of the siblings. 'Wuss' was David's, 'me too' was Carrie's, and 'I know' was Leigh's. "Turn on the news…where's my laptop?" Ross said, jumping up again and went to find it. Hallie switched to CNN and it was talking about financial stuff, MSNBC had something about an abortion clinic being shot up, and FOX had five people sitting around a table talking about the upcoming elections. Ross plopped down on the couch next to Hallie and started poking around recent news. On the Drudge Report he found a headline, 'Terrorist Expert Says Attack Imminent.' Ross clicked on it and there was a video link. He didn't recognize the man speaking initially, but then he noticed the name at the bottom of the screen; Dirk Madison. Ross heard his father mention the man many times. They listened intently to what Mad Dog told the reporter and sat stunned. As the camera swung up and to the right at the end of the video, Ross noticed something. He dragged the video back and stopped it just before the end and paused it. They both stared in disbelief; it was David standing just off stage with a pistol in his hand.

"Oh my God!" she cried, "That's your brother…isn't it???" Ross just nodded his head; still in shock at what he was seeing. It was surreal and he was trying to reconcile everything in his head. "Well, what do we do?" Ross looked out the window at the retreating sun, now casting silhouettes from the buildings. He grabbed his phone and tried to call David, but the phone immediately went to voice mail. Standing up, he glanced at the Bug-out-Bags in the corner of the apartment; then at the clock on the wall.

"We get the hell out of this city! Get Kate, now!" He ordered. "Tell her to grab her pack."

Hallie started crying as she started for the door. Ross grabbed the water bladders and started filling them from the sink. He watched as Hallie stood idle, holding on to the door knob, but not turning it. She was sobbing.

"I'm sorry babe." He said apologetically, "I know this is crazy, right? But, I know we gotta get out of here…it's not safe." He hugged her close for several moments before she turned the knob on the door.

"I'm okay. I'm okay." She said, quietly, "I'll get Kate." Ross released her and watched as she slipped out the door. He wanted to stop and think this through, but the reality was that there wasn't anything to think about and time was critical. Returning to the sink, he continued to fill the bladders and load them into his pack, which was now quite heavy. The door opened and the girls stepped in. Kate had her pack on.

"Take your pack off; we have to fill your bladders." Ross directed.

"No need. I filled those hours ago." Kate answered back. "That guy on the news that everybody said was crazy; didn't seem so crazy to me…so, I filled them up. Especially, after seeing your dad's video."

"Landon, do you think we should we load the SUV now?" Carrie asked, "Just in case?"

He looked at her. She was visibly shaking. "We can if you want to, but I want to see what the President has to say; he comes on at four o'clock Arizona time."

"The terrorist expert guy said 9/11 was the day…he was my dad's friend. What more confirmation do you need?" she pleaded. "What if the power goes out and we can't get gas?"

"We got all the gas we can take; tanks are full." He responded flatly.

"No we don't…I just drove the 4-Runner and it only has a third of a tank." She argued.

"We're not taking the 4-Runner any farther than my work; ten minutes away. We have time to see what the President says. Plus, we have a few days until 9/11. Let's just calm down and see how things go."

"What? We're flying?" She yelled. "When were you gonna tell me about it???"

"Hey, it was your dad's idea, remember? You saw the video." Landon said defensively. "Besides, it was my back-up plan, really. Not the primary method of escape." He lied. "But, I've been thinking lately that if something does happen, we can fly almost all the way and it will be a lot safer than traveling through all those cities in the dark." He told her of what he planned, except for picking up Derek and Karen. He'd meant to, but there just didn't seem like a good time to sneak it in. If something really did happen, he'd tell her when they got there. She probably wouldn't care as much then, due to being overwhelmed by the events. And, if nothing did happen, he wouldn't have to explain at all.

"Fine. It's probably not a bad idea, but you should have kept me in the loop." She fired back at him, "I'm still gonna put the packs in the 4-Runner." Then, she stormed out to the garage.

Landon thought maybe he should give Derek a heads-up, so he stepped out to the backyard and made the call. Derek confirmed he had set everything up, as asked. He'd even received the walkie-talkie Landon had sent last week. Now, came the hard part.

"Derek, I really appreciate this, dude. But now I'm gonna tell you some crazy stuff…" Landon started.

"Does it involve this guy on the news and the power grid going down by terrorists?" Derek cut him off. Landon was caught off guard by the question. "Because if it is, I feel better about things."

"Huh? You do?" Landon was confused.

"Yeah, bro…I figured that if you were going to steal an airplane; you had either lost it, or there was something really big coming. So, what do we do now?"

"We wait. If…er…when it happens, go to the appointed location as we discussed."

"Thirty minutes, Mr. President." The Chief of Staff warned.

"I want the Joint Chiefs, the Director, Homeland Security and the Secretary of Health and Human Services behind me in the frame of the camera. Shows solidarity and will give the American people confidence." The President ordered.

"Yes sir." The Chief answered. "It's as we discussed."

"Any word on Madison?"

"No sir. Billings PD lost them. The FBI is analyzing any and all media, videos, and HUMINT. They can't hide—the whole country knows them now." He sounded confident.

"I don't want *ANYBODY* talking to them, except our own people. It would be better if they resisted arrest and weren't able to talk at all…"

"Yes sir. Agreed." He wanted to change the subject. The President didn't need any more frustration before he addressed the nation. "Sir, your family is safe at Camp David and the Sec Def is airborne in the Nightwatch E-4B, call sign Venus 77."

"Good…good. I had a conversation with the Russian and Chinese ambassadors to ensure they understood that posturing of any kind would be viewed as an act of aggression and dealt with as such." The President paused to light a final cigarette before the address. "Like buzzards and vultures, they are…waiting and watching. It stands to reason they had intelligence on this and chose to remain quiet. Just makes me want to…" He stopped short, grunted and took another long drag off the cigarette.

"Tape up the headlights and I'll finish up on the windshield," Drew said, addressing David. "Nate can get the driver and passenger windows."

"Well, looks like you're finally gonna get the paint job you wanted, ol' timer." David quipped. Mad Dog picked up a roll of tape and hit David in the back of the leg with considerable effort. It stung and he had to rub it out for several seconds.

"You'll learn," Mad Dog said sternly, but with a smile on his face. "...you'll learn or die!" Everybody laughed. It was good; stress relief was badly needed. They hadn't expected to survive the takedown of the television station. At the very least they should have been captured. David thought of the redoubt and their new friends. He wanted to talk to Mad Dog about it, but the decision was his alone. They were good men and would be valuable to have with them. David had not yet met Drew's wife and kids, but he was sure they were of the same quality. If they stayed here, or even in their mountain cabin; their survival would not likely last beyond early spring. Sustained survival was much more complicated than eating elk or deer meat all the time.

"Hey, Drew," David began, "Tell me about your family."

Drew turned around slowly and had a puzzled look on his face. "What family?" he responded.

"Well, your wife and kids." David said slowly, now confused at how Drew responded. Drew and Nate looked at each other and started laughing.

"I ain't got no family...none that I know about anyway. Do you know something I don't?" Drew said, still laughing.

"Well, you told me you had kids...when we were back at the barn." David was still confused.

"Oh," Drew pipped back, "I just told you that to get you off guard. I thought you might hesitate to kill me just long enough for me to kill you! I ain't got no kids...wife either."

"What about Roxy?" Nate chided. Drew leaned into Nate as if he was going to punch him. Nate pretended to run away. Roxy was Drew's longtime girlfriend. It was amusing, but David would change the mood.

"Guys, I want to make an offer." David started. Mad Dog cocked his head and gently smiled. He knew what David was about to do and was pleased. It wasn't his place to invite these men to the redoubt. That was up to David and his family, but he was glad David was offering. It was a good decision in his opinion; both tactically and benevolently.

As they painted the AATREC, David explained the concept of a redoubt to Drew and Nate. It was more than just a cabin in the woods where you eat fresh game and fish. There were many other aspects of sustained survival to consider. He pointed out medical and dental needs as well as gardening, harvesting, and food preservation. Security, tools, infrastructure, consumables, and the building of a clan or community. The men were somewhat overwhelmed in what they heard as they had not considered any of these things—except one consumable; toilet paper. Nate was mostly surprised at learning about heirloom seeds. He used to grow things in a garden and thought he had that skillset covered until he realized the seeds he'd accumulated would only grow for one season.

"Wait, you're telling me if I harvest the seeds from my own produce, it won't grow?" Nate said emphatically.

"Nope, because those seeds are GMOs; or genetically modified organisms. The seed companies genetically modify the plants to not only grow bigger, they also produce sterile seeds or no seeds at all. The idea being that you have to come back to the store and buy them every year. It's a marketing and business development scheme." David explained.

"It's a damn rip-off is what it is!" Drew said angrily, "And let me guess; our government let them do it?!"

"Yeah, well, you're right." David agreed, "So, now that you understand, my father created a redoubt for us...well, mostly. He set aside a property about eight hours' drive from here that is perfect for a sustainable life and he buried a large shipping container in the ground that contains most everything we need to rebuild our lives…kind of a redoubt kit." David paused, glancing at Mad Dog, who still had a smirk on his face. "The thing is…to really be able to have everything you need for 'the clan' to function; you gotta have people with skillsets to complement the community. Like security and medical…dental…"

"Hey, POTUS goes on in ten minutes." Mad Dog reminded. "As much as I don't want to see him, I think we need to hear what he has to say."

"Okay, lets clean up a bit and get in the house. The TV out here is broke." Nate responded, "So does this redoubt have a mayor? I want to be the mayor."

David sloughed off the question and continued. "So, what I'm offering is an opportunity to join us at the redoubt…and if this 'Roxy' is someone special, then you may want to consider bringing her, because to leave her here…"

It was a solemn thought and changed the mood. They couldn't save everybody. Hopefully, POTUS was protecting the power grid and nothing would happen, but Mad Dog knew the grid was massive and even if mostly successful; many thousands would die. They cleaned up; all except Nate, who applied the last stencil to the front of the AATREC.

"So whadda ya think?" Nate beamed, "Whadda ya think of my artwork?"

The AATREC was painted to look like a military transport vehicle and matched current Army camo paint schemes. Nate's stencil was in large black letters and declared, 'Army National Guard.' Mad Dog shook his head and said, "Just leave me a couple of my spray paint cans so I can take that off when we get there!" It got a chuckle from everyone but Drew. He seemed to be in deep thought about something. He looked up at the men, and tapped the nose of the AATREC.

"I'm going to get Roxy."

CHAPTER 15

"Courage is being scared to death, but saddling up anyway."—John Wayne

"Mr. President; it's time," the Chief of Staff called out.

"Let them wait. We'll stall a little to make sure the stragglers get their TV's on. I want everybody to hear this," the President said arrogantly, as he continued to read over the scripted speech.

Most of America was tuned in to the broadcast. The press had done a good job of building up the event to entice people to watch. CNN, MSNBC, and the major networks had downplayed KULRs 'take-over.' Mad Dog was just that; a 'mad dog.' He was a poor performer and a rogue employee; a malcontent who became dangerous. However, FOX news chose a different angle. While they didn't afford Mad Dog any credibility at this point, they did resurrect stories concerning the instability of the power grid and interviewed subject matter experts who testified of its vulnerability. Mad Dog and David's pictures were all over the media. They were considered extremely dangerous because they had killed federal agents who were former elite Special Forces personnel. Video of the faux Schwan's AATREC was played over and over in hopes that someone could identify where it went. The last known sighting was just outside Red Lodge, Montana. It wouldn't take very long for the thug agents to figure out where it went and who helped them paint it.

"I want this changed." POTUS boomed, "I told you to pull that out! Words mean things!" He pointed to a particular phrase on the computer screen.

"Yes sir...immediately," the Chief of Staff cowed.

POTUS lowered his voice so only the Chief could hear. "What's the status?"

"They're fifteen minutes out, sir." He responded.

POTUS nodded, but was annoyed at the answer. He wanted to know all was taken care of before he gave the speech, but he knew couldn't delay that long. Madison and Wallace were loose ends and needed to be silenced.

The big truck had a deep drone as it rolled down Interstate-40. Leigh and Tanner were lulled to sleep, which is exactly how Mason liked to travel. They were just coming in to Oklahoma City and he had topped off fuel at the Fire Lake Grand Travel Plaza. He chose it because it was right next to the Grand Casino and hoped he might get a change to try his luck. Leigh was not about it, though. He argued they were on vacation and should have some fun. Leigh pointed out that it was not her and Tanner's kind of fun. So, it was 'gas-n-go' for the would-be gambler.

Mason turned on the radio and started searching for a good rock station. Leigh stirred and he thought better of it, continuing to find something softer. Instead, he found a talk radio station that was ranting about some whack job that shot up a TV station in Montana. They made an announcement concerning the imminent speech about to be given by the President and that they would postpone their conversation until he was done. Mason almost kept channel surfing, but thought in light of current events, he would listen. The speech was supposed to go on at 7pm. Mason glanced at the clock; 6:06pm Oklahoma time, POTUS was late—as always.

Kate's car was not the best mode of travel for long-legged musicians. The late model Ford Fiesta was packed full of their gear and even though Ross had the front passenger seat, it wasn't enough room for him. They were just coming into Chicopee on I-90.

"I'm hungry." Hallie said, "I haven't eaten anything today; do you think we could grab something for the road?"

"Yeah, me too." Kate said. "There's a burger joint right there next to that gas station. I'll get gas and you guys' get the food."

181

"Great. You know I can't eat that." Ross whined. "I hope they have salads."

Kate pulled into the station and Hallie and Ross went to the restaurant. It wasn't very clean. In fact, it didn't seem very safe either. Ross noticed several seedy characters eyeing Hallie and talking low. He reached into his jacket pocket and put his hand on the M&P Shield 9mm pistol—it made him feel better.

They made their order and Kate walked in. That caused yet another stir in the other patrons. Ross wanted out of there pronto and wondered what was taking so long.

"Okay, here you go." The server handed over the bag of food. *Clearly, there was not a salad in that little bag,* Ross thought to himself.

"Um…I think we had a salad?" Hallie had noticed too.

"No, you didn't order no salad." The server was insistent.

Hallie pulled out the receipt and looked it over. "See…here; a salad!" she barked, pointing at the line on the receipt.

"Fine! But you're gonna have to wait." The server snapped back.

"I want to talk to the manager!" Hallie elevated her voice. Ross was beside himself. One of the patrons, a very large man; stood up and started making his way slowly to the counter. The server who was clearly mad, had her hands on her hips.

"I am the manager!" She yelled, pointing to her name tag. "You got a problem???"

"Landon, I put all the stuff by the 4-Runner; can you put it in for me?" Carrie made it sound like a request, but he knew it was more like a directive. He looked at the TV. It was just two guys speculating what POTUS was going to say when he addressed the nation. Landon looked at his watch; 7:07pm eastern time. Late.

"Okay, but I want to watch this first." He replied.

"Watch what? He's not even on."

"He will be…any minute, now."

Landon looked back at the screen. There was a commercial on. Maybe he had time to load them and get back. He trotted out to the garage and picked up one of the packs; it seemed a little light. He unzipped the top access for the water bladder and looked inside; empty. Great, that would take more time. He would need to fill both first and picked them up, heading back into the house. He contemplated challenging her on the bladders, but thought better of it and started to fill the first one. He glanced at the TV; it was off.

"Carrie! Really? Why did you turn the TV off?" He yelled up the stairs. Landon picked up the remote and pushed the power button, then dropped the remote on the couch and went back to the sink to fill the bladders. After he filled the first one it, he put 3 drops of chlorine bleach in the bladder before he sealed it and slid it into the pack. As he reached for the second one, he realized it was quiet and glanced up at the TV; it was still off. He started to get the controller on the couch and a thought prompted him to look at the digital clock on the microwave—it was blank.

"Landon, the power is off!" Carrie exclaimed, as she walked into the kitchen.

"Yeah, I just realized that…" he said slowly as he grabbed the car keys and headed for the driveway.

"Well, do you think?" She started.

"I don't…it's not time for that…it's not 9/11 yet." He kept moving toward the door.

Landon went out to Carrie's car and got in, leaving the door open and turned the ignition key to 'accessory.' He fumbled with the radio for several moments, but all he heard was static. Carrie was now standing next to him and watching intently. He shrugged.

"Well, this isn't good." Carrie said as she looked around the neighborhood. It was still daylight, so there was no indication of power outage.

Landon thought of his cell phone and pulled it out of his pocket. It showed he had a signal—*that was good.* He thought about who he could call; *Derek—it would confirm things on several levels.* He selected speed dial for Derek. A message came on stating circuits were busy. He tried again; the phone answered on the second ring.

"Landon...I assume you called because the power is off down there too?"

Landon's skin contracted and the hair on his arms raised. His heart began to pound and Carrie noticed his breathing rate increasing.

"Yeah...it is," was all Landon could manage to say. Carrie gave him a quizzical look. Landon nodded back to her.

"I don't know how much longer we'll be able to talk, Landon...so if we get cut off or you can't get a hold of me again, I will watch for you and I won't turn on the walkie-talkie 'till I see or hear you. Okay?"

"Yeah...okay, sounds like a plan. Not sure if it will be today or even tomorrow...I gotta figure out how this changes things at my work...and if the power comes back on, then..." Landon paused, he was still in shock.

"Yeah, I didn't think of that...the power could come back on. We should wait, huh?" Derek looked for confirmation.

"Yeah, we wait...sounds like a plan." Landon responded.

"Okay..." Derek agreed, "Hey...uhh, thanks bro. Thanks for thinking of us."

"Sure, no problem." Landon's response sounded like he just acknowledged a 'thank you' from somebody he helped jump a car battery, but it was all he could get out at the moment.

The call ended. Landon just sat in the car and stared at the radio. Carrie would wonder who that was and he would have to answer. He should have told her the whole plan. Now, it would cause more stress in an already stressful situation.

"Well," Carrie began, "Who was that? They don't have power either?"

"Derek," Landon stated flatly. "It was Derek."

"The power is out there too? In Colorado?" She sounded afraid.

"Yeah, they…" Landon was cut off by the radio coming to life.

"Hey, we're back! Sorry folks, looks like we got a bit of a power failure. Nothing to worry about, our generators will keep us up for hours. So, back to our guest, school councilman Watkins; you mentioned the proposed levies will help with overcrowding, what about the quality of the teaching, will it be better now, too?"

Landon turned the station to try to find the presidential broadcast, but he only found three more stations that were transmitting, and they were all playing music at this point. He switched to AM and scanned through the stations—just music and some pre-recorded religious message from the pastor of Saddleback Church. Landon looked back at his phone; it showed he still had a signal. "What's going on?" Carrie demanded. "Why were you talking to Derek about things changing at work?"

Landon cringed. He was overwhelmed at this point and just wanted to escape everything, but it wasn't realistic. They had to focus. What was the next move?

"Okay, okay," Landon started, "Let's go back in the house and finish filling the bladders. I'll tell you all about it…everything."

The power kicked off, then on, then off again. The light from the windows was all that illuminated the restaurant. The kitchen and counter areas were mostly dark. Ross's eyes were trying to adjust as he gripped the pistol firmly.

"Wilma...is there a problem here." The big man asked in a menacing tone as he slowly started to push Ross to the side while engaging Hallie.

"Yeah, these fools think they got some kinda privilege." The manager said loudly as she addressed Hallie. "They think they supposed to get it their way...this ain't Burger Sling, honey!"

Suddenly, Kate pushed Hallie aside and delivered a bone crushing kick to the groin of the big man. He fell to the floor immediately. The manager tried to climb over the counter to engage, but she was severely overweight and her attempts were futile. Ross looked toward the area of the restaurant where the big man's friends were; they making their way to the counter area and two of them went to block the door.

"Not a good idea, boys!" Ross yelled as he pulled the pistol from his pocket and herded the girls toward the door. They all froze. He took a chance that they didn't have guns; this was Massachusetts and the average thug didn't just carry them around—at least these guys didn't. They got to the door and one of the two guys guarding it, stood fast. The other one fled.

"Dude, I will shoot you...get out of the way!" Ross yelled.

The man didn't move. This gave the thugs a bit of courage, and they slowly moved to surround the door area. Ross pursed his lips and gritted his teeth as he raised the gun to the man's head and started to squeeze the trigger. The man recognized the resolve and immediately raised his hands and slipped sideways away from the front of the door. The girls pushed the door open and ran for the car. Ross hung back a bit with the gun pointed at the thugs.

"Wilma; call the cops!" the big man groaned loudly, still lying on the floor.

"Yeah, Wilma...call 'em." Ross dared. "Let's see who they're gonna believe. I'll bet half of you are on parole right now." Ross asserted. "And, if that camera works..." he pointed the gun at the corner where a surveillance camera was aimed at the counter area, "...then, the police will see what really happened." No one moved.

The car pulled up next to the door. Ross looked back to see Kate motion for him to get in. He turned back to the thugs. They were still motionless. Wilma yelled some kind of profanity and Ross bolted for the car, its passenger door already open for him. As he jumped in, Kate tore off. The thugs burst through the door in time to hear Ross offer his goodbye and a little advice.

"Have a nice day...oh, and tell Wilma to stop eating so many of the profits! Tell her to eat my salad instead!"

"Hey, what did you two just do in there?! Oh my God!" Hallie exclaimed from the back seat.

Kate was driving like she stole the car as she looked over at Ross, who was looking in the rearview mirror to see if anyone was following them. He looked back at Kate and they stared at each other for a few seconds before they both burst out laughing. Ross raised his fist and they bumped knuckles.

The lights dimmed and then kicked off. The emergency lighting immediately flooded the room, followed by all the normal lighting returning and the floods then faded. The back-up generator had automatically come on line.

"What was that?" POTUS walked to the window to see the city mostly dark. "Get the general in here...get everybody in here."

The Chief of Staff returned after a few minutes with the Secretary of Energy. Both clearly didn't have any information yet and could only speculate until they received word from their subordinates. POTUS suspected as well, but he wanted them by his side when they got any news.

"Mr. President, we need to address the nation as soon as possible..." the Chief of Staff began.

"And, who is going to hear it? A token amount of people riding around in their cars?" POTUS didn't give him a chance to answer. "And, what do we tell them? Right now all they know is that some guy named

Madison claimed this was *going* to happen and that I *let* it happen...now it *has* happened!" He threw his glass of water against the wall forcefully. "You know how that looks! We're screwed here...where's the general???"

"Coming, sir. He was getting an update," the Chief responded meekly.

"Get my staff in the briefing room, we have to re-write the speech...think of a way to spin this. Tell my press secretary the broadcast is delayed until...oh, tell him an hour. Have him make a statement to that effect. That will give people time to get around a radio. Activate the Emergency Broadcast System."

"Mr. President." The general walked in. "Nearly the entire country is without power, save a few small pockets nearer generation sources. Our forces managed to protect only a few of the sub-stations before the attacks were carried out...there just wasn't enough time to get in place."

"I don't need your excuses, general, I needed you to do your job!" POTUS yelled.

"Yes, sir." The general said apologetically.

The Secret Service detail's lead agent entered the room. "Sir, we must evacuate you and the staff to the E-4 aircraft ASAP." He said assertively.

"No...not yet. It will take too long to set up the broadcast from there. We will go after the broadcast...we were caught with our pants down and all hell is going to break loose. General; initiate the martial law protocols as discussed." POTUS was flustered and it was painfully obvious.

The general excused himself to join the rest of the Joint Chiefs. As he walked down the hall, he began to formulate solutions for saving the nation—cursory top level thinking. He would share these thoughts with the other generals. Rounding the corner into the room, he sat down in front of the controlling military leadership of the entire United States. What would he say? He wasn't sure at this point. Because every thought he had so far—every plan—would be considered treasonous under the Uniform Code of Military Justice…

…but, he saw no other way.

Drew was arguing with Roxy. She had agreed to come with him based on his insistence, but once she got in the truck and listened to his explanation of where they were going and why, she was not happy. First of all, it was the most harebrained thing she'd ever heard. It was one thing to know about a federal agent hanging around the library; quite another to know why. Besides, Drew told her to pack for a few days and that he was taking her someplace special. Someplace special meant she brought dress clothes, not camping clothes. She couldn't live indefinitely in the remote wilderness sporting a high cut skirt and heels.

"Why didn't you tell me what to pack then?" Roxy cried.

"Cuz you wouldn't have come with me!" he replied.

"You're right! I feel like I'm being kidnapped right now—like I'm going to be some kind of breeding stock for an end of the world scenario in a B-grade movie. What about Susan, over at the diner? Why didn't you pick her?" Roxy queried. She's even *'easier'* to get along with, from what I understand!"

Drew didn't say anything. He was starting to get angry. She had seen that look before, and normally she would have backed off a little, but this was ridiculous. *The President is trying to take over the world and Drew wants me to hide in the mountains with him? What a freakin' story!*

"Well? I'm waiting…what's so special about me?" She pushed.

"Because I don't love the others!" he blurted out.

"Because you don't…" she stopped to consider what he said, "…you mean…you mean you love me?" He didn't answer and kept looking down the road. "You've never told me you loved me before."

"Well, I'm telling you now!" he said assertively. "Those boys back at the shop put it to me pretty hard. I could only think of one person I didn't want to live without...well, besides Nate Dog...and I can't marry him, so..."

"Well, halleluiah! I'm in good company with Nate Dog, huh? Top of the heap!" she was continuing her rant, but then it hit her. "Wait, what? Did you say 'marry?' You want to marry me?" The expression on her face started to change again. She tried to hold it back, but it was no use—a tear formed and rolled down her cheek. "You know, I've loved you for a long time...just never said it. And I've always thought you would be a good father..."

"Uhh, yeah...hold that thought." He cut her off as he leaned forward and closer to the windshield. "That ain't good." Drew saw several black suburbans parked just under a half-mile mile from the house. He slowed and pulled over. "Hand me them binos." He said pointing to a case on the floor board near her feet.

"What? What are you talking about? She said with a quizzical look on her face.

"The binoculars...by your feet, I need them!"

She handed him the case and he quickly opened it and glassed the area beyond the Suburbans. There they were; moving quickly and fanning out to surround the house and shop. He picked up his cell phone—no signal. Not good.

"Here," he said, as he threw the binos and the phone in her lap, "I'll be right back."

Drew slid out of the truck, pulled the colt python from its sheath under the seat and stealthily moved up the road to the first suburban. Then, made his way to clear each one. Once satisfied they were empty, he pulled out his Emerson folder and knifed the sidewalls of all the tires. Then, he ran back to the truck where Roxy was; she was shocked at what he was doing.

He opened the door and leaned the seat forward. Reaching into a sheath behind the seat, he withdrew a Sako 30.06 long rifle and laid it across the hood. He adjusted the power on the Leupold scope and scanned the killing field. He had to pick the targets carefully. Once the first round was fired, the gig would be up and the men would take cover. He just had to take the ones with the most cover around them, first. Also, the report from the rifle would alert Nate and boys in the house as to the threat outside.

"Roxy, honey...I need you to get out and get behind the truck where the metal is thickest; under the boom I guess...and crawl in there as far as you can."

She didn't argue and did as he asked. Drew moved forward to use the last suburban as a rest and shield; putting himself behind the engine block. Leaning over the hood, he selected his first target. The Sako was true to the sniper that pulled her trigger; the man's spine was severed and became shrapnel, exiting out his chest; he dropped like an early fall whitetail. The second target turned to investigate the rifle's report, only to succumb to the same fate. Two down, seven or eight to go...

The rifle report shocked the fugitives out of their laughter. Nate dropped his beer and it sprayed on the AATREC. Mad Dog and David grabbed the AR-10s and immediately took defensive positions. A second shot was fired, and a third. Then, it was answered by semi-automatic and automatic fire from several locations.

"Who is shooting?" David said to Mad Dog, now positioned in the corner of the window.

"I don't know...I don't see anything." Mad Dog answered. "But the first few rounds sounded like a large bore hunting rifle—the rest were probably AR-10s.

"It's Drew! I know the bark of that old Sako 'ought-six' anywhere." Nate cried. "We gotta help him!"

191

Mad Dog looked back at Nate, "You sure about that—the Sako, I mean?"

"Yeah, no doubt!" He replied.

"Okay, you go into the AATREC. There's two AR-15s in there; grab one and a bunch of the magazines. Get in this window and find a target. If you don't see one in about two minutes, fire anyway." Mad Dog ordered. "The kid and I are going out the back and when they hear that you have them in a cross fire, they'll return fire to the shop. Hopefully, we'll locate them and take them out from a flanking position."

"I'm on it!" Nate responded.

"After that, I'd get out of the window unless you want to be perforated!" David warned, as he turned to address Mad Dog. "We got about 30 minutes to take these guys out before the sun goes down to the point where they can use night vision against us—then we're screwed!"

"Good point! The tritium ACOGs on the ARs work well in low light, but are not ideal at night time. I do have a night scope in the AATREC, but there's no time to set it up—let's roll!"

As the sun set on the Oklahoma plains, Mason noticed a curious thing; there were no lights except for a house here and there. Those were likely generators. *That ain't good*, he thought to himself. Most of the radio stations dropping off line wasn't a good indication either. And then, there was the fact that POTUS pulled a no-show. He wanted to wake Leigh, but thought better of it. She would know soon enough and he wanted a stress-free drive if he could get it. Still, he was stressed about the situation. It just became very real. He was only slightly comforted by AR-15 behind his seat and hoped he wouldn't have to use it. There were several larger cities still in his path. The longer it took to get to the redoubt, the more chaotic things would become. He could jump off the interstate and take back roads, but he knew it would only be a short time before local people would start blocking those to keep 'outsiders' from entering. No, he would stay on the interstate for now and drive his butt off. They would be safer in about 18 hours or so. He would feel better after they cleared Denver; another 8 hours away.

The radio station stopped playing music for a special message from the Emergency Broadcast System. Mason listened intently as a curfew was just declared for a state of national emergency. The President would make an announcement within the hour as to the circumstances. Mason thought about the curfew. Should he pull over and stop to wait until morning to continue? No, if he got pulled over, he would continue and pretend he didn't know. He had to get there as soon as possible to minimize exposure to the crazies—and there would be crazies.

Several bullets cracked as they flew past Drew's position; several more hit the suburban next to him. *'Inaccurate fire,'* Drew thought to himself. Initially, their fire was directed at the wrecker, but his third shot clued them in that it was one of the Suburbans being used as a shield. While the AR-10 round is more than capable of hitting and killing him, Drew knew the assault version of the thug rifles had an effective sighting range of about 300 meters, but they were just over 800 meters—perfect for the Sako. He wondered about Roxy since the first volley was concentrated on the wrecker, but he was fairly confident the area he sent her would protect her, unless they were using armor-piercing rounds. He didn't think so.

Drew scanned the shop with his scope. Two men came out the back and dispersed; it was David and Mad Dog. He scanned back over the area where the thugs were hiding. Based on the flora and terrain between them and the shop, the thugs wouldn't likely have seen them come out. His friends would undoubtedly be moving to a flanking position. He wondered where Nate was; probably still in the shop.

Several more rounds hit the suburban behind him, but he couldn't see where they came from. One thing he did know—they came from a position closer than the last volley did. Drew was more excited than

193

scared. He had been actually enjoying this, but the last volley reminded him of just how much danger he was in. These guys were experienced pros and it was only a matter of minutes before they would take him if he didn't get help soon. There were at least six of thugs left.

A volley of shots rang out from the shop and into the general area of the thugs. Drew saw movement from another thug—it was a head! He quickly acquired the target and fired. Pink mist! "We're down to five, boys," he whispered to himself. Suddenly, a volley of rounds hit his Suburban—the gig was up! He dropped lower to shield himself behind the engine block and wheel rims. He knew they were coming—one was laying cover fire while the others were undoubtedly advancing. If he stayed where he was, he would be dead in moments, but to run from the cover of the suburban was not much of an option. He listened for a pause in the firing to indicate the thugs were swapping magazines. They would be fairly close by now; within a couple hundred meters.

There it was; a lull in the firing! He bolted down the side of the suburban and back toward the wrecker. The thugs saw his feet and sprayed auto fire. One of the skip-shots hit the heel of his boot and ripped it off; sending him off balance and spinning. He landed beside the front wheel of the second Suburban. Everything was now moving in slow motion for him; adrenaline pumping through his body. As he lay on his side, he could see under the vehicle; two men charging less than 50 meters away, weapons at the ready. *This is it,'* he thought, tucking into a ball behind the rim of the suburban.

Boom! Boom!—two shots rang out from somewhere near the wrecker, then three more—different from the crack of the ARs. It was a shotgun! Drew pulled the Colt Python and charged around the front of the suburban. The two men lay in the dirt; one was down for the count, but the other was only stunned as all the buckshot had impacted the bullet-proof vest. Drew made quick work of him with two shots to the head. He turned toward the wrecker raising the pistol to charge.

"Drew...you alright, honey???" Roxy yelled, still holding his Winchester Model 97 12-gauge pump. It had been behind the seat in a scabbard just under where the Sako had been. "You got anymore shells for this thing?"

Drew smiled. *What a woman!* He trotted toward her and motioned for her to get behind the wrecker to safety. Just as he reached the front of the wrecker something hit him hard in the left shoulder and knocked him flat in the road. It felt like he'd been kicked by a horse, though initially he felt no pain. He tried to reach for his shoulder, but his other arm was pinned under him as he lay on his back. There was a burning sensation followed by the scent of warm blood. It reminded him of being on the wrestling team and being pinned—he couldn't move. There was more AR-10 fire…some from the area that would have been a flanking position. Then, more from the thug held area. It went back and forth with the occasional report from a smaller weapon, probably an AR-15 or M-4 near the shop—must be Nate. Drew was breathing deeper now and felt like he couldn't get his breath. He closed his eyes; maybe they'd think he was dead.

"Drew honey…oh my God, you've been shot!" He opened his eyes to see Roxy leaning over him.

"Get…get…honey, you gotta get…down…" Drew managed to get out the warning. "Get…" His eyes rolled back and he lost consciousness.

David and Mad Dog saw three men concentrating their fire toward the string of vehicles on the road; one firing and the other two charging, but they were out of range and too close to Drew for them to lay suppressive fire, so they concentrated their aim on the thug that was spraying the suburban. Mad Dog didn't think they hit him, but it kept him from spraying cover fire. Bullets suddenly ripped into their positions from the right flank. It was from the thugs that had nearly reached the house before redirecting.

"We're in a bad spot, junior!" Mad Dog said as he returned fire. "I'll keep 'em down, you make your way to their flank."

David was already moving in that direction. How many were there? He didn't know, but it was getting dark. He ran down a coulee into a

195

small draw. Mad Dog was still firing; that was good. He started to poke his head up over the lip of the draw when he heard it—"bloop!" It was the sound of a 40mm grenade leaving its tube. That was a game changer. It exploded somewhere near Mad Dog's position. Mad Dog's AR went silent. Moments later the thugs started firing again. Then, he heard a smaller caliber weapon—Nate's AR—but it wasn't from the shop. It was much closer. The thugs now trained their fire on Nate. David could tell the thugs were directly in between him and Nate and he would have to move again to get to their flank. Still no activity from Mad Dog's position—that wasn't good.

David heard more fire from the area of the vehicles; Whump, whump…whump, whump, whump…then two quick cracks of a pistol. He hadn't heard the report from the Sako for some time and feared the worst for Drew. His mind was racing; Mad Dog and Drew…both gone? He thought of Nate and could hear the smaller AR spitting death as he reached the end of the draw—time to rock. David jumped up from his position to clear the draw when he felt something grab his boot and pull him back down.

"Where you going, Junior?" Mad Dog piped. David looked at him like he'd seen a ghost.

"I thought you were…"

"There you go thinking again…" Mad Dog said with a toothy grin. "We got ourselves quite a skirmish here, huh?" It was then David noticed the old warrior was bleeding from various places around his head and side. He reached for the clot-kit he kept in the cargo pocket of his pants. "Don't bother…its only superficial. I won't run out of juice for at least another hour."

The crack of the small AR shook David out of his focus on Mad Dog. "Nate! We gotta help, Nate."

"Easy, cowboy. Nate has them pinned down and he's too close for them to use that blooper. If they try to move from their position, he'll nail them." Mad Dog was good, David had to give him that. "But, we aren't too close for them to use it on us—and I can tell you that thing stings a bit!"

"Then what?" David asked.

"Okay, I'm not going to be much help here. My left leg is keeping me from running." David noticed the blood seeping from a shrapnel tear in the senior man's pant leg. "These guys have no choice but to charge Nate's position and they know it. To try to move back, left, or right is suicide. Nate knows it too." The old warrior paused to grit his teeth while shifting position. "What they don't know, is that we're here on their right flank. When you hear one of them go to suppressing fire, you'll know they're making their move…that's when you'll make yours. But it's going to be tricky and timing is critical. The first guy will lay down suppressive fire, while the second guy moves to flank Nate. If he moves to the left, it's not a problem—you'll take out the first guy and the second guy will be caught in a crossfire from both you and Nate. But if the second guy moves to the right…"

"Then, he'll be coming right toward me." David finished the sentence.

"Right, and that's not a problem because you'll probably have the drop on him as he'll be focused on Nate's position. However, if the second guy turns toward Nate's flank before you get him, he'll be directly between you and Nate. It won't be safe for you to fire and if Nate engages him, he'll cut you down as well—remember; Nate doesn't know we're here."

"Then, I'll move parallel and closer to Nate's flank…" David started.

"There's no time, kid. The thugs are going to make their move in seconds…it's what I would do." Mad Dog coughed.

"And the first guy?" David already knew the answer—and it was risky.

"Provided you get the flanker, you'll continue to charge the suppressor…you should surprise him too, but that's a call you'll have to make on the fly."

197

Nate waited for what he knew was coming. While he currently had the tactical advantage and he knew they would try a flanking charge, he didn't know which side? He hoped from his left. That side was slightly higher than his position which gave the thug a small advantage, but it also would skyline the attacker. It was almost dark and if he came from the right, he would blend in and be hard to see. Nate glanced at the vehicles on the road and wondered about Drew. In his gut, he knew it wasn't good and wanted to be there to help, but these guys kept him from it. He thought about David and Mad Dog; their guns had gone silent after the grenade explosion. The reality that he was totally alone in this fight had just seeped into his bones—he was not going to win this one.

Suddenly, suppressive fire came from in front of him—this was it! Nate scanned back and forth to see where the flanker would come from. There; from the left! Two of them...that made three total, he hadn't figured on that. He would take the closest one first. Two shots cracked from the AR-15; one struck the thug's armor in the center of his chest, the other through his trachea. The thug fell like a sack of potatoes. Nate trained on the second man, about 20 meters behind the first. As he was about to pull the trigger the second man fired—but it was not at Nate. It was toward the suppressor. David! It was David; Nate could tell by his gait as he advanced.

The suppressor now trained his fire away from Nate and onto David. Nate popped up from his position to charge—they had the thug in a crossfire. As he began to fire, Nate saw David go down in his periphery. He'd been hit and from the way he fell; it was hard. The thug was swinging his AR around to engage Nate now, but it would be of no use. The smaller AR pumped several rounds into the thug's neck and head. It was over.

As Nate made his way to his fallen comrade, he saw Mad Dog limping in from his left. "Is the kid hit? Mad Dog yelled.

"Yeah, I think so. He went down over there." Nate pointed to a spot in front of Mad Dog.

The two men arrived to see blood coming from David's neck, just under his chin. It didn't appear to be arterial, but it was moderate—most head wounds were. He ripped open David's vest; there were at least two perforations into the outer shell. Mad Dog reached into David's cargo pocket for the clot-kit.

"You got this? I gotta get to Drew!" Nate said hurriedly.

"Go," Mad Dog said, "and, be careful…there's at least one more out there!" Nate disappeared into the darkness carrying a dead thug's AR and several of the magazines. The flip-up night scope accessory would give an advantage.

"Hang in there, kid…stay with me," Mad Dog muttered to himself, "You're the only friend I got left."

CHAPTER 16

"Heroes may not be braver than anyone else. They're just braver 5 minutes longer"
–Ronald Reagan

Landon and Carrie drove slowly into the parking lot at Williams Gateway where Landon worked. It used to be called Williams AFB and was well-known for flight training in Mesa, Arizona. Currently, it is for commercial use, having been re-purposed. The UND building was dark and no one seemed to be around. They parked and got out of the 4-Runner. Landon had a key to the building, but waited to scope things out.

"Where's the security guy?" Carrie whispered.

"I don't know…maybe inside." He responded, "But, under the circumstances and with the curfew and all, I'm not sure he's here at all."

Landon walked down the side of the building to the flight line fence. He looked through the fence out to the tarmac. The Seminole was still there. He knew from the schedule that no one had flown it since he had it filled up. He looked toward the tower; it was dark too.

"Let's go inside." He said. They made their way to the front door and he unlocked it. The light on the alarm system was flashing and he entered the code to disable it. *It must still be working off the battery*, he thought. He wanted to go straight to the key box, but thought he should look around first. After checking out the facility and was sure no one was around, he returned to the key box.

"Now, what?" Carrie inquired.

"Now, we go into the hangar and get the bolt cutters from the A&P mechanic's tool box." Landon's flashlight led the way. He had put a red filter on it so it wouldn't be readily seen from outside. When they got to the box, it was locked. Landon looked around for something to break into it and finally found a large flat screw driver on the bench. He pried open the drawer and got the bolt cutters.

"You need those for the key box?" she asked, "Seems like over kill."

"No, we need them for the fence." He replied.

"Well, why don't we just crash it with the 4-Runner?"

"You've been watching too many movies." He said rolling his eyes.

They made their way out to the key box and got the keys to the Seminole. Then, they proceeded to a place in the fence between two buildings where exposure was minimal. Landon started cutting the chain-link fence. He left strategic links intact to give the fence a normal appearance, but later would only have to cut four more links to create a hole big enough to drive through.

"Headlights!" Carrie whispered loudly.

Landon turned around to see the airport police SUV turn down hanger row. They would be coming right past the 4-Runner in about 30 seconds.

"Hide!" he told Carrie, "Over there by that bench."

Landon walked slowly toward the 4-Runner in a non-threatening manner. He knew they would see him. A moment later they turned on their red and blue flashing lights. Landon stopped. The spotlight was in his eyes, he held up his hand to block it. He didn't run or act surprised to avoid the appearance of guilt.

"Place your arms straight out from your sides and turn around." The voice said over the PA.

Landon complied. The men got out of the vehicle and approached him slowly with their weapons drawn, but not aimed. As they got closer, one of them said, "Aren't you one of the instructor pilots?"

"Yeah, Landon Swanson…I work here." He replied.

"Well, there's a curfew on, didn't you know."

"Yes, I did. But I'm a diabetic and I'm low on insulin." Landon lied. "I always carry some in my flight bag…in the building." He motioned using his head. "Can I drop my arms now?"

"Yeah, sure." One said as they holstered their weapons. "Do you have a key to the building?"

"No, I was kinda hoping someone would be here…do you have a key?" Landon lied again.

"Nope, sorry…are you completely out? You know you can go to a hospital for that if you need to."

"No, I'm not out. Got another day's worth."

"Well, you can come back in the morning. Somebody might be here then."

"Yeah, okay, thanks…I'm just a little freaked out with this power outage thing, ya know?" Landon tried to sound scared. "You guys hear anything about when power might come back on?"

"Your guess is as good as ours…listen, you need to get on home. Please get in your vehicle and leave the premises. We're going to make our way to the end and circle back to escort you out."

"Okay, thanks for understanding…I appreciate it."

"No problem…you have a good night." They got in the SUV, turned off the flashing lights and continued on.

Landon returned to the 4-Runner and when the police had gotten further down the road, he motioned for Carrie to grab the bolt cutters and run back to him. "That was close," he said. "It's only going to take about 5 minutes to finish their round and get back here."

"What now?" she sounded scared.

"Well, in the morning, they're going to discover the fence has been compromised and it won't take long for them to figure out who did it." He was thinking out loud. "Then they're going to come for me…I'm thinking that you should take the 4-Runner and leave. I'll squeeze through the fence where we cut and go out to the plane, take all the tie-downs off and preflight it…you come back in about 30 minutes and watch their pattern. When they go to the other end of the field, come in with your lights off and I'll meet you at the fence. I'll cut the last four links and we'll drive out to load our gear." He took a deep breath. "Then, I'll fire it up and we take off."

"I don't like it." She said, "Why can't we both leave and come back?"

"Because I would still need to get the plane ready and that takes too much time." He replied.

"Well, what about if we…" she was cut off.

"Look, I'm scared too, but this is the only way…" He paused. She nodded with tears in her eyes.

"Okay…okay, you're right." She agreed.

Carrie drove slowly off and as promised, the police SUV followed behind her. Landon made his way through the fence and out to the Seminole. He looked it over and removed the tie-downs. Then, he made sure there were no control surface locks in place. Landon opened up the door and slid in. He turned the key; dim instrument lights came on and he checked to make sure the fuel was still good. It was.

Carrie left the airport property and pretended to head home. Once the police turned around and were out of sight, she turned off her headlights and doubled back. It took her a couple of minutes to find the best vantage point, but she eventually found one. She could see the flight line and the building near where the fence was compromised. Now, she would wait.

Mason saw flashing lights ahead…a lot of them. It looked like a roadblock. He slowed the big truck and brought it to a gentle stop. An Oklahoma state trooper approached the driver's door.

"Evening, officer…some kind of problem ahead?" Mason tried to sound cheerful and unassuming.

"There's a curfew in effect. You're going to have to shut it down." The officer replied. Leigh woke up and seemed startled.

"What's going on?" She whimpered, "Why are we stopped?"

Mason responded loud enough for the officer to hear. "Well, honey, I guess there's some kind of curfew on and we're supposed to pull over and shut down." It woke Tanner up and true to form, the boy started crying loudly. Mason could see the officer cringe slightly.

"Look, sir…is there any place we can stop ahead…maybe a place with bathrooms?" Mason pleaded.

The officer stammered a bit, clearly he didn't like Tanner's wailing. "Okay, look…there's a rest stop about 30 miles down the highway. Go directly there and stay until morning. If for some reason you don't stop there, you'll be arrested. Do you understand?"

"Yes sir, yes sir…thank you!" With that, he drove off toward the rest stop.

"What was that all about?" Leigh asked, trying to settle Tanner down. Mason told her all that had happened so far. Afterwards, she just stared out the window. "So then…it has started. We should have left earlier."

Ross leaned over to see the fuel level—three-quarters of a tank. It wouldn't get them far enough. They would need more. He wondered if the power was out everywhere. Glancing at the cell phone, he saw it had a signal. He tried several times with various numbers before he got a line out beyond the recorded message saying all circuits were busy. Someone picked up.

"Hello?"

"Chris??? That you? It's Ross."

"Dude! What the hell? You guys got power up there?" Chris asked.

"Nah, man…I assume you don't either?"

"Nope. And, I finally got ahold of my cousin in San Diego—they're out too! If I didn't know any better I…" The line went dead. Ross checked the signal. It still showed two bars. He thought about trying again, but there was no point—power was out everywhere it seemed—just like dad said it would. "How the hell…" he muttered to himself.

"What?" Kate said.

"Aw, nothing. I just wanted to confirm power was out everywhere. My buddy in Florida said his was out and so was California."

"How come the phones still work?"

"Well, the towers have generators that run on batteries and gas or diesel generators. They won't last much longer." He took notice of the road sign in front of him. "Hey, where are you going?

"Springfield." She replied.

"Oh…no, we gotta avoid any big city. We need to stay in the backwater places as much as possible. I know it's not the shortest route, but it's too dangerous to be in the cities." He tried to be gentle in his assertion.

"Okay, I'll try, but you'll need to help me navigate." She replied. "Of course it won't matter much if we don't get some gas, huh?"

"Nope, you're right about that," he said, as he started scoping out potential sources. "You're right about that…"

Carrie watched the police SUV as it turned around again for the third time. She looked at her watch—18 minutes—on average it took them 18 minutes to make a round. She started the engine and drove with her lights off to the point in the fence where she was to meet Landon. He was there lying on the tarmac. As she pulled up he popped through the fence and got the bolt cutters from her. It only took a few seconds to clip the last four links and the fence wire fell away. They drove through without a scratch and pulled up to the Seminole and parked.

Landon threw the packs into the plane and slid into the seat of the small twin aircraft. He took a deep breath and looked at Carrie.

"Here we go, babe!" The first engine turned over and started quickly. He pushed the throttle forward and released the brakes. As they taxied, he started the second one and made his way toward the end of the runway. Carrie looked back to see if the police had noticed them. She didn't see anything. Landon was trying to get all the avionics up including the GPS. He nearly hit a taxi light and swerved to avoid it. They were taxiing too fast, but they really didn't have a choice.

"Oh-oh," Carrie exclaimed. "Here they come."

The flashing police lights were racing to the entry control point. Landon counted on that; there was no power to release the lock and roll the gate open. They would either have to go all the way around the end or find the hole Landon made. *That bought us some time*, Landon thought.

"What's that?" Carried cried, pointing to the other side of the runway.

It was another cop, but this one was inside the wire and closer—not good. They wouldn't make it. Landon looked over his shoulder at the first cop, still stopped at the gate and unable to get in.

"Hold on!" Landon yelled, as he did a 180-degree turn in the middle of the taxiway and turning on the lights. "The taxiway is going to have to be good enough." He pushed both throttles full forward. The engines roared to life and they began to race away from the second cop. It was so dark and the taxiway lights didn't work. He held his breath—they were bit heavy with a full load of fuel and all the gear. Landon checked the airspeed; still 12 knots below calculated take off speed and probably right at stall speed, but the end of the taxiway was coming up quick. He pulled back gently on the yoke and the twin buffeted a bit but nosed up and started to leave the earth. The end of the taxiway zipped under them as he continued on barely off the ground. He retracted the landing gear and continued skimming low.

"Pull up!" She cried, "Why don't you pull up???

"Ground effect." He stated flatly.

"What???"

"Ground effect!" This time he nearly yelled it. He couldn't see it, but he knew the fence was out there in the dark and he was trying to judge when to get all airspeed he could while in ground effect and still pull up before the fence turned them into so much twisted metal.

Now! He thought, as he pulled back hard on the yoke. The Seminole responded and they climbed out steeply. Landon watched the airspeed roll back a bit, but stabilize comfortably. He leveled off and started a turn to the north, turned off all the external lighting, and finished up the after take-off checklist. He didn't think fighters would be dispatched from Luke AFB to intercept him, but he wanted to make it as hard for them as he could. A curfew wasn't martial law but, he didn't want to take any chances.

"Well," he said, "there's no going back now." She gave him a kiss on the cheek.

"Whatever happens, Landon, I'm proud of you and I wouldn't want to be anyplace else right now."

He smiled back at her and she leaned her head on his shoulder. He felt vindicated, but he felt fear and excitement at the same time. *This was kinda cool,* he thought. There was no sound except the hum of the engines as he synced them up. However, that only lasted a few minutes before she broke their blissful moment.

"Hey, by the way…where are we going?" she asked.

He took a deep breath and responded. "Yeah, um…about that…"

Mason pulled into the rest stop. It was packed so he had to park on the grass. Everywhere he looked there were people, tents, campers, U-hauls, and all manner of rag-tag rigs. One group of refugees had built a bonfire near one of the cabanas and were standing around drinking beer.

"What's this?" Leigh asked, not believing what she was seeing.

"My kinda people!" He chuckled and popped the door open.

"Where are you going?"

"Just going to check things out." He answered.

He shut the door and used the keys to lock the truck. Then, he made his way around, starting with the bathrooms. Leigh watched him meander from group to group. Some of the conversations were longer than others. The group at the bonfire gave him a beer. Normally, she would have been a little upset at what he was doing, but she knew he was gathering information. At one point, a guy pointed toward a large fifth-wheel trailer in the parking lot. Mason finished the beer and went to the trailer. He stayed in the trailer for a good 15 minutes before coming out and making his way back to the truck.

"Well, this isn't going to be as easy as I thought," he said, as he got in the truck and locked the door.

"What do you mean," she said, "What isn't?"

"See that trailer I was in? Well, that guy has a ham radio set up and also a police scanner. He's been in contact with people all over the country. The big cities like New York, LA, and Chicago are in total chaos. I guess the military and National Guard forces have been unable to secure everything so far. They're spread too thin to have any real impact. He said the police in those cities aren't coming to work because they're staying home to protect their own families until the power comes back on."

"Well, did he say how long before the power comes on?" She asked, holding Tanner closer.

"The cops are being told weeks to months…maybe longer. But, the official government answer is just a few days. He thinks they're just saying that to deter people from doing worse things and that they might get prosecuted. But that's not the worst of it." He paused, scratching his head.

"What do you mean?" She sat up, and turned toward him. "What could be worse?"

"The President released an emergency broadcast about 45 minutes ago. He said this was an attack by terrorists, just like your dad said, but that guy named Madison…from the TV station takeover?" She nodded. "Well, he and your brother David were working together."

"What??? What do you mean…Like David helped him do it?"

"Yeah, and the President said that it was supposed to happen on 9/11 like your dad said, and that the government had it all under control, but Madison and your brother screwed it up and the terrorists did it early before the government could get in place to stop it."

Her eyes darted back and forth, she was thinking through things. "That's BS!" She puffed.

"Oh, I know…but the whole country doesn't think so. I didn't let on to these guys here about our relationship with your brother or anything." He took a deep breath. "And that's not all of it."

"Oh my God, there's more?" She cried.

"Yeah, somehow the terrorists have managed to spread Ebola all over the United States!"

She sat back in her chair, shocked. This was something she couldn't have imagined. Did her dad know all this? How could he? Why didn't he try to stop it? Maybe he did and that's why he's dead now.

"Sorry, babe. Seems like the end of the world, doesn't it?"

"What do we do?" She asked, tears rolled down her cheeks.

"Well, there's a curfew on and we can't travel at night, but these guys said that soon there's going to be martial law and all travel will stop to quarantine areas so the Ebola doesn't spread. FEMA is setting up camps to take care of people and we're all supposed to go there. Some of these guys say they aren't going; that they'll make their own camps. They invited us to join them." He held her hand and rubbed Tanner's head.

209

"And what did you tell them?"

"I said I had to talk to you first." He replied.

"What's there to talk about? We're going to the redoubt." She said emphatically. "You didn't tell them about the redoubt, did you??"

"No, no, no…of course not. But, under the circumstances, we might not be able to get to the redoubt. If they declare martial law, we're screwed—we can't get there from here. The roads will be blocked and we'll end up in one of those FEMA camps."

She looked down at the floorboard of the truck and thought about it for a moment, then she looked at Tanner and stroked his hair. "I want to be with my family and I think it's worth the risk…get us out of here—now."

He nodded. "Yes, Ma'am…we'll have to take small backroads the whole way. They won't have enough manpower to control them." He fired up the big truck. "Get out the map, I'm gonna need somebody to help navigate this. Also, we aren't going to have enough fuel now to make it all the way using the backroads. We might have to hike a couple hundred miles or so…you good with that?"

She nodded solemnly. He put the big truck into gear and started making his way toward the on-ramp. People stared as he passed them; quizzical looks on their faces. Tanner looked at his father and smiled. Mason hoped that was a good sign as they drove off into the darkness.

"There it is…over there." Kate said, nervously. "I know we gotta do this, but I don't like it."

"Me either, but we don't really have a choice." Ross responded. "Just pull up next to the fence and let me out…right there…there by the ditch. I can get under the fence by the culvert."

"Why don't we just go find a quiet street somewhere and get gas from parked cars?" Hallie asked.

"Because their tanks probably won't be full. Rental car agencies fill their tanks after every use so they're ready for the next customer." Ross tried to sound confident, but he was really nervous about his little endeavor.

Kate slowed and Ross got out. He looked around and decided to urinate. Firstly, it would give him a chance to scan around for any security people without looking too suspicious. Secondly, he really had to go! There was no activity he could see, so finished up and went back to the car.

"Okay, when you see me come back to this spot, drive back over and I'll fill up the car. We're probably going to have to do this three or four times, so be patient." The girls just stared back at him. Ross reached into the trunk and removed the five-gallon plastic gas can they found on the interstate and a small coffee can he found while dumpster diving. Then, he made his way to the fence and pushed the items underneath. His coat snagged several times as he made his way under. He could see the airport about a mile away. It was quiet and there was no traffic; only a dim light coming from the tower area. He made his way to the first line of cars. 'Enterprise Parking Only' was written on the sign in front of the cars. *Ironic*, he thought, *I pick a rental car lot to steal gasoline from, and it happens to be a company that laid me off.* Ross crawled under the rear of the first car and produced a Super Leatherman tool his father had included in the bug-out gear. He selected the punch tool and placed the coffee can as close to his working area as he could. Placing the tip of the punch against the tank, he popped the end of the Leatherman tool hard with his palm. It created a small hole and gas began to seep past the tool. He rolled the punch shaft around to make the hole bigger, then pulled out the punch and quickly slid the coffee can underneath to catch the fuel. It wasn't flowing very fast. At this rate, he'd be here all night. Going back to the Leatherman tool, he traded the punch for a cross-point screwdriver. He slid the can out of the way and placed the tip of the screwdriver over the original hole and used the same technique to drive the larger tool into the tank. It worked, the flow was significantly better. He replaced the can and slid out from under the car. There was gasoline all over his hands, arms and jacket. He knew it might be messy, but really hadn't thought about the smell. Not good.

After the coffee can filled up, he transferred the fuel to the larger 5-gallon can, and then repeated the process several times until the larger can was full. Reaching into his jacket pocket, he found a gum wrapper and rolled it into a plug for the hole in the tank. It didn't totally stop the fuel from leaking out, but slowed it to a drip. He stood and scanned the area for any activity—nothing. Making his way back to the fence, he found the girls waiting.

"How did you know when to come back?" He asked.

"Back from where? We never left." Kate whispered loudly. Ross just rolled his eyes.

"So what part of 'drive back over' didn't you understand? You'd have to leave to be able to drive back, right?" He said, annoyingly. "Whatever…"

Ross emptied the contents of the gas can into the car and then made his way back under the wire to get more fuel. It took over an hour to refuel the car and three trips. He went back once more to fill the gas can to bring with them. Also, he had to punch a hole in a second car tank before the whole fiasco was complete. After he put the full gas can in the trunk, he got back into the car and motioned for Kate to drive off.

"Oh my gosh, you really stink like gas!" Hallie complained.

"Yeah," Kate added, "It's gonna give me a headache."

Ross was really annoyed now. He'd just risked his life getting gas for them and all they wanted to do was complain about the smell. He took off his jacket and put it in the trunk. It helped a little, but his arms and hands would still smell. As far as he was concerned; it was good enough. As they drove off, he couldn't resist a parting shot.

"Oh, and Kate…" She turned to look at him; he was pointing at her. "Heads that look like yours…are supposed to ache!"

Nate cautiously approached the Suburbans. The first one was shot up pretty good. As he approached the second, he heard crying. He raised the weapon to his shoulder as he rounded the front of the vehicle and found himself looking down the barrel of a Colt Python.

"Roxy! It's me; Nate!" he said forcefully, "Don't shoot!"

Roxy dropped the weapon and turned her attention to Drew. Nate made a quick surveille of the area before he knelt near his friend. "What have we got here," he said hurriedly as he started assessing Drew's injuries. The shoulder was the most obvious and clearly displayed arterial bleeding. Judging by the pool under him, he was about to bleed out. He had Roxy place her palm on the wound and apply direct pressure. Once he was sure she had stopped the bleeding, he continued the assessment. There appeared to be no other wounds.

"Roxy, honey…we gotta get Drew to a hospital." Nate said as he checked out transportation situation. "Looks like it's gonna be the wrecker today, you were just a little too efficient in disabling the Suburbans, buddy," he said, addressing his unconscious friend. "Roxy, look behind the seat in the wrecker…there's a large first-aid kit; bring it to me."

Nate traded places with her on the wound. She hadn't been pressing hard enough earlier, Nate remedied that. Drew moaned. Good sign; he's able to feel pain and isn't totally unconscious. '2 by 5' Nate would have assessed, referencing his combat medical training. Roxy returned with the kit. Nate had her pull out the clot-kit and tear it open for him. He applied the life-saving device with pressure again. After a minute he checked for bleeding—it was down to a seep—good time to move him to the wrecker. Once they got him into the back seat, the bleeding had completely stopped.

"Roxy, honey. You got to get Drew to the hospital now." Nate ordered

"No, I can't...I'm too..." She started.

Nate grabbed her face and held it toward him so he could look her in her eyes. "Roxy, he'll die if you don't! Hear me? He'll die!" He paused to give her a chance to recover. "Now, you got this, girl! I have to run the last guy down. If he gets to town, they'll be mass quantities of reinforcements here and we'll all die. You don't want that, do you?" She shook her head. "Good...now go!" He gave her a kiss on the forehead. She got in the cab and shut the door. Nate collected the Sako and more AR-10 magazines from the dead thugs. She turned the key and the big truck roared to life.

Nate watched the rig accelerate down the road. He made his way to the area used by the 'suppressor' to keep Drew's head down while the other thugs had assaulted the suburban. There was brass everywhere; this was it. He carefully looked for tracks leading away from the area and out into the woods. He raised the AR and turned on the night vision scope. His initial scan bought up nothing, but the second one produced a bloom of light from the south end of the property. Judging by the light it was a headlamp in the red spectrum. If the thug had used white light, Nate would have seen it with the naked eye. NVG compatible green or blue and the scope would not have seen it at all. Yes, it had to be red. He thought about going back to the dead thugs for similar gear, but decided against it; the thug would just get that much farther ahead of him and besides, Nate's night vision would maximize in about 20 minutes. That would be an advantage over the thug. Also, he knew the terrain and the thug didn't—Nate only needed to close the gap.

Carrie was shallowly asleep. She was tired—drained, from the excitement. The drone of the aircraft engines made her sleepy, but the fear of the events would not let her slip into a deeper state. So, she was caught in the middle—in and out. That was good for Landon, she wasn't happy with him for not telling her the whole plan earlier, but now it was all on the table; Derek and Karen, the stop, everything. He didn't leave anything out this time. She would get over it.

Landon's concern now was that he really didn't get to preflight the Seminole, nor did he do run-up checks. There was no time with the 'po po' on his tail. He thought about switching magnetos to A and B, but there was no point now, was there? They were either fine or they weren't. Landon was always very meticulous and methodical, especially with flying. It nagged him that something might be wrong with the plane, though it was doubtful. However, his biggest concern wasn't the mechanical status of the plane—it was weather. There was a front moving into Colorado sometime tomorrow morning. He glanced at his watch. It *was* morning; 12:36 am to be exact. They would be in range of the walkie-talkies in about an hour. He hoped Derek was there. If he wasn't, Landon had decided to land on I-25 and abandon the aircraft. There was no choice, really.

One additional little detail to worry about; landing on the taxiway of an airport that had been closed for almost ten years. Fort Collins airport was now an industrial park. The main runway had a huge dip and rough spot about two-thirds of the way down—it was unusable. Commensurately, the taxiway he was to land on had heavy equipment parked on one end. Derek was supposed to make sure it was all clear and find some way of lighting it for Landon. A taxiway to land on at a closed airport, the weather is moving in, no lights, no ATC, no ATIS—this would be an even bigger challenge than previously thought.

He was right.

CHAPTER 17

"Let whoever is in charge keep this simple question in her head (not, how can I always do this right thing myself, but) how can I provide for this right thing to be always done?"
— Florence Nightingale, Notes on Nursing: What It Is, and What It Is Not

Mad Dog slipped the composite armor plate out of the David's vest sleeve and examined it, then flipped it over; both rounds had been stopped, though it was clear the impacts had forced material to punch into David's sternum and ribs. While the skin wasn't broken, the severe bruises told the story—he was gonna be sore.

"Ohhh...that really hurt!" David exclaimed, trying to sit up. "I couldn't breathe!"

"Whoa, Junior...lay back. Let's make sure you don't have any other major issues." Mad Dog gently pushed him back down.

David felt the pain under his chin and reached to his throat. He saw the blood on his hand. "What happened here? Did I get hit in the neck too?"

"No, it's superficial. You have the same thing going on inside each of your arms...it's called, spalling—the jacket of the bullet impacts the plate and essentially explodes or ricochets outward. The small fragments then pepper your skin and sometimes penetrate deep enough to cause bleeding. This vest's plates had a Kevlar fabric layer, which gives it an anti-spall capability. So, it could have been worse..."

"We gotta help Drew!" David said as he sat up. He winced and grabbed for his ribs. "Oh man, it feels like I got kicked by a horse!"

"Nate already went to help Drew." Mad Dog replied, looking in the direction of the road, "Whatever he found when he got down there, caused him to take the wrecker and head for town, pronto."

"Did we get them all? What's the SitRep?" David was still a little disoriented.

"Best I can tell, we got them all...of this wave anyway." Mad Dog said, as he tore open his pants where the 40mm grenade shrapnel had penetrated.

"You think there's more?" David asked.

"Oh, there's always more." He answered, "The question is; did the first wave get a call out or not?" Madison took his multi-tool out and used the pliers to pull a shard out of his leg. Blood oozed from the wound. He began to clean and dress it. "We have to get out of here, ASAP. Whether they got a call out or not, somebody is gonna come looking for them. The strange thing is that the sheriff's boys didn't hear the war and come barreling out here. They must have been told to stay away...federal jurisdiction and all that crap."

"Yeah, I know what that means—we weren't meant to survive this." David added.

"Exactly right." Mad Dog concurred. "Help me up, we gotta vamoose."

David helped him up and they made their way to the shop. Once there, they fired up the AATREC and drove out to the Suburbans and assessed the site. David noticed the Colt Python laying near a huge pool of blood and picked it up along with a shotgun lying on the shoulder of the road. The two dead thugs were relieved of their weapons and they stripped the Suburbans. A significant amount of ammo for the AR-10's as well as M-40 grenades were in the bounty. Of particular note was a large Pelican case containing a high-tech drone. David smiled and thought of Nate.

Mad Dog limped out to the place where the suppressing fire had come from, while David changed into his uniform. He noticed two sets of tracks leaving the site. The span between the tracks was fairly wide, indicating the men were moving fast.

Mad Dog returned to the AATREC and gingerly slid into the passenger seat. He thought it would be more believable if a uniformed, card-carrying, member of the military drove the newly painted vehicle. Just in case they were stopped. "Let's go, driver!' he piped. David complied. It was 2:42 am according to Mad Dog's watch—way past his bedtime. But he needed to apprise David of what he found.

"We didn't get them all."

"Huh?" David responded.

"Yeah, looks like two of them headed south into the forest. No blood trail. Their gait showed they were moving quickly—means they're healthy. I think Drew disabled all their vehicles, so the thugs took off to hide rather than follow the road, knowing some of us survived and would likely catch up to them."

"Where to?" David asked.

"Hospital." Mad Dog responded.

David grinned. "For that little paper cut?"

"Your daddy didn't beat you much as a kid; did he?" Mad Dog feigned like he was trying to get his belt off. David couldn't stop grinning. It's just what they needed after a stressful engagement—humor. This guy made him miss his dad.

"No, I'll live…but the way the wrecker tore off, somebody is in that hospital and we gotta check it out. If it's Drew and he can be moved, we need to take 'em with us. To leave him behind is certain death." Mad Dog said solemnly. "Certain death…"

Nate was an expert tracker. A skill passed down from his ancestors; the White Mountain Apache. His grandfather taught him many things in the summers that he'd spent in Arizona. Tracking was something he not only excelled at; it also enhanced his military career as a Pathfinder. His company commander commended him many times for the lost art; citing Nate's skill as being directly attributable to the survival of his unit in the Afghan mountains. On several occasions during patrol, Nate's interpretation of tracks left by Taliban forces resulted in avoiding deadly ambushes and saved many American lives as well as achieved the capture of a major Taliban leader.

This thug was smart. He was using techniques to confuse anyone that may be tracking him and he discontinued the use of his headlamp. Nate had been very careful not to reveal himself, but despite that fact, the thug knew he was being followed and that made him very dangerous. Nate had to change tactics.

The thug clearly had a weapon craft skillset that was equal to—or exceeding—Nate's. He was probably ex-special forces and was recruited by the intelligence community because he was the best of the best. For Nate to go head to head with this man on equal terms was not a good strategy. The thug had an AR-10 and possibly a grenade launcher. Nate needed a force multiplier and that would be found in the long gun. Drew's Sako 30.06 had a much better standoff range than the AR-10. Nate thought about the terrain and the direction the thug was traveling. He knew of only one place along the projected path that he could take advantage of a shot in excess of 400 meters— Beartooth Draw. It would require Nate to double the pace of his adversary in order to be in place when the thug passed by below him. The risk of being countered was low, but it would afford only one opportunity to make the shot. If Nate was unsuccessful or the thug chose a different route, it would be difficult to re-engage before the thug made it to town. He knew the rifle almost as well as Drew and he knew it was sighted dead-on at 300 meters. They had practiced shots up to 800 meters and so he was fairly confident of a distance half of that, but Beartooth Draw was known for windy conditions. He hoped this would not be the case now. He looked skyward. The moon was nearly full and would be behind him for the shot—one good plus, anyway.

The increased pace wasn't the issue. It was the climb. Or, was it the beer and pizza that Nate lived on? He decided it was probably both. If he survived this mission, he promised himself to get in better shape. His heart was pounding and oxygen was a commodity, which reminded him of another factor he would have to deal with when he got to his hide. Controlling the effect of pulse and breathing for a shooter is as important as any other factor; it only takes the uncalculated influence of one of them to foul a shot. Hopefully, there would be time to rest before the thug passed through. He tried to imagine himself in the thug's position—moving at a good pace, but having to spend time removing tracks or sign as well as checking his six-o-clock position for an adversary.

Nate came to the edge of the clearing. He used the night vision afforded by the AR-10 he'd taken off the dead thug that shot David. Slowly he scanned the general area he expected the thug to pass through. Nothing, except—a large buck whitetail deer. That was a good sign the thug was not yet in the area. Nate took the opportunity to quickly move across the open area to his hide. It would save time and energy, as staying inside the tree line was a much longer hike. He tripped a couple of times, but arrived relatively unscathed. He looked down to where the buck had been—it was gone. Probably because Nate's scrambling over the rocks spooked him. Then again, it could also have been the thug. He hoped not.

Fifteen minutes had passed and Nate was thinking the thug had taken a different route, when there was movement on the edge of the draw. The optic on the AR was not good enough to define what it was. Carefully, he brought the Sako up and used the Leupold scope to view the same area. Movement again—it *was* the thug! He was moving like a well-trained sniper, but just a little too fast to be effective. Probably because he thought Nate was behind him. It was a calculated—but bad—risk.

Nate watched as the thug made his way to a respectable ambush point and then set up for a shot himself. It was very sobering to observe, because if Nate had continued to track the man to this point, he would have been likely killed right here. Nate lined up the shot. He could not see the head or feet—only the thug's torso and hip area. Knowing the thug was wearing body armor, the shot would have to be in the lower portion. The hip gave him the best chance of success, but at 400 meters the target was small; effectively, about an 8-inch diameter. He checked the wind and it seemed calm. Nate took a cleansing breath and released it slowly to a hold. The reticle seemed stable and the crosshairs were steady. He took another breath and did the same thing; this time applying metered pressure to the trigger. The Sako reported its presence, but the supersonic bullet would leave it behind as it traveled to the target. The rifle rocked back into Nate's shoulder and climbed slightly, but returned in time to allow Nate to view his prey through the scope as the bullet struck home. The impact clearly had a dramatic effect; the thug rolled over and off the small ledge where he had been perched. The AR-10 previously brandished, was still on the ledge above him. Nate actuated the bolt and stripped another round into the chamber. He could see the thug reeling and trying to return to his weapon, but it was no use—the bullet had traveled through both joints and left his legs unusable. Nate trained the Sako on the AR now—resting precariously on the ledge. He aimed slightly below the weapon to take advantage of the skip-shot effect. The Sako rocked again. The bullet struck the rock and skipped into the weapon's lower receiver, near the magazine well. Nate was pleased to see the weapon fly off the ledge and spin well below and to the right of the thug. There would be no getting the weapon now and it was very likely damaged. Nate relaxed slightly—he had won. Now, the smart thing to do was wait and let the thug bleed out. But, that's not what he wanted to do.

This was a man who, like himself, had served his country. Though, at some point that changed. Nate understood only feelings of patriotism, but the thug had made a decision to serve a tyrant—why? It angered him and it was the reason he chose to destroy the AR rather than finish the thug with a second shot. This man—this traitor—had shot his best friend and may have even killed him. Nate wanted the thug to suffer—to know he had been beaten—to know that Nate coming to finish the job.

Nate made his way down to the thug, careful to approach from a slight ridge. The thug was probably carrying a sidearm. He got close enough to see the man and made a half-circle around him; coming up from behind his head. As he walked up he could see there was no sidearm and the thug had his arms laid out away from his body. His breathing was heavy and death was close. Nate had seen it many times before. It would only be a few moments now. As Nate moved into view, the thug's eyes tracked his movement. The AR at the ready, Nate surveyed the damage—the hips were buckled in a grotesque way and blood was draining from a hole in his side. The thug said nothing as Nate could see his eyes start to close. There would be no parting statement—no eulogy. Nate thrust the AR above his head and wailed loudly; shaking the weapon into the night sky. The thug's eyes opened widely in fear, jolted from death's grasp. Nate immediately lowered the weapon to his shoulder and fired twice into the man's face.

It was a good death.

David parked the AATREC about two blocks from the hospital after dropping Mad Dog off around the corner from the entrance. Mad Dog surveilled the area for several minutes while David made his way back. Satisfied there was no one watching the hospital; they went in. There was lighting inside, but not to levels previously used when commercial power was available. David heard the generator running earlier as he made his way to meet Mad Dog. There were two nurses at the station in the emergency room. The waiting room was full and most were sleeping.

"Ma'am, we're looking for a friend that may have come in here about an hour ago with a significant injury…" Mad Dog began.

The nurse looked at Mad Dog and then at the pistol strapped to his side. "Are you the man that shot Drew?" she asked, clearly upset.

"What? No…he's my friend." Mad Dog said emphatically. "Why would I come here if I shot him?"

"Duh; to finish the job?" she replied forcefully. This was no ordinary nurse—this one had moxie! Mad Dog admired that—that and the fact that she seemed to have no fear of him. He glanced down at her name tag.

"Look, Phyllis...can I call you Phyllis? Ask Nate who we are...he'll vouch for us." Mad Dog pleaded a bit, which was not his style. David found it amusing. The woman was about Madison's age and must have been striking as a young woman—and she wasn't bad now. No ring on the finger, either.

"Nate...Nate Alchesay?" she queried, "He's not here...was he in the fight too?"

Mad Dog was confused. Where was Nate? If he didn't drive the wrecker, then who did? The gears began to turn in his head and he thought about the tracks leading from all the brass where the suppressor had been. The boot prints had been different, he just didn't put it together until now. It wasn't two thugs escaping—Nate had gone after the last thug.

"Well, who brought Drew in, then?" Mad Dog knew in his mind as the question left his tongue—Roxy. "Wait...is Roxy here?" A few of the patients started to stir from sleep now and the nurse took notice. Deciding to trust the men, she motioned for them to go around the nurses' station and down the hall. She met them there.

"Look, I don't know who you are, but I've known Drew since he was a boy delivering newspapers to my house. Why do you want him?" She was not about to back down without a legitimate answer. "The only reason I don't call the police right now is because you tried to warn us about the terrorist attack and I don't trust this president!"

Mad Dog was speechless. She had recognized him from the television station take-over. While he was trying to muster up a response, David took over.

"Ma'am, we really are friends of Drew and Nate...I don't know Roxy very well except she helped me in the library, but we'd really like to know how he's doing. Can you at least tell us that?" David was pleading now, too.

"Phyllis, he's asking for water...can he have it yet?" Roxy said, having walked up from behind them. She looked at David. "He's asking for you guys, too. Though, I wish he'd never met you!"

Ross put the last five gallons of gas in the car from the can in the trunk. He sighed, thinking about the process he was going to have to repeat if they were to keep going. It didn't please him.

"So, another rental car place?" Kate asked.

"No, I doubt we'd find one out here." Ross answered, "Just going to have to find some cars in a parking lot…Walmart or something."

"Hey, there's a lumber yard over there." Hallie spoke up, point out the window.

"Yeah, that might work." Ross agreed. "That delivery truck might burn gas instead of diesel…let's check it out. Drop me off in front of the gate."

Kate dropped him off and drove away to a safe distance and waited. Ross slid under the sliding gate and over to the truck. It had a big fuel tank on the side. Ross screwed the cap off and took a sniff—it was gas! He motioned for the girls to bring the gas can back. It was too fat to slide under the gate, so they had to throw it over the fence. It took six tries! Ross went up to the window of the building and looked inside—pitch black. He went around the back and found a small window that looked out over the lumber yard. It was probably used by the manager to see the operation. Ross picked up a cinder block that had been used to prop the rear door open and whacked the glass. It bounced off—Plexiglas. He hit it again, this time much harder and it split in the middle. Once more, and this time a triangular piece the size of a road cone pushed in. It took several more times before he could remove enough glass to gain entrance. Once in, he used the red LED on his headlamp to make his way around before finally finding rolls of tube hose. He selected the one that looked like it was used for a kitchen sink sprayer. Rolling several feet off the roll, he cut the hose. As he made his way out, he noticed several sizes of bolt cutters. Grabbing one, he made his way to the broken window, but not before hearing a familiar sound—and it wasn't pleasant.

The growl came from behind a stack of fiberglass insulation and judging by the low deep sound, it was a lot bigger than a Chihuahua! Ross ran for the window and threw the hose and bolt cutters through it. Then, he dove through himself and rolled into the lumber yard. The dog followed. Ross ran to a pile of stacked 2 by 4s and jumped on top of them. The dog tried several times, but could not get up, so he ran around to the other side. Ross took the opportunity to jump off the pile and run for the front of the building. He only got half way there before the dog closed the distance and pinned him against the wall.

"Where do you think he went?" Hallie asked; concern in her voice.

"I don't know," Kate moaned, "This is no way to travel. I need a shower and a good bed!"

"Me too! I know I stink...but not as bad as if I swam in gasoline." Hallie joked. They both laughed.

"He's been gone over 20 minutes...do you think we should check on him?" Kate said, as she opened the door.

Suddenly, they saw movement from around the building; it was Ross...and a dog! Ross would stop every so many feet and scratch the dog's ears, which the canine seemed to enjoy. He went to the truck, screwed off the cap to the gas tank and used the hose to siphon fuel into the 5-gallon can. Then, he sat on the side-step of the truck and scratched the dog's ears while the can filled. He waved at the girls.

When the can was filled, he went to the gate and used the bolt cutters to cut the lock and slid the gate open just enough to get himself and the can through. The dog tried to get through, but Ross blocked him. As he made his way to the car with the can, the dog began to bark loudly. He dropped the can and trotted back to the gate. Ross opened the gate and let the dog out, who seemed quite content to be near Ross's side.

"Who is this?" Kate said, scratching the dog's ears. She examined the animal for a few seconds. "I'm guessing half Rottweiler and half Australian Shepard."

"Yeah," Ross agreed. "That's what I thought too. His name is Blue."

Kate laughed. "He told you his name?"

"Well, in a manner of speaking…he had me pinned up against the building and was going to eat me. I knew if I could sound like I knew who he was, he might change his mind. He looked like a 'Blue' so I called him Blue. He just sat down and just looked at me, so…he's Blue!"

Ross made several more trips to the truck with the gas can, then he disappeared back into the building again and came back out with another 5 gallon gas can and two big 40 pound bags of dog food. He filled the cans and put them in the trunk along with the dog food. The girls just looked at Ross for a few moments before Kate finally said something.

"Whatever."

"How you feeling, gunfighter?" Mad Dog said, pointing to the bandaged shoulder.

"Feel like I got hit by a truck…kinda weak." Drew managed to get out.

"Think you can travel?" David asked.

"He's not going anywhere! He'll be in here at least a week." Phyllis objected.

Drew turned his head to face Phyllis. "No, he's right, Ms. Phyllis. If I don't get out of here, the guys that did this to me will come with more next time. We have to go."

Phyllis shook her head. "It's not safe. You have to be monitored for infection and that drain tube has to be removed later…" she paused to look at Mad Dog's leg. "And this one…who knows what he's got going on under that hack job of a bandage?"

"Madam, I take exception to what is clearly a work of pure genius." Mad Dog responded.

226

"Oh yeah, you're all geniuses…a bunch of rocket scientists! I can see that." She rolled her eyes and sighed. "Alright, well then…you!" She pointed to Mad Dog, "…get into Trauma Two and take your pants off. I'll see what I can do." Mad Dog popped a respectable salute and limped behind the curtain. "And you!" She pointed at David. "You got anything going on?" He lifted up his shirt to show the severe bruising and then raised his arms and tilted his head back to show the spalling damage. "Of course…I expected no less. I'll get Sally back here to help. The doctor went home to check on his family. He'll be back in about 45 minutes. You'll need to be gone before he gets back, he voted for POTUS…twice!"

"Bronco, Bronco, this is Cardinal; how copy?" Still no response from the walkie-talkie. Landon was worried.

"Maybe you should buzz the airport one more time." Carrie suggested.

"We are extremely low on fuel, babe. I need to have enough to line up on the interstate and land." He responded. Landon banked the Seminole away from Horsetooth Reservoir and toward Cheyenne. He would follow I-25 North until he was essentially out of fuel; then land and abandon the aircraft. They would be on foot after that—a scenario Landon hoped to avoid.

"Wait!" Carrie cried. "The airport…somebody is flashing their headlights!"

Landon continued the turn until he could see the airport. There *was* someone flashing their lights—it had to be Derek. The pick-up truck was on the northwestern end of the taxiway and his lights were streaming to the southeast. Landon continued his turn directly to the south, then turned east to extend for his downwind. He tried the radio again.

"Bronco, Bronco, this is Cardinal; how copy?" Nothing. Landon slowed the aircraft, brought the flaps to 50% and dropped the gear. They would only get one shot at this, then it would have to be the interstate.

"Cardinal…" The walkie-talkie crackled. "Card…"

"Bronco, this is Cardinal…" Landon replied, but again no response. "Pieces of crap! I should have gotten a better set!"

Landon dropped walkie-talkie in Carrie's lap and brought the flaps to 100%. The moon was slightly behind him and that helped, but it was dark and the buildings that lined the taxiway to his left were barely visible at this point. He turned the landing and taxi lights on, but they wouldn't be much help until he was nearly on the ground. Derek still had the lights on and it would become an issue soon, as they were directly in Landon's eyes.

"Babe, maybe he can hear better than he can transmit…tell him to turn off the lights." Landon directed.

"Cardinal…I mean Bronco…turn off your lights." She transmitted.

A few seconds later the lights were off. Landon could make out the outline of the buildings and picked an aim point. He slowed the aircraft as much as he dared. The end of the taxiway came into view and Landon made the correction to line up. Touchdown was only moments later. He chopped the throttle and got on the binders. They had plenty of room and actually had to increase power to make it to where Derek and his pick-up truck waited for them. He turned the Seminole around to face back down the taxiway for take-off. Then, he shut everything down and gave a big sigh of relief. As Landon got out, Derek was backing the pick-up to the tail of the plane and stopped. Landon noticed a bunch of 5-gallon gas cans in the bed of the truck. It made him smile; *this might actually work out*, he thought.

"Greetings!" Derek exclaimed, "Welcome to Fort Collins." Landon jumped off the wing and hugged his old friend. Carrie was close behind and Karen joined in as well. There were brief interactions before Derek brought focus to the group. "We need to hurry. There's a bunch of idiots riding around in the backs of pick-ups, claiming to be a security force to protect the city. In reality, their just a bunch of kids with guns from Fossil Ridge High School. I saw them earlier going up and down I-25, but it's likely they heard the plane."

With that, they offloaded the gas cans and started refueling the Seminole over both wings. Karen loaded their backpacks and food. On her last trip, she showed Landon a special cargo.

"Hope we have room for these." She said, smiling. "Derek broke into the Horse & Dragon Brewing Company—right over there—and filled a couple of growlers." She pointed to a building near the taxiway.

"Cool!" Landon said, smiling back "We'll make room." He called over to the other wing where Derek was, "Hey, where did you get this fuel?"

"From the Loveland Airport a few days ago…this stuff ain't cheap and at first they didn't want to sell it to me. I told them I was using it for my race car…high octane."

"You got a race car?" Landon asked.

"No…but they don't know that. There's right at 100 gallons here…that enough?"

"Should be…only holds 105."

Derek dumped the last of his cans into the wing and made his way to the other wing to help Landon, who was nearly done also. Seeing that, he went back to the pick-up to move it off the taxiway. Landon heard the truck fire up and wondered what Derek was doing. The truck moved off the taxiway and parked near the last building on North Link Lane. Landon looked at Karen quizzically.

"Oh," she said, "he thought maybe someday he might be able to get his truck…if this all blows over. You know how he is with that truck."

"Headlights!" Carrie cried, "Coming from over there!" She pointed to the north.

Two pick-ups were coming south on Lemay avenue toward the airport at a fairly high rate of speed. Landon motioned to the girls to get in the Seminole. He turned to look at Derek who was running back to the truck.

"Derek; forget whatever it is…we gotta go!" Landon yelled as he jumped into the seat of the plane. The left engine started, then the right. He looked back through the windows to see Derek slam the truck door and start running back toward the Seminole. He was carrying what looked like a rifle.

The pick-ups turned east on Vine and had cleared a line of houses to their south. As they raced across an open field, they saw Derek running with the gun and somebody fired at him. Derek looked at the racing vehicles and then at the distance he would need to cover to get to the aircraft. It was clear he would not make it in time. More shots came from the pick-up. Derek dropped to his knee and repeatedly fired back, aiming at the driver's side of the first truck. The truck swerved hard to the left and rolled. Derek watched as bodies flew like confetti out of the bed of the truck. A cloud of dust and dirt ensued as it came to a stop on its side. The second truck swerved to the right to avoid the first one and popped through the dust cloud in front of Derek. Landon watched in horror as the boys bailed from the truck and began firing. Derek gave as good as he got, but it wouldn't be enough.

"Help him!" Karen cried as she tried to push past Landon.

Carrie pulled her back as they watched the boys surround Derek's body and continue firing into him. One began firing at the Seminole and Landon heard several rounds strike the aft fuselage.

"We gotta go!" Landon yelled, as he shut the door and advanced the throttles. The aircraft rolled forward in what seemed like a snail's pace. Two more rounds hit the top of the nose cowl in front of Landon. As they raced down the taxiway, Landon saw the lights of two police cars going west on Vine toward the skirmish. He hoped they would jail the boys and throw away the key. Karen was crying uncontrollably and Carrie was trying to console her. The Seminole got to the end of the taxiway just as they reached take-off speed. He rotated the aircraft and it responded faithfully. Everything in him wanted to go back and fly over the field, but he knew it wasn't a good idea. In his mind, he kept seeing the scene of the boys pumping rounds into his friend—he couldn't shake it. He was furious and sick to his stomach at the same time. He looked over at the seat his that friend was supposed to be in;

there were the two growlers of beer. He felt tears well up in his eyes and a lump form in his throat. They had known each other virtually all their lives, and now Derek was gone. The small twin turned northward as the sun began to break the darkness—twilight. Landon looked back over his shoulder at Fort Collins, "Thanks, Derek." He said to himself, "I'll never forget what you've done, my friend…I'll never forget."

CHAPTER 18

"1-19. The term dislocated civilian is a broad term that includes a displaced person, an evacuee, an expellee, an internally displaced person, a migrant, a refugee, or a stateless person. (JP 3-57) DCs are individuals who leave their homes for various reasons, such as an armed conflict or a natural disaster..." -FM 3-39.40 Interment and Resettlement Operations (U. S Army Field Manual), dated February 2010.

"Dog fart!!!" Hallie cried out.

"Aww, jeez…not again! What did you eat, Blue???" Ross covered his nose.

"What were you thinking, Ross?" Kate blurted. "A dog, really? What happens when those two bags of food run out? What's he going to eat then, huh?"

"You." Ross quipped. "Well, no…I guess that's not a good idea."

"Why, because I'm too sweet?" Kate said, trying to be witty.

"No," he fired back, "because it would undoubtedly make his farts smell worse!"

They all broke out laughing and Blue started barking; not wanting to be left out. He was just happy to be there. Hallie was normally afraid of dogs, especially big ones, but Blue had won her over. They sat in the back seat together and had become fast friends. Hallie scratched his ears a lot, and she let him rest his head on her lap.

"Coming up on Logansport." Kate said, reading the sign. "What do we want to do? I know we still have the two gas cans in the back, but the fuel light just came on."

"Okay, go ahead and pull over before we get into the town. I want to have a full tank in case we gotta run." That'll get us to the middle of an Iowa cornfield before we need more."

"Sounds like a plan, Stan." Kate responded. "I have an aunt and uncle in Papillion, Nebraska. I think I remember how to get there. Maybe rest a day?"

"I don't know, Kate." He said, "Everyday this thing goes longer it will get worse, especially if we're in populated areas like Omaha. Were you close to them?"

"Oh, no...not really. We don't have to stop, I just thought if you guys wanted to..."

They continued on for a couple hours and had not seen any traffic for some time, when they came up on a tanker truck on the side of the road. Ross had Kate slow down, drive past it and pull over. They watched it for several minutes before Ross decided to check it out. The girls watched closely as he climbed up on the driver's side of the cab and looked in. He tried the door—it was locked. He got down and looked under the rig to see if maybe the driver was working on it. Then finally, he yelled to ask if anybody needed help. Nothing.

"What's he doing?" Hallie asked.

"Not sure..." Kate replied, "...maybe he thinks we can get some gas?"

The girls watched him climb up the ladder to the top of the tank, then back down again. He motioned for Kate to back up toward the truck. After she did, Ross got the gas cans, the siphon hose, and the bolt cutters from the trunk. He climbed back up on the truck and used the bolt cutters to get the lock off the hatch. He lifted the lid of the first tank and stuck his head partially in. Then, he lowered it again and went to the second lid and did the same thing. This time he seemed to be pleased with the findings. Ross ran back to the car, got the coffee can, and got back on top. They watched as he dipped the can into the tanker and poured the contents into the 5-gallon gas can. Then, he poured it into the tank of the car. After he repeated it, the car was full and he filled the first can back up. While he was filling the second one, a car pulled up behind the tanker and the driver got out.

"You broke down?" the man said, thinking Ross was the tanker driver.

"No, just getting some fuel…need any?"

"Sure! If you don't mind. All the pumps in town won't work without power. I was trying to get to my daughter's house in Peoria. I have money." The man still didn't know the circumstances.

Ross slid off the tanker and put the final gas can in the trunk. Then, he ran back and handed the driver his coffee can. "Help yourself." The driver just stood there like a spring calf looking at his first prairie dog. Ross trotted back to the car, got in, and waved as Kate drove off. The man never said a word.

"I don't know what's worse, you smelling like gasoline, or that dog's farts!" Kate complained.

"Well, at least both have something in common," Ross said.

"How's that?" Kate asked.

"Yeah, you can light 'em both!"

Phyllis might have been a nurse, but she had the skills of a surgeon. Mad Dog watched as she irrigated the wound on his leg and sewed him up. Then, she dressed the wound and handed him a bottle of antibiotics.

"Thanks, doc." Mad Dog said, trying to be coy. She merely waved her arm as she went into the next trauma bay where David was waiting. Mad Dog really liked her. His wife had passed on several years earlier and while he was lonely at times, he never really met anyone that made his head turn enough to want another 'noose around his neck.' He slid carefully off the examination table and made his way to David's bay. Phyllis was taping David's ribs. David saw Mad Dog coming up behind her and timed his question appropriately.

"Ms. Phyllis, you should come with us."

"Where we going, honey?" she responded, not even caring to look up. David grinned at Mad Dog.

234

"To the redoubt—a place to start fresh. It's remote, we have food and water there and everything we need to grow and maintain our existence." David sounded like a salesman.

"And leave all this?" She replied, smiling at David. "Aww honey, I appreciate it, but they're gonna need a lot of help around here soon. Especially with the outbreak."

"Outbreak? What outbreak?" Mad Dog asked. She looked up at David then back to what she was doing.

"You guys been living under a rock? The Ebola epidemic…the one the terrorists dumped on us."

David and Mad Dog just stared at each other. The silence confirmed to Phyllis that they had no idea. She looked back up at both of them and shook her head, then told them about the POTUS emergency broadcast and what she'd heard through official channels.

"By now there are thousands of cases all across the United States. Even Billings has 38 reported…so far." She paused, and dropped her hands on David's leg to balance herself. "Who would do such a thing?" Clearly, she was overcome by emotion. Mad Dog took the opportunity to comfort her by placing his hand on her back. She immediately, stiffened and shook off the sentiment, continuing to work on David.

"Kindly remove that appendage or I will sever it at the elbow!" She threatened.

"Yes, ma'am." Mad Dog popped, and pulled his hand back.

"Scimitar." David said, "The second part…that must have been the second part of it."

Mad Dog nodded. "How bad is it?" He addressed the question to Phyllis.

"Well, from a professional point of view, it's really bad. The last we heard there were hundreds of reported cases in all the major cities. That pretty much equates to thousands of cases that aren't reported...and now that the power is off, there's no way of knowing...," she paused to look up at them, "...there's no way of knowing how many now. I'm not an expert at the CDC, but if I were to make an estimate, I'd say millions of people will succumb to the disease eventually. Those in the cities are essentially doomed—without food, water and proper hygiene they have no chance. There are already thousands who've escaped the cities to hide in the rural areas, and are infected but don't know it; they will infect others in those areas. If you want to get an idea of what life will be like, look back in historical Europe during the advent of the black plague."

The room was silent; nobody spoke. Phyllis just kept working on David's spalling injuries. David glanced at the clock on the wall; 6:30 am. It would be daylight outside. He thought about how they would need to avoid other people on their way to the redoubt. That made him think of his siblings—they had much longer distances to travel and therefore more opportunity to contract the deadly disease.

"So, I read this study awhile back. It was kind of a 'end of the world' thing." Phyllis continued. "It had to do with catastrophes on a national scale. The thrust of the study was to help the government prepare for and respond to various events. They brought experts from many different fields to contribute; the CDC, Federal Reserve, Department of Energy, the military, etcetera. The idea was to identify preparations that could be made in advance, as well as result in creating 'pre-canned plans' that could be executed quickly in response to the events. Some of the events were pandemics, super storms, solar storms, economic collapse, civil unrest, and loss of the power grid..." She paused to concentrate on a piece of stubborn copper embedded in David's neck. She finally got a hold of it with a hemostat and plucked it out. David winced, but made no sound. She continued, "The interesting thing about this symposium of experts was that they found no matter what the event was, it would eventually result in loss of the power grid—and from there, all responses or plans would mostly be the same. So, if they planned for a worst case scenario of the grid loss, they would have most of the bases covered."

"I know this study," Mad Dog chimed in, "…I've quoted it several times. Even the Speaker of the House…uhh Newt Gingrich, briefed part of it to the House of Representatives. There was an initial interest, but of course like everything else it just fell by the wayside."

Phyllis nodded. "There was one particular part of the study that jumped out at me though; that being the effect of converging events— two or more that debuted simultaneously. In the case of severe pandemic paired with grid loss, the result would be a total killer…or in this case, a national killer—no chance of recovery."

"Our ISIS friends obviously took the study very seriously," David responded, "…our own government, did not."

"Well, yes…in a manner of speaking. The government plan was not to prevent the events, it was to respond to them. The cattle have left the barn, now we close the door and round them all up." She said.

"FEMA camps." Mad Dog added.

"Yes." She acknowledged, looking at him. "I went to some special training awhile back. It was to help set up and staff one of these camps. My expertise was, of course, in the medical field. There's a facility not far from here; it's a warehouse full of supplies and materials for the construction of a camp. Under the direction of FEMA and Homeland Security, we 'augmentees'—with the help of the National Guard—are supposed to establish the camp on a pre-determined parcel of land."

"When will they do that?" Roxy said, having come from Drew's room minutes earlier.

"They've already started. We were activated just prior to POTUS speech. I was supposed to go last night."

"Nothing but a damn internment camp!" Mad Dog grumbled.

"Yes…," Phyllis agreed, "it is exactly that. In addition to food and medical supplies, they also contain razor wire, chain-link fence, and burial vaults for mass graves. These facilities were confirmed under a House of Representative's resolution, referred to as H. R. 645, and are focused on providing aid to refugees under a humanitarian premise during disasters. I cannot fault the concept—it is a good idea to have these available. I do not believe in the conspiracy theory that they were created solely for the ominous purpose of interning American citizens for political control, but I don't discount the fact that a tyrannical President could use them for such a purpose. Like anything; good ideas, concepts, and inventions can be twisted for evil. I volunteered for this training as I believed it to be a good thing…and I still do. However, based on your assertions that were broadcast all over the country," she looked at Mad Dog now, "I fear they will, in fact, be used for purposes other than intended."

"Then, you need to come with us, Ms. Phyllis." Drew spoke, now standing in the back of the room with his clothes on. She shook her head.

"I'm better served here." She said.

"No!" Mad Dog exclaimed. "You are not!"

She turned to glare at the warrior, but did not see a flirting old man as was her previous experience. Instead, she was confronted by the face of a very serious and determined patriot. On the tip of her tongue waited the delivery of a curt response, but she held back to hear what he would say.

"You will die and your death will mean nothing. You will make no difference; save to possibly extend the life of a mere few who will eventually succumb to the same horrible end."

"You don't know that!" she fired back.

"I do know that!" He retorted. "The only survivors of this attack are those that planned to survive it—there will be pockets of them all over the United States—clans—that will need skills like yours to rebuild the country. Why would you stay here and waste a vital skill serving a futile few, when you could be making a difference in the lives of many?" Her eyes darted over his face. She could see the passion in his plea and she began to tear up. "Phyllis; your knowledge and abilities could be used—to not only care for these survivors—but to train

238

others to do the same. There will be no schools, no universities, and no teachers to pass these skills on to others, do you see?"

She turned her head away. "I can't...I...I just can't. This is where I belong."

"Nice speech." Everyone turned around to see the doctor standing in the back of the room. "Who are you people?" The doctor scanned their faces and came to rest on Mad Dog. He frowned. "I know who you are...if it wasn't for you, we would not be dying as a country!" He glanced down at the pistol strapped to Mad Dog's hip. "You need to leave...all of you! And, you can be assured the authorities will be notified as soon as possible." He turned and went to the reception area.

"You better go." Phyllis said hastily. "Here," she said reaching into a cabinet. "I put together some things you might need." It was a bag full of medical supplies, medications, and drugs. "Take it...and go, please."

"How about I just shoot him!" David said angrily.

"No, as much of a douche as he is," she said, "He's needed here...badly...as am I."

Drew hugged Phyllis and then they left. Mad Dog looked back once. Phyllis was holding the hand of a little girl and asking questions about her bandaged arm. He felt loss, though he hardly knew her. She was a very special woman. Very special.

"Anybody smell oranges?" Ross asked.

"Dog fart!" Hallie squealed.

"Hmmm, I don't think so," Kate said, looking sideways at Ross, "That one has a different odor."

"Ross!" Hallie barked, punching him in the shoulder.

Ross grinned impishly. Everybody loves the smell of oranges. Clearly, he had asked the question to ensure his victims would draw deeply though their nostrils and get a significant portion of his offensive concoction; thereby satisfying his intent to assault their olfactory senses. It worked on everyone except Blue, who seemed rather interested in the aroma and its source. The effect of the noxious gas was amplified by Ross' deliberate disabling of the window circuits by way of the lock-out switch. There would be no escape. Ross wouldn't stop laughing and the girls wouldn't stop beating on his back and arm. Bizarre humor had always existed in the Wallace family. In addition to finding pleasure in the discomfort others, observing one's behavior after being scared nearly to death or injured as a result of their own folly—also ranked high on the list.

"You need to control him!" Kate exclaimed to Hallie. "That's ridiculous! I mean, who does that???"

"Me." Ross said, simply. He had chosen his assault for when it was his turn to drive, thereby giving him sole access to the lockout switch.

Ross had intended to avoid Peoria by traveling south through Macomb. He wanted to cross the Mississippi River into Iowa in a rural area as his father had prompted him to do. Keokuk was his best bet. As they approached the river bridge they could see a roadblock on the Iowa side.

"Hi, is there a problem?" Ross said, in a friendly voice. The men at the block were dressed in a mixture of military garb, except for two policemen leaning on their patrol car.

"Yeah, you can't come here. This area is quarantined." The man said, maintaining distance from the car. "You'll have to turn around. Go north, to Fort Madison."

Ross surveyed the situation. This was not a quarantine to keep the infected in, it was to keep the potentially infected out. "Look, sir. We're not sick…or infected, okay? And we don't want to stop in your town. We just want to pass through—non-stop."

The man stepped back further and slightly raised his AR-15, but not quite to a firing position. The move caught the attention of the two police officers, who were now moving slowly toward Ross and the girls. "Whoa, whoa, whoa…hey we aren't a problem for you, okay?" Ross pleaded.

The first policeman spoke as he placed his hand on the pistol in his holster. "What's your business here?" he said firmly. Ross raised his hands and placed them on the open window ledge and pushed them out to demonstrate he had no harmful intentions.

"Sir, we've been traveling for a long time and like most people we have minimal fuel to get where we're going—which is to see my family in Montana. We don't want to stop in your town…we just want to cross the Mississippi and keep going. You're man here told us to go to Fort Madison, but they have the bridge blocked there too." He lied. He really didn't know if that were true, but felt like there was a reasonable chance these men didn't know it to be untrue. "I don't want any trouble; I just want to pass…please." Ross continued after they didn't say anything. "I mean…you could escort us across and out of town…we just want to be with our family." The cop looked at his partner and gave a quick nod.

"Jake; escort these people across the 7th Street Bridge into Missouri. Tell the boys on the bridge that they are not to come back over." The second cop started toward the patrol car. "Jake will take you to the 7th Street Bridge. From there you'll cross over the Des Moines River into Missouri…That's the best we can do." He looked into the back seat and saw Blue and cracked a smile. "He eat much?"

"All he can!" Hallie answered.

The cop addressed Ross again. "Son, if your intentions are anything other than what you said and you try to get into the town, you'll find we can be very inhospitable. All roads are blocked; into and out of Keokuk."

Ross surprised the cop with his response. "Probably a good thing to do, sir. In times like these we have to protect our own—it's the only chance this nation has under the circumstances. I hold no blame." The cop stood upright and motioned them through the blockade. It was a short distance to the 7th Street Bridge. Ross had planned on crossing into Iowa, but he'd just have to make adjustments otherwise.

After they crossed into Missouri, Ross drove a couple of miles and pulled over. He pulled out a map and assessed the town of Keokuk. It was essentially a peninsula between two rivers with only two medium sized roads coming into it. Those appeared to be easily controlled. Smart.

"Looks like we change our route a little bit. We'll just run south of Iowa along the border and then cross into Nebraska somewhere…maybe Rockport. Then, stay well south of Lincoln, Nebraska and turn north into South Dakota." The girls nodded. If we get any further than that, we're going to need more gas, though. Keep your eyes open for opportunities."

Ross wondered about Keokuk and other communities like it. Was this the way things would be in America? How many more times would they encounter this type of protective posture? He knew things would only get more difficult as the days passed. Soon, he knew people would begin taking from each other out of desperation and he wanted to be at the redoubt by then.

"Come on, gimpy!" David joked with Mad Dog as they made the two block trek to the AATREC. David wanted to get the vehicle and return to the hospital to pick up Mad Dog and Drew, but Mad Dog didn't want the doctor to see them get into the camper. It made sense, but it was also taking a long time to get the two wounded men down the street. Occasionally, David would see a curtain slide open and see faces watch them, but other than that, no one was around. He was glad there was no phone service.

After a few more minutes, they got to the AATREC. It took another 10 minutes to get Drew and Mad Dog settled into the vehicle. Mad Dog insisted on sitting up front with David, but David didn't think it was a good idea if they came on a roadblock. After all, he was the only one wearing a uniform. Mad Dog finally conceded the point and got in the back.

"Where to, boss?" David asked.

Drew responded before anyone else could. "We gotta find Nate." They all nodded in agreement. This meant they would have to head back toward the shop. That would be risky. David fired up the AATREC and put it in gear. Starting forward he immediately slammed on the brakes. Mad Dog rolled out of his seat and onto the floor. "Kid, what the hell are you doing?" Mad Dog barked. David looked back at Mad Dog as he rolled the window down and leaned out to address someone.

"Change your mind?" David asked coyly. It was Phyllis, standing in the path of the big truck. She walked around to the door on the passenger side and got in. Mad Dog was grunting trying to get off the floor to view her through the pass-through window. "Can we swing by my house? I need to get a few things." She said. David put the big truck back in gear "Yes, ma'am. Just point me in the direction."

She turned and looked back into the camper compartment. "Now look, mister…we gotta get a few things straight." She said, addressing Mad Dog with a serious tone. "It's hands off until after we're married. After that we'll play it by ear. And, I like a man with personal hygiene habits as good as mine or better. I'm thinking we're going to have to work on *your* part of the deal."

"Married???" Mad Dog said surprised. "Who said anything about getting married? Madam, I'll have you know…" She cut him off. "Look, killer…I'm old and tired and I don't have time for any long courtships; though there will be one. I recognize a good man when I see him, though you will require some behavioral modifications, I'm sure. Are you saying 'no' to my proposition?" Mad Dog shook his head. "Good. It's settled then." And she turned back around and addressed David. "Just go up two blocks and turn right."

Mad Dog twisted back around and slid himself up onto the chair. Drew and Mad Dog just grinned at each other.

"I'll be damned," He said, "I've never seen the like."

"She's a good woman, MD…and I happen to know she was a good wife, too. She was my mom's best friend." Drew said. "She does have some flaws…obviously, she isn't a good judge of character."

Mad Dog was still speechless and didn't even try a retort. He wondered about why Phyllis changed her mind and decided to come with them. Was it what he said? He wanted to ask, but he was still in shock and pleased at the same time. They stopped at Phyllis's home and she gathered some clothes, toiletries and a Ruger .270 with ammo that her late husband had used to hunt. Other than that, it was very light. Mad Dog still didn't address her—he was actually a little timid, which surprised him. The feelings were much like when he was a kid in 5th grade and crushed on Selene Dyckman. He had all these feelings of infatuation but was too afraid to talk to her—it was like that with Phyllis. He felt clumsy. The feelings stayed with him until they turned on to the road toward the shop. At that point, they fell away and Mad Dog turned to all business mode.

As they continued down the road, David saw a lone figure walking toward them carrying three rifles of some kind; it was Nate, heading to town. The AATREC slowed and came to a stop next to him. Nate ran around to the right side of the camper and opened the door. It was then Mad Dog noticed the shaggy artifact hanging off Nate's hip. It was the thug's scalp.

"Son, you will not get in my vehicle with that on your person!" Mad Dog barked. "I saw that kind of medieval crap in 'Nam and I won't have it—idiots going off the deep end, thinking they're some kind of warrior!" Nate shrugged, turned and walked away toward the back of the AATREC. Drew called out to Nate, "Wait! I'm coming with you." He scowled at Mad Dog as he struggled to get up, but before he could get to his feet, Nate returned to the doorway—without the scalp. He looked at Mad Dog for assurance that he met the conditions to enter. Mad Dog still was not pleased, but motioned for Nate to get in. Nobody talked for a few minutes. Nate seemed fine with Mad Dog's request as if he'd only been asked to clean the mud off his shoes before entering a house. Everyone was upset; especially Mad Dog.

"Son, I'm sorry I got on you like that, but why would you do such a thing?"

"I don't know. Seemed like the thing to do at the time. I thought my best friend was dead."

"Oh my God…Nate…Nathan…Nathan Alchesay!" David exclaimed, "I didn't put it together until just now. You're Nathan Alchesay; *the Apache*." Mad Dog looked puzzled, David continued. "Wait, see…Nate here is a legend. They called him 'the Apache' in Afghanistan. He scalped the Taliban soldiers that he killed. It scared the life out of the hajis. No one in his unit said anything because the psychological effect it had on the Taliban was devastating. Even the intel types used it as leverage during interrogations…Dude, you're the Apache! That blows my mind."

"Yeah, well it worked for a while until the politicians got wind of it." Drew weighed in. "A court martial was to be in Nate's future, but the White Mountain Apache tribe started a campaign to help him and the current administration didn't want the publicity. So, Nate got an Article 15 and was made to promise not to scalp people. They made him go to a shrink twice a week for a couple of months and basically passed off the whole thing as 'stress under war' being the real culprit. Nate here, was just a victim of war." Nate grinned, but didn't say anything.

"Damn, that's just wrong, Nate." Mad Dog shook his head. Nate still grinned, not knowing what to say.

"It might be wrong, but it isn't the same thing as what you experienced in 'Nam." Drew stuck up for his friend. "Nate wasn't some fruit bat who went off the deep end; what he did had real significance based on what his grandfather conveyed to him. I don't like it either, and I wasn't pleased to see the practice return, but I think we can give him a pass under the circumstances…don't you?"

Mad Dog took a deep breath and sighed. "Son, just promise me you won't do that anymore, okay?" Nate's grin slowly faded and he nodded affirmatively. "Good...I'll get over it, but I don't think I'll ever understand it. We need to get you reading the Bible."

Drew spoke up, "Oh, Nate reads his Bible...everyday, right Nate?" Nate's grin returned, and he nodded.

The AATREC turned around and away from the shop, starting its journey to the redoubt. Had they tried to return to the shop they would have seen a Blackhawk helicopter sitting in the yard and a team of thugs combing the premises. Instead, they headed up Highway 78 toward Absarokee, Columbus, and then west on I-90. They passed through several roadblocks with a mere wave; the Army National Guard ruse worked like a champ. However, just outside Livingston at the junction of I-90 and Highway 89, they ran into a checkpoint where an overzealous private would take note of strange circumstances.

"Hey, how's it going?" David said, looking down at the private from the cab of the AATREC. "ID please," was his only response. The private looked over the ID with scrutiny, he noticed the Air Force uniform. "Why are you driving an Army vehicle, Staff Sergeant?" the private asked. "I'm a TACP...a JTAC." David responded. The private didn't know what that meant, so he called over his staff sergeant. "Jack, this guy says he's an Air Force TACP, but he's driving an Army vehicle. I'm not sure what that means, but it seems a little odd to me." The staff sergeant smirked. "Well, he might as well be in the Army, because TACP's are embedded in the Army. They call in airstrikes and artillery for us. They're badass, Jimmy." He looked up at David and smiled. "Do your inspection and let 'em go." The private walked around the AATREC and used his mirror on a pole to check under the vehicle several times. When he got to the back, he noticed something peculiar hanging from the trailer ball and wondered of its significance. Obviously, it had been placed there on purpose. He continued his walk-around until he was back at the front and facing David. "Have a good one," he said, motioning David on.

As the AATREC pulled forward, the private pointed at the trailer ball. "Hey, Jack...why would they hang a piece of roadkill fur on the back of their truck?"

"I don't know, Jimmy…must be an Air Force thing."

CHAPTER 19

"Before a standing army can rule, the people must be disarmed; as they are in almost every kingdom in Europe. The supreme power in America cannot enforce unjust laws by the sword; because the whole of the people are armed, and constitute a force superior to any bands of regular troops that can be, on any pretense, raised in the United States."— Noah Webster, "An Examination into the leading Principles of the Federal Constitution." in Paul Ford, ed., Pamphlets on the Constitution of the United States , at 56 (New York, 1888).

"Whenever governments mean to invade the rights and liberties of the people, they always attempt to destroy the militia, in order to raise an army upon their ruins."— Rep. Elbridge Gerry of Massachusetts, spoken during floor debate over the Second Amendment, I Annals of Congress at 750, August 17, 1789.

Mason awoke with a start, as a heavy truck rumbled past on Highway-40. It was daylight. He'd slept a lot longer than he'd wanted to. He glanced at Leigh and Tanner; they were still sleeping soundly. The truck was parked behind a grove of trees at the Cheyenne County fairgrounds in Cheyenne Wells, Colorado. Mason had almost left the road a few times when he drifted asleep at the wheel, so he stopped and hid the truck behind the trees next to a baseball diamond. The big trucked fired up, but his family only stirred a bit as he made his way to a little gas station and convenience store he'd seen earlier. It was called the Kwik Korner and was only a few hundred yards from where he'd parked for the night.

Pulling into the pumps, he noticed a 20-something guy sitting out in front of the building. "Hey, can I get some fuel?" Mason yelled to him. "No power, mister…pumps won't work." Mason jumped down out of the truck and walked over. "Well, what if I could get you power." The guy thought for a few seconds before he spoke. "I don't know. The owner isn't here right now." Mason smiled, and pitched his best salesman persona. "I'll tell you what…I got a generator on my truck over there, that I can run your pump with…if you let me fill up,

I'll fill your car too and pay for all of it." The guy stood up and seemed excited at the prospect. "Yeah? Well, how would you pay?" Mason hadn't thought of that, but knew what the guy wanted to hear. "Cash is king…I'll even float you a little tip, whadda ya say?" The guy nodded.

Mason swung the truck to the first pump and got out tools to open the housing. This made the guy nervous, but Mason assured him that he would put it all back together when he was complete. After about 15 minutes, Mason had the generator and pump running, but the guy was concerned that the electronic display wasn't working. "Say, what's your name?" Mason asked. "JC" the kid responded. "Well, JC…you see the display won't work anyway because it uses credit cards, see?" He pointed at the slot on the face of the pump. "Why don't you get your car over here and we'll get you filled up after I fill this truck?" JC went to get his car and Mason started filling the big truck. After a few minutes the truck was full and Mason filled the car. JC kept looking nervously down the road both ways. "Is there a problem?" Mason asked? "Well, I'm not sure the owner would be happy…we're closed 'cuz there ain't no power, and I didn't know the display on the pump wouldn't work. So, how do we know how much gas came out?" JC stammered. "Look, here's two hundred bucks. There's no way we used more than that." Mason gave him the cash. "Now, here's the deal…you can tell your boss about this or you can choose not to…that's up to you, because there's no record of the fuel ever leaving the tank….but you have two hundred bucks in your hand, a full tank of gas and that ought to make somebody happy, huh?" Mason started putting the pump housing back together. JC just stood and watched. When Mason finished, he patted JC on the shoulder and bid farewell. As they pulled away, Mason looked in the rearview mirror to see JC still standing by the pump with the money in his hand. He smiled and wondered what was going through the guy's mind.

"Hey, that was some expensive gas you just paid for!" Leigh contended. "You feeling rich these days?"

"Paper money is about as worthless as used toilet paper right now…I think JC is figuring that out." Mason said chuckling a bit. "But, he did get a tank of gas for his own car…If he was smart, he'd just keep his mouth shut." He smiled at Tanner playing in his mother's lap. "I almost offered him five hundred bucks, but I thought that would tip him off…at that point you could offer a wheel barrel full of money and he would have declined."

They headed north on 385 toward Julesburg. From there, they intersected 26 in Nebraska and would eventually have to cross over I-25, but it would be well away from populated areas. The good thing was that they avoided Denver, Fort Collins, and Cheyenne, Wyoming. Also, they certainly had enough fuel to make it to the redoubt, with surplus. If they had another opportunity to top off before they got there it would be nice, but not worth any kind of risk. What Mason had just done, did incur risk, but it had worked out this time.

"What's the little town near the redoubt?" Leigh asked.

"Neihart…Neihart, Montana." Mason answered. "Near the Lewis and Clark National Forest…population; 51." He smiled. "My kinda place, though it's still almost an hour from the redoubt."

"Will we get there today?" she asked.

"No, I don't think so…but certainly the day after." He replied. "I know you're anxious, but we gotta be smart about this…and safe. We have to take every little backroad we can to avoid trouble…cuz trouble is looking for us."

"You look tired, Landon." Carrie said, concerned.

"I'll be okay." He said, looking back at Karen. She hadn't said anything since they left Fort Collins.

"We're almost there…only about 50 more minutes, best I can tell." He said.

"Why? Doesn't the GPS tell you?"

"Yeah, but the GPS has been acting funny…it might have something to do with the power being out. The ground stations report variances to the satellites…and they should be working, but there must be something going on with the ephemeris data, because I'm getting readings that don't appear to be very accurate. Finding the White Sulfur Springs airport might be an issue. We may want to consider going to Livingston airport, which is on I-90 and easy to see. Then, we could follow highway 89 to White Sulphur."

"Okay, then let's do that. What's the problem?"

"Fuel…it's going to be tight." He sounded concerned, but she knew he was always conservative in his estimates.

"So, just land in Livingston then." She said, sounding confident.

"Yeah, we can...but that's about 140 miles from the redoubt and we'll be on foot." He raised his eyebrows. "Think you can handle that? With the gear we have to carry, that's about a two-week backpacking trip." He looked for her reaction. "And, there will be snow, probably."

"Oh…" she said, flatly. "…and from White Sulfur?"

"About 6 or 7 days hiking." He replied. She thought about it for a few minutes before responding.

"Come on, White Sulfur!" She pounded the console in true cheerleader style.

They continued on to Livingston and found the intersection of I-90 and HW-89. There seemed to be significant activity on the roadways. Cars were backed up from what appeared to be roadblocks. Landon turned north up HW-89 and glanced at the fuel situation. They would make it, but not by much. He thought about Derek and then Karen. It seemed like a bad dream.

About 20 minutes later, Landon visually picked up the airport at White Sulfur Springs. It was designated a military airport, but Landon didn't see how as it was just a single strip next to the road with a few buildings next to it. Not at all like an Air Force base or something larger. He wondered about its purpose. Still, he was landing there without permission and didn't know if anyone would be there.

"Okay, babe…we're descending…strap in." He warned. Landon turned on final and decided not to make a radio call. What was the point? There was a slight crosswind, but nothing significant. He lined up on an initial heading of 010 and proceeded. The approach and landing went without incident. Landon taxied up to the ramp and parked next to a Cessna Skyhawk and shut down. There were only two aircraft visible on the ramp—now three, with the Seminole.

They quickly got out and gathered their gear. No one came to see them and there was no movement anywhere near the buildings. Landon threw the keys into the plane on the seat and shut the door. They started hiking straight past the last building and down a taxiway to what was probably a run-up area. Still, no one seemed to be around, so they walked across the field to the intersection of HW-89 and Big Sky Lane. From there, they continued to a cemetery on the south end of a golf course, just outside town. Landon bent down to tie his shoe.

"You know, I think we should avoid contact in White Sulfur Springs altogether. Let's hang out in these trees until dark, then we'll cut northeast through those fields and circumvent the town. Smith River is just north of town with trees and stuff; we'll camp there and figure out what to do next." Landon was concerned that the Seminole would draw interest and since they were the only strangers in the area, it wouldn't take much to make an assumption. "I don't know if it's safe to walk the roads or not. What do you guys think?"

Karen didn't speak, she just stared out where Landon pointed across the fields, and nodded her head. Carrie was worried about her, but didn't know what to do about it. "Well, that sounds good. I'm hungry anyway. Let's just stay here and eat." They found a shady spot in the trees where they wouldn't be easily seen from the road. Landon glanced at the tombstone Carrie leaned against to eat her sandwich. It read, 'Peace on your journey to everlasting reward.' He hoped it was a sign of what was to come…

…it wasn't.

POTUS was uneasy. He had initially instituted a curfew, followed by an escalation to martial law and next he would essentially assert an Executive Order; 'National Defense Resources Preparedness.' He knew that while there hadn't been much fanfare when it was originally signed; there would be now—especially from the conservative right. Of particular concern would be the ambiguous nature of the document and his implied interpretation. No one really believed the country would get in a state of turmoil bad enough to execute the order. Therefore, there was no reason to risk significant political damage leveraged by implications of racism, homophobia, and unwillingness to conform to political correctness—a familiar weapon used by the left and mainstream media. He counted on the conservatives to place their desire for re-election over a patriotic stand to do what their constituents expected. POTUS would express a need to employ the order to 'redistribute' resources in this hour of need—certainly that would be for the greater good and insure all citizens' needs were met. However, the undertow of his intention was to suspend the constitutional government as it was written—in short, he would gradually take control of the country with his appointed cabinet members and suspend elections until stability was assured. However, this would require a delicate shift and timing would be critical. There was disappointment in his progress concerning gun control and he had hoped to be further along at this point. He wanted desperately to ban all guns, but like the implementation of the executive order, it would have to be gradual and pick up momentum. His military—even if loyal to him—would not be strong enough to overcome the gun-loving citizens of the nation.

POTUS' plan was simple; like the proverbial frog placed into a warm pot of water that was gradually heated to boiling, he would slowly disarm the civil militia. The current state of violence in the cities by looters and thugs would be leveraged, even though the vast majority of them acquired their weapons illegally under existing laws. The first step would be to get citizens to voluntarily give up their weapons through a program to reward them with food and provisions that had been 'redistributed' from 'hoarders.' Next, would be a mandatory surrender of guns over a set period of time, with a promise to return them to their owners once stability returned to the country. Those that resisted would be considered criminals and summarily treated as such—even unto their demise. Gun sales records with the names and addresses of those who purchased them would be seized from all vendors and loaded into a database. This database would then be compared to those who turned in their guns. After that, a methodical search for those that had not turned in their weapons would ensue. Of course, anyone who expected to have their guns returned would never see it realized—the weapons having been destroyed almost immediately after they were given up. Yes, it would be bloody and stories of carnage would be plentiful, but eventually the nation would heal and a new Constitution would debut—one he had already written.

These things would all come to pass and while they were a source of uneasiness, it was the more recent news of a potential military coup that upset him. An informant had apprised him that the Chairman of the Joint Chiefs had secretly approached the Joint Chiefs with concerns of Constitutional violation. POTUS was disappointed in the general and those that would listen to him. Careful manipulations of the military leadership over the last seven years had all but ensured those loyal to POTUS replaced the patriotic constituency. Somehow, he had misjudged the general—that was a major game changer and had to be reconciled soonest; before he pulled the trigger on the executive order.

Chairman of the Joint Chiefs, General Nader "Slim" Pickens sat at his desk, stunned at what he'd just heard. His best friend since the Air Force Academy, Major General Mike "Rocky" Bannon sat across the rather large desk from him, nodding affirmatively. It made Slim angry and somewhat apprehensive at the same time. Bannon had just told him of a spy on his staff, Colonel Bastogne, who had warned the President of plans to remove him from office in the event there was an egregious assault on the Constitution or the American people.

"Technically, he could have you tried for treason, but it's unlikely he would do so as the facts surfacing during the trial would present serious issues for POTUS—the real traitor." Bannon said, solemnly. "To be honest, that only leaves him with one option…"

"Yeah…I'm sure it would be made to look like an accident or a terrorist hit." Slim responded. "Rocky, we're going to have to reach back into the SOF community…" Slim referred to the Special Operations Forces where both he and Bannon had made their careers. "…and soon. I don't see POTUS waiting on this; I'll be in a casket before week's end. Who can we trust?"

"Outside of select friends in SOCOM, not anyone I'd stake my life on…or yours," Bannon smiled, "but, that's still a pretty big list. I think our problem goes away if POTUS goes away and right now that means we need evidence…proof. There are several Congressional members that make no secret of their disdain for POTUS and if we can get something tangible in their hands…something they can use to remove him from office; then we're in business. If not…" Bannon paused, frowning, "…then our only alternative is a coup, and I think that would not be good for the country."

"I agree, but I can't take it off the table…it's a last resort." Pickens reached into his bureau and produced two glasses and a bottle of Macallan 18 scotch; pouring a couple of fingers in each glass, he continued. "So, what do the congressmen want us to produce for them?"

"Well, they know POTUS has CIA sewn up…the Director is in his stable." Bannon stated flatly. "They want Madison and Wallace…if they're still alive…to testify, I would assume."

"The two characters that took over the TV station?" Pickens didn't wait for an answer. "Not likely they are alive at this point. I got word of a skirmish in Montana with 'agency thugs'—there were bodies involved, but it's all cleaned up by now, I'm sure."

"I don't know, Slim…if that were true, CIA wouldn't still be looking." Bannon smirked. "You know, both those 'characters' as you call them—are ours?" He made reference to the men being 'special' and waited for a reaction. Slim looked up. "What do you mean?" He was interested. Bannon took a sip of the amber liquid and answered, "I mean, Madison was a Green Beret..." Slim nodded affirmatively, "Yeah, I knew that." Bannon continued, "...and Wallace is active duty...an Air Force JTAC." Pickens was about to take a sip himself, but stopped to look at Bannon. "I called his unit yesterday—he's cream of the crop, one of their best. They had nothing but good to say about him...and they told me they didn't believe a word of POTUS' accusations. To date, they have not reported him AWOL or a deserter."

Slim sat down slowly, clearly interested. "Do they have contact with him?"

"No, unfortunately, but they put one of his friends on the line, who told me Wallace inherited some land in Montana and that he planned to live on it someday. It was supposed to be fairly remote—might be a place for him to hide. It's what I would do." Slim nodded, "Yeah, hell I'd do that even if I didn't have to hide. Do they know where it is?" Bannon shook his head, "No, not really...a several hundred square mile area...but...they did say Wallace was TDY to the National Range just before he took leave and went to Montana—for a will reading or something...anyway, the point being that he has his equipment with him."

"Make a few passes with a fighter and see if he comes up on the radio?" Slim asked rhetorically?

"I was actually thinking of using a Combat Talon and putting his buddy on the radio." Bannon added, "Wallace wouldn't likely break radio silence, but if he saw the aircraft and recognized it for what it was, he might come up and listen...get any intel he could. Then, if he heard his buddy..."

"I like it!" Slim perked up. "Get him on a plane, ASAP."

"I already did...he flew in last night. He's at Malmstrom AFB, waiting for the Combat Talon that should be there in about 2 hours. It's the same crew you sent after the First Lady in Jordan." Bannon smiled, "They had just returned from their Middle Eastern rotation last week and weren't fans...of the First Lady, that is. They were apparently admonished for their crude behavior. I read them in on our little op already, and I've positioned a few other assets nearby...just in case."

Slim smiled and sat back in his chair, taking a sip of the scotch. "You have been busy. Why didn't you call and tell me all this yesterday...you had to fly up here from Tampa?" Bannon cocked his head, and Slim nodded, acknowledging the gesture. "Ahh...never mind, I got it...Rocky, you should have been a three-star by now...maybe a four. Hell, you should have my job!" They both chuckled over the comment. Slim hadn't had anything to laugh about for quite some time—it felt good. So did the scotch.

"I said, wake up!" A voiced stirred them, followed by a slight kick to Landon's leg. He had been dreaming about flying and the contrast between that and his current actual situation caused him to experience significant disorientation and anxiety. It took several moments for him to reconcile and calm himself. The voice retreated back a few feet and boomed at Landon again, "What's wrong with you...you sick or something?"

"Leave him alone! He's just tired." Carrie fired back.

When Landon finally settled in, he opened his eyes to see Carrie and Karen standing behind him and four men in front of him—carrying guns. He started to stand, but the men insisted he remain where he was; the sleeping bag still zipped around his neck.

"That your plane at the airport?" the biggest man asked. Landon nodded. "Why are you here? What's your business?"

"We...we're headed to our redoubt, er...our new home. We just flew in from Phoenix and this was the closest airport. We have to walk from here." Landon realized the pistol he bought was in the sleeping bag with him, though he didn't readily know where. He tried to move his hands and feet to locate it, but it made the big man nervous.

"You move one more time and I'm going to blow you away!" the big man yelled.

"Whoa dude, I don't want any trouble and judging by the four of you and the armament you're carrying, I couldn't give you trouble even if I wanted to!" Landon said, trying to stabilize the situation. "Look, we just landed late yesterday and didn't want to disturb your town; that's why we stayed here. Our plan was to travel south of town last night and make our way north...," he looked around and it was clearly daybreak, "...but as you can see, we overslept."

"How do we know you weren't planning something else...something more sinister?" A second man spoke.

"Well, I guess you don't," Landon agreed, "but, if you'll just escort us around your town, we'll be too happy to leave and not bother you folks any more. We don't need food or anything from you, our packs contain all the provisions we need...please excuse our intrusion. We mean no harm or burden."

The big man shifted his weight from one foot to the other, contemplating what Landon had said. "Phoenix, huh? Why didn't you stay somewhere around there? Why come all the way up here?"

"Because my dad willed land to us up here." Carrie jumped in. "Wallace, Robert Wallace is...was, his name." We have land about 45 minutes out of Neihart...We..." she was cut off. "I know who he is," the second voice answered. "He rented a backhoe from George a couple of summers' ago. You know him too; he's the guy that helped Susie that time she ran off the road and got hurt."

"Oh...yeah. Nice guy...decent." The big man lowered his weapon. "Sorry about all this, but we've had some stooges come up here recently and demand things they weren't entitled to...also, with this Ebola thing going around...we are pretty certain our town isn't infected like the larger cities and we want to keep it that way." He stepped back a few more feet, as did the other men. "Phoenix, huh? I'll bet there's a bunch of sick people there...you sick?"

"No, really…I've just been awake for over two days and…just tired. But, I understand your concern; you can't be too careful. Yet another reason we wanted to circumvent your town—so we didn't appear to be a threat in any way…sick, I mean." Landon stumbled for words, but got the point across.

"Alright, I appreciate that. My name is Jimmy…I'd shake your hand, but…"

"We totally understand…Is there some particular way you would want us to go around the town?" Landon kept the focus of his intent to vacate soonest.

"Yeah, you pretty much described the route. Although, if you stay too far south you'll run into the river. There's a bridge just on the northeast edge of town…you can cross there. I think you'll pretty much be safe to travel on the road most of the way to Neihart, but they have road blocks set up on both ends of town and they may not be as friendly as us." Jimmy said, advising caution. "Jessie here will lead you to the bridge. After that, you're on your own."

Landon eyed Jessie. Of the four men, Jessie was clearly the youngest—about 20 years old, he guessed. Jessie was also the only one that didn't lower his gun at this point. Jimmy noticed it and used his hand to push the muzzle of the rifle toward the ground. The other three appeared to be hard working men, but it was obvious they enjoyed their suppers and beer as well. It made sense that Jimmy picked the young thin man to walk with them.

"Be on your way then…" Jimmy directed, "…and good luck." He paused to tip his hat to Carrie. "Sorry to hear about your dad…he seemed like a good guy." Carrie nodded and partially smiled.

After a few minutes, the group was on its way. Jessie insisted they stay 50 yards behind him. He turned around several times to ensure it was adhered to, as well as catch a glimpse of the two women. Thirty five minutes later they arrived at the bridge. Jessie moved south on the road into town and motioned for them to continue north. Landon joked under his breath with Carrie that he knew what a leper felt like.

About a quarter mile up the road, Landon looked back toward the town—it was then he noticed Jessie was still with them about 50 yards back. He looked at Carrie and Karen, but they hadn't noticed. Landon stopped and moved slowly toward Jessie, who saw him and raised his weapon. Landon responded by raising his arms. "I mean no harm." He yelled. "I just wondered why you were still with us." Jessie didn't respond at first. It was as if he wasn't sure of his directions from Jimmy.

"Just making sure you go on your way and don't try to come back to town," Jessie yelled back. Landon nodded and waved. He turned back toward the women and once he caught up, the group continued on. Landon felt uneasy, but he wasn't sure why. Jessie hadn't really done anything other than to appear a little trigger happy and that made Landon nervous, but it wasn't what seemed to bother him. It was something else; maybe the way he looked at the women. He wasn't sure. The pistol was no match for the rifle, especially at this distance, but Landon thought it might be prudent to have a weapon just in case. He turned sideways to make it look like he was adjusting Karen's pack strap and used the opportunity to pull the pistol out of his pack pocket and tuck it into his pants.

They continued on for about an hour and Jessie was still trailing them, but now he was much closer than before. As they rounded a corner in the road, they came upon a small roadside picnic table recessed back in the trees. It seemed like a good place to stop and take a break, so the group made their way to the table. As they arrived, Landon looked back to see Jessie, but he was not in sight. "About time," Carrie spoke up, "That guy took his job too seriously." Karen didn't respond, but Landon nodded. "Yeah, kinda creepy."

They spent about thirty minutes to rest, eat a few Clif bars, and drink some water. "I'm worried about Karen," Landon said to Carrie. "She just seems lost...out of it."

"You would be too...if that happened to us," she responded. Landon nodded, "Yeah, I guess so. I just don't know what to do for her, you know?" Carrie smiled, and turned to look at Karen, sitting on the edge of the water. "She just needs time…a lot of it. It's one thing to lose somebody; quite another to witness the horrific way they were lost."

Suddenly, they heard a loud mechanical sound from behind them. They whirled around to see Jessie standing with his weapon pointed in their direction. "Whoa, whoa, whoa…we're leaving, Jessie!" Landon used the man's name to bridge familiarity. "Just give us a sec to clean up our stuff here."

"Shut up!" Jessie demanded. "You!" He pointed to Karen and Carrie. "Get over here, now!" Carrie was clearly upset, but she stood up to comply. Karen remained motionless near the water. "Tell her to get over her!" Jessie demanded again. "Now, or…"

"Okay, okay!" Landon raised his hands. "She just lost her husband yesterday and she's a little out of it." Landon exaggerated the relationship. He nodded to Carrie to go get her. "Just let my wife get her, okay?" Jessie didn't respond one way or another, so Carrie slowly made her way to Karen and led her back.

"Take your clothes off!" Jessie told the women. "All of 'em…right now!" Carrie started to cry, but Karen remained solemn and began to unbutton her blouse; displaying no emotion. Landon felt rage well up inside him, but tried not to display it. "You!" Jessie addressed Landon, "Git over there, by the table…and lay on the ground face down with your head pointing away from me!" Landon slowly moved toward the table and kept his right-side and back hidden from Jessie. "Hurry up! You know what's going on. If you do what I say, you can all be on your way and nobody will get hurt!" Landon knew that was a lie. Jessie could not afford to have anyone tell of his exploits. Jimmy seemed a decent man and if he knew of Jessie's crime he would likely take action.

Karen's blouse fell to the ground. and she began to unbutton her pants. Jessie saw the motion and turned his attention away from Landon. Carrie still had not started to remove any clothing and this angered Jessie. He began screaming profanities at her and demanded she do as he say. Her cries became louder and she dropped to her knees, placing her face in her hands.

Landon could take no more! He rolled over on his back and drew his knees up slightly to form a rest while drawing the pistol from his waist. Jessie caught the movement and began fumbling with the AR to bring it to a firing position. Landon had only fired a similar weapon once before with his father-in-law at the range, and even then only at 15 meters—the max design range for an M&P Shield. This distance was slightly further at 18 meters. Landon took aim and squeezed the trigger—nothing happened. He had not previously racked a round in the chamber. This gave Jessie a slight edge in the race for time, but in his haste the first round went to Landon's left and into the dirt. Landon racked the slide on the 9mm and fired twice just as Jessie's second round zipped past Landon's ear. The super-sonic crack was deafening. Landon's third round struck Jessie in the chest just below his right nipple, but the body armor did its job and safely terminated the round into the vest. However, the impact caused Jessie to fall back enough for his next two rounds to go over Landon's head. One of his bullets the hit concrete picnic table and ricocheted past the women. Carrie screamed. Landon's next round again hit the vest with little result, but the fifth round hit Jessie in the left side of his neck. The impact spun Jessie's head around and he lost his balance, falling face first into the dirt. The AR landed underneath him and was pinned. Landon immediately got up and closed the distance to his adversary, who was now screaming and holding his neck.

"Wait, wait, wait! I don't want any of this! I...oh my God; you shot me!" Jessie cried out. "Don't...don't kill me! Oh my God...I'm bleeding! Help...help me!"

Landon grabbed the AR by the butt and gave it a quick yank to free it from Jessie, but the weapon was secured by a single point harness and it slipped out of Landon's hand. Seeing an opportunity, Jessie grabbed for the weapon. Landon fired the last two rounds from the pistol into Jessie. The vest caught all the first bullet but the second one hit him in the right arm. Jessie let go of the rifle and grabbed his arm. Landon dropped the pistol and used both hands to secure the AR, this time breaking the sling QD as he yanked. He pointed the weapon at Jessie and backed up toward Carrie, nearly tripping over her.

"You okay, babe???" Landon yelled. He dropped to his knee. Jessie continued to scream while Landon watched him roll around in the dirt, holding his neck and arm. Turning his attention back to Carrie, Landon held and tried to console her. "It's ok, babe…it's okay. He can't hurt us now." Carrie looked up and saw the man reeling, then she looked for Karen. She had not moved and stood motionless with her pants around her ankles, staring at Jessie. Carrie stood and went to her, quickly pulling up her pants and getting her blouse back on. Landon stood over Jessie—he expected more blood especially from the neck, but the bullet had gone completely through and not hit the carotid artery or the jugular vein. He would live.

"You're the worst kind of scumbag, Jessie…the worst!" Landon said, harshly. "I really hope you die, but it looks like you'll live."

"You'll pay for what you did!" Jessie retorted, "Just wait until Jimmy hears about this! You'll see…"

"I'm pretty sure Jimmy is going to have a problem with what you did, Jessie…a big problem." Landon wanted to kick Jessie's arm in the worst way, but thought of how that might be viewed. "Get up! On your feet!"

"I'm shot! You shot me…get a doctor." Jessie whined. Landon had had enough, he wanted to beat this punk within an inch of his life. He certainly deserved it. Landon kicked dirt in Jessie's face. "I said get up!

Landon felt a hand on his shoulder; it was Karen. He turned to face her, but she still said nothing and only dropped to her knee to address Jessie's wounds. As a physician's assistant, Karen was responding to Jessie's cries. The gesture stunned Landon.

"Get her away from me! She wants to kill me!" Jessie protested, trying to scramble away from her.

"Shut up you idiot! She's a Physician's Assistant and is trying to help you…although, if it were me, I sure as hell wouldn't do it!"

Landon watched as Karen gently pulled Jessie's hand from his neck to examine the wound. The bleeding hadn't stopped, but it was fairly slow. Then, she checked his arm; it bled worse. Landon found that peculiar. He went to Carrie, who was shaking her head at the scene. Landon hugged her and felt emotion build up inside. This event could have gone a completely different way and they could all be dead right now. It made him shudder. It was then he noticed how badly his ears were ringing from the gun battle. He turned to look back at Jessie; Karen had him on his feet. Jessie just stared at the woman. She walked him over to the picnic table and sat him down. Landon saw his 9mm pistol lying in the dirt and went to pick it up.

Suddenly, Landon heard a scream and turned to the table. Karen was on the ground—Jessie had pulled a Beretta 9mm from his hip holster and was pointing it at Landon. "Drop the guns! Drop them now!"

Landon felt like a fool. In all the excitement, he hadn't thought about Jessie having another weapon, though it was clearly on his hip during the encounter. Landon had the empty pistol in his left hand, and the AR in his right, but it was not in a firing position. He dropped the weapons.

"Jessie...we could have finished you off, but we didn't. Karen even tried to help you." Landon raised his hands.

"You kicked dirt in my face!" Jessie yelled.

"Yeah, I was pissed off! You tried to rape my wife." Landon moved to his left, making himself a target away from the girls. Jessie followed him with the pistol. The holster was on Jessie's right hip, but he held the pistol in his left—maybe if they all ran, Jessie wouldn't be able to hit them—he was obviously right handed, but with a bullet in that arm he had to use his left. Certainly, he was in no condition to chase anybody.

"You know, I've been thinking…you're right, Jimmy wouldn't approve and I'm not sure what actions he would take…but, I don't think I'm going to take a chance to find out." Landon's blood ran cold—Jessie was going to kill them. This made the decision to run very easy.

"Jessie, you don't want to do this, man. This is murder!" Landon asserted, looking at the distance to the trees. It was a good 40 yards.

Jessie saw him glance at the trees and knew what Landon was about to do. He quickly raised the pistol to eye level to fire.

"Run!" Landon screamed, as he bolted for the trees. Landon heard the report of the pistol three times, though he didn't feel the bullets strike him. Everything was moving in slow motion and he felt as though lead were on his feet. Then, he heard much louder reports—louder than the pistol. He looked back to see Jessie fall lifeless in the dirt. A pink spray was in the air above the body as pieces of his head landed on the ground. Landon turned to look at the girls and expected to see one of them with Jessie's AR, but it was still in the dirt where Landon had originally dropped it. It was then he noticed the girls staring back toward the road. A large industrial work truck was stopped in the middle with its door open; a man wielding an AR was down on one knee, having just fired the weapon.

It was Mason.

CHAPTER 20

"Republic. I like the sound of the word. It means people can live free, talk free, go or come, buy or sell, be drunk or sober, however they choose. Some words give you a feeling. Republic is one of those words that makes me tight in the throat — the same tightness a man gets when his baby takes his first step or his first baby shaves and makes his first sound as a man. Some words can give you a feeling that makes your heart warm. Republic is one of those words." --John Wayne; playing Davy Crockett in the movie, "The Alamo"

"I like it!" Mad Dog breathed deeply to sample the air.

"I thought you would." David grinned. "Wasn't sure if we would ever get here, though."

They all walked around the property and discussed where each of them would want their cabin and the view they would have. It was exciting, yet sobering at the same time. It was new and fresh, but it was also likely where they would spend the rest of their lives and it reminded them of what was going on in the world.

"I thought there were buildings and such," Phyllis said, with a hint of disappointment. "What now?"

David smiled and nodded. "Well, a lot of work. We've been lucky the first dusting—or pummeling—of snow hasn't hit us yet. My dad planned for us to arrive basically when we did. This red rebar pin," David pointed to the item just to the left of the AATREC, "...is the entrance to a buried shipping container and it contains most everything we need to start our redoubt. It also contains things we need immediately; like shelter, food, medicine, and tools to survive until we can build more permanent lives...or achieve a state of sustainment. If we're lucky, we might be able to construct several cabins before the winter really kicks in...if not, we have cabin tents with woodstoves to get us through."

"Do you have an inventory of what's in there?" Phyllis asked, not trying to be difficult but still skeptical.

"I do, right here," he answered, already pulling it from his pack. Phyllis started reading the document. After a few minutes, she looked up. "I'm impressed. It will take some digesting, but this was well thought out…seeds for planting, canning supplies…the list of 'how to' books is extensive, too." She looked over her glasses at the men. "Well, what are you waiting for gentlemen? Get your shovels and start digging!" Everyone laughed. Mad Dog smiled at David and winked. He was proud of his new 'main squeeze,' though he hardly knew her. Everyone began to talk as David grabbed a shovel and started digging in the area of the rebar pin. He dug for a few minutes and stopped because he thought he heard something, but it faded. He started digging again and after about a minute, the sound returned—a low droning—it was definitely man-made. He stopped digging and looked around; it was getting louder.

"Wait! Do you hear something?" David got everyone to quiet down. He heard the sound more clearly now; it was unmistakable—an aircraft. "It sounds like a C-130." Mad Dog said, starting to look in the general direction of the sound. "Yeah, I think you're right. We need to get into the trees—quickly!" David exclaimed.

They left the AATREC where it was and sprinted about 40 yards to the tree line. David pulled out his tactical binos and scanned the horizon. Suddenly there it was, just clearing the trees about two miles away to the east. "It is a C-130." Mad Dog reported. David continued to look through the binos. "Yeah, but not just any C-130…it's a Combat Talon II…an MC-130H."

"Is it armed?" Phyllis asked. Mad Dog shook his head. "No, it has no weapons…not like a gunship." David lowered the binos and looked at him. "Well, unless you consider a BLU-82 or MOAB!" Mad Dog looked at him strangely. David grinned. "Daisy cutter?" Mad Dog asked. "Kinda," David responded, "same principle…but bigger."

They watched as the aircraft continued on its heading and disappeared. David started to dig again. Combat Talons were rare—even more so now that the Air Force was trying to retire them. They were being replaced with less capable aircraft in terms of sensors—the Talon having terrain following radar and other black boxes for covertly sneaking into and out of places that are politically denied. *Why was it up here?* David thought. *If they were hunting for David and Mad Dog, it would have been better served to send an AC-130 Gunship.*

"You sure about that plane, dork?" Mad Dog asked, wanting assurance. "Yeah, my dad flew those, remember? That, and the older Talon I too." Madison kicked a dirt clod off the end of the shovel for David, when they heard the aircraft again. This time, it was closer—about a mile away, but on a reciprocal heading. "He's flying a grid...a search and rescue grid," David said. "If he stays on that pattern, he'll overfly our little redoubt on his next pass in about 10 minutes...you better move the AATREC into the trees!"

Ten minutes later as predicted, the Talon flew directly over their position. Ten minutes after that, it flew about a mile to the east of them. It was somewhat comforting as obviously they had not been discovered, but it still made them wonder about why the aircraft was there. David didn't like it.

"You have a radio, don't you?" Mad Dog asked. "Yeah, it's in my gear that I took from the Jeep." He looked at Mad Dog strangely. "You aren't suggesting I contact them? They would DF us in a second, then if they did have a weapon or a bunch of thugs with parachutes..." David referred to Direction Finding capability—if he transmitted, the aircraft would only need two different vectors to lock in on their position.

"No, no...but if you just listened...you might pick up on why they're here." Mad Dog retorted. David thought about it, but he was still not a fan of the idea. The Talon would be using encrypted radios, HaveQuick, or SINGARS. Even if David could hear it; it would be static. But, Mad Dog insisted, "Never pass on a good intel opportunity."

Reluctantly, David set up his tactical radio and listened in scan mode. Within a minute he heard a transmission in the clear on UHF 243.00

frequency—the guard channel. "Junior; you down there? It's LT." David didn't respond. He waited until the aircraft passed three miles to the east. This time he heard the exact transmission twice more.

"Well?" Mad Dog asked, impatiently. David bit his lip and looked at him. "They're looking for us. They know I'm down here somewhere." David explained that during his training as a TACP, he and Lieutenant Wilcox became fast friends, even though it was considered fraternization because David was enlisted.
"Well, what do you think…is it him?" Mad Dog asked. "Sounds like him and he called himself LT, even though we both know he made captain a few months ago. I still call him LT and he calls me Junior…he'll always be LT."

"Is there any way you can think to authenticate?"

David didn't like it. It was too risky. What if they did have bad intentions? "Yeah, there's something we used to yell across the bars at each other…only he would know that."

"But, do you trust him?" Mad Dog pushed the point. David dwelled on it for a few moments, then answered, "With my life; without question." Mad Dog nodded, "Okay then."

David used the PTT or push-to-talk button. "Authenticate; Whiskey Tango Foxtrot."

"Tango Uniform!" came the quick reply. David looked up at the empty sky—somewhere out there was his friend. "Yup, it's him," he said looking at Mad Dog. "It's LT."

"Junior, come up Winchester." LT made reference to a radio frequency based on a famous lever action rifle; a Winchester 30-30, which translated to 303.0 on UHF. David changed the freq and responded with a double click on the mic button. A transmission came; "Junior, mind if I come for dinner?"

David looked at Mad Dog. "He wants to drop in on us." Mad Dog shrugged, "Well, how many?"

"Confirm dinner party."

"Table for one."

David turned to Mad Dog, "Just him." Mad Dog, shrugged. "Your call…" David looked at the radio handset as if the answer were written on it. "Well, they have enough signal intel by now to get within a mile of us…giving them our location won't make much difference." David rationalized.

"LT; Junior…standby for vectoring. I have you 10 o'clock and five mikes…continue on current track. Turn 90 degrees left on my mark…" David stood and ran into the center of the meadow to get a better view of the aircraft. "3…2…1…MARK!" The aircraft responded and made the turn. "LT; Junior…make 10 degree adjustment to the left." The correction was made. "On track, standby for mark."

Mad Dog walked up and stood beside David and watched the aircraft. It was driving right at them less than 2 miles away. As it approached overhead, David finished the vectoring, "Ready…ready…MARK!"

"Roger. Junior, order the appetizers, see you in a few."

The sound of the big plane droned away until it was silent. "You think anybody else heard that?" Mad Dog asked. "No, not likely; UHF is line of sight and short range, but just in case, I didn't want to give coordinates or compass headings…only clock positions and marks. Anyway, we need to clear this area, they're probably running the Twenty Minute Checklist right now."

Forty-five minutes passed and they had not heard the aircraft or the radio. This concerned David; had they been compromised? He gathered the group together and told them to prepare to leave the area. It wasn't well received, but they understood. Just as they were loading up into the AATREC, they heard a vehicle coming in from the south. Mad Dog and David bailed out of the camper and took defensive positions; Mad Dog on point, David and Nate on the flank. The rest were told to hide in the trees.

The vehicle was visible now, emerging from the first meadow. Drew precariously made his way out of the AATREC with his AR and joined

Mad Dog. As the vehicle got closer, it slowed until it stopped 50 yards out. The engine shut off. David held a bead on the driver as he opened his door to get out. Suddenly, there was movement from the rear of the big truck—several people jumped off. The last one clearly needed help getting down; there was no doubt who it was.

"Hold your fire, hold your fire!" David yelled loudly while standing up to expose himself. "Carrie…you are such a klutz!" David laughed as he ran to his sister. Mason and Leigh got out with Tanner and they all met near the back of the truck. There were plenty of hugs to go around—Carrie and Leigh flooded their eyes and looked like Alice Cooper. Of course, David told them so.

Mad Dog waved 'all-clear' to the group hiding in the trees as he made his way toward the new redoubt residents. Eventually, all of the redoubt community was standing together and everyone was talking at once. It was like 'old home week.' Introductions were made for Drew, Nate, Phyllis, Roxy, and Karen. Karen actually had a slight smile on her face. Landon was glad to see it.

"Ross?" Leigh asked. David shook his head. "I don't know. I haven't had contact with him." The group went silent. Carrie frowned, "Do you think he…" She stopped in mid-sentence, "…Do you hear that? What's that? I think someone's coming. They all got quiet for a moment before David recognized the sound. "Ahh…that would be our dinner guest." Seconds later, the Talon flew over and a single parachute deployed from the left troop door. As quickly as the big bird entered their world, it retreated until there was no sign it was ever there. The jumper landed 30 yards from them and quickly secured his chute. David ran up to him and gave a big hug. "LT! Long time no see, bro. I didn't think you were coming."

"Yeah, well, we just wanted to make sure POTUS and the boys weren't tracking us, so we made several 'simulated drops' in various locations. Keep your drop zone clear, they'll be back tonight with a supply drop—couple hours after dark…" he paused to look David over, "…damn glad to see you, boy!"

"Yeah, you too…so what are you doing here?" David cut to the chase.

LT laughed, "Oh…seems you two; especially him," he said pointing to Mad Dog, "…are on the POTUS most wanted list—you probably knew that already, huh? But, what you don't know is that you're also key to a congressional investigation. A several senators and representatives want Madison to testify against POTUS and his posse concerning what Madison said on TV." LT started taking off his parachute harness. "The Chairman of the Joint Chiefs is in hiding, but his friend—another general in SOCOM—is working with the politicians to put this together. They called the Det and here I am."

"Nice." David responded, "So, how is the state of the union?"

"Not good, buddy. Thousands have died in the larger cities from sickness or crime. Estimates are by the end of the month that number will be in the hundreds of thousands. It's chaos; nobody really knows what's going on. Reports vary, but this thing has likely killed the country…well, as we know it, anyway. The only good news is that the military is pretty much intact as they closed bases and posts almost immediately from the start to isolate from Ebola. There were a considerable amount of desertions; mostly guys wanting to get home to protect their families."

"So, the military is keeping our enemies from running us over?" Phyllis spoke up.

LT turned to her, "No ma'am. Ebola's doing that for us…we can't even get humanitarian aid from our allies…we might as well be lepers. POTUS has directed FEMA camps to stand up, but no one can tell if folks are infected or not. All it takes is one person without symptoms to infect a camp and it becomes quarantined. Communication is pretty much nonexistent…at least to the masses." LT looked around, "What you folks got going on here is the only solution I can see that might work. Smaller towns are setting up road blocks and barriers to protect themselves from thugs and disease, but without supplies or a way to get food and clean water it's only a matter of time before they…" he paused, seeing the faces of the redoubt group. "I'm sorry…but you asked." The group became quiet. It was a significant contrast of their mood from just a few minutes ago.

"So, what's the plan?" David asked. LT nodded, "Okay, so the General Pickens thinks the safest place for you is here until you testify. To bring you in and try to protect you would only make you targets. There are false searches being conducted west of here in Idaho—thanks to our military intelligence resources now supplying the CIA with bogus reports—keeps the satellite searches pointed there too. Tonight, a HSLLADS drop will be made for you. It will contain radios, crypto, an Iridium phone, batteries, a solar set for charging and some supplies. There are two AC-130 gunships and two Ospreys waiting for your 'beck and call' should you need them; located at Malmstrom. Use the Iridium to make first contact, and radios for JTAC ops."

"What's with the Ospreys?" Mad Dog asked.

"QRF; two teams of shooters on standby alert to interdict if needed…also, they'll be your ride out for testifying. You'll transfer to the Talon for the flight to DC when the time comes."

"That's a nice warm fuzzy…so, now the big question—right son?" Mad Dog put LT on the spot.

"Well, yes sir…" LT nodded, "Do I have to ask?"

Mad Dog looked at David; David nodded affirmatively. Mad Dog turned toward LT. "Son, we'll be there with bells on!" LT smiled, "Yes sir, I thought that you would." He turned and looked at the setting sun. "Well, I got about a 20 mile hike ahead of me to my EXFIL point…can't compromise you folks…and it will be dark in a couple of hours, so I better get humpin.' Junior; here's the freqs and crypto you'll need for your radio until you get the HSLLADS drop…and you might want to keep the DZ clear at all times." David gave him a thumbs up.

"What's hiss-lads?" Nate had to ask. "That a bomb or something?

"HSLLADS, stands for High-Speed Low-Level Aerial Delivery System. Talons have a special beefed up tail section that allow them to deliver air drops at high speeds. Other aircraft have to slow down to around 150 knots or so. If they're being tracked on radar, it will give away the position of the air drop when they slow down and the bad guys will know where to start looking. With HSLLADS, they have no idea as the aircraft can fly thousands of miles on a single mission."

"Cool." It was all Nate could think to say.

"Junior," LT addressed his friend. "Always good to see you, dude! See you soon." They shook hands and LT started trotting off to the east. David watched him leave and felt a sense of loss; quite a contrast to just a few minutes ago when he felt the opposite. As LT disappeared in the trees, David turned to the group and put on his best southern accent for Leigh, "Okay all ya'll, it's going to be dark soon, ya'll might want to get your packs out with tents and bags." Mad Dog grinned and pointed to the AATREC. "If the camper be a rockin'..." Phyllis raised her eyebrow and turned to David, "You can stay with the 'rocker' over there; let me borrow your tent." Everyone broke into laughter.

After the tents were set up and dinner was complete, David continued to dig. Mason grabbed a shovel off his truck and helped. The rest of the group conveniently migrated away from the diggers. Mason took the opportunity to apprise David of happenings earlier in the day.

"What?" David dropped the shovel and looked toward the group, now huddled around a fire near the tree line. "What did you do with the body?"

"We left it on the picnic table with a letter explaining what happened. Landon and I didn't think it was a good idea to go back to the town and risk confrontation...with the women, kid, and all."

"No, you were right...probably the lesser of the evils...but I met Jimmy too, when we came through. He seemed like a sensible guy."

"Sensible or not, if somebody shot my son, I'd be livid and probably 'un-sensible'...maybe worse."

"Son? Jessie was his son???" David said in disbelief.

"Yeah, when we went through town, he asked us to send him home if we saw him. Of course, the only time I saw him, he was trying to kill Landon...so I blew his head off."

"That ain't good. It's likely we'll get a visit before too long…I better let Mad Dog know."

Well, that's it…time to get out and walk," Ross reported. It was as far as they could go with the car. They had been refused access to the towns they came across; Ebola scare. So, there was no opportunity to get gas. "I figure we've got about a two month hike in front of us, and with winter coming…it's going to slow us down." The girls looked out the windows, Hallie spoke first, "It's already cold out there. Should we just stay in the car tonight?" Ross shook his head, "No, actually we need to start traveling at night if possible…it'll be safer."

They reluctantly agreed. After snacking on Clif bars and beef jerky for dinner and feeding Blue, they headed out on the road carrying as much as they could. Ross managed to squeeze the remaining dog food into airgaps in each of their packs. Kate didn't' like the idea because it made her sleeping bag and clothes smell like dog food, but she allowed it.

The three traveled for several days without much fanfare or incident, having avoided towns by walking around them at night. Water crossings were a challenge as most the time the bridges were co-located near or in towns. The water temperature and the weight of their gear prohibited wading or swimming. They made fairly good time and distance most days and were able to mitigate population avoidance until they came to Angostura Reservoir in South Dakota. Having avoided the road block near Smithwick, they traveled west on Smithwick Road and came upon a small community on the southeast corner of the reservoir. The map showed they would need to travel southeast to avoid it and find a river crossing on route 79. The alternative was to enter and cross the Black Hills. That started the conversation about the reality of making it to the redoubt in winter, regardless of the route. He had to admit to the girls he didn't think it was possible; that they should really consider a place to hole up for the winter and then continue their journey in late spring. Angostura was a good source of water and probably had fish as well as game nearby. It

275

was about as good as they were going to find before the snows really came. Still, Ross had no illusions about other things they would need if they stayed here; namely, a heated shelter.

He proposed a plan to approach the roadblock and beg to stay close by—and maybe work for his keep. If it was okay, he would come back for the girls, if not, he would do all he could to escape and join them at an agreed location. In addition to having a need for shelter, their supplies were very low and the weather was getting worse. It actually snowed lightly on two of the nights already. Ross left his gear with the girls at a vantage point where they could see him approach the roadblock. As he walked up, two of the men manning the barricade pointed guns at Ross and made him get on his knees while they interrogated him. Afterwards, he was allowed to stand up while they talked. They talked for quite some time.

"I wonder what they could possibly be jawing about." Kate said, impatiently.

"That boy could sell ice to eskimos…it's part of his spin to establish a rapport with people before selling…see? He's got them laughing about something." The girls watched for a few more minutes before they saw one of the men escort Ross past the barrier and into town—but maintaining a safe distance for bio reasons.

"Now, what?" Kate said, "We didn't talk about this part." Hallie blinked, "Well, I guess we wait."

It had been a several days since LT had graced their presence and they had heard nothing. Not that they should have, just that it was unnerving to not know what was happening. The evening he left, the Talon had come back and left them a good supply of ammo, food, toilet paper, tampons, MREs and various other sundries. The radios and extra batteries were a welcome sight. There was also documentation and an authentication matrix with a 'duress code.'

Their efforts to create a winter worthy camp were successful for the most part, but it was evident that building log cabins before winter was not feasible. They had harvested and prepared quite a few logs, but they needed to dry out and 'season' before construction. Four tents were set up and strengthened with the smaller logs, creating somewhat of a hybrid shelter. Each had a wood stove and they had accumulated several cords of wood to last them through the winter. The original cabin Ross and David encountered on their first visit was cleaned up and made serviceable. The women and Tanner slept in it and most of the meals were prepared there.

David had become their leader of sorts. It wasn't that they voted, but it was the natural order of things. Mad Dog was a like an advisor to David and helped balance things out. Phyllis was also an advisor and David relied on her heavily before making decisions for the group. At one point, David suggested to Mad Dog that he be the leader, but he declined saying he was a guest and that the property was owned by the Wallace family. All in all, it went fairly smooth and there was very little conflict. However, there was one directive on which David stood firm; no one was to approach the cabin on the lake behind their property. He would lead a small team—probably himself, Mad Dog and Phyllis—to make introductions when the time came. For now, he didn't want anyone to go beyond the property or be seen. His intent was to demonstrate self-sufficiency and good neighborly boundaries before approaching the Kitchenmasters. Yes, they were undoubtedly related to Rick Kitchenmaster who piloted the aircraft his parents were killed in, and meeting them was likely part of his father's plan, but David was adamant that contact would be at a time of his choosing. This is where he and Phyllis didn't agree. She felt their little community should be a democracy—that they should vote on such things. David was envisioning a republic; but for now he was charged with keeping them all safe and his rule would stand until such time as they were able to establish a governing process.

"I think we should raise the shipping container to above ground level, eventually." Mad Dog said, wiping his brow after splitting another pile of wood. David looked back into the ramp leading down to the doors of the container. "My dad said we should use it for a root cellar to store our perishables and keep them from freezing…like potatoes, onions, etcetera." Mad Dog nodded, "I didn't think of that…good idea!" The two men took a break from splitting wood to get a drink; it was then they noticed Phyllis and Karen walking across the meadow toward them. David smiled. Phyllis had been good for Karen—a mentor as well as a counselor. Mad Dog licked his hand and tried vainly to comb his hair. He and Phyllis had been getting along well; taking their nightly strolls together.

"Gentlemen." Phyllis started, "I'm to inform you of an invitation for dinner tonight with our neighbors, the Kitchenmasters." David felt his face flush red. "And how did this event come about?" Mad Dog could hear the tension in David's voice, as could the others, but Phyllis didn't flinch. "Mrs. Kitchenmaster was walking on the trail near our cabin and Karen and I introduced ourselves. She took us back to her cabin and we had tea and met Mr. Kitchenmaster. They're really quite nice people."

David was not happy about this. He had been very clear; or so he thought. "Phyllis…" he paused, not wanting to say something he couldn't take back, "…I feel directly responsible for the safety of our group as it's within the expertise of my vocation. I don't tell you how to conduct matters of medical or health related issues. If you had been wrong in your assessment, it could have risked all our lives, not just yours."

"I'm sorry, David…of course you're right." She took a breath and looked at Karen. Karen nodded. "Okay, so I might have stretched the truth a bit…I'm sorry about that too. Karen and I kind of went spying on our neighbors—who by the way, were spying on us—and we had a chance meeting with Mrs. Kitchenmaster." She raised her eyebrows as if begging forgiveness. David shook his head. He was still angry. "Phyllis, the men from White Sulfur Springs are a threat until we find out differently…we can't take chances. You really need to stay within our safety zone. I'm glad the Kitchenmasters are friendly, but they could just have easily sided with the townsfolk and…" Phyllis lowered her head, "I'm really sorry. That kind of infraction will not happen again." David felt bad, but he needed to make the point. An uncomfortable silence fell on the group. "Okay, well…what's for dinner then?" he said, wanting to break the tension. Phyllis looked up and smiled, "Grilled elk steak and potatoes and green beans!" She looked at Mad Dog, "...and, he makes his own beer!" That got a chuckle out of the old warrior. "Well, then...what time is dinner?" Mad Dog asked. "Oh; 4pm!" Karen said smiling at David. She rarely spoke, but clearly this excited her enough to say something.

David liked her smile. David liked her *period!* She was just his kind of woman, but he knew better than to engage her in a relationship. She had a lot to work through. Grieving was something that took time. He could wait, besides; there were important survival issues to focus on. David smiled back at her. "Okay, you two go get your party dresses on...and let the others know...They do know how many of us there are, right?" He asked, changing his tone slightly. "Oh, yes...they do...she said; the more, the merrier!" Karen was a beautiful woman; strong and capable. David held his gaze just a little too long. Phyllis and Mad Dog picked up on it.

David watched as the two women quickly made their way to the others. Mad Dog punched David in the arm. "You better watch out, Romeo...that one won't last long in this environment. I think Nate has his eye on her too!" David looked at Mad Dog, trying to keep a straight face. "What are you talking about? I'm not angling on Karen...she's still dealing with the loss of..." Mad Dog cut him off, "U-huh...yeah. Well, you can shovel that somewhere else, young sniff dork. I saw the look in your eye...and hers."

David didn't answer, but he did watch her walk out of sight. "Maybe someday...but not today." He pointed to the axe leaning on Mad Dog's hip. "You need to keep working on your heart attack ol' man...keep chopping." Mad Dog grinned like he had something on David—which he did. "Okay Romeo, I'm choppin,' I'm choppin'..."

It had been over an hour since Ross disappeared into the little community. The agreement was if he didn't come out in 90 minutes, they were to leave. "I'm cold," shivered Hallie. "It's going to be dark soon..."

"Wait!" Kate cut her off, "There he is!" Ross walked through the barricade and waved at the two men manning it. They waved back. He trotted across the field toward them and when he arrived he was excited. "Good news, ladies. We're in! They said we could stay here for the winter and actually have a place for us to stay—an empty building or house or something on the end of town. They only have one condition; we have to stay in it for two weeks without contact with the other members. Kind of a quarantine to make sure we aren't sick…then, as long as we pull our weight, they'll let us stay as long as we want!"

"Town?" Kate questioned. "There's like only 50 houses over there…that's a town?"

"Yeah, ever since the lights went out, they got together and decided to create their own town. Technically, they're part of Hot Springs, but Hot Springs is closed off and miles away. So, they call themselves, 'Not Springs.' Anyway, they're pretty friendly, but they have to be cautious with Ebola and all." Ross seemed sold. Kate would have been more skeptical, but she was freezing and motivated to take the town up on their offer. "So, now what?" She asked. Ross picked up his pack and petted Blue on the head, "Well, we walk that direction," He pointed to the west, "…we cross Angostura Road, then we walk between the houses to Shoreview and then take Sunset Lane to the end. That's where others stayed until their two weeks were up."

"Others?" Hallie was curious.

"Yeah, there have been others before us. Once we get out of quarantine, we get our own place. Ours will be down at the marina in a trailer. We'll be assigned jobs after that."

"What kind of jobs?" Kate said, "What did you tell them our skills were?"

"I said we were servers but could do about anything they needed." He replied, "Oh, and they like music, but don't have much to play…I think I can help with that too."

The four weary travelers made their way across the prairie toward their new digs. The mood was light; certainly better than earlier in the day.

Everyone was excited as they made their way past the old cabin and down the trail to the edge of the lake. There was lots of chatter and Mad Dog was at the center of it. David noticed he was holding hands with Phyllis as they led the group. Nate and Drew stopped to skip rocks on the water every so often. As they rounded the corner, they were met with the smell of grilling food. *Hickory,* David thought to himself. It reminded him of his father and the smoker they had at home. He thought of the Kitchenmaster's and their relationship to his parents. They must have known them as mom and dad spent all their spare time up here. Nate tripped while throwing a rock and his whole foot went in the water. Everyone broke out laughing as he shook his shoe of excess water. The look on his face was priceless. Drew chided him and Nate punched him in the shoulder—before remembering it was the very one a bullet had passed through. Drew howled and Nate repeatedly kept saying he was sorry. David found it amusing and started laughing. He heard giggling from behind him; it was Karen.

"You have a twisted sense of humor, young lady." David chuckled.

"Oh? And what about you?" She responded, with a twinkle in her eye.

"Okay…" He said. "Busted!" They both laughed and continued to walk toward the cabin, going around Phyllis, who began to examine the reinjured shoulder while scowling at Nate. David glanced at Mad Dog as they passed him. There was that grin again. David ignored it, not wanting to give Mad Dog the satisfaction of ribbing him about Karen. He looked back at the herd, still bantering along behind him. What a crew, he thought, smiling. They approached the steps leading to the cabin as David heard Phyllis chastise Nate, "You made it start bleeding…now we have to leave the tube in for another week!" Drew groaned and Nate started with the apologies again.

David heard the screen door open and Karen spoke first to make introductions; "These are the Kitchenmasters." David was looking back at the 're-wounded' and disgruntled Drew, the overly apologetic Nate, and the scolding nurse—he started laughing. He put out his hand to shake as he turned. Then, he froze. Karen saw the smile slip from his face; turning white like he'd seen a ghost. In a way, he had; there before him was none other than Robert and Katrina Wallace— his parents.

CHAPTER 21

*"We hold these truths to be self-evident, that all men are created equal, that they are endowed by their Creator with certain unalienable Rights, that among these are Life, Liberty and the pursuit of Happiness.--That to secure these rights, Governments are instituted among Men, deriving their just powers from the consent of the governed, --That whenever any Form of Government becomes destructive of these ends, it is the Right of the People to alter or to abolish it, and to institute new Government, laying its foundation on such principles and organizing its powers in such form, as to them shall seem most likely to effect their Safety and Happiness. Prudence, indeed, will dictate that Governments long established should not be changed for light and transient causes; and accordingly all experience hath shewn, that mankind are more disposed to suffer, while evils are sufferable, than to right themselves by abolishing the forms to which they are accustomed. But when a long train of abuses and usurpations, pursuing invariably the same Object evinces a design to reduce them under absolute Despotism, it is their right, it is their duty, to throw off such Government, and to provide new Guards for their future security...
In every stage of these Oppressions We have Petitioned for Redress in the most humble terms: Our repeated Petitions have been answered only by repeated injury.* **A Prince whose character is thus marked by every act which may define a Tyrant, is unfit to be the ruler of a free people."* –*
Declaration of Independence, July 4, 1776

As Ross and the girls approached the end of the street, they could see the house on the right was surrounded by a tall chain link fence with barbed wire on the top—it looked like a makeshift prison. Ross stopped and turned to the two armed escorts who joined them at the first road and followed them to the house. "Hey, what's this?" he said, pointing to the fence. The front door of the house opened and a man came across the small yard and opened the fence gate. He stayed at a safe distance and spoke loudly. "I'm Richard Davis; kind of the mayor of 'Not Springs.' I'm sorry about the appearance of incarceration here, but it's what keeps us safe. Please don't be alarmed." He left the gate open and moved to join with the two escorts. "You don't have to stay there and you are free to leave now, if you so wish. In fact, you can leave at any time after you stay with us, but unless you submit yourselves to quarantine for a full two weeks, you are un-welcome here and must move on." He paused to see their response. Blue responded with a low growl, sensing uneasiness. "I don't like it," Kate said under her breath so Ross could hear it. "Dogs are a good judge of character," she petted Blue on the head to reassure him.

"I'm sorry folks, I know it seems harsh, but put yourselves in our position; if we just let folks wander in and out of town, we incur significant risk." The mayor sensed their hesitation. "Look at it this way, if we didn't want people here at all we wouldn't have built this little facility...we care, alright? But, we have to protect ourselves. If we wanted to harm you, we would have already done so." He pointed to the escorts with guns.

"He has a point," Ross said softly, "and, quite frankly...we don't have much of a choice." The girls nodded. He addressed the mayor. "So, we have to stay in the house the whole time?"

"Oh, no..." Davis chuckled, "It's not like that...ah, several times a day, the gate will be unlocked and you can come outside and walk down through the camp ground to the lake, but please don't approach anyone. The escorts will observe you from a distance and tell you when it's time to return to the house. They volunteer for this and have families of their own to tend to; you understand?" Ross nodded. "Good...well then...welcome! I'd shake your hands, but that's going to have to wait for a couple of weeks."

"We good then?" Ross addressed the girls. "I guess, but I wish there was another way. Seems creepy somehow," Kate said, reservedly. "Yeah, I feel ya," Ross agreed. They walked into the gated area and up to the front door. One of the escorts locked the gate behind them and said, "Hey, if you need anything, let us know." He walked away to the house that was opposite on the cul-de-sac.

They checked out the house—it was nice—nothing special, but it was mostly clean and had beds. That made Hallie very happy! She plopped down on one and fell back. "Oh, how long has it been?" Ross laughed, "Too long!" The only thing that seemed strange were the crayon markings all over the walls in the living room, hallway, and some of the bedrooms. Clearly, kids had stayed here before them. "Some people's kids!" Kate piped.

David sat at the table with his father and Mad Dog. His sisters were cuddled on the couch with their mother. The mood was surprisingly subdued considering a reunion of this type. There were so many questions to be answered. Robert Wallace didn't push the information. He knew his son needed answers, but he needed them in his own time and in his own way.

"Why, dad?" David began, "Why would you drag us through your deaths like that? Couldn't you have reached out to us…let us know???" David felt joy, happiness, anger, hurt, and pain—all at once. He didn't know how to resolve these feelings.

"No, I couldn't. POTUS had to believe we were gone. They would move heaven and earth to find us and the first place they would start would be with you kids. There is nothing they wouldn't do to get what they want—horrible things. Most importantly; they also had to believe none of my damning evidence had been conveyed to you. POTUS had NSA, CIA, and a number of un-named resources watching your every move, bugging everything. Had there been even a slight slip in a whisper, you would have been tortured to death, along with your siblings. I knew you would try to find out what happened to us. The tenacity you demonstrated to investigate our deaths was proof you knew nothing that could be held against them." Robert paused, a tear in his eye. "I'm sorry, son…but there was just no other way."

David nodded; it made sense. "I understand, dad…but it doesn't hurt any less. I'm having a hard time accepting you're alive…and you're sitting right in front of me! Does that make any sense to anybody?" There was a silence for several moments before Leigh found the statement humorous and began to laugh. It was infectious and within seconds everyone was laughing. This is what they all needed. The conversation lightened considerably after that.

The cabin was full and Katrina Wallace was in heaven—it's what she lived for. Still, she was not totally content; one of her flock was still missing—Ross. David was on the porch with his dad to watch the sunset on the water. She walked up behind him and rubbed his shoulder. "So, nothing on your brother...not even a little?" David turned to her and gave a weak frown. "No, mom...nothing. The last contact I had with him was over Facebook when I told him to leave Boston. If he left when I said, he should be okay...and Ross responded that he would." David tried to sound reassuring. "It's a long way from there to here and the population is much more dense...he knows he needs to avoid these areas. Also, he may have decided to hole up somewhere through winter...it's what I would have done in his shoes." Katrina thought about it for a moment before she patted his shoulder again and turned to go back inside. She opened the screen door and stopped. "Wait, doesn't he have a radio...for you kids to call each other?" David nodded, "Yes, and it's an HF long range radio, but it's a low wattage...only five watts. Unless he's within a few hundred miles or gets a great skip, he won't be able to contact us." She nodded weakly and turned to go. David continued, "But mom..." She looked back. "...we'll still be listening for him...twice a day, at the appointed time." She smiled. "When is the next one?" He looked at his watch. "In a little over an hour." She nodded and went inside.

David watched her go before turning to his father. "I have one more question, dad...how?"

"Ahh, well...there is a sad part to our story. Rick Kitchenmaster—a dear friend of ours and experienced pilot—was very ill with stage-4 pancreatic cancer. He had weeks to live and they suggested hospice. Rick knew of our situation and technically does partly own the land this cabin sits on, but it was willed back to a shell corporation that we all essentially own—you included. He loved to fly and did not want to die in a hospital bed. So, we flew to Destin, Florida and were seen in various places around town and on the beach. When it came time to leave, we waited until an hour before dawn, all piled into the plane, and taxied out. When we got to the end of the runway, your mother and I got out and made our way to the fence under the cover of darkness. Destin airport is tiny and serves private and corporate aircraft, so it was fairly easy. Rick took off, climbed to altitude, set the auto-pilot, and decompressed the aircraft. It was a very painless and peaceful death...much better than what he would have experienced."

That satisfied David for the moment and he thought perhaps he should update his father about everything that had happened so far. Robert was particularly surprised about the Ebola outbreak. He knew there had been hints of a biological attack, but had assumed it was nerve or blood agents. The impact of those would have been significantly smaller as they are harder to deploy and are relegated to smaller areas; unlike a disease on the level of Ebola. David mentioned the effort to bring POTUS to justice.

"I need to go, then. Your testimony may be considered 'hearsay.' Only Mad Dog and I had direct interaction." Robert paused, he could tell David didn't like the idea. "It's dangerous, and if something does happen; you need to be here to take care of your siblings...and your mother."

Ross looked at his watch; only a few minutes until the transmission window. He grabbed the pack and got the Yaesu FT-817ND radio and antenna, and went outside. It was almost dark now, but he could see. The 'escorts' were nowhere to be seen. They likely thought Ross and the girls were in for the night. He looked around for a place to string the antenna; finally deciding to throw it up on the roof. He connected it to the radio, powered it on and listened for a few seconds before selecting the frequency. Reaching into his pack pocket, he retrieved the COMSEC matrix and waited. It was a beautiful night and he hoped for good propagation. At exactly 7 minutes after the hour, Ross transmitted; "Bandar, Bandar, this is Prelude; how copy?" There was no response. "Bandar, Bandar, this is Prelude...how copy?" This time there was a crackle and a partial response; "Prelu---...Ban..." Ross got excited, that had to be them. He spread the matrix on the ground and used his headlamp red LED to read it. "Bandar, Bandar...this is Prelude...authenticate Lima Papa." He heard nothing, so he repeated. Again, nothing. Ross waited two minutes and tried again, but with no luck. He was deflated. He almost had them, didn't he? It had to be them. His watch confirmed the window was closed. Maybe tomorrow night. Ross broke down the radio and went inside. In his mind, he replayed what he heard over and over. He told the girls. Kate asked, "Well, how do you know it wasn't somebody just returning your call? I mean; they heard your call sign and who you were calling…couldn't they just have repeated what they heard? You didn't get an authentication, right?" Ross was even more deflated, she was right…it could have been anybody. He nodded. "Yeah, that's true…well, there's tomorrow night…I'll try again then."

"Oh my God, was that him??? Was that Ross?" Katrina wailed. David looked at his dad and then addressed them all. "Yes, I think it was. While we didn't authenticate, 'Bandar' and 'Prelude' couldn't have been a random happenstance…especially not at exactly seven minutes after the hour. Even if somebody took the radio and the COMSEC matrix, the transmission time was not included. That information was only in Dad's video to each of us." David looked up, this time smiling. "Yup, I'm pretty sure it was him!"

Katrina hugged Robert's neck tightly. "Oh, thank God…he's okay…he's alive." She paused to look at David and then asked the question; "So, that means he's close, right?" David thought about the atmospheric conditions, the five watt radio and answered. "Well, I'd say so…of course skips have been known to…," he paused, thinking about his mother's feelings. "Yeah, mom…I'd say he has to be within two hundred miles or so." Everyone seemed happy with the assessment and Katrina visibly relaxed. It was a good way to top off the evening.

After everyone had eaten and consumed significant quantities of homemade beer—an IPA, of course—it was time to relax in front of the fireplace. It wasn't 'Savannah Marie' from the Peoria Artisan Brewery, but it was pretty good. David sat in a big leather chair and just observed the 'herd' interact. He hadn't really thought about what life would be like at the redoubt, but he sure didn't expect this; *it wasn't going to be too bad,* he thought... *not too bad at all.*

Ross had gotten up early and watched the sunrise. He looked out over the lake and thought about his siblings and what they might be doing. Hallie and Kate were still sleeping and would probably continue to do so upwards of nine o'clock. He wanted to take Blue for a walk down by the reservoir, but the escorts were not waiting outside the gate like usual. They had been every day before. Ross looked in the direction of the house on the other side of the cul-de-sac where one of the escorts apparently lived. There was no activity.

Just then an unpleasant odor passed Ross's nose. He turned into the breeze in the direction it would be coming from. The only thing it could have been was the garage building next to the house, just on the other side of the fence. Ross had seen men take an occasional deer or antelope in there and figured that's where they butchered the animals, but they hadn't been there lately. He wished they cleaned up better, the smell was putrid. The escorts had brought them food every so often, but it was always vegetables or oats—never meat. Ross had been resigning himself to chicken for the last couple of years and swore off beef and pork, but either one of those sounded pretty good to him now. He had eaten deer before, but not antelope and wondered what it tasted like. Then, another smell made its debut; this one he recognized—it was a stockyard—probably the one just north of the community that Ross had seen when they surveyed the area. His thoughts were interrupted by the sound of someone walking down the road. Ross turned to see 'Mayor' Davis and the two escorts approaching the gate. Ross met them there.

"Good morning! You're up early," Davis declared.

"Yeah, I was kind of hoping to walk the dog," Ross replied.

"Sure, no problem," Davis answered. "These gentlemen will open the gate for you." The Mayor motioned and one of the escorts opened it.

"Say, I really just came down to bring good news; we're going to see about letting you guys out a little early—would you be up for that?"

"Wow that would be great!" Ross said excitedly. "But, it hasn't been two weeks."

"Well, we were talking and decided to take into consideration that you said you hadn't had any contact with anyone since the day the power went out—so, it's been longer than two weeks." Davis paused, as Ross started walking toward him to shake hands. "Whoa, hold up—we still need to check you out though. We have a nurse practitioner in our community and she wants to examine each of you tomorrow morning. Provided everything is okay, you'll be free to walk among us."

Ross stopped and backed up a few feet. "Sorry, I was just a little anxious…Well, that sounds good. I'll tell the girls." With that, the Mayor waved and turned to go.

"Oh, Mayor?" Ross had one more question. "I noticed you guys use the garage over there for a slaughter house and I was wondering if we could get some meat with our vegetables."

"Meat is hard to come by, son. Every once in a while somebody gets a deer…maybe then."

"Well, what about the stockyards…don't you have cattle?"

The mayor looked back at Ross and frowned. "Nope, our friends north of us in Hot Springs have chosen not to share their wealth. They control the stockyards. They're actually the ones that called us Not Springs." Davis stood staring back at Ross for several moments. "Anything else?"

"No…no, I'm good. Guess I'll learn more about the lay of the land later." Ross waved and took Blue down to the lake for a much needed walk. He couldn't wait to tell the girls, but nature called for his four-legged friend—that would come first.

Later that evening, after the dinner of their remaining Clif Bars and some potatoes they got from the escorts, Ross announced he was going to try to make radio contact again. The girls were chatting it up and stayed in the house. He was thankful for that—they were driving him crazy with their excitement to meet other women in the community. Ross could still hear them with the door closed as he threw the antenna on the roof and attached it to the radio. He glanced at his watch; a minute to go. Turning the radio on, he selected the frequency and immediately he heard a voice; very clear and distinct, "Prelude, prelude; this is Bandar…how copy?"

Ross almost fell over! "Bandar; this is Prelude…can you hear me?"

"Prelude…have you 5 by 5. Authenticate Foxtrot Papa." Ross hadn't taken the COMSEC matrix out, nor did he have his headlamp ready. He was so excited he almost peed himself, but that soon turned into frustration as he checked his pockets several times, looking for the device and couldn't find it. Finally, he opened up the matrix and held it up to the light escaping from the window to try to see. It was then he realized the headlamp was actually on his head.

"Idiot!" He said to himself. Switching it on, Ross located the authentication response. "Bandar; authenticating with Charlie, X-ray…say again, Charlie, X-ray!"

"Roger, Charlie, X-ray…Damn, big brother; where've you been? Is everything okay?" It was David. Ross became emotional and a lump formed in his throat. He could hardly answer.

"Yeah…yeah, we're good. We're going to winter here in South Dakota… Angostura Reservoir."

"Hey, before we lose contact, give me your GPS coordinates." David asked.

Ross fumbled around, turning the matrix over to see where he'd written them down on the back. He read them out to David twice. David in turn read them back, but in the background Ross heard a woman's voice say, 'I love you.'

"Who was that?" Ross inquired.

"Oh, it was Leigh. She and Carrie made it up here. We're all here except you." David lied; it was his mother. He turned to her and spoke solemnly. "Mom, I know you want to talk to him, but trust me—he doesn't need to know about you and dad over a radio call. It wouldn't be good for him. I'm sorry."

Katrina teared up as she stared at the radio and she nodded. "I understand—it's just been so long since I heard his voice…I…okay, I'll be quiet."

David returned his attention to the radio, "Hey, listen…these batteries don't last very long and the little solar charger dad included in your pack takes a long time to charge the battery. As much as I'd like to keep this conversation going, we should probably get off for now."

"Okay, cool…I really miss you guys!"

"Yeah, we miss you too! Bandar; out."

Ross was just beside himself! He couldn't wait to tell the girls. As he disconnected the antenna from the radio, he thought of his siblings and wanted to strike out tomorrow for the redoubt, but that wouldn't be smart and he knew it. He looked down at the lake and took a deep breath. It wasn't a bad place to spend the winter, but now waiting would be harder knowing everyone was there but him. He would just have to be patient—not something he was good at in the past.

David plotted the map to identify Ross's location. It was about 430 miles as the crow flies; 600 miles if following roads. The little radio was pretty good. He could hear Europeans on it all night, but reaching back to them would be a different story. It depended on the ever changing propagation. Sometimes it was great and other times not. He marked an 'X' on the exact point where the coordinates lined up. Katrina stared at the map.

"That's where he is, huh?" She asked.

"Yeah. Actually looks like a good place to hole up. Lots of water, probably fishing and hunting…you know it would only be a nine hour drive, if things were different…" David gave her a hug. "We just have to be patient, mom. He'll get here." He smiled at her. "Let's go tell the others!"

The next morning, the girls got up early. They were excited to finally get out and meet their new friends. Last night, while Ross was talking to David on the radio, the girls had washed their best clothes in preparation and this morning they busted out the 'war paint' so as to look as presentable as possible. Ross laughed at their antics, but it didn't seem to faze them. Mayor Davis showed up at the gate with a woman named Beulah; the nurse practitioner. She had a mask on and latex gloves. Ross thought she looked more like a jack-hammer operator. She was a large woman and appeared weather-worn; like she had spent a lot of time outdoors. The term, 'battle axe' came to mind—something his father would have said.

"Okay, who's first?" The Mayor asked.

"First?" Ross questioned back.

"Yes, we can only take you one at a time. Once Beulah clears you, you'll be temporarily separated from each other until all three of you are cleared. We can't have the cleared mixing back with the un-cleared. Basic rules of medical decontamination. You'll be examined, and once cleared you'll go to your new home in a trailer near the marina. The girls were very excited and finally settled on Hallie going first. Ross didn't even try to throw his hat in the ring—he knew better. "I'll go last." Nobody was listening and that was fine with him. He was in no hurry to have big ol' Beulah groping him—he shuddered.

"Oh," the Mayor said, "do you three want to live together, or does one of you want your own place? We have several open trailers down at the marina?" They looked at each other but no one spoke. "Okay, well you don't have to make up your mind now. It can be settled later. Just give it some thought."

With that. Hallie walked away with Beulah and the Mayor while the escorts locked the gate. Ross thought about the potential arrangements; it would be nice for him and Hallie to have their own space, but they would leave as soon as spring weather would let them. So, it really wasn't a big deal. Still, privacy for romantic interludes would be nice.

CHAPTER 22

"... May we with Gods help spend the comeing year better than the past which we purpose to do if Almighty God will deliver us from our present dreadful situation..." From the diary of Patrick Breen; member of the Donner Party — December 31, 1846

Ross came running back to the house from the lake. He had caught two brown trout and there would be meat for dinner tonight! The gate was open and the escorts were sitting on the porch of the other house. They waved as he ran by. Blue trotted along behind him and barked, sensing his master's excitement. He ran through the gate and into the house. Kate was sitting at the table sewing the pocket on her blouse.

"Look Kate! We got dinner!"

She looked up and smiled. "Nice, but I don't eat fish."

"That's cool, all the more for me and Hallie. You can chew on those old potatoes." He chuckled. "They haven't come to get you yet?"

"Nope. Probably not coming until tomorrow. Hallie and the mayor came by on their way down to the marina. The nurse had to deliver a baby. So it's just you and me tonight, big boy."

"So, Hallie went to the marina?" He sounded disappointed.

"Yeah, she's going to pick a trailer and work on it—clean it up a little so you love birds can nest."

Ross smirked, that would be good. He could do with a little 'nesting' right now. Dumping the fish in the sink, he searched for a skillet and some oil. There wasn't much flour left in the cupboard, but it would be enough. He heard Blue bark and went to see what the issue was. Some men in a pickup were backing into the garage. It was obvious they'd been hunting from the way they were dressed in camo. Ross waved at the men. They waved back.

"What's all the racket?" Kate complained, still messing with the blouse. "Some hunters in the slaughter house," he answered. "Maybe the mayor will share some with us." She looked up, "What kind of meat?" He shrugged, "I don't know…deer…antelope…maybe elk." She looked puzzled. "Elk? What's an elk?" He laughed, "You'll see. If we don't get it here, we'll definitely get it in Montana."

The fish tasted great. Ross had found some blackening spice in the cabinet and seasoned the fish with it. Kate tried the fish and actually liked it enough to finish half of one. Ross ate the rest. He was stuffed. Wandering outside, Ross looked up at the stars and was blown away. "Man, you don't see that in Boston," he said to himself. Ross had a routine of walking laps around the perimeter of the fence every night. Blue followed him around for a couple of laps before he realized they weren't going anywhere and decided to lie on the porch. Ross was in deep thought about his siblings and imagined what they would be doing at this moment. As he made his way around for a fifth lap, he found himself nearest the garage. Ross was curious and wondered about it. He looked back at the house across the cul-de-sac; all the lights were out—it was late. On his sixth lap, he was reminded of the chain-link fence near the back of the house. Over time, the rain had washed the soil from underneath and he thought it might be possible to squeeze under. He wondered about what might be waiting for him to pilfer. He wouldn't take much—just a little. What if he got caught or they found out—would they kick them out of the community? He didn't think so. He was getting out of 'jail' tomorrow anyway.

Ross got on his belly and slid under, snagging himself several times. It was tighter than he thought, but he eventually got through. Quietly, he made his way to the garage and looked in the window—too dark to see. The headlamp in his pocket would remedy that, but it would also be quite visible to anyone else that might be looking in the direction of the garage. He decided to try the door. Blue heard him and started barking. It almost scared Ross to death. He trotted toward the gate and let the dog know it was him. Blue stopped barking, but now he was whining because he wanted to be with Ross. "Shhhhh, be quiet, dog!" He scolded. Blue went back to the porch. That surprised Ross; somebody had trained him well.

Ross looked back toward the garage. It was too tempting. He made his way back to the door and tried the knob—it opened. He went inside and shut the door. It was really dark and his eyes would take time to adjust, so he decided to use the red LED light and cover it with his hand to reduce the beam even more. Carefully, he made his way into the stall of the first bay. He could barely make out a carcass hanging in the center, its freshly skinned hide piled up on the floor below it; too small to be an elk, it was a deer or antelope and was hanging by its hind quarters. Ross turned off the light and reached in his pocket to retrieve the Leatherman Tool as he made his way to look out the window slot in the garage door. He looked back toward the house and surveyed the yard, then toward the escorts' house. All was quiet. Stealthily, he made his way back toward the carcass and selected the knife from the tool. He would only take a little. Donning the headlamp, Ross moved toward the carcass but would leave it off until he got closer. He tripped on something and crouched down to find a meat saw. *Great place for that,* he thought. *They must have used it to cut off the head.* He could just make out the forelegs now, hanging below the headless carcass. If he could take a little of the neck meat they'd never know it was missing. He crouched down and turned on the lamp to red. The first thing he saw was a small hand where there should have been a hoof—he gasped and fell back on his butt; scrambling away from the carcass. The headlamp bobbed up and down as he retreated crab-style; illuminating more and more of the hanging body as he got farther away. As he approached the wall, his hands got tangled in something—fabric—his head whirled down to see what it was. They were clothes Hallie's clothes!

The realization of what he was seeing overwhelmed him and he immediately vomited. His face contorted and he began to shake. "Oh my God, oh my God…" he said over and over to himself. Without thinking he turned once more to look at the center of the garage. The light cast over Hallie's entire form hanging lifeless before him; a large portion of her thigh was missing. And, of course, her head.

Kate sat in bed and was filing her nails while she read the scribbling on the walls around the room. There was a lot of it. Somebody must have been mentally deranged to do all this. It was like they just went crazy; scribbling and writing everywhere. She suddenly realized that a kid could not have done it. First of all, the words used were not simple. Secondly, the markings were too high on the wall for a child to reach. She focused on the scribbling and could make out words; 'meat locker' and something about 'who needs refrigeration?' Kate stood and moved closer to something she couldn't quite make out. She cocked her head sideways and it became clearer; 'you are food for them.' "What the hell?" She said out loud. Suddenly, she heard Blue barking again, but this time it was much more urgent. She ran to the back door of the house to find Ross, but he wasn't there. So, she ran outside and headed toward the barking dog. Blue was near the fence, barking at something—a figure crouched outside the wire. As she got closer she realized it was Ross. He was tucked in a ball and rocking back and forth. "Hey! What are you doing out there…get back in here! What's the matter with you???"

Ross rolled over on his side and looked up at her. "They're eating her, Kate…they're eating her right now!" Kate shook her head and tried to reconcile what she was hearing. "Eating what…?" Then, it hit her all at once—the writing on the walls, Hallie being gone, the uneasiness she'd felt since they got here, 'Not Springs' being denied access to the stockyards. She felt the blood start to leave her face and then her brain—she felt her knees buckle—and then darkness.

Kate's eyes began to open. The morning sun was pouring in the window and making her squint. She looked at the foot of the bed and Blue was on the corner looking at her. She started to move and realized someone was holding her—it was Ross. Sitting up she looked back at him, puzzled. He just stared back blankly. She started to remember the horrible dream and thought of telling him about it, but then why was he holding her? She was confused. Slowly, the memories from the night before crept into her consciousness and she began to realize it wasn't a dream. She screamed out and began to shake. Ross grabbed her and pulled her back. "It's okay, it's okay…shhhhhh, you gotta be quiet. They'll know that we know." Kate sobbed for half an hour before she got quiet and just stared at the wall. Neither one said anything for nearly an hour. Finally, she drew a breath and said a single word.

"Cannibals."

"Yes," he responded.

"What do we do?" She started to cry. "They'll come for us today…"

"No, I don't think so," Ross countered. "They have no power for refrigeration. This jail is essentially a way for them to preserve meat until they need it—keep us live on the hoof. They have enough…" he paused, choking up.

"Don't say it…please don't say it." She whimpered, "I can't…"

"Okay, okay…" he held her closer. "But, I'm betting they come by today and give us some story about having to delay the medical check and our move to the trailers…something to stall us. We need to act like we suspect nothing, or the gig will be up."

Blue started barking. Ross slipped off the bed and made his way to the front door. The hunters were returning to the garage. He watched as they used the side door rather than open the larger bay door as they had before. Mayor Davis was with them, but he didn't go inside; choosing instead to stay near the truck and smoke a cigarette. A few minutes later, the men came out and called Davis into the garage. One of the escorts went with him. Several minutes later, they all came out and the hunters left; the escorts and Davis came toward the house. Ross swallowed hard, opened the door and made his way toward the gate, putting on his best poker face.

"Good morning," Ross tried to say cheerfully.

Davis took a last drag on the cigarette, dropped it to the ground and snuffed it out with his boot. Looking up at Ross, he exhaled the smoke and squinted one eye. Ross could tell, something was different in the Mayor's demeanor.

"So, you had fish for dinner last night?"

"Oh, yeah," Ross piped. "It's been a while since I had any. It was really good and..."

"U-huh," Davis cut him off. "The reason I know you had fish, is because it's on the floor of my garage over there."

Ross felt his blood run cold. The gig was up. He had vomited in the garage and forgotten about it. He glanced at the escorts, their weapons slung across their chests. It would take several seconds to train them on Ross—probably felt safe behind the locked gate. He felt his hand tighten on the pistol in his jacket pocket. He wanted in the worst way to empty the mag into Davis and these men, but the reality was that he would not be able to get them all before they him cut down. Then, they would take Kate. It was a losing situation.

"Yeah, sorry about that," Ross answered. "Quite the operation you boys have going on here. You always been cannibals!?" Davis smirked, and shook his head. "Nope, that's something relatively new for us...but it's pretty good, you should try it. I can't wait to try your friend in there," he referred to Kate. "She looks to be a bit healthier." Ross's face flushed red and it was visible to Davis—it was all Ross could do to keep the pistol in his pocket. The smirk dropped off the Mayor's face and a frown replaced it. "We have to do what it takes— nothing personal—but we have mouths to feed. You're not the first, and you won't be the last." He turned to go.

"See you in Hell, Davis!" Ross shouted out almost involuntarily.

Davis didn't even look back. He just waved his arm and replied, "You might...you just might at that...but you'll be there a lot sooner than I will; save me a place."

Ross went back into the house and told Kate of what had happened. She was beside herself and began to cry again. He did the best he could to console her, but it was no use. There was only one thing that would be of any comfort and that was to fashion a plan of escape.

That afternoon, the 'escorts'—now guards—were more diligent and they filled in the hole under the fence, but it was not much of a fix. Also, several of the community members came out to stare at them— women too. Ross and Kate stayed in the house, not wanting to give them the satisfaction. It angered Ross greatly; he thought only a handful of the people knew of the source of the meat, but it was clear now that they all knew.

As the sun went down, one of the guards remained—that would make escape harder. Now, Ross knew why they did a poor job of filling in the hole under the fence—because it really didn't matter with a 24-hour guard on site.

David turned on the radio and selected the frequency. He had not heard from Ross since the first time he called. It's not that David was worried or anything, but he sensed in his spirit that something just wasn't right. He couldn't explain it. It was the appointed time and they had just finished dinner. His parents' were there to listen, as was Mad Dog.

"Do you think he'll call tonight," Katrina asked David.

"I don't know," David replied, "…I mean, there's no reason to, really. He needs to save his battery power, so just calling to chat isn't something I expect. But, we have to check in at the appropriate times…you know?" She nodded.

The radio crackled to life, "Bandar, Bandar; Prelude…how copy?" Katrina squealed with joy.

"Prelude; Bandar…authenticate Bravo, India." David challenged.

"Michael, Romeo." Came the response.

"Hey, big brother; what's the word?"

301

There was a long pause—so long that David thought they lost the signal, but the answer eventually came. "Cannibals...I'm in a lot of trouble little brother...they...they ate my girlfriend...they ate Hallie..."

"What??? Where...What???" David was frantic and Katrina began to cry.

"Yeah...," Ross said, in an almost monotone voice. "They killed her and...we're in a lot of trouble here. They have us in a makeshift jail...well, now we realize we're just livestock...umm, I don't know what to do. I have a pistol, but they have assault rifles...and... and there's a lot of them...only two of us."

Mad Dog looked at David. "I expected this kind of behavior, but not this soon." David stared at the radio for several seconds before keying the mic.

"Can you escape?"

"Yeah, I think so, but it's cold here. I don't know where we'd go...also, they would undoubtedly come after us."

"Standby..." David grabbed the map and began to scrutinize the terrain. His eyes darted over every pixel; searching. He keyed the mic again, "Okay, write this down...I'm going to give you some coordinates." David read the coordinates off and had Ross read them back. "Okay, now tonight you need to leave there—right now—and get to those coordinates. Hang on big brother, I'm coming!"

David turned to Mad Dog, "Sign off with him, would ya? I gotta make a phone call. He jumped up, grabbed the Iridium satellite phone and ran out into the darkness. Robert and Katrina looked at Mad Dog strangely. Mad Dog knew what the JTAC was thinking and he knew what hell would soon be unleashed on the unsuspecting town of Not Springs.

"It's about to get real, folks...it's about to get real."

Ross signed off and went in the house without breaking down the radio—he had no time. Kate was to observe the position of the guard and warn Ross when he started to come around to the back, and she did—but just barely in time. Ross would have to wait until the guard went back to the front before he could break it down and retrieve the antenna. Ross told her of the conversation and that his brother was coming to get them. She wanted to know how and when, but Ross had no details. He told her of the GPS coordinates and the need to plan a route to where David would meet them. Ross loaded the coordinates in the GPS and looked at the moving map—the point David sent was north of an airstrip, near the river. "As the crow flies, it's about five miles away. We can do it in a night easily. I'm going to guess he's got some way of flying over here if he wants us to get to the airport."

Ross went to the bedroom and grabbed a pillow off the bed. He dug in his pack and produced a roll of electrical tape. He held the pistol in his hand and wrapped the pillow around it. Then, he had Kate pull a black garbage bag over it and wrap it with the tape. It would have to do.

Kate went out to the yard near the back fence and waited for the guard to come by. She spoke to him just as his eyes focused on her in the dark. He was clearly startled and used his flashlight to illuminate her. This part of the plan worked well, as now the guard's night vision was compromised enough for Ross to work his way around the house and sneak up on the unsuspecting man. Kate tried to make small talk and asked for a cigarette, but the guard wasn't reciprocating the friendliness.

"Come on, I just want to talk to you." She begged. "Ross won't talk to me…he's all freaked out."

The man had a twisted grin on his face and simply stated, "I don't talk to my food."

That was the last thing he'd ever say. Ross crept up close enough to aim the pillow apparatus at the guard's head and fire twice in rapid succession. The first shot was relatively quiet and struck the man in the left eye socket; the second was louder than the first and hit him just in front of the ear. He dropped like a stone.

CHAPTER 23

The most difficult thing is the decision to act, the rest is merely tenacity. –Amelia Earhart

Mad Dog watched as the MV-22 Osprey left the redoubt and disappeared into the night. David had made contact earlier using the satellite phone and LT coordinated the extraction. The final details of the mission would be completed in flight, but the concept was simple; transfer to the Combat Talon at Malmstrom AFB, the AC-130 Gunship and the Talon would then proceed to the Hot Springs airfield where David and LT would HALO in and secure Ross and Kate. The Talon, carrying six members of SEAL Team II, would then initiate an airfield seizure operation with the gunship providing Close Air Support, if needed. David, LT, Ross and Kate would then exfil on the Talon and fly back to Malmstrom. It was overkill considering the resistance expected, but there was no reason to take chances. If all went well, the blacked out operation would take less than 6 minutes. Except for some uncharacteristic noise coming from the airfield, no one would know of their presence.

Ross cleared enough dirt from under the chain-link fence to slide under and secure the dead guard's AR-15 as well as the keys to the gate. Then, he and Kate took their gear and quickly escaped from the jail. Ross was concerned that the second shot fired from the pistol might have been heard, but so far there was no response. He left the guard laying where he was—*they could eat his ass now!* Ross and Kate wanted very much to recover Hallie and give her a proper burial, but it just wasn't feasible; they only had a few hours to get to the airfield.

Kate, Ross, and Blue had a fairly easy go of it. They headed north past a few sparse houses. If anyone was in them, they were asleep. Eventually, they came to the highway that led to Hot Springs and decided to offset to the west several hundred yards just in case someone was searching for them. There were lights at the feedlot and as they got closer they could see activity. Kate counted seven armed men guarding the cattle. These must be the men that Davis said had denied him access to the beef. Ross and Kate would need to move much further west to the river to avoid contact and then follow it up to the coordinates David provided. Ross was concerned about the additional time it would take for them to go around, but they had no choice. It was bitter cold and Kate shivered visibly. "Keep moving, it'll help keep you warm," Ross said, as he petted Blue's head. The dog didn't seem bothered by the temperature.

David checked LT's HALO rig and then LT checked his. They were an hour out now and the sun would be up in just over two hours. The Loadmaster set the lighting to a dim red color, allowing for their adjustment to night vision. In another 30 minutes, he would turn out all the lights. The drop would be from 17 thousand feet—only a thousand feet below the orbiting gunship. David had not completed a lot of HALO, or 'High Altitude Low Opening' parachute drops since he got qualified—and only two had been at night. Under different circumstances he might have been more concerned—nervous even— but his brother was down there and that was his focus. David prayed his brother had made it to the point north of the airfield, otherwise he and LT would have to travel to the coordinates Ross provided at the jail and break them out. The sun would be up then and they would have to be extracted at a later time. The gunship would stay on station to support their escape, but the Talon would return home. They considered using the Ospreys rather than the Talon, but the Joint Special Operations Task Force (JSOTF) commander was not keen on using those assets for this operation, especially without tanker support. David was just happy to get support at all, as this was essentially a mission of a personal nature. David and LT implied to the commander that Ross was an additional witness to support the Joint Chief's agenda, but they didn't actually state it. If they pushed harder to acquire the Ospreys, the commander may have contacted the general directly and then the whole mission might have been scrubbed.

David made his way to the cockpit to thank the crew. As he climbed the stairs he noticed very low dark green lighting—NVG compatible. He stood next to the Flight Engineer, who handed him a spare headset that was plugged into the instructor pilot's position. "Hey gents," David started, "I just wanted to thank you boys for the ride."

"No problem; happy to do it." The pilot answered.

"You know, my dad flew these…he was one of the original cadre."

"Oh? What was his name?"

"Robert…Bob Wallace." David said, but none of the men seemed to know him. "Yeah, he retired in 1998."

"I know him." A voice said over the intercom. It was the loadmaster. "We flew together in the 7th Special Operations Squadron…I'm sorry for your loss. He was a good dude." David didn't let on that his father was still alive. Just then a rotten odor filled the cockpit. The Flight Engineer was at it again.

"Howdy!"

Ross checked the GPS—only about a quarter mile to the coordinated point. He wondered if his brother was already there. "Five more minutes, Kate—then we can rest." She only nodded and kept trudging on. How would David get them out? Was he even coming? Ross looked southward to see if anyone was tracking after them, but they were now below the bluff near the river and couldn't see. He knew the airfield was above them somewhere and listened for aircraft, but it was quiet. Blue trotted a few yards in front of them as if he knew where they were going.

He glanced at the GPS again—62 feet to go. "Okay, let's get to those trees."

"Is he here?" She said; a quiver in her voice.

"No, I don't see him. But he'll be here—I know it!" Ross tried to sound confident, but inside he knew there could be things beyond his brother's control. They found a good hide in the trees and Ross deployed Kate's sleeping bag. She crawled in and he zipped her up, then he had her hold on to Blue. Once they were secure, Ross crawled to the top of the bluff to get a view of the airfield. There wasn't much to see except the feedlot lights just southeast of the field. He looked directly south to the jail—didn't seem to be any activity. He would wait.

"Sorry, sir—no joy." The co-pilot said, referring to his attempt to make contact with Ross on the radio. David wasn't that concerned. He hadn't told Ross to be listening outside of the normal contact time, but it would have been nice to know that he made it to the airfield.

"Twenty Minute Checklist!" the Flight Engineer called on interphone. David made his way to the back of the Talon and acknowledged the call with the loadmaster. The aircraft was extremely noisy and he could barely hear anything except the engines and a bunch of high-pitched cooling fans. His heart was pounding a little harder now. LT gave him a thumbs up, "Hang in there, Junior—we'll get 'em out!" David nodded. The loadmaster seemed intent on listening to something on his headset and made his way to David. Leaning in, he said, "Hey, the pilot was just in contact with the gunship; now in orbit over the airfield. He wanted you to know they have three contacts near the north end of the field by the river. It looks like two people and a dog." David leaned back with a puzzled look on his face. "A dog???" The loadmaster nodded, "That's what the man said!"

Every once in a while, Ross thought he could hear something in the sky well above him, but he wasn't sure. At first he thought he was hearing things, but an occasional bark from Blue below him in the trees confirmed that he wasn't—Blue heard it too. Was it David? He didn't know. The sun would be up in about an hour; if David didn't get here in the next 30 minutes or so, they would have to leave for a better place to hide. The Mayor and his minions would be looking for them. Suddenly, Blue began to bark loudly and would not respond to Kate's attempts to quiet him. Ross looked down the hill at them—was someone coming? Then, he heard it immediately to his right—a fluttering in the air. He turned to look just in time to have a boot land next to his head as someone ran past him. The figure only took a few steps before he stopped and a parachute collapsed behind him.

"Hey, big brother…any bad guys in the area?" David said softly.

"You scared the hell out of me!" Ross cried. "I almost crapped my…" he didn't finish his sentence before a second chute glided in next to David and startled Ross again. "Damn!" he jumped up. "Are there any more I should know about?"

David laughed, "Nope, this is it…You okay?" He said, coming over to hug his brother.

"Oh, man, I'm glad you're here!" Ross said, a tremor of emotion in his voice. He watched David and LT gather their chutes and put them into a bag. Ross looked around for a few moments before he asked, "So, how we getting out of here…we walking?"

David smiled, "No; our 'Chariot of Armageddon' will be here in a few minutes." He paused to return to a radio conversation with somebody. "They'll be here in ten mikes."

Ross heard Blue barking again and realized Kate and Blue were still down below in the trees. "Hey, I gotta get Kate." David followed Ross down the hill, Kate was just re-attaching the sleeping bag to her pack when they arrived. "Kate, this is my brother, Dork. Dork; Kate, Kate; Dork." David smirked at his brother and then extended his hand to Kate. "Glad to meet you…name is David….and who is this guy?" he said, addressing the dog. "Ahh, this is our security specialist; Blue." David smiled, "A perfect addition to the redoubt."

They gathered up their gear and climbed back up to the airfield. LT announced that the Talon was about two minutes out. Ross strained to look down the runway, but couldn't see anything. Moments later he heard the big plane reverse pitch on the props as it loomed in front of him. The aircraft turned around on the runway and he saw several figures fan out in all directions to form a perimeter. "Those are the SEALs...let's go!" David prompted.

"SEALs? You brought SEALs?" Ross said, in disbelief. David motioned for them to hurry. The ramp and door was open and they ran right up into the back of the aircraft. The loadmaster quickly secured them into webbed seats. Blue tried to run back out of the aircraft. Ross could tell the noise hurt his ears. The loadmaster caught the hint and provided an extra headset for the dog. Kate had to hold it for him, though. The SEALs came back in next. Ross felt a surge as the brakes released and the Talon powered up to leave as suddenly as it came; within seconds they were airborne. Kate realized they were finally safe and emotion took over. She leaned over on Ross and began to cry. It made Ross think of Hallie. He missed her and thought of where she was; hanging in a garage, waiting to be eaten. David unbuckled and squatted in front of them "You guys okay? One of the SEALs is a medic." Ross nodded, "Yeah, we're fine...I was just thinking about Hallie, is all." David asked what had happened and Ross gave him the quick version of the story; ending it with Hallie's current state. David looked at Ross in disbelief, then he stood and made his way to the flight deck. Moments later, Ross heard the engines roll back and David returned. "Come on, I want you to see something."

David and Ross went up to the flight deck. David handed Ross a headset to put on and put one on himself. "Look over there," David said, pointing out the window on the pilots side. "That's where you were staying." Ross could see the reservoir. His eyes tracked up from the lake to the jail. The Talon was about a mile away in a gentle bank, circling the area. "You say, the northern most building is the one Hallie is in?" Ross nodded, "Yeah, and the jail is right next to it."

David selected a radio at the IPs position and keyed his mic, "GHOST one-seven, this is TALON two-six—confirmed; structure north of primary target is also cleared for engagement...Bring the rain." Seconds later, a stream of fire emanated from well above the Talon and descended toward the jail and the garage like lasers in a sci-fi movie. Ross had never seen anything like it. The buildings erupted into a brilliant fire and lit up the night sky.

"Willy Pete, er…White Phosphorous." David said, "There won't be anything left…just ashes." Ross watched for several minutes before the Talon climbed away. He felt emotion overtake him and tears formed in his eyes. "Thanks, bro…thanks…for everything. I couldn't have hoped for a better burial." He squeezed David's shoulder. "It's been a hell of an ordeal—I don't think anything could shock me now!" David smiled and started laughing. "Oh yeah? Well, try this on for size; mom and dad are alive and well—living at the redoubt!" Ross just stared blankly like he'd been gut-shot. "Yeah, it's true—long story—they live in that big cabin we saw on the pond. I'll let them explain it to you."

David had never seen his brother at a loss for words, but that clearly did it for him. The look on Ross's face was priceless. "Well? Aren't you going to say something?" David chided. Ross looked up from staring at the floor and glared into David's eyes with a strange expression. "Yeah…what the hell is that smell?"

"Howdy."

As the Talon climbed away carrying the last remaining members of the redoubt, the sun began to bless the morning sky, casting shadows on the Black Hills below. They would all be together now, facing a new world and a new life. Commensurately, thousands of miles to the west, a troubled president gazed at the latest report of who might be still under his leadership and who might be under General Pickens; the Chairman of the Joint Chiefs. It was very late, and he hadn't slept yet. The tray full of cigarette butts was nearly full; a half-burned specimen now sending its curling trail up through the light of the dim desk lamp. A door opened and the Chief of Staff entered briskly.

"What is it?" POTUS challenged curtly.

"I thought you might want to hear this soonest!" COS said excitedly. We have Madison and Wallace narrowed down to a forty square-mile area in the Montana wilderness."

"Send our people in?" POTUS asked rhetorically.

"Three teams are assembling as we speak!"

"Excellent!" POTUS popped. "Excellent…Once they get confirmation, I want to be notified immediately." The COS nodded affirmatively and left the room. The partially deposed world leader stared deliberately into the darkness beyond the light cast by the desk lamp, contemplating the demise of the two men. Slowly, the smoke trail from the nearly expired cigarette came into focus. Picking it up, he placed it into his mouth and leaned back in the chair taking a long slow drag. A wicked smile forced one corner of his mouth to curl up. "You can't hide from me, boys." He seethed, "I always win in the end…I always win…"

Praise be to the Lord my rock, who trains my hands for war, my fingers for battle.
– Psalm 144:1, Holy Bible

www.ingramcontent.com/pod-product-compliance
Lightning Source LLC
Chambersburg PA
CBHW071127200626
46817CB00018B/2326